One Million Project
THRILLER ANTHOLOGY

40 gripping short tales
Compiled by
Jason Greenfield

Horror – Ghost – Mystery Suspense
Thriller - Crime Detective

Index: Genre – Title – Author

THRILLER: Continued **Page**

CRIME-DETECTIVE

Copyright

OMP Thriller Anthology

Dedication

This book is dedicated to 3 groups of people: The dozens of contributors (writers, promotional artists, media, admin, tech) who gave of their time and skills to help a good cause, the charities and activists who spend every day trying to make the world a better place by helping others and finally, you the reader, who bought this collection and have helped contribute towards raising ONE MILLION POUNDS and making this a globally known cause. Thank you all. Jason.

Acknowledgments

Our story writers – 40 wonderful writers whose names you'll find in the index and at the head of each story. Our cover designers/artists - you'll find their names at the end of each story.

COMPILING EDITOR - JASON GREENFIELD

OMP: THRILLER PROJECT MANAGER -SOLEIL DANIELS

OMP: THRILLER EDITORS – S. L. BARON & SOLEIL DANIELS

MAIN COVER DESIGNS - D.J. MEYERS

MAIN COVER LOGO DESIGN - CLAUDIA MURRAY

FORMATTING AND IMAGE EDITING - DECLAN CONNER

PUBLISHER - OMP PUBLISHING: WITH ASSISTANCE FROM KATE ANDERSON & DARK INK PRESS

Introduction

Welcome to the OMP, a project very dear to my heart and years in the making. Before you lies a journey into 40 varied and fantastic stories by 40 different writers including myself. Hopefully you will be thoroughly entertained as well as gain the satisfaction of knowing your money is going to a good cause.

The collection you see before you was born out of two separate notions of mine that didn't seem very workable on their own. Firstly, having written several novels, I wanted to do a collection of stories but even when I had the idea of adding other writers to it, it seemed like it didn't have much chance of standing out among the millions of other EBooks and print books on Amazon and elsewhere.

My second notion was a deep desire to do something to help people; having watched programs on the homeless, and experienced the agonies of a relative contracting cancer (my mother - now many years in remission thankfully) these were the two areas of charity that I wanted to raise money and awareness for.

However I had no idea, how I, a mere writer, could ever be in a position to do anything significant.

Then suddenly a synapse sparked in my head and it all made perfect sense! What if I could combine my short story collection with the charity issue - now I have a hook for one and a vehicle to raise money for the other! Ideas came fast and furious ... I would build up a network of creative people (and promotions/media folk) - writers to contribute the stories and artists to do covers. The primary goal would be to raise money for our chosen charities and as a secondary goal, the work of the creative people within would have exposure to a large audience. Many more ideas and strategies have come of this since then and hopefully there will be huge global word of mouth to make this project a success.

It's called the ONE MILLION PROJECT as that is an aspirational figure - raising £1,000,000 (and hopefully more) and so far we have four anthologies debuting in early 2018 with more books and other projects within the OMP brand to follow.

100% of the profits of this collection are going to charity so I really hope that you will give the wonderful, generous and talented people who have given their time, skills and effort for free, a look and check out their other projects - all our writers can be found via their personal bio and links at the end of their stories. Please support them and if you like the collections (see links at end for the other OMP anthologies) please tell all your friends to download and help spread the word.

NOTE: OMP THRILLER presents a variety of different genres including Horror, Thriller, Mystery and Crime. Stories are of differing lengths (with a few writers choosing to do multiple mini stories so in fact there's more than 40 overall!) - While standardizing the look of the collections, I've tried to keep the individual characteristics and style of the writer intact where I can.

Now without further ado, I present 40 great stories

Enjoy.

Jason Greenfield.

Bill

Dan Pullen

"Bill" is about a man being guided by forces outside his control. Bill calls these forces "the tendrils." Has Bill tapped into the secret communication network of the universe, or is he just another unhinged, misguided human drifting through life on the strings of the unseen?

Dawn

The tendrils sent Bill his awake message, and he opened his eyes. He received the message to get out of bed, and the tendrils pushed him along to the bathroom to start his morning routine.

In the mirror, he examined the patch of eczema that was growing on his left elbow. He felt the messages for the itch coming from a tendril through the floor before they finally hit his elbow, and he struggled against the tendrils urging him to itch it. Instead he followed the tendrils prompting him to reach for the hydrocortisone in the medicine cabinet. He felt soothing waves rush into his elbow, working those itch messages away into the sink and walls and floor. Until a new stronger itch sensation blossomed from deep in his flesh, and a crushing wave forced his fingers to work his nails deep into his skin. Deeper and deeper he probed, the information forming cyclones of pain and pleasure through his arm and out into the surrounding area. The cyclones would hit against the sink and mirror and come spinning back at him, sending new sensations through his face and chest and legs. Finally his fingers worked all the way through the skin and sinew to his bones because the itch had become lodged deep in his marrow. When he finally hit the marrow, though, he felt the presence of a little girl, just about 8 years old. He could feel the tendril that connected them, connected their bones. He felt the corruption inside her and tried to scratch it off her bones. He felt her writhe from the pain he was causing her and tried to slip back down the tendril that connected them. He was caught in the tide of information that streamed into the girl's body, a piece of his consciousness endlessly bobbing away on the energy field that propelled our existence.

Back in his mirror, Bill began to shave.

Telephone

Bill opened the door and picked up the receiver to the Last Phone Booth. He picked up the phone book and tested its weight.

"Three pages," he mumbled, "damn kids. No respect."

Bill punched in the number 146528, one number higher than he had dialed yesterday. He heard three rings and a click then a woman's voice.

"Hello, this is Marie."

Bill felt a sudden pull on his neck. The phone booth shifted into six different fragments of pictures. One he had seen before, on a summer night sixteen years ago. He smelt the fire and felt the warmth of bourbon in his blood. He felt Marie's arms fall around his shoulders and her breath by his ear. He felt a tendril move through the night air and place her lips, gentle and wet, on his neck.

"Marie?"

"No, let's say Gloria instead."

"Okay. Gloria. What do you have for me?"

"There are currently seven swans in the pond across the street from the Lateral Building, in Quincy Park. Two of them are planning an insurrection."

"Which two?"

"They will be marked."

"How?"

"They will be marked."

"Understood."

There was a long pause. The receiver clicked twice.

"Do you have anything else for me…Marie?"

"Gloria. And no."

Message

Bill propped his left leg up on the tile wall of the bathroom, the hand dryer blowing a hot stream onto his damp pant leg. The bathroom door flung open and Charles Portney stuck his head in.

"Head's up, bud, LePuke is looking for you."

"Thanks, man."

Charles began to exit but poked his head back in and nodded toward Bill's leg.

"Puddle."

Charles exited with an "Oh," which relieved Bill. It hadn't rained for three days.

At his desk, Bill fought against the keys being pushed up at his fingers by the tendrils. He tried to stay on task: input the serial numbers off the parts inventory into the MES. When a particularly strong tendril pulled at the base of his hippocampus, Bill's eyes fluttered shut and his back went rigid. He could no longer fight against the forces bombarding his body, and the tendrils took over completely. His fingers rapped out an alphanumeric sequence: ef6has9fjfjoasinf8hf. When the tendrils released him, Bill studied the sequence. He heard footsteps making their way toward his cube, so he jotted down the sequence and backspaced it out of his computer. It was Nancy from HR.

"Hi, Bill." She was speaking in that whisper tone she had, the one that everyone can hear. "Steve wanted me to come over and see if everything was all right. He said you were late again today?"

Bill thought Nancy's loud whisper had evoked a "shh" from one of his co-workers, until he realized the "shh" was actually the sound of the ocean. The sound of the waves from Long Beach had found their way into the air conditioning system. These waves were the same he had heard when he was seven, sitting with his uncle after playing catch in the surf.

The familiar thought of "He's getting sand down there" entered Bill's mind, and he was overcome with the sensation of the sand particles on his crotch. Bill lurched to his feet, startling Nancy.

"It's everything all right, Nance, just is everything, y'know." As he rambled, Bill swept up his notebook and laptop and shoved them into his messenger bag. "Gonna lie down, home, gonna take a sick." The particles of sand were migrating through his body, carving tiny tunnels into his legs and abdomen.

Nancy followed Bill as he half stumbled down the hall. "Now, Bill, I understand, but you're not, er, you're actually out of sick time, Bill. If you need time off we're going to have to submit a leave, or maybe you can talk to Steve and work something out. Bill? Let me just give you a form."

"Mail me," Bill said as he reached the stairwell and shut the door behind him. The hot air of the stairwell warmed his body and deadened the sensation of the sand burrowing through him. He took the stairs three at a time, slipping once on the second floor, until he was out the back exit and on the sidewalk.

Bill couldn't recall the eighteen-block walk from his job to his home; he wondered if possibly he had been disassembled there on the sidewalk and reconfigured there in his living room. It was a phenomenon he had theorized long before, though there was no good way Bill knew of to test this theory. Instead he rifled through a stack of notebooks in his coat closet. Not finding what he was looking for, Bill took a deep breath and reached out for a tendril to guide him. He felt the tendril's wave come at him from behind the bookcase and rode its energy down to the spare bedroom, the one he used to share with his sister. He opened several boxes and emptied their contents onto the floor. He finally found what he was looking for, a journal marked "9/27/93-11/14/93." He leafed through the pages of notes and drawings until he came to a series of several alphanumeric sequences under the large header "PAGER." He walked back to the living room and retrieved the notebook where he had written down the sequence "ef6has9fjfjoasinf8hf." His finger traced through the list, trying to find a match to the sequence.

Finding nothing, Bill sat down on the edge of a large plastic storage tub. He'd been positive he'd seen this sequence before and was sure it was in the list of messages he had received from his pager in 1993. It was then he felt an array of small tendrils pulling at and manipulating the fingers on his right hand. They were tapping out a long, complex pattern, a pattern that would seem completely random to the casual observer. Bill opened his old notebook and ran his fingers over the page. His fingers were only hitting the letters e, f, h, a, s, o, i, and n, only the letters contained in his encoded message from earlier in the day.

"Only j is missing, and the numbers."

It was just then that Bill heard a dog bark. *Neighbor's dog, Maxwell, pit bull, bull frog, Jeremiah, that's the j.* A large tendril came crashing through the picture window behind him, riding on the heels of Maxwell's bark. It bent Bill's spine and forced his head up to see the large number six he had painted on the ceiling, surrounded by other smaller numbers and symbols Bill didn't understand.

"That's it, that's all, just the nine and eight. Have to find them."

Bill threw both notebooks into his messenger bag and made his way to the front door. He climbed a series of invisible steps that left him wedged against the ceiling, unable to reach down and turn the door handle. Bill expanded his body until his weight and size pushed the invisible steps to the floor. He turned the handle and exited out to the front lawn.

Needle

Bill walked along Marbledale down toward Hudson. He felt no data activity other than the usual ebb and flow of the tendrils feeding him the data that was his reality. He was looking for some link to the numbers eight or nine. Walking past a bodega, he saw a knitting needle lying across a storm grate. He picked it up. The end of the needle read "Size 9."

Looking around, Bill scanned the environment for a number 8. Jogging a bit further down Marbledale, he saw an establishment called Vinny's Pizza, which was located at #8 Hudson St. Stepping into traffic, a man in a yellow car honked his horn and made an offensive hand gesture toward Bill. Bill then waited at the corner for the signal to turn and headed to Vinny's Pizza.

Bill saw a few patrons eating, a kitchen in the back, and an old arcade game in the corner by the cash register. A plump little woman said, "Sit where you want, hon," as she waddled out from behind the counter carrying a menu.

Bill couldn't feel anything important about the place or any of the patrons. He saw a sign for a unisex bathroom at the other end of the counter, so he headed there. He opened the door, but it was empty. He walked back into the kitchen and saw nothing of interest. He was about to open the door to what he assumed was a closet when he heard a voice say, "The fuck" and felt something grab the back of his shirt. Bill turned to see a man, just about the same height as the little plump woman and with the same pinched face, grabbing him and pushing him out of the kitchen. The man pushed Bill all the way to the front door and forced him through to the sidewalk.

"Stay the fuck out. Weirdo."

Bill straightened his shirt. He scanned the street for another number 8. Then he noticed he was still holding the knitting needle. Holding it out in front of himself like a divining rod, Bill felt a large tendril slide toward him from underground and take hold of the needle. Bill followed its pull.

The needle took Bill all the way down Hudson, taking a left onto Grace Lane. He walked through the basketball courts at Peaford Park and over onto Wellsview. Under a large billboard for a lawyer's office, Bill saw the abandoned Millner Building. The lawyer's phone number was one of those 800 numbers. The needle took Bill around the back of the building to the receiving dock. Next to the big dock door, Bill pulled the handle on the receiving entrance and walked inside.

The Millner Building had been abandoned since Bill was young. He knew they used to make some kind of paper product, and he knew that the site was sitting unused all these years due to some dispute with the EPA about ground contamination.

Bill followed the needle to the back of the dock and into an office area. He found a stairwell outside the offices and followed it down. Here the ground was damp and the air was heavy. Bill thought he could hear a fan running, but he didn't feel any kind of breeze. He walked to the end of a long hallway and found a large metal door. He twisted the handle and went in.

The room Bill entered was completely dark except for a square area of pale light in the center of the room. Bill looked up but couldn't see a ceiling and couldn't see where the light might be coming from.

"Hello?" he said.

"What do you want now, fucker?"

It was a woman's voice, husky and broken. Bill spied into the darkness, but he couldn't see anything.

"Hello? Hello, I'm Bill. Is that you?"

Her voice became hostile. "Don't come near me, fucker, I swear I will kill you this time."

"Marie? Marie, it's me, Bill."

"I don't care who the fuck you are. I said I would kill you this time!"

Bill jumped back when he saw an arm flash through the square of light in the middle of the room. It looked like it was holding a small strip of wood.

"Stop, it's me, it's Bill. We talked on the phone this morning. Marie, it's me!"

"Just fucking kill me, stop playing these fucking games with me! Just kill me, just kill me, just kill me!"

Bill felt her retreat to the back of the room, and he stepped forward into the light.

"I'm not going to hurt you. I found you. Marie, I called you and I found you."

"My name's not Marie, you fuck. Just do what you're gonna do, you sick fuck."

Bill felt two tendrils push through the ceiling, one coming down on him and one on Marie, just as he heard a voice from behind the door bellow, "I told you to shut the fuck up, bitch."

"Marie, the tendril, get down."

"The fuck are you talking about?"

"The tendril, lay on the floor. Lay down, Marie."

"I told you, I'm not MARIE!"

Bill lay prone, his right cheek pressed against the cold concrete. "The tendril, the tendril, the tendril," he whispered.

Bill could feel a wave of corruption push through the door, spearheaded by a large figure. Bill heard three quick steps and a voice say, "Bitch, you're gonna get so—" before he felt the toe of a shoe jam into his ribs. He saw a man stumble into the square of light, and all at once he heard the man say something unintelligible, and that sound was followed by a sharp, wet thud.

The next sound Bill heard was a shuffle toward where the thud happened. "You killed your friend, asshole. His skull's split to his brain, just like I'm going to do to you!"

Bill rose to his feet. "He's not my friend. I'm your friend, I'm Bill. We talked on the phone. I came to find you."

The woman stepped into the square of light, brandishing the

piece of wood. "I'm serious, asshole. I'm walking out that fucking door. I'm serious."

"Marie, it's me, it's Bill. I found you."

"My name's not Marie, asshole, it's Gl—"

Just then a tendril lifted Bill's hand toward the woman's chest. The knitting needle he held slipped right into her heart, the same way a key fits into a lock. The woman mouthed some words that Bill could not hear before collapsing to the ground.

Receiver

Bill stumbled into the Last Phone Booth and struggled to reach the receiver. Ever since he pierced the woman's heart with his knitting needle, he was being bombarded by strange sensations. Instead of feeling the slow surge of data being downloaded by the tendrils, he felt the tiny spirals of data being deconstructed and heading back to the collective. It was as if the whole world were a series of never ending drill bits that we all had to walk through. The first spiral he felt formed in the woman's chest where his knitting needle shared space with her flesh. Bill could feel that he had not pierced her skin or flesh, not technically, and she did not bleed. Instead, the space between the molecules of the knitting needle and the space between the molecules in her flesh had lined up so perfectly that they had come to occupy the same space. The molecules interlocked, and as this double set of data began traveling back to the collective along the same path, that's when Bill recognized it as corruption.

For the first time, Bill could comprehend data at a collective level. He felt the block of corruption leave the woman's chest and break into millions of pieces. He then felt those pieces be pulled back up along tendrils to be delivered to different points in space time. Each time the corruption reached a new point, it infected the reality or the receptor receiving it. A man slapped his wife. A boy began vomiting. A tree began to blight. Bill could feel all these events at their different points in space time. Then they faded away, replaced instead by the downward spirals of data exiting Bill's existence. It was against these forces that Bill worked to lift his hand, pick up the receiver, and dial the phone.

"Hello?"

"Yes, it's Bill."

"There was a pause. "You already called today."

"I know, but I need help."

"You can call again tomorrow, as scheduled."

"Marie, Gloria, whoever you are. I killed you. I killed you, and now all the data is going the other way."

"This is Celeste, please call back tomorrow."

"No, I need help. I can't move like this, it's too much. I need to know what to do."

"Thank you, please await further instruction. Goodbye."

Bill was about to hang up when he heard the voice on the other end say something. "What was that? Did you say something?"

"I said, it's a strange paradise, isn't it?"

The words "strange paradise" hit Bill in the chest. It was the same hit to the chest that Kenny Flores had given him in the sixth grade. The one that knocked the wind out of him in gym class. The hit that kept Bill awake some nights dreaming about all the things he should have done to Kenny Flores that day.

A feeling like the itch of a sunburn formed in Bill's chest and radiated outward through his limbs. The sunburn left his body and created a cocoon around him. He could no longer feel the push and pull of data running through him, though he could feel its existence in the environment outside his cocoon. He looked at the phone receiver in his hand and heard a click and a dial tone. He put the receiver back on the cradle and opened the phone booth door.

Not knowing what to do, Bill walked the three blocks back to his house. He was still aware of the data going back and forth outside his cocoon, but for the first time in years, he was disconnected from the stream. It was a surprisingly lonely feeling.

Bill drifted home. His thoughts were clearer than they had been in years, but the events of the day were still racing through his brain. He was so lost in thought, he didn't notice Charles Portney standing at his front door until he was halfway across his lawn.

"Hey, man, just wanted to check on you. Heard you freaked out a bit on Nancy today. Everything cool?"

Usually the sight of someone at his door would send Bill into a panic. Inside his home were the stacks of journals and videotapes and the symbols he drew on the walls. If Charles entered his home, he would see the food wrappers and dirty plates and stained carpets. He would see it all, and Bill would be exposed. But today, instead of panic, Bill felt a sense of relief. A part of him knew this had all gone too far, and he was relishing the idea that it could all end if he just opened the door and let Charles see his secret.

"Yeah, guess I just needed to clear my head, ya know?"

Charles nodded. "You wanna get a beer or something?"

Bill shook his head. He coughed, and both he and Charles rocked back and forth on their heels for a moment. Without the push of the tendrils, Bill had a hard time making a decision. Looking down he exhaled and felt a weight leave his body.

"You wanna come in?" he asked, and Charles shrugged and nodded. Turning the key to his door, Bill's mind laid out all the possible things Charles could say once he saw inside Bill's house. As he opened the door, the breeze swept over Bill and filled him with relief. Until he looked inside, and all his possessions were gone. Not his basic furniture or the pictures on the wall, but his journals, his videotapes, the garbage, the symbols painted or carved into the wall. It was all just gone.

"Nice place," he heard Charles say behind him.

Bill entered slowly and scanned the room. He could feel that the cocoon of emptiness that had surrounded him now extended to the dimensions of his house. He was further away from the tendrils than he had been since he was twelve. The only thing he could feel was Charles' presence in the room. He knew he had to act as normal as possible.

"Sit down. Do you want something to drink?"

"Beer?"

Bill said, "No beer," as he walked into his kitchen.

"Anything then."

Bill opened the fridge and saw there were indeed five beers left in a six-pack container. He pulled out two and walked back into the living room. Looking at Charles he could see Charles was saying something. It was then Bill noticed the only thing he could hear was the sound of rushing water and of his own heart beating. He handed Charles the beer and sat down, shaking his head in an attempt to come back to the reality of the living room.

"...just some sort of indicator, right? Like some way for people to know when they walk in —it was like this when I got here! Right?"

Bill could tell this was one of those moments where he should laugh, so he gave Charles a smile and a chuckle, but he sensed it was delivered too late. Charles took a sip of his beer and then placed it on the table. He took a deep breath and folded his hands.

"It was a good run, Bill."

"Sorry?"

"Look, we've enjoyed your work, you were always dependable. But after today, we can no longer keep you around. You're a liability."

"You're firing me?"

"No, we're disconnecting you."

Charles reached out and put his hand on Bill's shoulder. Bill felt every molecule in his body rend from each other. The molecules then rushed out through the walls of Bill's living room and into the air above. Here they were each picked up by an awaiting tendril and transferred to larger data structures below.

A Reality

Bill opened his eyes to a white room with a large window to his right side. A network of tubes and wires sat astride his bed. A woman in hospital scrubs walked in wearing a bright smile. "Morning, Bill, how did you sleep?"

Bill attempted to ask the woman where he was, but the only sound he heard from his mouth was a weak "The tendrils."

"Oh, yes, the tendrils. How are the tendrils today, Bill?"

Bill wanted to tell her he could no longer feel the tendrils, but again the only thing he could say was "The tendrils."

The woman smiled at him and checked the instruments surrounding Bill's bed. A moment later an older gentleman entered.

"How is he?"

"He's good, all his signs are normal."

"Does he look right to you?"

The woman paused to look Bill over before giving the man a shrug and a shake of her head.

"Something different," said the man. He bent over the bed and flashed a bright light in Bill's eyes, looking inside them closely. He stood back up and stared at Bill for a moment. "Something different," he said again.

"You think he's okay, Dr. Cleary?"

Dr. Cleary nodded and turned to walk out of the room. He walked down the hall and entered his office, exchanged his hospital jacket for his raincoat, and proceeded to the parking lot.

After a light supper and an attempt to complete the crossword he started that morning, Dr. Cleary retired for the night. He found his wife, Judy, already in bed, reading.

"You all right, dear?"

"Yes, it's...there's a patient I'm a bit concerned about."

"Oh?"

"Yes, well, he's a catatonic, and he's donating, er, he's a match for his sister's bone marrow. So the mother is allowing him to donate his to his sister and all. I was for it, but…today he seemed different."

"Different how?"

"Just…more alive I guess. Maybe it's just me, but he seemed to be, I guess, anxious today. Like he knew what was coming."

"Did he say anything?"

"No, he can't talk, he can't know what we're doing, he—I had no problem with this when I thought he couldn't know. We'd sedate him, keep him comfortable. But now…"

Dr. Cleary's wife jutted her hand to her husband's shoulder. "Roger, you're bleeding."

A tingle on his forehead prompted Roger Cleary's hand to reach up. Pulling it away he saw a smear of blood on his palm. "How curious."

His attention was drawn to a sudden, splitting pain from the middle of his forehead to his hairline. He began shouting and Judy pointed at him yelling "Oh my god, oh my god" over and over. Reaching up, Roger could feel what seemed to be thick sticks probing and pushing under his skin. He tried to push them down, but they opened his skin and began worming their way over his flesh. Roger's eyes rolled back, and he began slapping at the finger-like protrusions coming from his forehead.

Judy jumped out of the bed and threw herself back against the wall. A noise like the vacuum cleaner when it catches the bathroom rug emanated from her husband's mouth, and his skull was expanding to an extraordinary size. The skin that was split back to Roger's hairline suddenly broke all the way to the back of his skull, and a human hand erupted from the gash.

In his mind, Roger now heard a voice saying over and over "I'm sorry, I'm sorry" and "the corruption." He almost made the connection from the voice to one he'd heard earlier in the day, but his mind shut off before it could complete the thought.

Judy screamed as a man emerged from her husband's engorged skull, covered in blood and masses of tissue, saying over and over the words "I'm sorry."

Bill wiped the blood from his eyes and saw a woman in a nightgown and robe pressed against the wall. She was screaming and pointing and thrashing her head back and forth.

"Shh," Bill said as he pushed his way through the hole he was in. "Shh, the tendrils, they'll hear you."

The woman did not comply but threw herself on the bed in front of Bill and reached out to touch the mass of tissue he was extricating himself from. Bill looked down and saw she was reaching for something that looked oddly like a face, but she stopped herself from actually touching it.

"Be quiet, be quiet!"

Bill freed himself from the tissue sack he was in. When the woman would not stop screaming he reached for the bedside lamp and swung it at her head, only to have the cord get caught on the bedpost and the light hit against the mattress, crumpling the cheap lampshade. Shadows rocked back and forth on the bedroom wall as Bill yanked at the lamp. A spark sounded, and the light went out in the room, and Bill felt his arm fly toward where the woman's skull had been. The next sound Bill heard was his panting breath filling a silent room. He collapsed on the bed, about to say "I'm sorry," when he felt the corrupt touch of a tendril push through the wall and stand him up. Bill walked out of the room and closed the door behind him.

The End

Find Dan Pullen at the following links:

Twitter: @danpullenbooks

Goodreads:
https:www.goodreads.com/author/show/2427506.Dan Pullen

Cover by Zach Saltos.

The Bones of my Friends

John Dodd

Introduction - "The Bones of my Friends" was originally an idea for a full-length novel where the main protagonist was to go beyond the confines of the chamber and into the world beyond, where they could learn all about the things they'd missed in the time they'd been gone. When I was asked to write for the OMP, I considered that there's only so much self-discovery you can do with someone who's never known anything else, so I took a shorter, sharper route to the story that you find in the following pages.

I restarted writing at 25 when I realised that the competition I lost at 13 was to a fellow pupil who just copied out the last pages of *The Sea Wolf* and changed the names. In 2014, I took a challenge to write a million words in a year that I beat with a week to spare. I'm a swordsman, weightlifter, organiser of games' conventions countrywide, and analogue writing enthusiast who takes it to evangelical levels. If you find me with less than three pens and two notebooks on me, I'm unprepared.

It's been thirty years since I ate my last companion when I hear the noise in the antechamber. I pause in the third step of Rhatari and un-flare the sun sponges from my back, then move silently to the back of the vault to collect my sword. The door rattles as someone tries the lock on it, and I lift myself up on the ropes attached to the ceiling, swinging without noise to the perch above the door.

A loud crunch, something slamming against the door; not the same size as me, not as strong as me.

Can't be one of the Brigade...

Another crunch, something speaking quickly in a language I don't understand, and a faint metallic clicking from the lock. I lean over, adjusting my weight to allow me to reach down without overbalancing. The lock turns, and the same voice speaks. I hear something backing up from the door.

Careless. No thought that there could be someone in here...

The thump of a boot against the door, and it flies open; two figures wearing metal armour charge into the room, one going left, one going right. I wait.

If it were me, the real threat would be coming in after the distraction.

A third figure in bright clothing; a fourth wearing what looks to be the skin of a dead animal. They look around the room; the one in bright clothing takes out a book and starts to read from the page, pointing at the vault door. The two armoured figures move back towards the antechamber door, the bright-clothed one moving towards the vault. It raises the book and starts to trace the lines of the seal as I move above the armoured figures.

"Evinida," it speaks, and I stop as the word ripples in the air, the seal changing colour from dull grey metal to a faint pearlescent blue.

Loyalty...

I hang in the ropes above, looking at the door as the bright-clothed one moves its small, delicate hands to another part of the vault.

"Sohas." The seal goes silver, the edges starting to glow

Strength...

Its hand reaches again and traces the line of the silver, reaching the end; it turns the page in the book and looks back up to the vault. I switch my position, anchoring myself to the rope with my feet as I hang down, looking at the armoured figure below. I blink as my training kicks in, and I look around the rest of the room.

Breathing, therefore needs air; makes sound through air. Helmet strapped on, no neck guard...

I reach down and pull the figure's head back, putting my sword in the gap and down into its chest. As it goes rigid, I drop down next to it without sound, moving quickly as I use my body mass to turn the first over, hurling it towards the one wearing the animal skins. As the bodies crash together, I'm already moving, the second armoured figure turning to watch its companions as both tumble to the ground.

Turning away from me...

I step in again, pulling the head back and pushing the sword in. Unprepared, it has no chance; its head goes back, and whatever warning it had goes with it to the ground. I step forwards as the one wearing the skins struggles to throw its companion's body from it, the Bright One turning, its face going pale as the blood drains to its limbs to prepare it to fight.

Too slow, not a soldier...

I put my foot into the Bright One's chest, the impact knocking it against the wall as the other rises up, drawing two short, curved blades and shrugging the animal skin from its back. Markings adorn its entire body as it weaves a pattern in the air. I move in as it makes a measured step forward, both weapons in constant motion, and I sway as one of the blades misses me by a narrow margin. My return strike is faster, but it moves aside, recognising I'm stronger, the blade cutting close again. I spin back, keeping the blade between us as the marked one keeps its blade in contact with mine and follows me like a wave.

Faster than me...

I growl as the blade slides against my skin, not breaking the surface but creasing it. The Marked One smiles and follows up with a strike towards my eyes. I drop my sword and move into the strike, snapping my head forwards, letting the blade strike my armoured forehead, the metal glancing off harmlessly. I look up, seeing the look of shock on the Marked One's face. My hands close on its hands, and I pull hard; there's a sound not unlike leather snapping, and the Marked One staggers back, staring in shock at the arms I hold in my hands, then at the ruin of its shoulders. I step back as it slumps to the floor, then lies still.

I drop the arms and turn back to the door, moving in silence to the door and looking around.

No companions, no spare packs, no beasts of burden... Looters...

I pile the three dead in the corner and tie the Bright One's hands behind its back, leaving it propped up against the far wall. The smell of meat is strong in the room, and I feel my insides react on a primal level.

We can survive on sunlight, but it doesn't feed the true hunger...

I move towards the bodies, pausing as I look down at them.

Be wary of what you eat, but eat while you can; there may not be another time; take what you need, but leave the rest behind...

The words of Alpha flow back to me across the gulf of time, its sacrifice so that the Brigade would continue through the gift of its flesh. I consume the heart of the Marked One first.

A worthy adversary should be rewarded appropriately.

So long without meat, I feel my muscles singing as the energy flows up into them, not the cold energy that I get from the sun.

Hot like blood, like a drug; this is what we were supposed to do, to be; we were never meant to exist as long as this. We were made to consume our enemies, to feast upon them and take their strength into us to use as our own.

I look at the body and remember the surge of information I received from Alpha when I consumed its brain. What has happened in the world since I came here? Does the war still rage?

Do I still have purpose in this world?

I reach down and take the brain of the Marked One, turning it over in my hand for a second before consuming it. My eyes close as the force of knowledge explodes within me, opening to a terrible hunger. I dig into the heads of the other two without finesse and devour what I find there. I turn to the Bright One and pause as the random memory of the Marked One echoes in my brain.

Aline, her name is Aline.

I stop as the memory digests, turning back to look at the Marked One.

It had thoughts for her. Not just thoughts...

There's a curious sensation in my chest: not pain, not muscles moving, something else. I put my hand on my chest, probing for what it might be. No damage, nothing else, but a sharp pain in my shoulders and the memory of something else, a flash of an image, one of the Brigade holding two arms aloft.

Not one of the Brigade, me... This is the last thing the Marked One saw...

Another feeling in my chest, moving up to my head, like a buzzing there, a feeling of heaviness. I shake my head and look at the armoured figures, the memories filtering in faster than I can sort through them.

Never trained to deal with anything beyond the influx of memory, and what I learned from Alpha isn't enough...

There's a kaleidoscope of bright lights, and I crouch with my head in my hands as my vision blurs with the pressure: a thousand memories, thoughts of training, of travelling. A bright day, the wind in my hair, the Bright One turning to look at me, its mouth widening as it shows its teeth, but not a display of aggression, something else. The sensation in my chest again.

Emotion...This must be emotion...Should have left the brain alone...

I rise up as the memories finish filtering in, taking a step forwards, then across. The movements feel natural, even though I've never done them before. I move again, one hand over the other, crossing my arms as I step through.

Eskran Mila, first movement of Tine Discipline...

The Bright One stirs against the wall, and I force myself back to the present, turning to look back at the other bodies. Before now it wouldn't have concerned me, just another enemy, but now, now there's something else in my head.

Wouldn't do to leave the bodies where friends could see them...

I frown, picking up the bodies one by one and climbing over the ropes to get to the ledge above, leaving each of them piled up in a heap there before dropping back down. I look around the chamber and move towards the Bright One.

Aline...

I shake my head again, trying to clear the thought, standing still as the Bright One opens its eyes and looks around, its gaze coming to rest on me. Its eyes open wide, and it scrambles backwards.

"Rehin tahel. A dechetel. A DECHETEL." The words get louder as it pushes back against the wall.

I hold up one hand, waiting for the words to filter through the memories. The Bright One squirms in the bonds and looks up at me.

"A dechetel," it says again, my head buzzes as the memory filters. "I obeyed."

"O..." *I haven't used my voice in a long time.* "Obeyed?"

"You're not it." The Bright One looks at me and frowns. "Who are you?"

"Brigade One Alpha," I say, my voice thick with dust. "Why...are you here?"

"You..." It frowns, its fear of me evident, but its fear of disobeying me even stronger. "Something like you sent us."

"I am the last." My frown mirrors hers. "There are no more like me."

"There's one outside," it says. "Bigger than you. Said it would kill us if we failed."

"You have nothing to fear. If I wanted you dead, you would not have woken." I nod for emphasis, not giving it time to think about what I've said. "Tell me the name of the one that sent you?"

"Brigade One Zenith." A look of uncertainty in its face as it looks me up and down. "Like you, just bigger, much bigger."

"Zenith?" I ask, then my own memory reasserts. "The least of us?"

"Least of you?" There's a half laugh in its tone before it looks up and then averts its eyes, stilling its mouth. It waits a half second, then it looks up at me. "Are you serious? It's three times the size of you, and it's never been beaten."

"Zenith?" I frown as the Marked One's memories come through.

A hundred years of war; an invincible warlord that learned from the brains of those it killed; a fighter without parallel. A monstrous creature able to break anything.

I try to reconcile my own memories of Zenith, the runt that we left behind at Xern, with the memories of the Marked One. Even accounting for them being smaller than me, the creature in front of them is massive beyond reckoning, looking like one of us, but showing the signs of uncontrolled growth—the muscles overbuilt, the skin hardened over in layers of armour. I close my eyes to try and keep the image, but to no avail.

"What did it tell you?" I ask the Bright One.

"Gave us a book." It looks down at the book it dropped. "Told us to come in and open the vault, bring whatever was inside, out."

"Why didn't it come in itself?" I ask.

"Doesn't fit in here." The Bright One looks puzzled. "Promised us it'd leave our homelands alone if we succeeded."

"Did it tell you what might be in here?" I frown. "Did it warn you about me?"

"No, it just said to come down and open the vault." It pauses. "Where are my friends?"

I open my mouth to speak, and a shard of memory spikes deep inside.

The Bright One, clad in black cloth, the others to each side of us, a cord of red binding all our hands.

"I…" The uncertainty is new to me; I can't say that I like it. "Aline, I…"

"How do you know my name?" Aline's eyes go wide. "Where's everyone else?"

"Gone." My words are hollow now, the realisation of what I've done sits like dead metal in my chest as I hold my hands out to forestall her protest. "I am the guardian of this vault. I have been for more than four hundred years. I thought you were here to loot it. I…"

"Where are they?" Aline looks me in the eye. "Where are my *zucha*?"

Zucha, Bound in blood

I close my eyes and tap my chest. "Here," I say, my voice taking an accent unnatural to me. "They are here, in me."

A moment of silence, and I open my eyes to see Aline looking at me in disbelief. I tap my chest again, and my other hand moves quickly into three positions. Her eyes flicker down to look at my hand, and she looks up at me with her eyes wide.

"Inosh…you can't be." She shakes her head, the realisation of what I'm saying not getting through her disbelief. "You're not him."

"I am all he was." My voice still carries the accent. "All they were."

"Was?"

Damn it.

"Was." I speak softly. "I am sorry. You were all dead the second you entered this chamber. Zenith would have known that; he sent you to your deaths."

"How?" I see her expression change, still not believing what she's hearing. "How can he be within you?"

"I take the knowledge of my enemies…" I say, trying to skirt around telling her how I can do it. "His knowledge, his…*being* is a part of me now."

"Prove it…" She looks at me, her eyes hostile now.

"Aline…" I look her in the eye, trying to find a memory that would help. "It is not now, but forever. It is not just this life, but…"

"All lives." She finishes the sentence, her brain hearing the words, but her heart not accepting their truth. "We are strong…"

"For those who have no strength of their own." My hand reaches out to hers, my claws cutting through the bindings.

She opens her hands and flexes, my hand reaching out to press my index finger against her palm. Her hand snakes around mine, her index finger pressing against my palm in return, a reflex action.

She draws her hand back as if stung, her mouth opening wide as some semblance of understanding enters into her consciousness. Her hands come up to cover her mouth, and tears form at the edges of her eyes. I reach out on impulse, but not my impulse, *his...*

She recoils from my touch, and I bring my hands back instantly, the rejection like a knife to me.

Take what you need; leave the rest behind.

Alpha's words are hollow in my mind. Without the specialised training, I could not have filtered out the emotions that came with the brain and heart. I look at Aline, stepping back into the square of sunlight in the middle of the room, the sun sponges on my back flaring. The influx of energy speeds the memory absorption, and another thought comes back to me.

I look to each of the others, Aline shaking her head, as we stand outside the antechamber.

"We do this, and Zenith will leave our homelands alone," I say. "We'll have time to make a defense against the horde."

"You don't believe that." Gres shakes his head, the helmet scraping against his gorget. "He's not going to stop till he rules the world."

"But if he doesn't start with us," I say, "we can raise an army to fight against him."

"Your idealism will be the death of you," Talren snorts, her voice muffled through the plate helm.

"Maybe," I say, "but not today."

"All right, come on." Aline points at the door, then looks at Gres. "Reckon you can break that?"

"Faster than he can pick it." Gres looks at me and grins. "Come on..."

"You came here." I keep my words slow. "To give your people another chance against Zenith."

She doesn't say anything, her eyes steady on me, her uncertainty clear.

"I cannot..." I search for the words again. "Make right what I have done. I cannot give back what I have taken. Do you understand that I bear you no malice?"

"Where are my friends?" Her eyes are still fearful.

I shake my head. "Gone."

"Where are they?" Her question is more forceful, and I lean back.

"Gone." I shake my head again. "Aline, I..."

"YOU DON'T CALL ME THAT..." she howls at me, her finger prodding my chest to no effect. "YOU...you don't..." Her hands cover her face, and she sobs quietly.

I start to reach out, my rational mind overruled by the impulse within my chest, then pull my hand back again.

I'm not him...I'm not him...I'm not him...

I sit in silence just beyond the square of sunlight, a sensation hard to describe, like my hearts are in my stomach. I hold my hands together, a jumble of words spilling into my head. I close my eyes and concentrate, trying to find words from the meat digesting within me.

"It may be he shall take my hand," I murmur, "and lead me into his dark land and close my eyes and quench my breath..."

"It may be I shall pass him still." I open my eyes to see Aline looking at me. "I have a rendezvous with Death."

She stops and looks me in the eye, her head cocked to the side. "How...how do you know these things?"

"I am him." I still don't have the words, and I feel the heavy sensation in my stomach grow. "I..."

Either tell her or end her...

The rigidity of what I learned from Alpha sits strong in my head; there are no other options.

"I ate his brain..." I say. "Our kind were made to learn from those we defeat; we learn by consuming them and taking what they were."

Her eyes go wide as the words register in her ears, her head shaking from side to side in disbelief.

"I ate him." I nod. "I now *am* him..."

"You can't be him..." She stares at me. "You can't be..."

I step back into the sunlight, and the sun sponges flare again, the digestion speeding up.

The creature leans forwards, crouching down to bring its head level with mine, the sun sponges on its back flaring massively, its eyes glowing with power as it drinks in the energy of the world around it. It looks at the camp below, then over at the small entrance on the side of the mountain.

"That..." it growls, the words coming clumsy from a mouth evolved to tear and consume flesh. "That is where the last of my kind is. You go in there. You bring it to me, dead or alive, and I'll spare your people. You'll be allowed to go home again."

"Is it like you?" I ask. "We can't beat it if it's like you."

"Like me?" A rattling of overgrown vocal cords that passes for laughter. "I was once like it, but it left me behind, and now I want what should have been mine all along. You will bring it to me. I will do the rest; it will be no threat to you."

"So why can't you do it?" All eyes turn to Jener as he looks up at the creature. "Why do you need us?"

The creature's arm snaps forwards and yanks Jener into the air, its mouth opening wide to encompass his whole head. The sound of snapping bones and tearing flesh echoes for a few seconds as it chews before discarding the body to the side.

"Because I just ate..." the creature says. "And it might have disagreed with me. Any more questions?"

"Zenith ate one of you before you came in here," I say slowly. "Did it not?"

"It did." She nods, looking uncertain.

"Is it so hard to believe that I am any different?"

"If you ate someone, you could not be him," she says, her certainty returning. "Inosh would never eat people."

"He ate meat." I shrug. "He particularly enjoyed beef."

"He did." She nods, then shakes her head. "It's not the same."

"It is to me. I am the last of my kind." I think for a second and then nod. "The second to last of my kind, along with Zenith."

"Why does it want you?" She frowns. "Why you, why now?"

"It wants what I have." I tap my forehead. "It was left behind in the mountains when we were sent here to guard this."

"And what's in there?" She points at the door.

"I don't know." I shrug.

"You came here to guard something, and you don't know what it is." She sounds incredulous.

"I was told to guard this, along with twenty-four of my kind," I say. "We lost six of us in the taking of the castle outside, and the rest of us waited for our orders."

"Orders?" she asks.

"Alpha was told that we would be given other orders when we'd finished what we came here to do."

"But you're Alpha." She frowns.

"I am now." I nod. "I started as BR1S, Brigade One Slaughter, Master of Close Quarters."

"I don't understand." Her frown deepens.

"When we consume a living creature, it becomes a part of us." I open my hands to her again. "Like Inosh, we take all that it was and make it a part of ourselves. We live a long time, but we eventually need to eat, which is why they sent so many of us. When the sunlight was no longer enough, we consumed each other until we received other orders. When we consume one of our own, we learn their skills, and we take their rank if it is higher than ours."

"How many of your own did you eat?"

"So you believe me?" I ask, sidestepping the question.

"How long have you been here?" She makes an equal sidestep. "How long really?"

"When we came here, we'd just put down the Sertian emperor," I say. "They sent us from his throne room to here."

"That was five hundred years ago."

"To me, that could have been yesterday," I say. "We don't age the way you do. We don't learn except by the destruction of others."

"Why did they send you here?"

"We don't know." I shake my head. "Alpha was the only one who knew our orders, and when I consumed it, it had no answers."

She nods and walks around the room, her manner completely changed, no trace of any fear in her eyes. "So you remained here, for all those years, and you never thought to go outside and see what had happened to the world you left behind?"

"Duty." I nod. "It is all we have."

"Where are my friends?" She turns to face me.

"Close by." I look closely at her, the claws sliding out of my fingers as I look around the room, my ears turning outwards. "You're no longer afraid of me...Why?"

"Where are they?" She looks around, then up, seeing the blood dripping off the ledge above.

"I did not want you to see them." I remain still. "I did not know that killing was wrong before..."

"No, you didn't." She turns to me, her mood growing jubilant. "The stories that Gres told us, that Zenith grew strong by consuming all those it defeated, those were all true, and in sending us here, it's delivered us you."

"*Delivered?*" I start to pace back and forth, keeping my eye on her. "You cannot take me from here; this is my duty."

"There is a world outside that needs you more than the world that sent you here," she says. "Your masters, whoever they were, are gone, long gone, and with them, your duty."

"It is not for me to dispute their orders." I frown as another memory surfaces.

"You shouldn't have come for me." I look through the bars of the cell as Gres brings the hammer down on the lock. "Our orders were to hold the line."

"Orders be damned." Gres grins at me and pulls the door open. "Sometimes you need to tell them where to get off."

I put one hand to my head as the conflicting emotions spiral around inside me, feeling a heat in my chest as I pace towards Aline, my claws sliding out. She opens her arms wide to me, presenting a target of her chest and throat. I stagger back as another memory surfaces.

"He's the enemy." Talren hefts her sword and looks at the unconscious guard on the floor. "We should end him."

"He's done nothing to us," Gres says. "He was just holding the door as he was told to. We don't kill when we don't have to."

I curse in three languages new to me, and Aline steps forwards into the sun, her hair now so bright as to be blinding.

"You must help us," she says, her fingers reaching out to me, the familiarity of her touch from the memory of the dead within me. "We cannot stop Zenith, but you can."

"It has grown beyond my capacity to end." I shake my head. "Even with the skills I have, I cannot defeat it on open ground."

"But it lacks your discipline," she says. "If you had been it, you would have devoured all of us without pause."

"BR1C," I say. "Control. Master yourself and nothing may deflect your will."

"And if it had that, it would not rampage through my world as it has."

"If it had that, it would have all of me, and I do not know what else it has learned in the years since I saw it last," I growl. "My memory of it is a scrawny beast not worthy of the regiments; it must have grown strong feeding on vermin and carrion."

"But now it controls more than half of my world." Aline puts her hand under my chin and tilts my head up to look into my eyes, stepping forwards. "And you can stop it."

"I cannot risk what I have falling into the hands of someone who would turn it to dark purpose." I step back, even as the mind of Inosh compels me to step forwards, the sun sponges on my back folding in as I step out of the light.

"You truly become all the things you eat?" She looks me in the eye.

"On my honour, *zucha.*" I hear the words a split second before I realise they were said by me.

By him...

"Did you..." She pauses for a second. "Eat all of my friends?"

"I did." The truth is known already; it makes no difference to speak it.

"Then you know what they know; you know what's going on out

there."

Burning kingdoms, the blasted ruins of civilisations in many countries, like a red tide of fire over the land. At the front, Zenith, always Zenith.

"I know." I nod. "But I cannot leave here."

"Do you not see what we're up against?" She takes a step forwards. "How can you stand there and not want to help us? You can't be all the things they were. They would have given anything to end the slaughter."

"But they knew that sometimes the hardest fight is the one you can't fight," I say. "They would have been slaughtered by Zenith, so will I, and your world will fall all the quicker."

"No..." She draws her dagger. "You will come out to face what you left behind."

"I will not." I hold my hand out, palms up. "I cannot kill again."

"Then only one thing remains." She smiles, her dagger turning in her hand till she's holding it overhand.

"You cannot harm me." I shake my head. "I will not hurt you."

"Oh, I know." She nods. "But I want to be with my friends again, and my friends are in you."

"I won't..." The very thought is anathema to me now. "You can live. I will not kill you."

"This is not life." She waves her dagger towards the outside. "This is waiting for Death, and I'm tired of waiting."

She plunges the dagger inwards, the blade sinking in up to the hilt. She looks down with a puzzled expression, then her legs give way, and she crashes to the floor. I'm by her side in a second, the panic of the other three coursing through me. She looks up and half smiles as the blood flows down her tunic.

"Let me be with my friends." She reaches up to touch my face. "Pl...."

Her hand drops away, and her body goes limp in my arms. I stare down in horror as the primal scream of the other three builds in my throat, the chamber amplifying the noise back to me tenfold. I sit and cradle the body in my arms, and the cold logic of Alpha repeats in my mind.

Take what you need; leave the rest behind.

I look down at the small body in my arms and feel the pull of three minds within mine, the need for their friend to be with them.

I am them; they need her.

I try to turn away, to leave the body, but the pull of my own biology is strong and the pull of the souls within me stronger still. The crack of bones beneath my fingers, a wet slurping noise that sends a shudder of revulsion down my spine, and the deed is done.

Another kaleidoscope of thoughts explodes within me, but this one more focussed as if the thoughts were the only things in the brain.

The fields of Senslan on fire, the inhabitants slaughtered to the last.

The castle at Otri reduced to rubble, a thousand years of history broken asunder.

I feel the heat in my heart, a blind, bottomless fury at the crimes that Zenith has committed.

The sacking of Angor, where the pyres for the dead raged for weeks afterwards.

I feel the body drop from my hands as the knowledge suffuses me, my claws digging into my palms as I feel the weight of Aline's misery upon me.

The creature stands before me, it's arms held forwards, palms up. "I will not kill you," it says.

"This is not life." I feel the despondency of my failure. "This is waiting for Death, and I'm tired of waiting..."

A spike of pain in my chest as I feel the memory of the dagger, and I open my eyes wide. I look down at the swords upon the floor, utterly alone, my friends all gone, never to talk to me again, never to see them, never to hear their voices again. I take up the sword and weigh the balance.

It could penetrate my armour if you knew where to put it.

I stop as the sword seems to move of its own accord, and I place the sword at the junction point of my armour, pausing as the cold commandments of the Brigade stir within me, holding back the raging emotions for a second.

Take what you need; leave the rest behind.

I pull the sword back with an effort of will; I understand Aline's last thoughts, and it will not be long before I am compelled to act on them. But Zenith has not my training; if it wins, it will take everything that I am; the emotions will come through before the training, and if it's hard for me to hold these thoughts, these impulses, back, it will be impossible for it to before it's too late. I stagger upright, looking down at the bodies of my victims, at the bones of my friends.

I will win and kill Zenith, or Zenith will win and end itself...

Aline's smile is on my lips as for the first time since I got here. I step out of the chamber and into the cold air of my last day.

The End

To connect with John Dodd, follow these links:

website: www.theodd.com

blog: www.millionwordman.blogspot.com

He can also be found by typing "millionwordman" in any search engine.

Cover by Author.

Fingers and Hot Steel

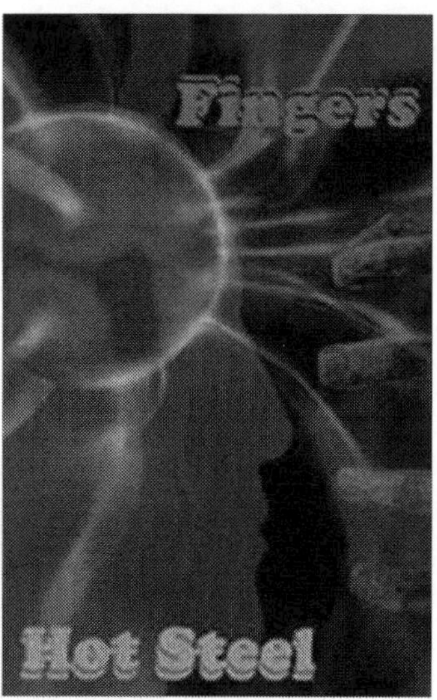

Mike Cooley

Introduction - Mike has been writing science fiction and fantasy stories for many years. His writing has an edge to it. He enjoys exploring the dark and surreal landscapes of the mind. Fingers is followed by Hot Steel.

***

Fingers

I didn't want to cut it off, but when it moved again, I had no choice. The silver finger twitched and sparked, with gold wires extending from the cut end like nerves. I was down to three fingers on my left hand and two on my right. I held the blade with my left and watched the shorn digits flex like inchworms trying to crawl across the dark wood of the desk. The dim room around me smelled of dust and pain.

My face was the color of mercury and emotionless, contrary to the turbulence within. It was dark outside my window, with only the reddish-yellow glow of a streetlight piercing the night. The only sound was the hum of the power grid. Even the familiar rasp of my breath was missing—along with the thud of a heartbeat in my ears.

They had warned me about the adjustment period. One of the fingers curled, then rolled off the desk. I tried to grin at my reflection in the glass, but my metal lips resisted. One thing they hadn't mentioned when they had told me my thoughts would be accelerated a thousand-fold was that the depression would hit like a tsunami. There were still marks on my neck where I had tried to saw my head off.

I kept my brain in a jar on the bedside table to remind myself that I wasn't real anymore. It floated serenely in an amber fluid. My thoughts and dreams had been drained out and poured into this cybernetic matrix. At first it wasn't that bad.

Then Didra had jumped.

Our new android bodies were extremely repairable. We would all live forever. If we wanted to. Many didn't. Couldn't handle the stress. Every bad thought multiplied. Every small step toward depression becoming an ocean of despair. Every glance in a mirror a reminder of all we had lost. Every touch of skin, artificial.

I looked down at the glittering fingers. Traitors. I felt hostility rising in my circuits. On the wall above me, the monitor blinked red. I knew they were watching. They hadn't expected the first years of our immortality to be rife with suicide.

I wanted to jump, like Didra. But they had reinforced all the windows and sealed the rooftops. It turns out you can be heartbroken without a heart. I drew tears running down my face like raindrops under my green irises. Behind my eyes, my synthetic brain glowed blue. Jagged bolts of thought flickered across the surface.

One of the remaining fingers on my left hand flexed against my will. I chopped it off. It was going to be hard to masturbate with only two fingers on each hand. Luckily, I had no sex organs anymore. AndroidTech considered them disruptive.

It's too bad we had ruined the atmosphere and never left Earth. We could have stayed real. I pulled my fingers slowly across the desk, feeling the intricacies of the wood grain, a reminder of trees that no longer existed.

I smashed the jar, crushing the remains of my organic brain between my hands. Amber fluid dripped onto the floor like blood. I smeared the gray matter on my face and chest.

I stood up, ran across the room, and bashed into the wall—over and over. And over.

Until they came for me.

Hot Steel

The smooth, cold steel of the Beretta felt reassuring against my thigh as I entered his office. I let him sit back down before I shot him. Then I closed my eyes and held my dad's gun between my breasts, letting the heat from the barrel work its way deep into my tattered soul. I remembered the night I dug him up to get it. He had insisted it be buried with him. I pushed the slide release and slid it off, holding it beneath my nose, my long, dark hair hanging down to my shoulders. The smell of powder and hot metal sent shivers down my spine. Dan stared at the ceiling, blood oozing from the hole in his forehead. There was less blood than I expected. Time to switch to hollow points.

I left when the sirens got loud, after clicking the barrel back in place and sliding the 9mm into the holster beneath my short black dress. The security cameras perched in the ceiling of the office complex had a good view of my breasts as I looked up and smiled. My nipples were hard from the killing. I could hear the sound of wings on the other side of the gateway. Flapping ponderously as they waited for me. Outside the sky was blue and dotted with clouds. It was a warm summer day. The *Tribune* at the newsstand had a grainy picture of me on the front with the caption "Femme Fatale Body Count Rises." I was just getting started.

I slipped two loaded fifteen-mags down my shirt where they nestled sweetly between my breasts before I left my apartment on the South side of St. Paul. I licked the barrel of my trusty 92FS and rubbed the side of it against my face like I was getting prepared to suck it down my throat. It was cool and dark...just waiting and waiting for me to flick off the safety and blow someone's brains out. I had a list. It was three days since Dan. And a week since I started. There were police everywhere, but they didn't seem to recognize me. At the edges of my vision, the dark wings flickered up and down, edging closer.

The bank was fun. Shooting that many people made me wet. The iron grate separating me from Hell creaked open on its rusty hinges, and I could smell the decay of the river. The sky was grey and filled with bats. I could hear a hum like the sound of a power transformer about to blow. I slipped another mag in the Beretta and stopped at an Irish bar to use the bathroom. The blood spatters didn't show on my red dress. I wiped droplets off my face and hands. The blood tasted salty. There was a glimmer of recognition in the bartender's eyes. I leaned over and ordered a Guinness, letting my succulent tits erase his suspicions. I could hear the Beretta whispering its sweet song into my mind as I drank.

Sam was last. I shot him in the balls when he answered the door. The look on his face was priceless. My dad's gun radiated heat and happiness. Charon was calling for me: *"Melissa. Melissa."*

It wasn't time yet. I pushed Sam to the floor on his back and kneeled over his face with my knees on each side and held him down as he bled to death, not giving him the release of a quick death. His struggling got me off as I rubbed the tip of the warm Beretta against myself.

The police came and examined the body as I sipped lemonade on his couch. They didn't seem to notice me.

***

"So, what's her story?" asked the doctor as he watched the green lines tracing across the display. He tapped the side of the machine out of habit and jotted down notes on his clipboard. The girl was pale, dark-haired, and very beautiful.

"Taken hostage during a bank robbery," said the nurse. "They took her home, to her own house, and raped her. Then they shot her dad when he got home from work. Then they shot her three times and left her for dead."

"Next of kin?" asked the doctor.

"She's got no one. It was just her and her dad, and he didn't make it."

"No brain activity," said the doctor. "Time of death—" He looked at the clock, jotted it down, and flicked off the ventilator.

***

I pulled back the slide and ejected a brass shell from the chamber as the coroner zipped up the body bag over Sam's cold, dead eyes. The shell *pinged* onto the glass table in his living room and rolled off onto the white carpet. I pulled the action back and unloaded another shell, and another, until the mag was empty. Then I set the gun down on the table and walked outside.

The sky was crimson and full of pterodactyls. The moon hung large in the sky like a rotting melon. I stepped onto the boat at the edge of the river, and the char of brimstone flooded my nostrils. Charon helped me off on the far side, kissing the back of my hand, and told me to walk towards the light.

***

The nurse reached into her pocket and felt the cool, dark steel. And the list. She went to the front desk and punched out early.

The End

Connect with Mike Cooley at the following links:

Website: https://mikecooleyfiction.com

Twitter: https://twitter.com/last writes

Cover by Sunni Seckinger.

Tocsin

Brian Bogart

Brian Bogart is an American author of dark fiction and horror/fantasy. He has written stories most of his life and has been a fan of the genre since the age of seven. His approach to storytelling is a tad macabre at times but tries to capture the nuances of the humanity and sometimes, inhumanity, beneath the surface. You can find him and his works in various places online. Dream Darkly and Keep Writing.

Alice finds herself in a Clockwork Wonderland. But what horrors lurk in this twisted fantasy world? Will she survive? Will she make it to the Tower? Time is a harsh mistress in the gloom of an alien landscape. Dangers await her as she makes her way through this unsettling tale.

***

Tocsin (noun)
1. An alarm bell or signal.
2. A warning; an omen.

The Hatter had said a great many things to Alice. Some were

nonsensical to the logical mind and others profound. He and his guests may have been locked in a never-ending tea party, but that did not mean she would remain trapped in Wonderland in a similar fashion. Time had arranged a different punishment for her offenses.

"No tea parties for you, little girl," the voice boomed in her head. The voice was foreign yet familiar, like a forgotten shard of memory piercing her ears.

She held her small hands to the sides of her head and focused. His taunting was a distraction, just one of many in this place. She clenched her fists, lowering them to her sides. Her childish heart began to beat in rhythm to the sounds around her. She was determined. She was a girl who saw things to an end. She was no Mad Hare, after all.

Alice glanced to the left and saw a crooked wooden sign. It read: Clockwork Wilds. She pondered the name a moment then stared down the dirt path ahead.

It was a forested area, dense with odd trees and shrubbery. She bent down and began crawling through the limbs stretching across the entrance. Emerging on the other side, the name on the sign made sense.

She now stood in the shadowed confines of the wood. Her eyes widened in fascination. All around, she was surrounded by tall blades of grass and sunflowers. Monstrous oaks stretching so far into the darkened sky above that their leaves and moss formed a seemingly endless canopy above her. Thin shafts of light from the gibbous moon gave the illumination of her surroundings an ethereal tint.

This was all an illusion, though. These were not Nature's creations. Wood and grass, the petals of the swaying sunflowers—these were all whirring mechanisms of abstract machinery. They had been painted to appear real, but the mimicry ended just beneath the surface.

The tree limbs were alive, the rotating and telescoping arms flailing madly. Each segment was comprised with circular layers, grinding together as they sparked and spun. They seemed angry in their motions, reaching for anything and everything that dared come close.

The petals of the sunflowers seemed to breathe, opening and closing in unison. Alice took a cautious step forward. The grass underfoot was not grass at all, either. They were sharpened spikes of glass, cold and scraping the soles of her doll-like shoes. This frightened her more than the groping branches. A simple fall or even heavy step could prove a bloody and fatal mistake. She swallowed hard, her legs trembling in her stockings. She took two more steps. An errant shard of the grass hung on the material, down by her ankles. It was only a slight tear. Though it barely scratched the flesh, it warned her of the possible finality of the test before her.

The ceaseless whirring and turning of gears around her began to amplify. The sunflowers rose and leaned forward to meet her frightened face. She caught her own wide-eyed reflection in the panes of glass nestled in the dead center of the blossoming petals. Each one was adorned with the hands of a clock, spinning as if brought to life at that very misstep. They seemed to sense her soft skin had been in danger and eager to witness even more. She caught herself from staggering back. The hands of each clock continued to spin before slowing to a stop in unison, at precisely the same position.

"Time waits for no one, sweet Alice," the voice chided, bored by her lack of urgency. "Your task is simple: Go to the clearing in the center of the wood. Climb the Great Oak Clock tower there. When you reach the top, ring the Bell. That is all. Very simple."

Time then laughed. The very vibrations of his wicked cackle sang the sharp needles beneath her feet into a frenzy and each metal monstrosity in the forest hummed in response. The noise was like thunder in her head. Alice winced and tried to focus on anything but the noise, noticing that there seemed a layer of fog in the distance. Thick and white like steam. She guessed that it would be hot on her skin, as well. Too hot.

"When the hands of the clock come together, in this forest you shall remain forever. If, by Fate's mercy, you do succeed, I will still enjoy how much you bleed!"

With that last word hanging in the musky air around her, every clock within view began ticking. It was the sound of an old grandfather clock, slow and meticulous. The pistons all around pounded with such force that her own heartbeat felt frail by comparison. Her chest hammered in anxious rhythms that made her nearly cry.

Alice stifled the tears. She was certain she would need to save them for when she reached to top of the damned clock tower and shouted her victory above the steel and iron tree lines. Shout it right into the face of Time Himself, if He dared ever to show it. She took a deep breath. Ignoring the tree limbs and blades buzzing above her, she let out a yell that filled her heart with courage.

"I'll climb your stupid tower and ring that bell! Cut me you may, but break me, you will not!"

She took a long look behind her. She waved goodbye to the safety of her previous adventures and walked further into the shadows ahead.

The first few paces were the worst. She walked with a brave elegance, despite each blade of sharp glass tearing into her shoes. She avoided her tiptoes, especially. What had first seemed to require dainty movements proved the opposite. If she took great strides, propelling herself with constant momentum, the soles of her shoes would catch the sharp bits only randomly. Her knees stayed as straight as they could, and for a very long time, it seemed that would be enough. After ten minutes of traversing the hungry teeth of fake grass gnashing angrily underfoot, she teetered forward.

She caught herself immediately but not before the tip of her right shoe caught between two blades, snagging it. She lifted her leg and rested her foot against her left knee. Her balance was a thing of grace, but the shoe shredding and spinning into the hungry mechanical abyss below was anything but. Bits of it were flung high into view before being pulled down and away like a piece of driftwood in a storm. Bits of stringy leather was all that was soon left. The buckle from her shoe danced and clanged on the surface.

Shards of glass shattered, scattering into her face. Alice shielded her eyes. She was careful to keep her balance. She noticed that the shoe's buckle had succeeded in stopping the blades from moving. For how long, she couldn't know. She laid her foot down gingerly. Tiny pinpricks of pain nipped at the tender soles of her feet. It stung but it was bearable. Though her stockings were torn slightly they provided a bit of cushion. She made her way hastily to a large tree trunk in the distance. She did her best to ignore the lawn as it screamed back to life behind her.

She sat down and crossed her legs. Her foot was throbbing. Pursing her lips and squinting, she tore a part of her dress and wrapped it around her wound. It was bleeding, ruining her stockings. She wriggled her toes, thankful but annoyed. What once had been pure white was now stained a dark and sticky pink. She pouted and applied more pressure. After a few moments, most of the bleeding had stopped, but the tiny lacerations would take ages to heal. Walking would be painful, and her heart sank into her stomach when she considered the climb she may have ahead of her. She glanced at her other shoe, the heel of it chewed thoroughly, and slid it off. She tossed it over her shoulder, into the glassy jaws behind her. The crunching and grinding pleased her.

"Better the shoes than me. Hope you choke on them," she said under her breath.

She glanced at the clock-faced flowers. Forty minutes or perhaps less. It was hard to tell with the steamy fog rolling in. She stood up and practiced walking on her foot. The ground here was solid, if a bit moist. She could feel the muddy texture seep into the stockings and between her toes. It was the first expanse of something natural in a most unnatural place. She prayed there may be more ahead. Maybe a Cheshire smile in the dark or a tasty treat with proper instructions. Even those wonders would be welcomed in the rusted shadows that threatened her here.

Alice turned her focus to the sloshing of the mud instead of the incessant sounds of the clockwork. The sound of time ticking away was maddening. Her eyes felt heavier now as she stared through the fog and into the darkening wood. She shook her head. This was no time for sleeping. Of all the places she had seen in this land, this area filled her with the most uncertainty. She could still see the tree limbs observing from the shadows like angry cobras preparing to strike. Some were sharp and bladed while others appeared to have twig-like fingers. Two heavy branches lashed down at her, the serrated edges falling less than an inch from her nose. Alice screamed and fell to her knees.

The mud was warm and thick, splashing up into her eyes, drenching her arms. She wiped the muck away the best that she could, but succeeded in smearing it more than anything else. She coughed as some touched her lips and, though she knew better, licked them out of curiosity. She regretted that. Not only was it acrid but also viscous. Wiping her hands on her dress, she stood and noticed that the mud wasn't mud. It was an odd mixture of black and red. It reminded her of oil. She imagined the machines here would bleed a similar substance, if harmed.

"Maybe it belongs to both the forest and its victims," a girl's voice whispered from behind her. Alice turned, sloshing the mud as she stood. It was a child's voice. It could almost have been her own voice from years ago. Her heart panicked in her chest as she worried that in this nightmare, it was.

She could hear faint laughter. It did not seem malicious, but it had a nervous quality. Alice watched as another limb fell. This was followed by another and then another, blocking her original path. That had to be the way, though the Forest itself refused to let her continue. She stepped forward, careful of not catching her dress in the whirring limbs as they snaked around her. She swore she could hear the ticking of the Clock Tower somewhere high in the treetops just beyond. She kicked mud unto the branches as they knotted around each other. The metallic hiss that followed was like the sound of a crashing train uprooting the tracks as it spiraled out of control. They did not enjoy that, and this made her laugh.

"Moan all you want. Whether through there or some other way, you're not stopping me."

The faux oak trees seemed to stretch and groan, breathing their own sarcastic reply. The shy girl's voice sang into the air again, splitting the steamed fog beginning to gather. Alice noticed the fog was indeed hot but not quite as searing as she had originally thought. Her dress clung in places that a girl's dress should not because of the mud and steam. She began to sweat and tendrils of her hair became matted to her face as she followed the voice.

"Come on. I know the way. I went there once. Here, you can't stay."

"Cute," Alice scoffed. "Keep talking then. I'll follow as best I can." She did not know if the voice could be trusted, but it was getting hotter and the fog becoming thick. If it led her closer to the tower and out of the mist, she would play along.

"Should I sing you a tune? Weep like a widow? The shortcut's not far, just follow this kiddo!" The laugh that came afterwards calmed Alice. She found the silliness of her rhymes charming. She would remain cautious, though.

The voice led her down a separate path, one with actual grass. Thick bushes of red roses glistened with dew on either side. The trail seemed normal compared to everything else here, if a bit overgrown with wild vines and brush. No groping branches and sharp objects to avoid. Even the ticking of the clocks seemed faint and distant. Looking back, she could still see the myriad of clocks taunting her.

Alice jumped as a figure darted past her, giggling. She reached her hand out in protest and dashed ahead to where the girl had disappeared. A large oak tree stood there, a clock carved into the fungus-covered bark. It was a crude design, like a children's drawing. She held back a scream when she noticed that the jagged wood held small bits of torn cloth and bloodstained clumps of hair.

Had the tree eaten the girl? She glanced around anxiously, picking up a rotted wooden branch from the grass. She poked at the splintered bark, lifting the fabric and turning it. It was the same color of her dress and seemed the same material, as well. The small hairs began to dance on her pale arm. A sense of dread hung in the air, thicker than the steam and fog she had left behind her.

The rustling of leaves above her drew her attention. She clenched the branch in her hand tight and forced it up and into the low hanging limbs. A small hand reached down, first waving and then yanking on Alice's makeshift weapon. She pulled back with a grunt. There was a loud cracking sound. Two limbs fell, slamming into Alice's shoulder on the way down. She winced and focused her eyes.

Sprawled at Alice's feet, laughing uncontrollably, was a frail little girl of perhaps seven years of age. She sat up, hugging her legs to her chest, and rocked back and forth. The strange girl's hair hung in her eyes, oily strands of blonde only slightly darker than her own. Her dress was shredded in multiple places, the skirt edges frayed. Her eyes were wide and wild. Catching her breath, the girl stood up and brushed the dirt from her knees with a sigh. Her arms were bruised with lacerations running this way and that. The cuts looked deep and possibly, infected.

She was thin, her frame almost skeletal. In fact, the only thing that seemed healthy was her voice and her eyes, though they sat deep in their sockets. Her lips drew back in a thin and cracked grimace before staring up at Alice. Recognition danced behind her sunken eyes, and she smiled. It was a toothy grin that reminded her of a certain cat she had met earlier, although these teeth were less sharp and seemed worn and decaying. It seemed innocent, despite the rotted appearance.

"Torn my flesh and ripped my dress. Perhaps you'll end up less a mess."

The girl licked her dry lips, watching intently as a butterfly fluttered around her head before landing on her nose. She opened her mouth as if in astonishment. The look on her face was endearing. The red and gold wings spread and folded a few times, and the girl giggled, like it was tickling the tip of her nose. Her tongue flicked out and upward but not to return the favor. In one quick motion, the butterfly was gone, her tongue dragging it into her decaying mouth. Locking eyes with Alice, she chewed quickly, spitting out bits of its wings in slight disgust. Alice gagged, her stomach cramping as her throat burned. She held her hands to her mouth, fighting the urge to puke.

The little girl smiled and then apologized. "Sorry, but I've been here so long. I eat what I can, whether right or wrong."

"Yuck," Alice said. "Exactly how long, may I ask?"

The girl's eyes rolled upward and to the side in exaggerated fashion. She rubbed her stomach and picked at her teeth with the jagged fingernail of her hand, spitting out another piece of wing. Satisfied, she pointed to the tree with the poorly etched clock.

"Hard to say, but given that tree... I'd gather it's been at least two years or three. Maybe even more, but this is my fate. I'll guide best I can, but not through that gate."

The child pointed excitedly at a large iron gate a few yards away. Vines and sharp thorns wove in and out of each bar, and Alice realized that if it had not been pointed out, she may have never seen it. It rested amid the thicket of violet and crimson rose bushes, obscured save for the sound of rusted hinges as the gate rattled. An uneven breeze could be felt just beyond, and Alice was certain that the clearing was close. The Tower would not be far now. Her confidence in this was certain, and she turned to face the girl one last time.

"There? I can sense that it isn't very far from here! Thank you, miss. You've been very helpful, indeed!"

Gathering her dress, she started to run towards the iron gate. The girl let out a desperate cry, lunging towards Alice and locking both arms about her waist. Her skin was cold and damp. It felt as if her flesh would eat away the material if left pressed into it for too long. Ignoring the repulsiveness of that thought, she sank down to her knees, removing the girl's arms and placing them at her side.

"No!" she wailed. The tears forming in her eyes were frightening and dark. They resembled ash and smeared like wet mascara as she sobbed. Alice felt the urge to pull her close, to give her a hug. The girl's tongue began running across the cracked sores of her lips. The ashen tears trickled down, and she licked away the soot as they approached her mouth. Alice shuddered and decided against it.

"What? Don't cry. Is there something more? I really must go, little one. With or without you, I can't waste too much time. Do you want to come with me? You know the way, after all. You can help me and be free, too!"

The girl pushed away, shaking her head in a violent and frightened manner. She rubbed her arms as she hugged herself and began pacing. The tears began to gather in the corners of her eyes, her dark lids batting them away. She began murmuring to herself and pulled out tufts of hair, her scalp splitting and flaking away.

"No, no, no! I can never go! I've been once before, you see. The Tower waits for you, not me. The forest is hungry and lies in wait. No room for two, beyond that gate!"

The girl turned, skipping at first, before bounding away. Little footprints and kicked up flecks of dust were all that was left. Alice could still hear her rhyming in the near distance, nervous and gleeful in equal measure. She could barely make out her last words.

"...whatever you do. Remember it is not one, but two!"

Two? Two. What was two? Alice thought on her parting words a moment. Perhaps there were multiple doors. Maybe she would have to ring the bell twice. She did not know exactly, but she was certain that it was secret knowledge, wisdom that would help her. She gestured a goodbye into the dark woods behind her.

"Thank you. Be safe. I will thank you properly, once I am free! This place is no home for one so small," she said, through cupped hands.

She listened for a moment, and once again the forest was almost silent. She could hear the clocks again on the other side of the gate. Pushing up on the rusted latch, she placed her hands against the iron bars. The hinges groaned in protest, but she lowered her shoulder and pressed against it, digging her heels in the dirt. The gate finally surrendered, and she fell forward into the shadows.

The gate closed behind her with a loud and echoing clang. The latch locked back into place. She pulled on the gate, but it remained shut. This was just another distraction. She had wasted too much time, and the spiraling clock hands decorating the trees screamed at her from all sides.

Ten minutes.

Alice ran. She brushed the snaking branches away, hopping over a few crudely implemented tripwires along the way. Her heart raced, and the sound of it in her head was dizzying. The ticktock of the forest made her wince, and she gritted her teeth against the urge to scream back twice as loud. The grassy area just ahead was a welcome sight, for the lurching trees gave way to a small clearing. Not the clearing she needed, but she was closer. She knew it. She had to be.

Pausing to catch her breath, she saw in the first clearing a large red brick wall. It reached so high above her that it was impossible to see what lie beyond it. Flowers bloomed along the stretch of it.

Sharp thorns adorned the petals of each in an exaggerated and cartoon-like fashion. She almost let out a squeal when she noticed that the wall also had giant oak doors embedded on the left and right.

"Door one or door two, I presume?"

She smiled at her own joke. She glanced in the direction of the first door and considered it. Shaking her head, she reached for the knob of the second door. The knob was like fire in her grip, the iron searing into her palm as she turned it. She was sure it would leave a scar. She frowned and pushed the door open.

Cobwebs adorned the doorway, tangling about her when she stepped through. She was like a careless fly in a web. Tiny little legs scuttled into the trees away from the door. She plucked the silken strands from her hair and dress in disgust. There was movement all around her, the trees teeming with activity. Spiders and perhaps other creatures, though it was hard to be certain. Thousands of tiny eyes were watching her. They studied her movement, keeping their distance. Biding their time. They screeched a starved and inhuman pang that made her cringe. She was sure that any moment some horrible thing would lunge, and that caused her flesh to inch up her spine. It was like the spindly legs of spiders crawling under her skin.

Alice could see the Tower in the distance. It was not as tall as she had feared. It rested just above the trees and was dwarfed by even the wall just behind her. She was certain that she could make it in time. If she just ignored the noises that swarmed all around her, she would be home soon. The one place she had never wanted to be but now longed to stay. Gathering the bottom of her tattered dress, she bolted forward with renewed determination. The sounds of the hungry forest creatures behind her continued to follow.

Crooked steps of rotted wood and stone led around the outside of the Tower. Scaling up the outer wall proved challenging. Her stockings snagged more than once on the jutting edges of stone along the way. The wood splintered and cracked as she climbed. One misstep and she would fall. She looked behind her. The eyes she had previously felt on her were now visible below. Unblinking and uncaring, they watched with anticipation. Blood pounded in her head, and waves of dizziness rushed at her. The dark sky weaved in and out of view, but she would make it.

Slabs of stone fell away as she ran. They tumbled and shattered as they collided below. Alice jumped over the window sill ahead and into the Tower itself. The sounds of tiny legs filled her ears again.

She watched as the shadowy spiders moved in tandem, thankfully away from her. They were a large black mass, undulating like a river flowing downstream. They scurried up and over the clutter of the room and out of sight. They were nesting inside the bell itself now, waiting for her to pull the rope.

Despite this, she would pull it. Not once but twice, just to be sure.

Her heart began thundering as she hurtled forward on trembling legs. Her blood coursed violently, her head swimming with anticipation. Almost giddy, she glanced at the rope dangling from the bell. She saw the shadows of hundreds of erratic movements all around her and even more from inside the bell itself. Her fingers twitched nervously as she grabbed at the cord.

The cord seemed heavy and alive. She could feel it pulsing in her grip. It was sticky and rubbery, the texture of melted latex. She swallowed hard and tightened her fist around it. Bits of the rope oozed between her fingers, dripping slowly to the dusty floor. She moved her feet out of instinct. Globs of it landed with a squishing sound, followed by the skittering chatter of the bugs. They stayed hidden, but the noises they made seemed like laughter.

She pulled.

The gonging of the bell started as a faint tone, widening and spiraling in musical echoes. She felt vibrations all around, and the spiders began to fall, drenching her hand. Her hand remained steady. It no longer looked like her hand but instead a gloved and hellish mockery of one. The itching movements of the bugs as she prepared for another pull was maddening. They wormed their way between her fingers, their tiny legs and teeth pricking her skin in a constant frenzy.

She pulled again.

The eight-legged beasts began to rain down again, scattering and spinning as they fell. The sound of their bodies hitting the floor was like the soft, continual sound of rain pattering against glass. They inched towards her. She stared in disgust and began stomping at them. The feeling of their round abdomens crunching against her stockings brought tears to her eyes, and she gagged. Her eyes widened as she watched a few tend to some of their injured brethren. They spun their webbing, forming makeshift slings for those with shattered limbs. It was equal parts fascinating and unnerving.

Then in one quick motion, they paused. Their beady eyes fixated on the floor, and for a moment, they seemed satiated. Hairy mandibles opened and closed, chattering their secret language in excitement. Alice had started bleeding. She noticed now that her hand was covered in tiny cuts, small bites that did not hurt at all. In fact she felt numb all over, except for her face. A puddle of blood pooled at her feet. That was the reason for their distraction. It was feeding time. They began to drag their oral appendages in the red mess beneath her. She did the best she could to turn away. Given the toxin in her veins, it was a wasted effort.

Alice sensed her knees and body stiffening before she began to rock back and forth. She closed her eyes to brace for a fall. She knew she would not feel it if she did. The venom had guaranteed that. She could almost sense a numbness in her very brain, a slowing of thought and understanding. The end of being anything at all. It worked slow but efficient, and what she glimpsed next made that fact seem a blessing.

Eight monstrous legs stabbed into view around her, each adorned with sharp and coarse hairs. The limbs seemed mechanical in their movements but not like the plant life she had witnessed earlier. Those had seemed man-made, the work of a skilled madman. These spindly legs seemed borne not of anything dreamed in nature. They were the creation of an insane god, deprived of all sense of decency. Each hair dripped with the pungent gore of nightly feasts and conquered beasts.

She heard the thud of each step as the legs positioned themselves on either side of her. Her vision began to dim, but she saw the moist ends of its hungry mandibles teasing the sides of her face. It seemed to coax her, an almost reassuring gesture that it had done countless times before. She decided that she could not bear to watch. Instead of closing her eyes, she focused on the window and the starlit sky behind the beast.

In the distance, stretched high against the moonlight behind it, there was a second Tower. The girl's voice seemed to scream in her head.

Two. Not two doors or two pulls.

Two Towers!

All of her confidence withered away. She stared at the silhouetted structure just out of reach and tried to laugh, a final act of bravado. It came out instead as a scream. It did not last very long, though. The spiders were already crawling into her mouth. They choked her cries and replaced it with their own starved and skittering noises as they fed.

The End

Connect with Brian Bogart at the following links:

Wattpad: https://www.wattpad.com/user/DreamsDarkly

Facebook: https:/ www.facebook.com/DreamsDarkley

Twitter: https:// www.twitter.com/DreamsDarkley

Cover by Nadimah.

Trance

Joe Stanley

I think we all wish for magic now and then. What it would be to bend reality to your will, to make problems vanish, to create the opportunities you will never have...But would it be so simple? Can you ever really get something for nothing? And what of those unfortunate souls whose desires differ from your own?

Here in the Abyss, magic is real, but it is not a dumb force. It pulses with a life and will of its own. The would-be magician would be wise to remember it returns upon the sender and acts with consequences unforeseen.

Still, never mess with a wizard, especially a dead one...

A Tale from *The Abyss*

1

Early in my youth, I grew a head taller than my friends. By the time I was a teenager, I was as large as any man I have ever met. They described me with words like strapping and strong, and many anticipated a career in football for me.

But I had no interest or talent for sports, and more, I had no time.

On our family's little plot of ground, I became the beast of burden. My father filled my head with a sense of guilty duty, complaining that it cost too much to feed me. Though I worked long, hard hours under a burning sun, he said I was lazy and whipped me like a dog.

He was the only man I ever feared.

I found him one evening slumped in his chair. His hateful black heart had finally failed him.

Secretly, I rejoiced in a wicked way. I wept as they lowered him into the Earth, but those were tears of joy rather than grief.

That, I believe, was what damned me.

My poor mother, who was far more mistreated than I, was finally free. To my dismay, she followed him soon. I very much resented those who said she had gone eagerly to join him in the hereafter.

Now alone in this world, my nightmare had only begun.

The bank foreclosed on our farm. My father had mortgaged it to worthlessness. I had lost not only family but home as well.

For those troubles, which seem as nothing now, I damned myself more by wishing for my own end. But as I have said, my soul was already forfeit.

I advise you to be ever cautious in the thoughts you dwell on and in what feelings you let fester in your heart. Though I have never trusted preachers, they are indeed correct in their notion of dark forces about in this world.

Ever such things listen for stray spirits like my own.

I found work where I could as a laborer and, with it, a contempt for the only life I had ever known. But surely I may be understood as to why, for the road I walked was a hard and twisted one.

With each beat, my heart filled with anger and despair. Each day of life was more burden than blessing, and again and again, I pleaded for the end.

Those things that listen stirred to life. How cruelly they granted me a false reprieve.

My talent for growing things from the soil won a permanent position in the estate of Denault.

That family was known across the county in the wicked gossip whispered across fences and at church picnics when the sun began to set.

Though most involved the grandsire Elmer, his descendants were known to wallow decadently in the fortune he left behind.

Among them, the round and repulsive Alvin found an interest in what he called my "simple mind."

Like his grandfather, Elmer, he held interest and talent in the black arts.

2

Alvin offered me, from his own funds, more than my salary to participate in experiments.

He made me vow to keep such secret. I had no objection, at least not at first. Now, I think, what I say does not matter. For in truth, I cannot remember all the details nor do I believe anyone could recreate the effects he achieved.

They were strange experiences. Sometimes I was made to sit before objects or images while he read or chanted. Sometimes this was done in simple English, sometimes in a tongue I did not recognize.

Long hours I spent sitting in colored lights that shifted hues. Yet, sometimes the sessions passed so rapidly they were over in what seemed only moments.

I was made to hold items, to repeat words I did not understand. I was given odd jewelry to wear. All of it seemed silly, and many times I found my employer to end our work in a state of frustration.

He was, however, kind to me and never blamed me for what he must have felt was failure. While I had no idea of his true aim, I admired his persistence and marveled at his vast, albeit seemingly useless, knowledge of strange things.

This continued for several months. I feared with all certainty he would grow weary of the effort and I would be abandoned. Yet, he persevered.

Though I tried to focus or relax as he requested, I often slipped into a state not unlike a daydream. At times, these were heavenly; still others were visions so horrible I will not recount them here.

I had a sense of travel to some distant place far beyond this world.

When I woke from these experiences, it was to my own voice speaking, yet fading, as I returned to this Earth.

I asked only once what had happened. Alvin simply replied that we had made progress. By his expression, I was left with no doubt of this. While I was relieved to see him pleased, I was also disturbed by what felt like a growing ignorance of his designs.

And I was troubled by nightmares, which began to haunt my sleep.

Some shadowy and unseen monster pursued me across a blackened and blasted realm, which alone brought dread as I had never known. What this assailing force or being intended of me was a terror to which that horrid land paled.

My only source of comfort, indeed my only hope, was the voice of Alvin calling to me through the atmosphere of that hellish domain. In the sense of refuge and safety it provided, he became something of a savior.

In those dark times, he was more than just a man to me: He was a keeper of great wisdom, a wielder of incredible powers. He was my guardian and protector.

He became the embodiment of words like "Lord" and "Master." I humbly, eagerly, obeyed his every command.

For he had brought a purpose to my being.

3

There was nothing he could do to diminish my adoration of him. You, no doubt, will see the problem therein, which I could not.

Even though he spoke less and less to me, it was enough I merely be in his presence.

He could, by simple and wordless gestures, direct me. I knew, for instance, where he wished me to stand or what task he desired my strength to accomplish. It was as though I was privy to his very thoughts.

Even this I did not question, though. I knew only bliss all the while. There was a strange satisfaction in simply knowing what it was, more than merely existing, to be real.

I felt privileged to glimpse his inner circle of friends, though I could not dare to count myself as one. Such was how far above me he seemed.

Among them, one constant companion was the sniveling and rodent-like Lucas. He was quite the contrast to the noble lord I served.

I disliked and mistrusted Lucas, but I had faith that the master, in his wisdom, had reason to associate with such rabble.

I took no small pleasure from the fearful glances the rat-man gave me. Still, he looked upon me in a way that I felt more of a thing than a person. Sadly, there was a truth in that impression as I would come to see.

The master was a collector and sought to add to the library of his grandfather a tome of great importance. As they spoke, I learned attempts to purchase the book had met with no success. This troubled the master greatly.

"That he refuses to part with it for even a small fortune is bad enough. That it rests in the hands of one too incompetent to recognize its power…" he lamented.

The scheming rat smirked, which enraged me, though I obediently stood in place. Then he spoke.

"Why not just go and take it?" he asked. The vileness in the inquiry was as base and vulgar as the one who asked.

"Take it?"

"That's right. Just go around one night, let yourself in, and take it."

The master looked both skeptical and intrigued.

"He's in bed by sunset every night," Lucas informed him. "He keeps it in the parlor by the pool. The damned fool never even locks his doors. He's there all alone."

"Are you offering to get it for me?"

Here Lucas poured himself some cognac and swirled it in a snifter. He wrinkled his face as though he actually pondered the question.

"You know," he said at last, "for just a fraction of what you offered him, you could have it from me. All I would need is a little muscle, in case things go wrong."

Glancing reluctantly at me, he asked, "What about him? Would he do it? Will he... obey me?"

"He will do anything I tell him to," replied the master, correct as always.

4

We drove through the darkness along back roads that went mostly untraveled. They carried us to the edge of a great estate.

"You don't say much, do you?" he asked, not so much for want of an answer but because his nerves were straining. The worry in his features was clear, and his expression was one of pain.

The car rolled to a stop, coasting to a dark and quiet spot beside the road.

He took a flask from his pocket and downed a long, slow gulp.

"All right," he said, getting out. A moment later, he was back at the window, irritated.

"Come on," he commanded. "Follow me."

The master had been clear. I was to obey Lucas. I did not care to, but I greatly desired to serve the master faithfully. Ere, I must obey.

We walked along a game trail that slithered through the trees. Beyond our own footsteps, the sound of buzzing insects filled the silence. He glanced side to side along the way, his guilt haunting him with fear.

We emerged from a tree line. Across the clearing, a beautiful house stood lonely and quiet.

"Get down," he hissed, crouching in the shrubs. I followed suit. He watched the house for a long while and took another large drink from his flask as he worked up his courage. There was no sign of life from the darkened windows.

"Let's do it."

We approached the house and went around it until we reached a pool. It was a splendid place, marking the man who lived here as one of great wealth and taste.

Lucas tried the doors. His reflection grimaced at their refusal to open. He produced a pocket knife and slid the narrow blade between them. With an impressive speed, he had them open.

"Wait here unless I call you," he whispered, disappearing inside. There followed a few moments of relative calm, though I could hear him fumbling about. Then there came the crash of breaking glass.

An angry voice demanded, "You! What the hell are you doing here?"

A noisy scuffle ensued. In a few seconds, Lucas was calling, "Help! Help me, damn it!"

I entered to find Lucas on the floor yelping as the man bent a fireplace poker over him with several blows.

"The police will help you when I'm through!"

I caught the man's arm and spun him around. He shrieked as I lifted him and hurled him with terrible force across the room. He struck the corner of a heavy cabinet and crumpled to the floor.

A groaning Lucas staggered up. And, finding the poker, he made to return the beating he had just received. But, with his arm raised, he stopped before a single blow had landed.

"Oh shit..." he whispered as he studied the still and silent body. Its eyes were open, and a deep red pool spread out across the white marble floor.

"Oh, God, no. You killed him!"

5

After Lucas frantically scoured the room for evidence of his presence, we made our way back. At one point, we stopped while he was sick on the side of the trail.

As he spat and gasped, he lifted his eyes to me. The moonlight left deep shadows in the crevices of his features. Through them, I could see the whole was twisted by revulsion and fear.

I was aware of a sympathy for him. This was tempered by a strange amusement. He had played at being something, a criminal, and now he knew what it was to be that thing at last. The taste was not as sweet as he had anticipated.

But, to this, my mind's own turmoil was a tidal wave to a drop of rain.

There was a faint voice screaming within me, driven to its frenzy by guilt and horror. It cried from someplace, deeply buried, like a long-discarded memory. Above it, a cold and silent wall gazed down with disaffection.

I began to realize, more than this mere human drama around me, something was dreadfully wrong.

Lucas recovered, and we continued on our way. He mumbled and muttered to himself softly. I could not hear him, but I understood nonetheless.

When we were in the car, he dug for his flask and tipped it back. Cursing, he flung the empty vessel to the floorboard. His breathing was ragged, as though he stifled a scream or tears. Then he turned to me.

I did nothing but turn my head in response. He flung himself back into the door, terror in his beady, little eyes. He remained there for a time after I turned back.

Soon the motor was running, and we careened away along the weaving, bumpy road.

The master sat at his desk as we entered his study. His old-fashioned quill danced across some journal or ledger. He didn't even lift his head.

Lucas began to babble, and the details spilled out in a nearly incoherent chain. The master simply raised his finger, and Lucas fell silent.

"Yes, I know," was all the master said for a time. He gestured to my place, and I took it. When he finished writing, he continued.

"I know all about it, Lucas. I was watching. The book," he

demanded.

Lucas' face soured in anguish, but he snapped free and produced the tome. The master opened a drawer of the desk and removed a stack of bills. Lucas moved like a puppet, making the exchange.

The master's eyes greedily consumed the book, smiling.

"I'll never do it again," Lucas whispered. The master chuckled.

"Oh, yes, you will," he corrected. "This is only the beginning, Lucas. You'll do whatever I ask or the sheriff will receive all the information he needs to put you away."

Lucas snarled and stepped forward. With one stride, I intercepted him. He screamed, jumping back, terrified and beaten.

The master poured himself a drink and laughed as Lucas fled.

6

I resumed my place and began the wait until I was needed.

The master read and drank for several hours. He whispered and smiled to himself until his eyes could no longer focus. Then locking the book away in his hidden safe, he staggered across the room.

He looked up at the portrait of his grandfather and cackled loudly.

"I have it," he slurred. "Do you hear me? It's mine!"

The painting stared as a soul gazes across eternity.

"All those years you searched for it. With just a skimming, I can see why. Oh, what secrets it will reveal to me."

He began to laugh louder and louder. The portrait smiled slyly, but I could see it did not smile with him.

"That's right, old man, to *me!* How long I've stood in your shadow, listened to stories of how great you were. Well, I have everything that you had, and now...I have more!"

The mournful face of the painting stared down. The master could not see how its eyes were fixed upon him.

"I will go where you have never gone," he vowed in his drunken stupor. "I will achieve that which you feared to dare."

If the painting's face could have asked a question, surely it would have been, "How far is far enough?" or, better still, "How far is a step too much?" But the silence that smote his ears was the only thing the master heard. It set him ablaze with the madness of fury.

"I—" he began, belching, "will sunder this meaningless world. I will rise up and throttle the gods. Everything, all of it, will be mine!"

I could not determine if the image wore an expression of pity or contempt. Perhaps, it was both. I had never seen the master in such a state.

Suddenly he stiffened and looked around as though he had heard something. His empty glass fell from his trembling hand and shattered. The sound snapped him out of his confusion, and he laughed.

He staggered over to me and smiled. He stank of booze, but I forgave him for his outburst. Surely, I told myself, this indiscretion deserves it; few of us would be able to conceive of the troubles he must know.

Laughing, he plodded away to sleep it off.

In an instant, the air grew colder until it was as ice upon my flesh. There was a sensation like fingers tickling my spine. I heard what I thought were whispers from the corners of the room.

I pondered what I had seen. A spark of anger smoldered within me. It grew until I quivered and burned despite the frigid air.

Things had changed. I no longer desired to serve Alvin. I wanted to leave that place, to break the trance that fixed me to him. But there I stood, perfectly helpless, held against my will.

Then I saw that the painting's eyes had turned to me. We shared a smile.

7

The master's growing collection swelled as our loathsome task was repeated. Soon, a score of homes had been violated by our invasive expeditions. We avoided more bloodshed for a time.

On one of these occasions, our target was a small, private museum. Creeping through the darkness of the midnight hour, we gained entry, and Lucas went quickly to his work.

Out of a desire to prevent murderous complications, he had grown in his nefarious talents. He was quieter and worked with a speed that confessed his desire to be done with it.

I stood near our point of entry, waiting.

Within my sight, a grotesque ceremonial mask stared through the gloom. It was a hideous construction but more revolting for the disturbing familiarity of its composition.

It was a face to hide a face. Meant to empower the wearer by means of terror, it now hung on the wall as a landscape or portrait might.

I could not believe the owners did not recognize the leathery face to be nothing less than human flesh. Surely, they would have buried it simply to honor the hellish suffering endured during its harvest.

Their remains displayed as art should truly anger the dead. It seemed to drip with malignant rage. What misfortune its silent screams and curses must bring...

I heard a voice, high and shrill, more comical for its attempt to sound authoritative.

"Hold it right there!" it demanded. I moved toward the sound.

Lucas stood illuminated by a flashlight beam. A security guard, bald and overweight, held a revolver on him.

"You just bought yourself a ticket to prison..." the man taunted.

"Prison," Lucas repeated.

As I moved closer, I saw the guard's lips turn up in a sinister sneer.

"You've got another choice," he said then lowered his voice to a whisper. "All you have to do is give me an excuse."

He slid the hammer back, its click like thunder. He meant to shoot.

Here, I lunged at him. Seeing me from the corner of his eye, he wheeled and fired twice. My fist came down on his forearm, shattering the bones and sending his hateful weapon clattering across the floor.

His remaining arm was no match for both of mine. I seized his head and twisted it until a third bony crack sounded loudly. He followed his gun to the floor.

In the spinning flashlight's radiance, I caught glimpses of Lucas' stunned and horrified face. He blinked and shuddered as his senses returned.

Snatching up the torch, he threw its beam on me, dumbfounded by what he saw. He stared at my wounds, and, having nothing better, he finally pleaded, "Come on, come on..." as he started for the door.

Our drive back home was spent in utter silence. Lucas trembled and clutched the wheel as if for life, as if to keep his mind anchored in this world. Like the sudden throwing of a switch, his tremors stopped.

The miles rolled on.

8

"Shot?" questioned the master with no small amount of disbelief in his voice.

Until then, I had assumed the master had been watching, that he knew all.

With timid steps, he approached me, staring at my chest. Opening my shirt, he gave my wounds little more than a glance before he staggered back, shaken.

"My powers," he stuttered after a large swallow, "are greater than I knew..."

"What are you going to do?" Lucas demanded.

The master's frightened and confused face regained its composure. To Lucas, he replied, "Nothing."

"You can't leave him like this! He needs a doctor."

The master shook his head.

"Look at him!" roared Lucas. "Look how pale he is. Look at the circles around his eyes."

The master said nothing.

"Alvin," Lucas begged. "Alvin, please! For the sake of my mind! Tell me, why isn't he bleeding?"

The master walked slowly around his desk, never taking his eyes off me. He eased himself down and sat a moment before he answered.

"The magic," he whispered. "The magic binds him to my will. It is so powerful not even death can break the spell."

"You've got to help him..."

"What do you think I can do? I can end the spell with a single word. He will fall over dead. Is that what I should do?"

There was no sincerity in his words; a maniacal smile twisted his face.

"Alvin, he must be in terrible pain. Maybe...maybe it would be better to let him die."

Indeed, I wanted that.

"His pain does not concern me," stated the master as he gestured to my place. I took it. Lighting a cigar, he continued, "All that matters is that he obeys."

Incredulous, Lucas shook his head.

"This is beyond cruel. This is inhuman."

The master hissed.

"I am more than human, Lucas. I would have thought this might prove that to you."

"No," grumbled Lucas, "not more than human. *Less.*"

"Mind your tongue!" growled the master. "Should you ever doubt me or dare to disobey, you remember his freakish state."

Smiling wickedly, he went on. "It's nothing to the Hell I can bring down on you."

Lucas only stared.

"Now," the master went on, opening a drawer. He removed another stack of bills and tossed them on the desk.

"The item?" he inquired.

Lucas produced an ornate blade: a dagger engraved with strange designs. He looked from it to the master and back.

I noted I was too far away to stop him if he tried. I kept my place.

With the reluctance he might have surrendered his very soul, Lucas made the exchange.

He looked at the cash and sent a mournful glance to me. He turned to leave.

"Lucas, I have almost everything I need. Soon, no more will be required. I promise you a great reward."

Lucas walked out into the night.

9

Our excursions had grown so numerous that, when the master announced our final task upon us, Lucas' face was as emotionless as my own.

The heavy door, which Lucas had started with a prying bar, required all my strength to wrench open. Its hinges screamed through the dark, but we carried on heedless of the din. For there was no fear of any substance that we might arouse the denizens within.

Stairs of dark gray stone, cloaked in dust and grit, gave our steps a grinding, scratching voice as we descended. At the bottom, Lucas paused, his lamp throwing yellow-orange light through cobwebs and onto the crumbling masonry beneath them.

But soon we moved again by countless niches that climbed each other to the arched vault above. Within them, crumbling boxes held occupants who would never awaken to any sound.

Some were in such state as to have all but disintegrated. Dark gray objects of distasteful familiarity could be seen among the rubble and detritus.

Lucas would not look upon them. He consulted his map far more often than required and looked ahead but never to the side.

Which, I wonder, is more horrific to conceive: That some lingering presence still peers out from those dark hollows, or that nothing remains to gaze out?

How I envied the thought of that oblivious rest. But there came subtle challenges to the sole hope and dream within my heart.

As we searched a seemingly endless hall for a single name, there were strange stirrings in the shadows just beyond our light. Were they more than a sinister effect of a flickering flame? And how strangely the small clouds of dust continued to swirl with odd and suggestive shapes...

But these were forgotten as, at last, we located the one we sought. We placed it on the hallway floor, and Lucas began his accursed breaking of its seal. When the lid was lifted, we paid a brief and silent tribute to the sleeper.

Lucas pulled on his heavy gloves tightly, each in turn. Reaching in, he labored for a short time to seize the item of our sojourn. But he withdrew his hands and hissed a troubled sigh. All within had shifted at his efforts.

Swallowing loudly, he unfolded his knife. As the blade did its work, he gasped and groaned and cried as if the edge cut into his own flesh. In his exasperation, he cast it aside. His pulling became more forceful so that a foul creaking and cracking issued forth.

When it finally came free, he stared, mystified, as it was wholly free of flesh though his gloves were fouled with grime. Turning it around, he shared its timeless gaze, pleading with his moistened eyes.

He placed it in his satchel, and we lifted the remainder back into its place.

We turned back. Before us, faint impressions receding; behind us, others advancing. We, who had desecrated the place of their rest, deserved no less than their wrath.

Yet, they let us pass.

10

"The skull," the master demanded. He crossed the room and tore it from Lucas' hands.

Lucas stared at the soiled gloves he still wore. He closed his eyes with a weariness beyond mere physical exhaustion.

The master studied his prize, his expression one of triumphant spite. It was as though he sneered into the face of a beaten enemy. He raised it and looked beyond its grim grin to the portrait.

He was comparing them with a hateful glimmer in his eyes.

Walking back to his desk, he placed it irreverently down. Its empty orbits fell on me. Rather than taking his comfortable seat, he leaned against the desk.

His sparkling eyes painted Lucas with a glare of ill will.

"Rules..." he began, his voice smooth and deep...almost hypnotic. "Of all the people I know, that scum like you would be so troubled by the breaking of meaningless rules."

Lucas recoiled as though he had been slapped but said nothing.

"I promised you a reward. You have certainly earned it."

Lucas trembled with tears in his eyes as if he knew what was coming next.

"To me," the master commanded. "Kill him."

Helpless, I felt my foot step forward. But at that very moment, I saw the faintest flash light up the eyes of the skull.

I looked at Lucas. He was resigned to his end. Slowly, I turned my eyes to the door and then back to him.

"I said kill him!" thundered the master.

Lucas' own eyes widened in surprise. I turned mine to the door again. In an instant, he was through it.

Then I turned to Alvin, to my....*master.*

"Damn you!" he roared. "How dare you disobey me?"

I took a heavy step forward, lifting my hands.

"No!" he screeched. "Stay back!"

I made one more step before the coward spat his word.

The constant agony my wounds had brought me was nothing to the surge of pain that came. I clutched toward them, nearly crumpling. Blood began to flow.

I wanted to fall to the ground, to be truly dead. I could have almost thanked him.

But to feel the ebbing of my state, neither living nor dead, seemed a loss as precious as life itself.

I had never been my own man. I had never made a mark upon this world I could claim as my own. And I would not leave until I had.

He watched, frozen, as I straightened myself and came forward. He gasped as I seized his throat and began to squeeze.

His face discolored: first red then purple then blue...

My own hands were changing. They darkened and weakened.

I willed all my strength into my hands, which were naught but bony claws. My vision faded, but I saw his eyes roll into his head. We collapsed to the floor.

Until life had left us both, I squeezed.
I squeezed until I was nothing more than a still, withered corpse.

The End

Connect with Joe Stanley at the following links:

The Ghostly World (website): www.jonathanharker.co.uk

Wattpad: https://www.wattpad.com/user/JoeStanleyAuthor

Facebook: https://www.facebook.com/JoeStanleyAuthor/

Cover by John Riley.

Good Intentions

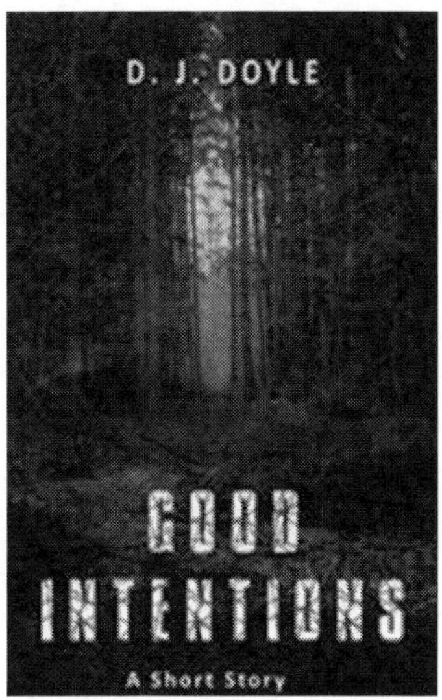

D. J. Doyle

D.J. Doyle is a horror/thriller author with a published novel, *The Celtic Curse: Banshee,* and novelettes, "Hades' Gate" and "Red." All are available on Amazon.

***

"Boo!"

"Ahh! Stop. Stop joking around," Jennifer said to her jesting boyfriend, Aron. She dropped the screwdriver from her hand. "You're going to give me a heart attack one of these days. You'll be sorry then."

"You know I'm only kidding. I can't help it. It's just too easy," he laughed.

"Yes, but I'm up this stepladder trying to fix this curtain pole. If you were any good at DIY, it would be you doing this...being the man!"

"No need to insult my manhood."

"I'll be doing more than that to your manhood, if you keep it up." She giggled.

Jennifer stepped down while holding onto Aron's shoulders, who could have reached up and tightened the loose screw without any effort. Aron couldn't even change a light bulb. He grew up pampered and pandered to: their servants did everything. That was before the market crash four years prior, when the family lost everything. Aron's father was found, in his favourite car, with a gun in his hand. His mother had the car destroyed a week later. A good education allowed him to get a well-paid job. Jennifer was a grafter. She had her first job in a laundrette at the tender age of twelve. Then worked in a supermarket weekends while she attended college. They met in a local coffee shop. Aron "accidentally" picked up her coffee, but it was all a ploy to talk to the woman who he found attractive. They had been dating for five years and had their ups and downs, yet they always pulled through.

"You need to stop doing DIY and housework. It's time to get ready. We have to check into the hotel, and we have a table booked for eight o'clock—that's in four hours. Susan and Rick will be here in thirty minutes. So get a move on."

"Where are we going again?" she asked as she opened her wardrobe door. Jennifer browsed through her dresses and inspected her line of shoes down below, trying to pick the best match.

"The Fort Lodge Hotel. It's in the middle of nowhere," Aron replied.

"Never heard of the place. Right, I'm going for a shower and will put my face on."

***

Rick pulled up and parked their car outside. He smiled at Susan. Her vibrant red hair flowed like silk and suited her emerald green dress. His confidence and sense of humour had won her over. A large Jewish nose had been the butt of many jokes growing up, so he worked on his charm to talk to the ladies. They walked up the drive to the porch, and Susan rang the doorbell.

"Do you think she has an inkling?" whispered Rick.

"No, not a clue. I talked to her yesterday. She has no idea."

The door opened, and Aron stood there with a big grin.

"Hey, guys. Come in. Jennifer is nearly ready. She's dressed, makeup on. Just doing her hair now. I have a bottle open. I hope red is OK."

"Sure, Aron. I'm thirsty as hell," said Rick.

Aron poured out four glasses. Jennifer came down the stairs in the blue dress Aron adored. She tossed her long brown hair over her shoulder with a black leather bag, the last thing that remained of her grandmother.

"Wow, you look amazing, Jennifer," said Susan.

"You do, too! Look at you in that dress. And Rick, very handsome in a shirt and tie."

"Hey, what about me? Do I look good?"

"Of course you do, honey." And she kissed him on the cheek.

They chatted for a few minutes, discussing their hopes of what might be on the menu that evening and the luxury they would experience on their romantic weekend.

The cab turned up outside, and they heard the impatient driver bang on the horn. All four finished the remainder of their wine in one go.

"Good. We're all gonna have a good time."

***

"Are we all strapped in?" asked the driver. He heard multiple clicks from the back. "Fort Lodge Hotel it is. I'll be doing the back roads as it's quicker from here," he said and slid the safety hatch shut.

Excitement filled the air; Jennifer hadn't been away in quite a while. She and Aron struggled with their first-year mortgage payments, so they needed a short break. They were finally back on their feet. The girls talked about the latest dish Susan had tried from her favourite cooking show, while the boys laughed at the Trump and Clinton memes going around their office.

Jennifer glared out the window. They had turned off the main road and were on a long, windy country road, only lit by the full moon. Tall trees stood on both sides of the road. Some were so overgrown, the long branches curved over and the leaves brushed against the top of the car. Jennifer found the sound quite soothing. Then she spotted some movement in the bushes and was convinced she saw a head pop up. *That's odd,* she thought.

"Where is this road? I've never been here before. It's so creepy," said Susan.

"There used to be an old asylum near here. It closed down over twenty years ago, I think," Rick told them.

The headlights on the car were not strong enough to see further than a hundred yards.

"There's something in the road up ahead," said the driver.

They were unable to hear him, so Rick instructed him to open the hatch.

"I said...there is something in the road up ahead. I can't see what it is. It's blocking the whole road."

As the car got closer, they could see a large fallen branch. A mist began to flow through the trees like a river and gathered all around them.

"I'll get out and have a look. See if it is not too heavy to lift and move out of the way."

The driver's door eerily creaked as he opened it. Rustling noises came from beyond the trees. However, he could not see anything moving. He ducked back into the car to grab a flashlight and walked over to the obstruction in the road. The driver shoved the branch with his leg to test it. It shifted about a foot. *Maybe we could move it, after all*, he thought and beckoned Aron to help him.

Aron slid out of the back seat, leaving the door ajar, and followed the light that shined directly in his eyes. He could not see a thing, so he raised his hand to block the rays.

"What's that noise?" Jennifer asked. "It's like moaning."

As the driver waited for Aron, the others in the car saw them coming. All they could see were silhouettes of people creeping forward with their arms stretched out.

"Who are they? What are they doing?" asked Jennifer.

They lurked towards the inattentive driver and reached out.

Jennifer and Susan yelled at him to turn around. "Watch out. They're behind you!"

Rick struggled to get out of the car as his shaky hands tugged at the door handle. He shouted to warn them.

Five zombies mauled the driver and dragged him to the ground with more lunging on top. They heard a shriek of pain, blood spraying out of the heap. Bits of flesh and intestines propelled into the air. The women screamed.

Aron stood frozen, facing the space where the driver had stood. Jennifer hollered for him to come back. Tears welled up in her eyes and trickled down her cheek.

"What the fuck is going on?" Susan said.

"I think they're...zom...zombies," replied Jennifer.

"Don't be silly; zombies aren't real," quipped Rick. "C'mon, Aron."

"What the fuck do you call them then?" Jennifer bellowed.

"They're probably escaped lunatics from the asylum I told you about."

"That closed down years ago. That's what you said, remember?"

"Well, maybe I was wrong."

More zombies came from the bushes. They headed straight for Aron, grunting and moaning.

Aron turned to run, though it was too late. They hauled him down to the ground and lugged him over to the side of the road as they fought to get their pound of flesh. His body disappeared under the mass of zombies.

Jennifer bawled, unable to breathe. She gasped for air.

"Rick, get back in the car and shut the doors. Don't make any noises," instructed Susan. "I've seen enough zombie movies to know they're attracted to sound and light. We need to get out of here, fast." Susan's heart pumped with adrenaline, and she knew Jennifer was in no state to think straight; she needed to keep control of her emotions and take command.

Rick climbed into the front to make their getaway. Instead, an alarm invaded the night's stillness. Sweat seeped down his forehead into his eyebrows. *Fuck, what have I done?* he thought. The noise rang through their ears, and the zombies perked their heads up to listen. More came from the trees on either side, all heading for the car.

"Turn it off!" Susan shouted. "Fucking turn it off, now!"

Rick fiddled with the dials and buttons. All the lights came on inside the car, and they could barely see outside anymore. He finally switched the alarm off, then he turned off the lights.

Susan gasped; Jennifer screeched. The car was now surrounded by zombies.

***

They saw faces covered in blood, old and new, with rotting flesh exposed. Their clothes were tattered, and their black and brown, blood-covered teeth made Jennifer gag. Susan jumped up in her seat as they clawed at the windows.

Jennifer became enraged. "Bastards!"

"How are we going to get out of this?" whimpered Rick.

They did not respond. The two women didn't know what to say.

The car rocked back and forth as the zombies desperately tried to get at the people inside. Rick roared at them to get away, but that fell on deaf ears. The windscreen started to shatter as a zombie pounded on it. It was the driver.

***

"They will eventually get in. What are we going to do? I don't want to die like this," said Susan.

"I'm getting us the hell out of here," Rick said and tried starting the car.

The door opened beside him, and he was yanked out.

"Help me. Help," he begged, then it went quiet. Susan slammed the door shut.

The trunk door clicked and started to open. Zombies poured into the back of the car and reached for Jennifer and Susan.

"Those fuckers are not getting me," Jennifer stated.

***

She searched for something to defend herself with. Nothing. She checked through her bag in case she had her pepper spray. She didn't, not that the spray would affect them. Rummaging some more, Jennifer found a screwdriver and remembered she'd had her bag on the floor when Aron frightened her earlier on. It must have dropped right in.

Jennifer aimed for the three zombies with their arms reaching through the headrests on the back seats. In the corner of her eye, she saw Aron approaching the car. Covered in blood, he did not look like the Aron she knew, not the Aron she fell in love with. *He's a zombie now.* She noticed Aron holding something in his hand.

Jennifer lashed out and stabbed each of the three closest zombies in the crown of the head. She heard a crunch from the bone cracking with force. Blood squirted like a pulse all over Jennifer. She did not expect that from "the dead." Some got into her mouth; it was sweet flavoured.

***

Horrified silence spread across the crowd of zombies. One lifted her hands to her face and screamed at the top of her voice. They backed away in terror. Jennifer glared at the blood on her hands and body. She stared at Aron coming her way. He held a small opened box in his hands. A diamond ring sparkled under the moonlight.

***

As they grabbed the driver, they ripped his shirt and trousers and squirted fake blood. They covered his face with grey and brown putty to make it look messy and threw fake flesh into the air above them.

Aron lay on the ground while they made a mess of his face and clothes with more putty and fake blood.

Rick was gagged and dragged away before being let in on the plan. He giggled when he spied on Susan and Jennifer from behind a bush, so frightened on their own.

Aron took the ring from his pocket and took a deep breath. This was the moment that would change their lives forever.

***

He trembled at the sight of the slaughter. "Jennifer, it was all a joke. I was going to ask you to marry me."

The End

If you would like to know more about D.J. Doyle and other projects she is working on, here are some helpful links:

Website: http://djdoyleauthor.com/

Facebook: https://www.facebook.com/DJDoyleAuthor/

Twitter: https://twitter.com/djdMar123

Cover by: TheCoverGirl

Tails

M.W. Johnston

I don't consider myself a writer. I'm just a person who likes to write. For as long as I can remember, I have loved stories. Loved to read. Loved adventure. Over time my writing has changed. From writing stories about quests and magic, to stories that are more transgressive, tackling taboos, and causing a little controversy. My biggest influence is despair and the dreary reality of life. I don't particularly like happy endings.

"Tails" is a story about a man looking for perfection and the devastating effects it can cause.

Editor's Note - the subtitle refers to a collection of horror stories by different writers, taking place at the same horrific location - the Bradford Hotel, where every room harbours a fiend or victim!

A Short Story for the Bradford

Once upon a time, there was a man who demanded perfection from everything in his life. Driven by an unrelenting case of OCD, he religiously pursued the one thing that evades us all.

A teacher once told him that practice makes perfect. And so he practiced until there were no more jagged edges in his life. Another person once told him that nobody is perfect, and he punched that person in the mouth. It was a perfect punch—one he'd been practicing.

He cut away the things in his life that weren't perfect. His unpredictable family with their unpredictable ways. His imperfect friends with their spots and scars and blemishes. He sacrificed the things that most other people crave: love and friendship.

He couldn't abide imperfection.

His body was a temple. Symmetrically perfect. Flawless.

His was a life of straight lines. The perfect horizon. Everything was ironed out. No creases.

But it was all about to change.

Regardless of how much he tried to ignore it, he couldn't suppress his most primal urges. That thing that all humans desire. The intimacy of the opposite sex. However, it didn't prevent him from looking for perfection. He could maybe forgive a stray freckle for one night of dispassionate sex. Or even a minimal chip on her nail polish.

He once made a woman leave because she hadn't shaved her vagina. And another had a small mole on her breast that made him ill.

But, on the night of his unfurling, he'd thought he'd found her. The one thing that had eluded him for so long. The perfect woman.

The bar was quiet. The pianist played some soft jazz in the corner. The man approached the bar, ordered a Glenfiddich, and asked if it could be put in his own glass: a crystal tumbler he brought with him, wrapped in a red velvet handkerchief. Perfectly perfect. The barman didn't flinch and poured him a glass. The man turned, drank, surveyed the room, and spotted her immediately.

She was looking at him. Their eyes met. He was already making deductions and calculations from where he stood, absorbing her from across the bar, while the piano jazz swirled around him.

She didn't smile or blink, and she didn't look away.

They both waited patiently for the other to move; both of them making entirely different observations of one another. He was waiting for a sign, an indication of her imperfection, something that would turn him away rather than lure him in. But nothing happened, and the pianist continued to play, and they continued this silent, motionless dance. Until, without meaning to, the man moved forward, drawn in by this strange woman's irresistible presence.

He slid into the booth beside her, placing his glass on the table on top of a napkin. She still hadn't blinked. They didn't speak, not at first. He searched her almond-shaped face and let his eyes roam over her. It was fruitless. Her skin was smooth and white and perfect. Her green eyes shone bright in the shade, and her auburn hair left him astounded. The woman had him bewitched.

And then they spoke, and he allowed her voice to wash over him. So sweet. So, *him.* She laughed, and it was like the first time he heard jazz music.

It continued back at his place. She undid her dress and let it fall to the floor. She flicked it away.

She stood naked before him. He ran his hand down between her perfect breasts, over her smooth belly, and down to her vagina. He trembled as his fingers searched for anything crooked. He kissed her lips and slipped his fingers inside. She let out the softest moan and her breath clouded his face, and he took it in, letting it fill his lungs. She was wet, and he brought his fingers out and sniffed them. It engulfed his senses like the scent of a rare flower.

He pushed her onto the bed and dragged his lips down her body. She pulsed and twisted in all the right places as his tongue flicked out and played with her clitoris. He took it in his teeth and gently squeezed. She shuddered. And when he came up and entered her it was like they were supposed to be. He felt a shift in the world around him, like everything was falling into place. They were two halves of the same soul finally coming back together.

Then he turned her over and the world shifted again. It became cold and dark, and he was alone in a long, windowless corridor. As she writhed below him, his erection faltered, and went soft. At the base of her spine, just above her perfect ass, there was a tail. A stubby, ugly, little thing that looked like a thick, fleshy Dorito.

His jaws quivered. He fought hard to keep himself from throwing up. She turned over and watched him. Her face was expressionless. Her eyes were cold. He told her to leave, and she got up without question. She picked up her dress and gave him this piercing look as if she knew something he didn't. Her green eyes were now grey. She smirked and left him standing there. He watched her leave. She stepped out of his house, still naked. It was raining outside.

***

Something was different the next day. His head was full of rusty spanners, clanging and scraping together, giving him a migraine and hurting his teeth. His sinuses were completely jammed, and his face felt swollen and ready to burst. He checked himself in the mirror, but he looked fine.

Then the tinnitus started. A high-pitched ringing in his ears that scraped the underside of his skull and hurt his bones. He put a finger to his ear and felt something hot and sticky. When he drew his finger away he saw that it was blood.

He ran to the bathroom and checked himself in the mirror again. He had to rub his eyes to make sure he wasn't seeing things. There were two long, thin strands hanging out of his ears, and they were twitching. Cold dread swept through his body. He grabbed one and tugged lightly. The pain was horrendous, blurring his vision and throwing the room into a spin.

He bit down, grabbed the strand, and yanked it hard, like tearing a plaster from a cut. There was a ripping sound and more terrific pain, and something squeaked. He fell to the floor, screaming in agony. Blood poured from his left ear, and in his hand he held a small, shivering field mouse, covered in his own blood. He squealed and chucked the mouse against the bathroom wall, where it left a bloody print.

He scrambled to his feet, grabbing onto the sink to pull himself up. He slipped on the tiled floor.

He looked at himself in the mirror. The mouse had left a gaping hole where his ear used to be, torn to bits and bleeding. However, there was another tail hanging from his right ear.

He passed out when he tore that one out.

***

Days passed without incident. His head was wrapped in a thick bandage, covering the wounds on either side of his face. He hadn't left the house. He hadn't cleaned or washed or cut his fingernails. Things were starting to fall apart.

Then, on the eighth day, his nose started bleeding. Both nostrils opened up. Fear clawed at his heart. The mirror confirmed the unthinkable: two more tails. One hanging from each nostril. Twitching, like before.

He cried then. Hot tears burned his cheeks. He couldn't breathe. He screamed in anger, tearing his throat, punching the floor, breaking his knuckles. He grabbed both tails at once and pulled. The noise was terrifying. A clawing, tearing sound and the crunch of broken cartilage.

He flopped to the side and allowed the two mice to bounce away, leaving little bloody prints on his floor. He curled into a ball and allowed the pain and the grief to consume him.

***

His face was constricted and white. Blood seeped through the bandages on his head. A crusty wound dominated the place where his nose used to be. The world shrunk around him, closing him in, suffocating him. The weeks passed in a blur of twisted pain, heartburn, and relentless diarrhea.

He would wake up in blinding agony, with heat crawling up his throat, and a stabbing pain in his bowels. Nightmares conquered his sleep. He would see her, naked and smiling, with a huge, sweeping tail dragging behind her.

Sometimes he found himself in strange places, shivering and crying. He woke in a phone box once, with an empty bottle of vodka and a few pills lying next to him. Another time he woke in a strange room, in a stranger's bed, next to a transvestite, and his arsehole was burning.

He stumbled through each day, not knowing if it was a nightmare or reality and never knowing if there would be another attack.

On one of these days, he stumbled into the Bradford Hotel. It was a place he'd heard about, on the other side of the water, and a place he never wanted to see. And yet, he found himself drawn to it like a moth to a flame. Something about its crumbling façade and cruel reputation made him feel like he'd find some kind of peace.

And so he checked himself in, wandering past vagrants and vile people to get to his room. He heard people shouting and crying and screaming. He fell into his room and sucked in its cummy scent. And, almost immediately, he had another attack.

He crashed to his knees as his stomach contracted. He wretched and choked and threw up. Something long and thick dropped from his mouth, hanging over his lips like a deranged tongue. He pulled it out, feeling the creature slide up his throat, and it slopped onto the floor, followed by a torrent of acidic vomit.

Through the tears in his eyes, he saw the iguana. It licked at his vomit then started to slowly move away. But the man snatched at it, grabbing it fiercely. The lizard scratched with its claws, and the man bit into its green, scaly skin. The lizard made no sound as the man devoured the poor creature, including the tail.

***

The next attack came just a few days later. It was a brutal day. His bowels shifted like tectonic plates, causing horrendous flatulence and follow through. Shit ran down the inside of his legs as he cowered in a ball, crying.

Then it came. He felt it sliding out, all long and hairy and swinging. He wrapped the tail 'round his wrist. It was longer than the others. It felt strong. He pulled. The pain was indescribable. He felt his insides explode. The smell was overwhelming. The scream that escaped him was demonic, and the thing just kept coming.

Then his backside collapsed, and shit poured from him like a river. Relief washed over him. And then he heard the screech of the spider monkey. It bit the hand holding its tail, and the man swung the little monkey up and smashed it on the floor. The monkey screeched and tried to escape, but the man held firm and swung the little bastard like a pillow, slamming it off the floor on each side of him, bringing it up in a wide arc and throwing it down again. Blood and fur and shit and guts flew in every direction. The monkey fell silent, but the man continued to smash it around until he too fell silent.

Things settled. The pain eventually subsided. He started to eat and sleep. No more nightmares.

He embraced his imperfect environment. He wandered the Bradford and got to know some of the other residents. He learned how things worked and who to go to. He learned that you could get almost anything from certain people. He even found himself a job. It turns out that some men have a fetish for sticking their cocks into bloody holes. It paid well.

Months passed. He was making a name for himself. He enjoyed being where he was. He hadn't felt this good in a very long time.

He woke one night, desperate for the toilet. His latest client lay sleeping beside him. He stumbled to the toilet and started to pee. It burned. He looked down and saw a cascade of blood pouring out of him. Then it stopped, like something was blocking it. He squeezed, because he could feel it building. Very slowly, something edged its way out of his penis. It was long and pink and fleshy. The room around him started to spin and the tail started to twitch.

He allowed the tail to wrap 'round his finger and he pulled.

The End

Connect with M.W. Johnston at the following places:

Amazon: 10 by MW Johnston: https://www.amazon.com/10-M-W-Johnston-ebook/dp/B012UVJ2NC

Wattpad: https://www.wattpad.com/user/MWJohnston

Cover by Author.

Don't Go In

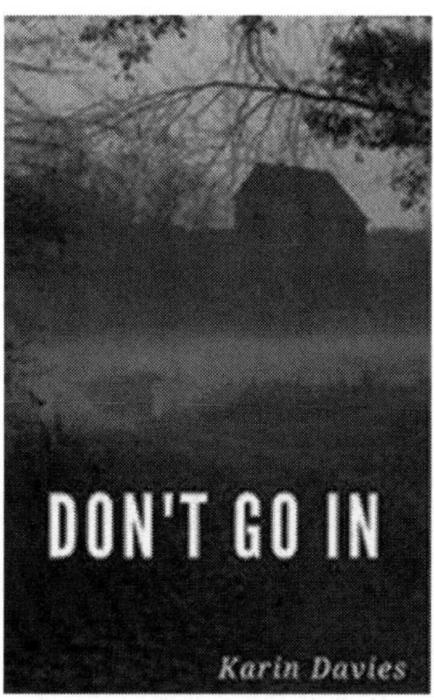

Karin Davies

I live in the incredibly beautiful town of Aberystwyth where, as well as having glorious coastal views and wonderful rolling mountains, we are known to have the highest ratio of books to people in the world. I live with my partner and our three children and so time to write is currently scarce. I have always loved writing and look forward to a time when I can do more of it. I hope you enjoy reading this collection of thrilling stories!

In this story, a beautiful summer's day is about to turn into a nightmare for six unsuspecting friends as they take shelter in an abandoned mansion. Little do they know the horrors in store for them when they fail to heed the generations-old advice of mothers: 'Whatever you do, don't go in.'

***

The heat of the day has been close to blistering. Waves of haze still obscure the air despite the big, fiery orange sun that is midway through setting. The sky is painted deep pink, hot red and warm purple. The sporadic breeze is warm but cooler than the thick, heavy air it had to fight through. From the verge of the hill, one can see down through the trees and spattering of houses to the glistening sea. For a few moments, the view is untainted. A small bird flits across the scene and perches itself on a thin branch before starting to twitter melodiously. Yet, the glorious day does not lift my spirits as much as the static charge that is slowly building in the air did. Centuries of waiting will come to an end before daybreak.

A loud screech smashes the silence to pieces. The little bird flies away as laughter and chatter successfully drives away the peace. In spite of the disruption, the six figures make for a lovely picture as they are silhouetted against the sun—the painted sky contrasting wonderfully with their blank canvases. As they move further up the hill, the sun lowering behind them, their features become easier to distinguish.

Of the six, four are male, their beach shorts hanging low on their toned waists, and the flip-flops on their feet *flip-flopping* stickily to the road as they walk. One is typically preppy: his blonde, slicked hair falls seductively over his bright eyes while his brilliantly perfect teeth glisten in a way that enhances his cupid-bow smile. The male next to him appears more athletic. He is shorter, yet his muscles are more defined. His hair is dark, short and spiky, his smile warm and his laugh genuine. On the opposite end of the line is the eldest of the group. He oozes a quiet authority although his deep hazel eyes are full of merriment. He too has dark hair, but it has golden highlights and is devoid of spikes. The fourth male is between the two females. His eyelashes are long, his cheekbones well-defined and his skin flawless. It is clear that he is the hunk of the group despite his egotistical personality.

To the left of the hunk and hanging on his every word is a leggy brunette—the producer of the screech that shattered the tranquillity mere minutes ago. Although superior to her friend in looks, she is more materialistic than intelligent. On the opposite side of the coin, and the hunk, is a pretty redhead. Her hair is cropped short, and her smile easy. She wears a bikini like her friend but also has a long wrap around her waist. She possesses more intelligence than even she is aware of, and there is a dullness to her eyes that suggests there is something inside just longing to be unleashed.

Prodding their minds with my own, I quickly determine they have spent the day at the beach —twenty-minute walk from their current position, yet this is much preferred to the countless minutes that would have been wasted trying to find a parking space nearer to the sand. They had parked underneath a big oak tree a hundred yards into a private drive that is just shy of half a mile long.

Rumour has it, the great house the drive belongs to is cursed. So strong is this belief—so real the fear—that the surrounding area has been left untouched and the nearest house, in each direction, is a five-minute walk from the gates to the bottom of the hill. No one in living memory has seen the house. In fact, many of the older folks often go so far to say the thing must have collapsed by now; yet not a soul is brave enough to find out, although a lot of people talk about it. Mothers of generations of children have warned them, 'If you are brave enough to go see the house, make sure that is as far as you go. Whatever you do, don't go in.'

As the six enter through the gateway, an enormous rumble of thunder causes them to jump almost out of their skins. They all turn to look skywards, puzzled as to where the thunder came from when, just moments before, the sky had been clear. Fat drops of rain greet their upturned faces, causing five of them to run for the car; the redhead just laughs.

'Clara! Come on!' shrieks the other girl, raindrops running into her eyes.

'Ashley, get the car open!' cries the preppy lad to the muscular one.

'I'm trying!' Water pours off his hair into his eyes and onto his hands, making the simple task of getting the key in the keyhole very difficult.

'Give them here!' demands the hunk as he moves to take the keys from Ashley. There is a slight tussle between the two as they fight for possession, then, after some interference from myself, the keys are on the ground and sliding away down the hill in a river of rainwater. 'Look what you did!'

'Me?'

'What happened?' yells the girl who isn't Clara. 'Get the car open.'

'We can't,' answers Ashley.

'We can't stay here, that's for sure,' shouts the eldest of the group. 'Let's go to the house.' This suggestion is met with a chorus of responses, none of which can be heard over the downpour. Clara, who has stayed where she is, twirling slowly and humming to herself as if she were at home taking a shower, quietly heads along the driveway. It takes a few seconds for the others to realise, but when they do, they are quick to overtake her—cursed or not, the group wants shelter from the rain.

The first glimpse of the house and its garden causes the group to pause despite the downpour. The creepy building may have been empty for as long as anyone could remember, yet its sheer size and empty, soulless windows cause the group to shudder with fear. They hesitate a moment: Is the house really cursed? A clap of thunder, and the group throws caution to the wind and heads for the porch, desperate to get out of the rain.

If they waited for the flash of lightning, they would have seen the shape of a man watching them from one of the uppermost windows. I am the servant of the house. My Master vanished hundreds of years ago, but I can feel my Master's presence. The time for his return is nearing. It will be soon.

Back on the porch, there is some debate over if they should knock or walk straight in, and who should be the first to do so? While they squabble, I use my mind to twist the doorknob, causing the old, heavy door to open slowly. The group stops bickering and stares at the door before stumbling across the threshold and almost falling into a heap.

'We should stay together,' announces Ashley. Everyone murmurs their agreement and enters the lounge.

Now the fun begins.

The preppy lad lingers in the doorway for a moment too long. I get into his head, causing him to forget his friends and move up the ornate wooden staircase. It is a trick I learned from my Master, and I have become very good at it over the centuries. The lack of moon shining outside prevents Preppy from noticing how perfectly kept the landing is: not a cobweb or mislaid piece of furniture anywhere. He also fails to see the figure watching from the shadows.

Picking the first door he comes to, he opens it and enters the room beyond. 'Sweet!' he whistles to himself as he spies a closet filled with dry clothes. He rustles through the contents, discarding those he dislikes onto the floor, until he finally comes across something he appreciates. He pulls on a red jumper before starting to remove his wet shorts. He tugs on some loose-fitting sweatpants and, with a satisfied smile, falls back onto the bed. He doesn't even have time to scream before the knives that have been carefully concealed under the thin mattress end his life.

With one down, I turn my thoughts to the others. They are all sitting in silence, afraid in case the haunted house hears them.

'I'm going to look for candles.'

'But, Ash,' says the girl who isn't Clara, 'you said we should stick together.'

'I did, but I need some light; this darkness is barbaric.'

'Well, if you see...' But Ashley is already closing the door behind him.

Following my nudges, he enters the kitchen. There are saucepans on the cooker, each filled with a thick glutinous liquid. Rising a ladle from one of the saucepans, he sniffs, his nostrils filling with the magnetic scent. Instinctively his tongue protrudes, but he stops short of actually tasting the liquid. Dropping the ladle, he rummages around some cupboards before yelling, 'I've found some matches.' He strikes one and looks around, hoping some candles will jump out at him. Instead, what he sees sends shivers down his spine. 'I did not just see that!' he mutters to himself as he squeezes his eyes shut. Slowly he opens them again. The darkness is blinding, but the lack of sight welcome. He fumbles around some more until, at last, he finds the candle being offered to him. Breathing deeply, he strikes another match, his hand shaking as he raises the flame to the wick of the candle. The darkness peels away to confirm what he had seen.

As his eyes absorb the sight before him, Ashley finds himself frozen to the spot. On the floor in front of him is—what must once have been—a human. There isn't much of it left, just some sinew and a skeleton bearing deep teeth marks in places. Thinking back to the pans causes him to shudder with fear. Sidestepping his way towards the door, he notices a footprint, a bloody footprint. Pushing the candle forward to get a closer look, he realises the print belonged to an animal, possibly a cat but much, much bigger. Gripped by terror, he gasps and makes to run, dropping the candle and eliminating the small flame in the process. He nearly makes it to the door before feeling a shift in the air behind him. Slowly it dawns on him that he is not alone, that he had never been alone. He turns slowly yet fast enough to glance the figure of a man before it shifts shape. Being as black as the darkness, the gigantic cat is almost impossible to see. Yet the murderous glint in its eye and the shine of its jagged teeth shine brightly, instilling pure fear into Ashley's heart. The mouth opens wide, gently at first as if in a yawn, but then the teeth are bared. And Ashley prays.

'Ashley?' comes a girl's shaky voice. 'Did you say you found some matches?' The kitchen door opens slightly, and the leggy brunette stares into the gloom. She takes a step forward and jumps as her foot connects to something. Bending down, she wobbles a little unsteadily, shakily she reaches out her hand until her fingers brush against a firm yet soft surface. Instantly she recoils. 'Get a grip, Rose!' she scolds herself on hearing the box of matches rattling softly. On standing, she lights a match and calls 'Ashley' once more before forgetting who Ashley is and turning to walk away, leaving the kitchen door to close softly on the ravaged body of her friend, who had been just inches from her reaching hand.

Rose moves slowly, trailing her hand along the wall. When her fingers come into contact with a door handle, she grips it and opens the door. Lighting a candle and stretching her hand out in front of her, she realises she is in a bathroom. A big window allows a small glimmer of moonlight to shine into the room, dispelling the darkness temporarily.

'At least it has stopped raining!' Rose exclaims to herself before making her way towards the window, where she is certain she has just seen several candles. She is right. Striking another match, she lowers the flame towards one wick then another until a warm, glowing light starts to flicker away the darkness. The slight warmth of the candles causes Rose to shiver. Noticing there are soft and surprisingly clean towels on the side of the bath, she starts to undress. Selecting a towel, she wraps it around herself, but then I enter her head and tell her the cold in her bones will not be so easily dispelled. Following my lead, she decides to test the taps. If she is surprised to find water running out of them, she is even more so when the water started to run hot and swirls of steam began to mingle with the smoke from the candles. Bending down to put the plug in, Rose notices a bottle, and with a quick twist of her hand, the cap is removed and a generous measure of bubble bath is poured into the water. With the air warming, she drops the towel and opens the window a crack. As the swirling steam makes its escape, Rose sinks into the bath. The chill in her bones is instantly relieved. A sigh of happiness starts to escape her but is replaced by a scream when I remove the filter I have fitted over her eyes, allowing her to see what she has really gotten into. Then there is silence.

The scream echoes along the corridor to the rest of the group. Clara and the hunk jump up, both wanting to help but terrified. The eldest of the group, who had been dozing, fell off the sofa before groggily finding his way to the hallway. The other two make to go with him until I suggest they stay behind. Wiping sleep from his eyes as he stumbles through the darkness, he tries each door he comes to until he reaches the bathroom door. The smell hits him before the door is fully open and causes him to sink to his knees and vomit.

Despite the candles having been blown out by the breeze coming in through the open window, the sight before him is all too clear. Knowing what he will see, he raises his head to see the bath where Rose's body is already unrecognisable. What Rose had believed to be water had burned through her silky skin until only patches of it remained—the power of suggestion is such a wonderful thing. Ian whimpers before crying fat tears complete with shoulder shaking sobs. His misery becoming so loud and all-consuming, he fails to hear the padding of feet as they creep up behind him.

The padding paws stop; the muscular shoulder blades jostle in preparation, a small snarl escaping, then I jump.

Without ever knowing what had happened, Ian finds himself in the death bath with the girl he has always been too shy to admit he loved.

Standing over the decomposing bodies, I return to my human form. The presence of my Master is overwhelming now. My head starts to lose focus, and I have to forcibly prevent myself bowing to no one. I can feel his power as if he is standing next to me, yet he is nowhere. He must be close by, but why has he...It is then the thought hits me, and I realise just how blind I have been. The servant has been toyed with just as much as the pathetic humans have.

As Ian's body starts to rot with Rose's, the hunk is starting to make his move on Clara. Maybe it is the fear causing him to lean in to kiss her, or maybe he has always wanted her. Either way, his actions have nothing to do with me. Neither did hers.

Clara smiles sweetly, welcoming the pressure of his lips on hers. The silence is pierced by an ear-splitting shriek. My keen hearing tells me the walls I have kept clean for so long are now splattered with blood.

Footsteps start to approach. On bended knee I bow, head lowered with the knowledge my Master has finally returned and, not only that, my Master has tricked me all night long in allowing me to think it has been my power manipulating the humans. I should have known that despite my centuries of practising on foolhardy daredevils, I am not powerful enough to do all that has been done this night.

A shadow falls over mine. The footsteps stop.

'Welcome, my Master.'

'Arise, my silly, faithful servant,' answers a sweet, singsong voice. Startled, I risk raising my head and am greeted with the sight of Clara's slender frame.

'You expected Hank the Hunk?' She laughs.

'Yes, my Master. You have never before taken female form.'

'I am more powerful now. I have learned many things. The world will fear me like never before.'

Looking up, I witness Clara's body melting slowly into nothingness and being replaced by the tall, pale figure of my Master. His dark hair shines, his eyes gleam and his sharp teeth glisten as he throws back his head and laughs manically.

The End

Cover by Susan. K. Saltos.

Loose Change

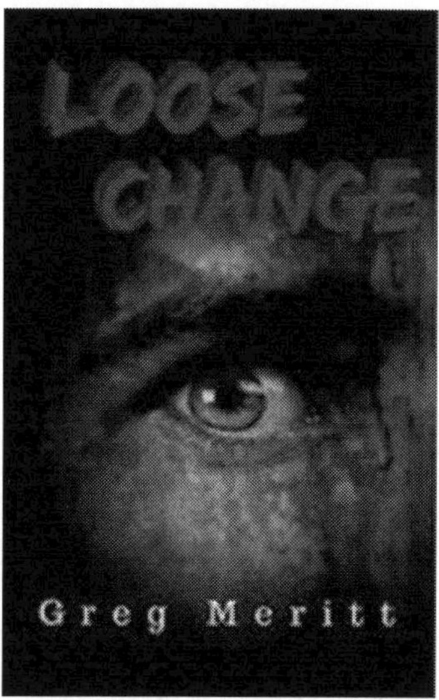

Greg Meritt

I have loved reading and the world of imagination ever since, as a teenager, I read Stephen King's *The Stand*. I have always enjoyed writing my own stories, too, but had to put that on hold for around 35 years (I think I forgot about it actually) to work and raise a family. In late 2012, I began writing again (don't know what compelled me, but I had to) and my short story "The Attic," received 18th place out of 5,900 entries and was included in the *Writer's Digest* 2013 short, short story competition anthology. What a thrill! And Mardibooks, the London-based publisher, also included my work in an anthology. Another short story, "Affliction," was an editor's pick on Book Country, an online website run by Penguin Books (now defunct, unfortunately).

The Adoption, available on Amazon, is my first full-length novel. I live in the beautiful Pacific Northwest with my wife and three wonderful adopted children, ages 11, 10 and 8. I write in the early morning hours before work, and I am currently working on—at readers' request—the sequel to *The Adoption*.

The short story, "Loose Change," was born a few years ago from a contest held on AuthorStand (also gone now), a community of writers sharing their work. I believe the prompt was something like: Write a story about what happens to a character who finds some loose change. And this is what I came up with. What can I say? My mind leans towards the macabre, the strange, and the just plain weird.

Oh, and I love reading, movies, nature, road trips and hanging out with my wonderful family. Thank you for taking the time to read.

***

I was walking down Front Street when I noticed it glimmering in the early morning sunshine like a wink. As I bent to pick it up, I heard a voice say, "Don't!"

"W-what?" I said, bewildered. I stood up with the shiny quarter clutched in my fist as if it were a winning lotto ticket instead of a measly twenty-five cents.

I turned toward the sound and was met with the frightened look of a young woman who appeared to be homeless. She sat among the dried-out, overgrown grass and weeds in the abandoned lot beside the 7-Eleven. Next to her was a shopping cart packed with overstuffed garbage bags, pots and pans, blankets and a dirty pillow. These items were secured to her home-on-wheels by a rope, which was entwined like a snake through the sides and bottom of the dilapidated cart.

"Oh...oh...no," she gasped. She clamped a hand over her mouth; she looked as if she had just seen the end of the world.

"What is it? Are you okay?" I asked. I realized then I was probably speaking with a mentally ill or drug-crazed person. But upon closer inspection, I noticed she was *clean* and her eyes were lucid, unlike most of the homeless population. She was young, twenty-five to thirty years old would be my guess.

"That money you took, it's cursed."

"The quarter I found on the sidewalk? What do you mean cursed? You're crazy," I said, dismissing her with a wave of my hand.

I began to walk away when she hollered at me, "That's the devil's quarter! He laid it there himself. Has a deal with God for one more soul!"

I shook my head, stuffed the quarter in my jeans pocket and kept on walking. Sunday morning walks were a ritual for me. I was fifty-two now, and my good doctor explained to me how important exercise was for the old ticker.

Two miles and forty minutes later, I was standing on my porch, breathing deeply of the crisp March air, my fingers fiddling with the quarter in my pocket.

I went inside. I was immediately hit with the aroma of frying bacon and the delicious smell of black coffee. I could hear bustling noises coming from the kitchen; I made my way toward the sounds and smells. I found Katie, my wife, cracking eggs with one hand and pouring coffee with the other. She was a great multitasker.

"Morning, handsome," she said without looking up.

"Hi, honey. Are the kids awake?"

She looked up. "Are you kidding me? If I had a nickel for every time you asked—"

"You'd have a dime," I interrupted. And suddenly I didn't feel well. Instead of causing me to salivate, the smell of greasy bacon was making me nauseous. "I'm going to check on the kids," I told my wife as I hurried upstairs.

I barely made it to the toilet before I threw up. Leaning against the marble counter, I stared at my reflection in the bathroom mirror. I watched in numb horror as I began to rapidly age. It was as if forty years were being crammed into the space of seconds: I went from a healthy, vibrant fifty-two-year-old to a wrinkled, withered man of ninety or a hundred.

I closed my eyes, shook my head. When I looked in the mirror again, the old guy was gone. My disbelieving countenance was staring back at me, jaw slack, eyes wide.

I splashed cold water on my face and walked from the bathroom to the bedroom. My fingers touched upon the forgotten quarter in my pocket, and when they did, the young homeless woman's words screamed in my head: *"That's the devil's quarter! He has a deal for one more soul!"*

I took it out now and looked at it. My mouth dropped in surprise; the coin in my hand began to pulse and glow, and as I watched, George Washington turned and smiled at me. His lips parted slightly; fangs protruded from his upper gums. He looked directly at me and winked; I dropped the quarter at my feet and backed away with a whimper, like a beaten puppy.

A couple of seconds later, my thirteen-year-old daughter, Peggy, was standing in the doorway. She gave me a funny look. "Are you okay, Dad?"

"Uh huh...Yeah, thanks, sweetie. I was just thinking about something."

"Penny for your thoughts!" She grinned.

"Right now I don't think my thoughts are worth that."

"What's that?" Peggy asked, ignoring me. She walked toward the quarter lying on the carpet.

"Don't! I mean...it's a quarter. I dropped it. Get dressed, honey; your mother is making breakfast."

"I'm not hungry. I'm going over to Sara's. Her mom promised to take us skating, and then we're going out for pizza."

"Sounds fun," I replied with a thin smile. "But you really should eat some breakfast, honey. You know what they say: Breakfast is the most important meal of the day." I furtively glanced at the dropped quarter lying on my bedroom floor.

***

The Devil's Quarter.

Yeah...right. Maybe I should make an appointment with Dr. Selby.

"Okay, okay, I'll eat something...I'm not going to Sara's for an hour anyway," Peggy said. "Dad, are you sure you're okay?"

I cleared my throat. "Yes, of course, I am," I said, trying to convince myself.

"Then why are you just standing there staring at a quarter? You're weird!" She bounced over to me and planted a kiss on my cheek. Then she bent down to pick up the gleaming piece of metal off the floor.

Thinking fast, I grabbed her shoulders and spun her around. I hugged her playfully, kissed her cheek and told her how much I loved her. And as soon as I released Peggy from my grasp, I bent down and plucked the poisonous change from the floor before my little girl had a chance to touch it.

"If you want money, you'll have to earn it," I joked half-heartedly.

"You're losing it, Dad...what am I gonna do with a quarter? Can't buy nothing with that."

The sudden spasm in my stomach and lower intestines had me racing back into the bathroom, the quarter still clutched in my hand. "Tell your mother I'll be right down!" I said to Peggy as I slammed the bathroom door.

Before I was halfway to the toilet, I felt a sharp pain in my lower bowels, as if an invisible hand had grabbed my intestines and squeezed. Quickly dropping my jeans around my ankles, I collapsed onto the seat; the second my flesh touched the porcelain, liquid poured out of my body as if I were dissolving from the inside out.

Unable to help myself, I peered down between my slightly parted thighs and into the toilet bowl. The clear water had turned a deep purplish-red. I was clutching the quarter so hard that my fingernails were biting into the flesh of my palm. I tried to scream then, but all that came out was an exasperated gasp of confusion and fear. I threw the cursed quarter across the bathroom toward the far wall and watched as it rolled on its edge and then spun crazily like it was being sucked down a whirlpool: round and round and round she goes. Finally tiring of the crazy spin, the quarter wobbled and fell on the linoleum, tails up. *Heads you win, tails you lose,* my mind whispered. *I lose.*

Suddenly I felt better. Tentatively, I looked between my legs again and was blessed with the wonderful sight of clean, clear water. Almost crying with relief, I stood up, belted and zipped my pants and walked over to the quarter. I squatted on my haunches and stared at it, careful not to touch it, wondering what to do next.

"Peter, are you okay?" Katie asked from the other side of the closed door. I never heard her come upstairs. She sounded concerned.

"I'll be out in a minute," I replied.

"Okay." She hesitated for a second and then said, "Breakfast is ready."

"Be right down."

My wife left and went back downstairs. I continued to stare at a piece of metal produced by the United States Mint, which now lay harmlessly on the floor of my bathroom. I couldn't leave it here; what if my wife picked it up? Would she get sick? Would terrible things happen to her?

No, I had to get rid of it somehow. Although I was scared to pick it up, I had no choice. Taking a deep breath, I plucked the coin from the floor and hurried toward the bedroom window. As I was crossing the room, my hand began to heat up. It felt like I had reached into an open fire. Once more, I dropped the quarter to the floor, half-expecting the carpet to burst into flames.

No flames; no fire.

I walked to the window, parted the drapes and looked down to the street below. Empty, at least for now. I slid the window open and removed the screen. Without any thought of who may find the cursed piece of metal, I quickly plucked the quarter—which was now cold—from the carpeted floor and threw it as hard as I could out the open window. I watched it roll down the street, bounce off the curb and come to rest next to a storm drain. I remember thinking: *Some kid will pick it up and shove it in his pocket and take it home and put it in his piggy bank. And that will be that.*

Now that the cursed quarter was out of my home and away from my family, I felt a hint of relief. But there was a nagging feeling that this wasn't over.

Taking the steps two at a time, I hurried downstairs. "I have an errand that's urgent; I'll be back in about an hour," I told Katie.

"What errand? And what about all this food I just cooked?" There was a slight irritation in her voice, but her eyes told the real story: She was worried.

"Yeah, Dad, breakfast is the most important meal of the day, remember?" Peggy chimed in. She was at the table, a freshly-made breakfast of eggs, bacon and waffles on the plate in front of her.

I felt nauseous again.

"I'll explain later, I promise," I said, praying I didn't vomit a spray of blood in front of my wife and child.

I rushed out the door and bolted down the street to where the quarter had come to rest next to the storm drain.

It was gone.

I looked left and then right; the streets were empty. *Maybe it rolled down into the storm drain, after all,* I thought. I looked at my watch: 9:05 a.m. It had only been an hour since the homeless woman informed me I was doomed, but it seemed as if an eternity had passed.

I went back to the house, jumped in the car and headed to the 7-Eleven, to the place where I first laid eyes on the gleaming twenty-five cent piece. My stomach cramped again; sweat was dripping in my eyes. Looking in the rearview mirror, I noticed my skin had yellowed, as if my liver had given up on me and quit processing my body's bile.

A few minutes later, I reached the convenience store at the corner of Third and Blanchard. As I feared, the woman was gone. "Shit, shit, shit," I mumbled under my breath.

I pulled into the 7-Eleven's near-empty parking lot on that early spring morning, trying to collect my thoughts, which had taken on a life of their own. It seemed I not only was losing control over my physical body but my mental state as well.

Looking out through the windshield of the car, I spotted the woman in the store purchasing what seemed to be a pack of smokes and a can of beer. I fumbled for the door handle, and as I did, I noticed my hands were not only shaking, but they had become, like my face, a discolored yellow and were mottled with dark brown liver spots. These were the hands you might find on a ninety or hundred-year-old man, not on a vibrant, healthy fifty-two-year-old.

Before I could get out of the car, the young homeless woman opened the passenger door and slid in next to me. Much to my surprise, she smelled like perfume and fresh air instead of alcohol, stale smoke, and vomit.

"Where's your cart?" I managed, my voice now raspy and hard.

Without a word, she slid closer and then wrapped an arm around me; it was strangely comforting.

"What…what is…is happening…to me?"

"I already told you," she whispered, her breath hot next to my ear. She flicked the lobe with her tongue. I shivered. "It wants your soul."

"It?"

"The devil falls under many names but takes no gender."

"W-why me?"

"Your heart is filth, Peter Hammond, and so is your soul. You have sex with prostitutes while away on business trips; you embezzle money from—"

"I don't embezzle money!"

"You embezzle money from your firm," she continued, "heavily padding your expense account while pretending to do your job. You care nothing for others; you shun the less fortunate and pretend they don't exist. You act as if you care about your fellow man when in truth you are out for yourself only. You are an egotistical—"

"Fuck you!"

"—maniacal wretch of a man, preying on the misfortunes of others."

"I got rid of it, you bitch," I laughed crazily.

"Check your pocket."

I reached into my pants pocket and pulled out the quarter. When I held it up, I noticed my fingernails were now yellow and cracked with age. I bolted from the car and ran into the store. I grabbed a bag of potato chips and threw them on the counter with a dollar bill and the tainted twenty-five cent piece. The clerk quickly made change and took a few steps back. I knew I must look crazy.

When I climbed behind the wheel, the woman was gone along with the sweet smell of perfume and freshness. What filled my nostrils now was the smell of decay, rot, and putrefaction.

My mind reeling, I headed home. As soon as I turned right onto Pebble Beach Drive, I heard a noise behind me. Keeping one eye on the road, I peered over my right shoulder. The woman was in the back seat. But she was no longer the young, homeless woman from the convenience store; she was now a hideous thing. Her eyes were dark, almost black, and her lips were gone. It was as if they had been burnt from her face. Pus oozed from open sores.

The thing climbed over the seat to join me. "You forgot this," it hissed, holding up the quarter. It grabbed my face and rammed its tongue down my throat. The smell was awful; the taste even worse.

So this is what death tastes like, I thought.

Then it grabbed the wheel and yanked hard to the right, sending us through the guardrail and to the rocks below.

"Welcome to hell," it whispered seductively in my ear as I plummeted to my death.

The End

Connect with Greg at the following:

Website: www. gregmeritt.com

Twitter: https: //twitter.com/greg_meritt

Facebook: https: //www.facebook.com/gregmerittauthor/

Cover by Tracy Blair-Funnell.

The Creature from Beyond the Coffee Cup

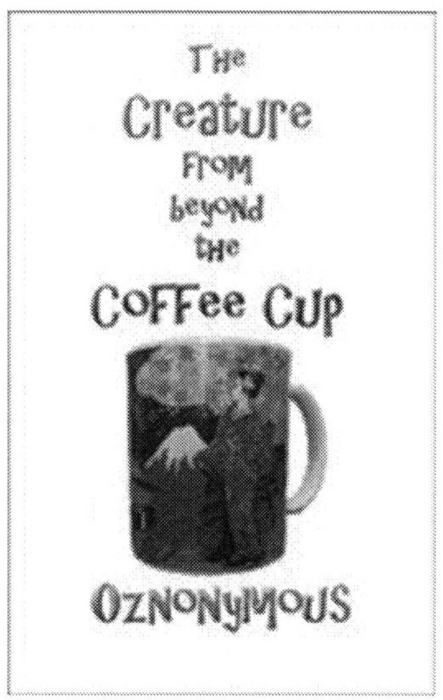

Oznonymous

Oznonymous (a.k.a. D. J. Meyers) was born and raised in Melbourne, Australia. A writer of poetry and short stories from the age of ten, many years were spent writing the words and music of songs. Fourteen years ago the itch to write a novel was scratched, and after several attempts, these completed tomes were placed on the Internet for review by others. Lessons learned and style adjusted, *The Renaissance Series* was born. *Tales of Yorr* became the first of these, focussing on the legend of the skeleton in the car park and the myths of history's winners. This was followed by two loose sequels: *Birth of Venus*, which delves into the life and loves of Sandro Botticelli and *The Whispering Mime* – a reconstruction of Elizabethan England and the origins of one particular bard named William. A sci-fi novel, *Sentenced to Obscurity*, was released in 2016 under the pseudonym of Oznonymous.

"The Creature from Beyond the Coffee Cup" precedes the forthcoming novel *Reviews from the Dead.*

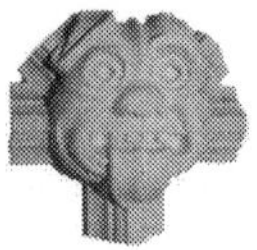

For all those who have lost someone and wished there was a cure

Part One

Kindergarten

Behind the fringes of willows at the end of Sandford Grove, there is a bluestone wall topped with shards of glass. Whitewashed many times, the paint added no thickness to its defenses, nor did it disguise the accusation — **MURDERER** — the stain of letters, a metre high, always bled through.

Sun setting on the structure, the colour of an aging paperback, a lone figure studies the graffiti. He makes a note on his tablet, folds its keyboard over the screen to place the device into sleep mode, and presses his finger to the intercom.

"Who is it?"

"Doctor Zafiropoulos."

The cast iron gate set into the bluestones clicked and swung inwards, its operation remote, the manor beyond even more so. Ivy clung to the house's decrepit brickwork. The web of dormant, brittle tendrils was born of decadence rather than a style to complement the three contradictory towers. One an inverted cone, the second a mansard square, while the third formed a rectangular steep peak. A porthole, of sorts, inhabited this final tower, glazed in four segments with a cross set in between that bled rust through its metal joints.

A path of solid chimney bricks led to the house, its edges manicured, the sand grouting clear of any weed or blade of errant grass. The doctor stepped along this toward twin marble lions that guarded the three steps up to the front door. The gate slammed behind him, yet he didn't break stride.

Stained glass kookaburras chuckled at the visitor as he strode through the gaping doorway and into the grand hall. A row of the owner's ancestors glared at him from the walls. Their eyes followed his confident passage through to the library. This wasn't his first visit.

The entrance closed in behind him, its ominous click a tut of a tongue yet to be convinced by the psychiatrist's methods.

He sat behind a reading desk, switched on the overhanging lamp, its apron of leadlight depicting some of the more macabre scenes from Shakespeare's tragedies, and turned his attention to the patient stretched out on the chaise longue. The question mark shaped back of the furniture was cushioned with pillows as velvet as the doctor's speech, which complemented his initial probe.

"Who are we today, son, Charlie Wattle or Ozwaldous Jones?"

The young man's thoughts strayed from the worn, pin-cushioned leather beneath him to the dust that sprung up from the doctor's notepad: particles of imagination, which drifted across the room beneath the lamp's awry light.

***

One might wonder how, as narrator, I could follow the good doctor's progress then know the inner workings of Charlie Wattle's brain. Is it a trick of the pen, the exaggeration of a fertile imagination, or do I have a bigger role to play in this tale? I'll leave those quandaries to your curiosity and delve into Charlie's head, reaching from the outside in.

***

Twenty-four years of age and surrounded by the tomes with which his mother had homeschooled him, Charlie balled up the knuckles rapped daily by his undertaker father's ruler. Used to measure the bodies of the dead by night, it bludgeoned knowledge into the young man as most other teens enjoyed the warmth of the Australian sunshine.

Charlie wiped sweat from the flesh so devoid of sun, he imagined it translucent, but thankfully clear of the melanoma his generation would falter from in years to come. If only he spent his dormant hours conjuring a cure from the myriad thoughts the psychiatrist attempted to mine.

What number therapist was this one? Twenty-nine? Almost three per year since...he masked the thought, but the inference had been spotted by the psychiatrist, who ventured his next question.

"Tell me about Lucy."

No, not L-L-L-Lucy... Even Charlie's inner dialogue stuttered at the mention of her name.

The doctor attempted to press his advantage.

"You'd—"

"*You had,* Doctor Zafiropoulos." Charlie's mother appeared in the library doorway, her tone enough of an arctic dunk for any young man. "There are no contractions in this house, except when my boys are plunged into an ice bath for impure thoughts about the sluts in the local village strip."

She placed a tray on the desk by the psychiatrist, the coffee there steaming in defiance of her chill disposition.

"You were saying, Doctor?"

"Yes, Charlie... *you had* just returned from a stint as an exchange student in Japan. How did that experience affect you?"

Under his mother's glare, Charlie rectified the slouch he'd formed, nestled as he was in the low-backed chaise longue. He focussed on the bookshelf beyond the psychiatrist's perch.

He remembered Japan. That was just before... before his fourteenth birthday. Six weeks at an exchange school in Hakone, by the banks of Lake Ashi, beneath the ominous presence of Mount Fuji. The mountain was a hotbed of perfection, ancient customs, and propriety—not unlike his home and the looming shadow of his mother.

Allowed a single souvenir, he bought a delightful coffee cup. The scene on its exterior depicted a geisha crossing a vermillion bridge beneath cherry blossom, with Mount Fuji in the background. He'd only drunk coffee out of the cup once. His mother's shriek as the hot beverage melted away the geisha's kimono to reveal unadorned flesh was enough for him to drop the offending vessel to the kitchen table. In the mêlée of cane blows and straps that followed, Charlie's prized souvenir tumbled to the floor and shattered.

His mother made him sweep up the shards and the coffee dregs, but in his first act of defiance, he didn't deposit the refuse in the rubbish bin. He hid it behind the back garden's only surviving plant, a ragged diosma that attracted blow flies with its putrid pink flowers.

Pieced together over countless hours in the solitude of a darkened attic, Charlie discovered to his horror the cup leaked when he attempted to wash off the remnants of the coffee. He never drank from it again. Its festering remains lurked behind an 1823 second edition of Mary Shelley's gothic masterpiece, which he spied beyond the psychiatrist's shoulder.

"If you would rather talk about something besides that day, tell me where you met Lucy."

"Kindergarten." The word slipped out as if a spectre through a mausoleum wall; an unwanted presence with an otherworldly volition—much like Charlie's imagination.

His mother's admonition echoed in from the hall. "It was a preschool, Charles. Your choice of word is a foul Germanic creation. We do not mention the War in this household. Too many sons were lost to their lust for power."

He knew she dusted the ancestor's paintings, and he pictured each hung Wattle with a scowl.

Charlie stuttered out his correction. The structure of his sentence, crafted to endear pride from his mother, masked his nerves. "Preschool, of course." He drew breath. "Lucy wore a daffodil-coloured dress, with white polka dots. She had hair down to her hips." He bit his lip, fearing the anatomy mentioned might draw another rebuke from his mother. It didn't. He cringed at the contraction in his thoughts and continued. "Her hair was braided, a random Rastafarian, tied off with ribbons that matched her dress." He swallowed and sucked saliva between his front teeth.

"Go on, Charlie," the psychiatrist urged.

"We were all running along the path."

"What have I always said about running wildly, Charles?"

His mother's voice reminded him of a chalk screech on the preschool's blackboard, and he continued with a wince.

"We were pushing trolley cars, weaving between slides and monkey bars. I followed in the wake of Lucy's ribbons; the breeze she created as she ran was a sunny day with a breath of apple. I didn't... I did not see the bend in the path, but I felt the metal crossbar of the climbing equipment as I slammed into it face first."

A tear bobbled on the rim of his eyelid as a tingle etched through his gums like the stump of an amputee.

"The words of my teacher floated about my head amidst the stars... *He'll lose those teeth, along with the adult ones coming down. Feed him baby food and they might hang on...* trailing prepositions and contractions mingled with stardust on flitting eyelashes, all held together by Lucy's fingers, entwined in mine as I lay on the playground path."

"Focus on the facts, Charles."

His mother's words another collection of nails hammered into the coffins his father prepared daily, the geyser within Charlie exploded.

"Shut..." *the fuck up*...the final three words steamed out of his ears, but not past his teeth. He threw his head back, clocking his skull on the rosewood trim of the chaise longue to the chime of the cuckoo clock. The timepiece was another anomaly, having originated in the Black Forest, but this antique had been crafted long before the Twentieth Century wars. Charlie concluded his sentence with a more peaceable structure. "The door please, Doctor Zalphabet."

"Zafiropoulos."

"Sorry, Doctor Zafiropoulos, I can't...cannot, concentrate."

The psychiatrist complied with his patient's request, yet in the passage from desk to door and back, he did not notice the fermentation spilling over the edge of the coffee mug, which lurked behind the *Frankenstein* tome.

"Please continue, Charlie."

"Lucy wept over my bleeding form, each teardrop a spherical translucent rainbow."

"You've used that word before, Charlie."

"Have I?"

"Yes. Is that how you'd prefer to see yourself, as invisible?"

"If I were, I wouldn't see myself." Mixed metaphors and failed ones were another of his mother's bug bears.

"True." The psychiatrist scribbled in his notebook. "You've been well educated, Charlie. You are a credit to your mother."

"She says I'm a failure, and she wasn't impressed with Lucy. I remember her words, 'Who is this girl, this village slut,' she yelled as she hovered over me in the preschool's playground. 'Luthy,' I replied through mangled teeth, 'Luthy Offerman.' She tore my hand from Lucy's with a sentence of a phrase, 'We do not fraternize with Germans, Charles.'"

The psychiatrist wrote on his notepad again, each sentence a sentence of its own. The patch on the elbow of his jacket polished the wooden surface he rested it on, as he polished his diagnosis. "When was the next time you saw her, Charlie?"

Every day in my head and every night in my dreams, came the fragment of a thought that clung to his flesh. His words in open company were more discreet. "I saw her every day at primary school and during my first two years at high school. The other kids called us Peanuts, and kept asking if I had a dog named Snoopy. There were no dogs allowed in the Wattle mansion."

"Did your mother know about your friendship?"

"No."

The scrape of the psychiatrist's pen across pristine paper shivered down Charlie's spine, a spectre across the tombstone he'd yet to imagine for himself. Funeral directors for generations, the Wattles were not a clan who celebrated death with gaudy memorials, only creepy portraits. Charlie felt these shaking their heads at him from the hall as the mould in his coffee cup fermented further, spilling from the fractured vessel and over the shelving.

"Are you still friends with Lucy?"

"No."

"Why not, Charlie? I've always found such early and intense friendships last long into adulthood."

Charlie's fingernails caught in the leather seat of his mother's antique chaise longue. He wished it was the flesh on her face as the psychiatrist's glare fixed on him from beneath the halo of the reading lamp.

"You know why!"

"No, Charlie, I don't."

"Everyone in Yarraville knows."

"I'm not from the Western Suburbs. I live on the other side of Melbourne, Charlie."

The continued repetition of his name clawed at Charlie like the fodder in a penny dreadful. His father's collection of Westerns filled two shelves here, fully catalogued with special editions. A nod to his mother's mantra—*'Do not be a snob, Charles. There is writing designed for everyone in God's kingdom.'*

"When was the last time you saw Lucy?"

"Don't make me say it."

"Contractions, Charles!" exclaimed his mother from the hall.

"F..." the letters of rebuke Charlie intended were severed in his throat by the memory of the cane his mother so often wielded. "F-f-fourteen... my fourteenth birthday, you bastard."

The psychiatrist's mobile phone rang. Its ringtone, the opening notes of *I Feel Fine* by The Beatles, grated. Guitar feedback followed by a rolling riff: something else from the Sixties, another link to his pathetic name. Charlie Wattle closed his eyes and waited for the specialist to answer, to relieve the tension. He didn't and the phone played on into the verse. Imagination his salvation, Charlie conjured a version of the doctor's voicemail greeting:

Hi, you've reached the message bank of Doctor Nick Zafiropoulos.

I'm currently in a session with a patient who is tied down to a leather couch. I have electrodes attached to his temples, and I'm about to press the big red button. If you're brief, I might return your call, but my response is bound to be shocking. All correspondence will be treated as confidential, unless the word count is 125 or less. If so, my secretary will quote you on our Twitter account—'The Things People Say Under The Threat of electroconvulsive Therapy'— Beeeeeeeeeeeeep...

"Tell me about your fourteenth birthday, Charlie."

The return to therapy shocked Charlie into answering. "There was a knock on the front door. There was no intercom in those days. I was upstairs. My bedroom faced the front gate, and I heard it squeak. Mother always has the windows open, even on the most bitter of winter days—*fresh air and fresh thoughts lead to godly minds.*"

"Wise words, Charlie."

"If you believe in all that s-shit."

"Charles!" How did she hear through a solid wooden door with lath and plaster walls for surrounds? "There will be soap in your mouth when the good doctor is done."

"Soap?"

The doctor's query wrought a smile on Charlie's face. He lowered his voice to a whisper in response. "It's not so bad if you catch it early, break it down, and blend it with real strawberries."

"You're joking?"

"Nope. My brother sorted that out years ago. He claims to be a psychic. Perhaps you should see him and flatten out his head."

"You mean straighten—?"

"No. He's a bastard. Get a good steamroller over the top of him and the world will be a better place."

The psychiatrist shuffled in his seat. "Why don't we concentrate on your visitor?"

"Lucy." Charlie sighed, closed his eyes, and lay back on the chaise longue.

Part Two

The University of Life

Charlie Wattle remembered hanging out of the first-floor bedroom window, the afternoon sun warm on his face. He watched as Lucy skipped along the path, patted each of the marble lions who guarded the stairs, climbed the three steps, and reached out to the brass doorbell.

His mother's shriek, a tireless wheel on virgin asphalt, drowned out the chimes. "Who is ringing at this hour? Dinner is almost on the table."

The door squeaked open, the only mouse to survive in these halls under his mother's poisonous regime.

Lucy spoke without fear. "Hello, Mrs. Wattle. Is Charlie home? I've come to play."

"We do not use contractions in this house, young lady. Charles!"

He remembered rushing down the grand staircase, pausing at its final turn. Torn between light and dark, he thought his face matched the creases of his disgruntled ancestors. Charlie chose light and bounded down the remaining stairs, careful to tread on the centre of each one to avoid wearing the carpet at the edges. He emulated the swivel hips of a race walker across the entrance hall, as to run was a sin, and grabbed his friend's hand without drawing breath.

"Hi, Lucy."

"Hello, Charles." She giggled as she replicated the dourness of the mansion's matron.

His mother's words dripped faux concern. "If you climb onto the roof, fall down and break your legs, do not come running..."

The words faded to a shrill whistle beneath the thickness of the lath and plaster walls as the teenagers scurried upstairs. First floor attained, the hidden panel to the attic was pressed in the appropriate places, with the secret finger formation, and opened.

"What is this place, Charlie?"

"My tree house."

"Don't you have a gum tree or a willow in the backyard like everyone else?"

It was at that moment Charlie Wattle felt the spark of the future pseudonymous Ozwaldous Jones within, and created his first furphy[1]. "We've got a few roos[2] loose in the top paddock, so it's a bit dangerous out back at the moment."

"My dad's got just as many silly jokes, Charlie. He said you were a few sandwiches short of a picnic. You don't need odd anecdotes, you're weird enough as it is, and just as I like you to be. You're my

[1] A rumour or story, especially one that is untrue or absurd.

[2] Kangaroos.

dragonfly: beautifully fluorescent, with an eye for every detail, and that fabulous Wattle sting in the tail. Take me to unimaginable heights, Charlie."

They climbed the stairs, lit by a single swinging globe that brushed their shadows across the sullen walls within the narrow, dogleg of a cavity. On the top landing, he paused to search for the main light switch. Bakelite and cracked through, he flicked it with care. It sparked, yet the action illuminated the vast expanse of the attic beneath its three towers and extended gables.

"Wow! What a great place, Charlie. My house is old, but nothing like this. And you have spider webs and everything. I love creepy old houses. What do you do in here all day?"

"I don't spend all my time in here. I have another place—one my brother is shit scared of." He bit his tongue on the trailing preposition. "Come on, I'll show you."

Charlie led his friend through the attic to the base of the largest tower, and clambered up the wrought-iron, spiral stairs. Rusted and quivering with the weight of the two teenagers, it held by the swollen threads of its russet screws. At the top, he reached up to a latch on the ceiling, pulled back on the handle, and the roof opened. The open hatch framed a sky-blue day. He dragged himself up and held his hand out to his friend. Their fingers entwined, and he lifted her onto the roof of the tower. She did not avert her eyes from the heights as his brother did and, hanging over the edge, she marveled at the grotesque gargoyles, still drooling after an earlier spring shower. She spun up on high with the sounds of music imagined in her ears, before hanging over the edge of the fleur-de-lis railing again, shouting at the top of her voice.

"Hold me around the waist, Charlie."

***

The scribbling from the psychiatrist continued in the background, a feather tip of a whisper from things unsaid, as Charlie remembered his fourteenth birthday. His detached version of the tale was ominous.

"What did you do next, Charlie?"

"I didn't... she did."

Distancing himself from her actions, he spoke in her excited tones. A spectre of a past lost, his voice bristled in the hairs on the psychiatrist's arms.

***

"Come on, Charlie, grab me, I want to fly." He did as she asked, and she leant further out with arms stretched wide. "I'm the queen of the world."

Her hair a kite of daffodil-bows and braids, he sniffed its apple perfume as the strands flapped against his face. Charlie had never held Lucy in his arms. The sensation stirred things unmentionable, the words of his mother dogging him.

"You scrub that thing until it is red raw, young man, and do not entertain any of your father's thoughts about those dirty little sluts in the village."

Charlie enjoyed the rise and fall of his friend's supple waist in his hands and her squeals of delight. If only her joy had lasted. The dreaded tones of his mother wrenched him from the moment.

"Get your hands off that little slut, Charles Wattle."

The limpness that enveloped his arms infected other areas, now even more unmentionable. Shoulders slumped, he turned. "She's—"

"Contraction!" The chalk scrape of his mother's tongue on the air forced a correction.

"She is my friend. My only friend."

"I know what she wants, what she wants to hold, and the money she can squeeze out of it."

The orbital muscles beneath Charlie's eyes twitched. His neck matched the involuntary tic. "I d-do not care what she wants to hold. I only care what I want, and if I c-c-can-not hold her, Mother, no one will."

***

The scrape of the pen ceased. An awkward silence was followed by a nervous tap. Charlie Wattle clamped his mouth shut. The psychiatrist gave his patient time as the swing of the cuckoo clock's pendulum continued, tick upon tick.

"What happened next, Charlie?"

His answer was more of a whimper than a memory. "She said she wanted to fly."

"But what happened."

Charlie leapt up from the chaise longue. "I don't remember...don't make me remember, you fu—"

"Charles Oedipus Wattle! Curb your tongue and answer the

question."

He collapsed to the couch, his mother's words reverberating between his ears as they had for twenty-four years, punching each eardrum in turn. Charlie felt like clocking the doctor. He elbowed the cushion of the chaise longue instead.

The fermentation of his coffee cup matched his mood, engulfing Shelley and spilling over shelf after shelf, until it soiled the floor. He closed his eyes again. The psychiatrist misread his mood.

"Go on, Charlie."

Despite his reluctance, some part of the memories flowed.

"I remember her falling...from the tower...a butterfly in daffodil, flapping in the evening breeze."

Charlie didn't reveal his most vivid image from that day: Lucy's body on the solid, red-brick pavement at the rear of the manor, her legs and arms swimming at impossible angles.

"What else do you recall, Charlie?"

"There was no cake."

"Was there ever cake in this household, Charlie?"

"Are you kidding? Mother makes the best sweets. She lays them out on the coffee table in the lounge room, but only the brave get to sample them."

Catching onto the mood of the manor, the psychiatrist asked, "Why, what's the punishment?"

"Notoriety."

"I don't understand."

Charlie sat forward on the chaise longue, salivating at the thought of the desserts. "Picture a couch, built for five adults or seven children. Line them up on it and tantalize them with pavlova, shortbread, and cake. Picture the same classic fifty's couch covered in plastic to preserve its fabric from falling preserves. Every move a child makes toward the sweets is accompanied by a crumple. Lean forward— *crumple crumple.* Pickup cake— *crumple crumple.* Sit back to stuff face— *crumple crumple*...and repeat. Every move, every thought of a move, every delicacy sampled...all noted and stored away for a gluttony accusation."

"You're not overweight, Charlie."

"I was too bloody scared to eat!"

"You're not afraid now, though. I can see the defiance in your eyes. What happened to Lucy Offerman?"

Charlie flopped back onto the couch and buried his face in its fabric. "Don't make me remember that."

"You must! One can't hold onto that kind of grief without consequences."

"Ha! You have no idea. They might not have put me away, but they locked me in here for ten years. The authorities should have gaoled us all."

"Why, Charlie? What did they do?"

"They made me bury her."

"What! Who?"

"Lucy, you moron."

"Wasn't an ambulance called?"

Charlie rolled off the chaise longue and stood. "You're joking, right? She was buried with the refuse— in the backyard."

The fermentation from the coffee cup oozed across the floor and pooled at the psychiatrist's feet. Charlie thumped his palms down on the reading desk and stared at the doctor.

"My brother stood point with his slingshot as I dug, while Mother lectured me from the good book. I could see her lips moving, but I couldn't hear the words. I still can't."

He spat out the contraction as the dregs of the coffee rose up, forming a fermented hand.

"Why did you make me remember that, you bastard?"

"Now calm down, Charlie. I'm sure there is a perfectly good explanation for the events you've envisioned. You clearly have a vivid imagination."

Contractions and adverb abuse tore at Charlie's psyche as the psychiatrist wrapped up his probing.

"Perhaps we should end our session here, Charlie."

The hand of mould swept down toward the doctor's neck: a glowering, gelatinous, fermentation of hate, angst, and forbidden desire.

"You're damn right it ends here."

He slouched out of the library, every strike of the shovel that buried Lucy shuddering through his fingers.

His mother waited.

"Do you feel better, Charles?"

"Yes, Mother."

"Did you leave a mess?"

"Nothing that cannot be mopped up and buried in the back garden."

Charlie wiped a slither of froth from his lips and paused by the grand staircase, its guardian gargoyles carved with garish delight by a Wattle ancestor. He patted the closest creature, as Lucy once had. His mother rested a hand on his shoulder, a brief anointment rather than a comforting embrace.

"We all remember our first, Charles. Your father was mine. He is like a good Protestant. An *Amorphophallus Titanum*, putrid and erect once every seven years."

Charlie cringed. His mother had a habit of drawing parallels to his father's prowess, although what he did outside the house and at work no one really knew.

"When are they going to find a cure for this, Mother?"

"There are no cures for some of God's more insidious maladies...and certainly not for you. Finally, you are a true Wattle, Charles."

The compliment was worth a rebuke, yet he bit down on his tongue until it bled, his thoughts betraying him. *No! I'm no longer Charlie Wattle. I repress that entity into my inner monologue—I am Ozwaldous Jones.*

The End

Connect with Oznonymous (a.k.a. D. J. Meyers) at:

http://www. thegargoylechronicles.com.au/

Cover by Author.

To Save Lives

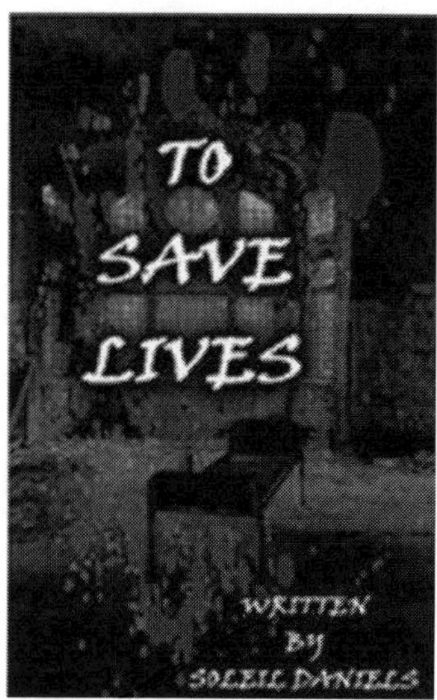

Soleil Daniels

Soleil Daniels enjoys writing many things, but she has the most fun when delving into the darker imaginings. She uses everyday happenings and scenarios, twisting them to make a normal activity into something that would leave some people wondering why. Like, take field dressing, skinning, and cleaning a deer; now, imagine that deer is a person . . . yeah, Soleil wrote a story about that, and she enjoyed it. That is not this story.

The story that follows is one of many things. It's dark, but it's also a story about love, betrayal, and creation. "To Save Lives" is a spin-off short story of one of Soleil's longer works, a series known as *Halfborn*, and it features one of the four main types of vampires in the series. These vampires are known as Abominates, and this short is about two of them that have gone astray.

1. The Plan

"We're known as the worst of the worst. The putrid. The ones that should not be. The Abominates. But, what if we could help humans who'd thought they'd lost a loved one? What if we could help them keep the people they care so much for but fear they have lost to sickness and disease? Would they agree, even if it cost more than they could ever imagine?" Calvin mused, more so to himself, but he turned to make sure Daphne was paying attention.

"I'm not sure I'm following, Cal. How exactly do you mean 'help them keep the people they care so much for'?" Daphne shook her head, puzzled.

"We take the humans that are one step over the threshold of death and we transform them. We convince their families—their loved ones—to ask the hospitals to take them home and live their final days, maybe hours, there. We do this under the pretense that we can save them. We promise the families that there's no reason for the person to die."

"Why? What's the point? If it's to feed, I find the hassle seems far too much."

"An army, Daphne. A defense against our enemies. The Inborns. The Wraiths. We'll truly be transforming those who knock at death's door. We'll give those families their wish of more time. Though, I believe it won't be exactly what they'll expect," Calvin explained as if it made all the sense in the world.

"I don't know. There's something about it that doesn't fit. Building an army that way, well, don't you think that someone else would have already done it if it were possible. Besides the transformation being so difficult, to begin with, there has to be a reason why we've never heard of anything similar being done." Daphne walked across the room to Calvin and smoothed the crease that had formed between his eyes with her thumb.

He knocked her hand away. He'd lived nearly seventy-five years more than Daphne as an Abominate. Her blood-need had only been awakened eighteen years before that night. In a way, she was his sister as they had both been turned by the same Abominate, Petra, but Daphne was also his lover. He despised the fact that she would disagree with him. He'd had more experience, and unlike him, she'd never attempted to transition a Newling. He had two attempts under his belt. Both of which were failures, but he'd since then studied the history of the Abominates, the turning process, and also gone to medical school, learning all he could about the human body and how it functioned. He used the knowledge he learned of both humans and Abominates to devise a plan to make the transformation process easier and more successful. At least, that was his hope. Yet, Daphne doubted him.

"I see that you're angry with me, Cal, but all I'm saying is, we should at least talk to Petra or another of our kind before moving forward," she said, showing him just how little faith she had in him.

"Petra?" he said, the anger tainting his voice nearly tangible. "Petra! The beast who transitioned us and then left. Sure, I had a decade with her, but you? She dumped you on me when you were barely six months transformed. You were still a Newling. You were still in need of your creator. And, you want her to, what? Help with a plan I've spent twenty years devising. I think not! Besides, she's probably still chasing down that impossible creature. Determined to claim a mere Halfborn is more than what it truly is. She's lived too long, and she lost her mind centuries ago."

"I'm not trying to upset you, Calvin. I'm just not sure about this. Please, we should, at the very least, question another of our kind. What's a little more time—"

"No!" Calvin boomed. "I will do this whether you're by my side or not!" He turned and left the room, slamming the door hard enough that he'd heard the frame crack.

2. Terry Stone

"You can wake my baby up? My sweet Terry? The doctors here say there's nothing to be done, but you seem so sure that's not the case," the woman said, her tears leaving streaks through the layers of makeup coating her face.

Calvin knew he'd have to put up with emotional people. It didn't mean he had to like it. In fact, he despised it. Babbling, leaky humans. Even though he used to be one of them, he couldn't ever remember being so ... sniveling. As he was, and had been for nearly a century, he had wants—needs—but nothing so strong that he'd cry. Not even in the sanctity of being alone.

"I do believe that, yes, my colleague and I can bring him back to a conscious state. I won't promise it will work, as it's experimental, but I feel it will be successful, Mrs. Stone."

"But, why do I have to have him taken home or to a private facility? I don't understand why you can't do the procedure here."

Mrs. Stone wiped at her reddened nose with a tissue.

"At this stage, the procedure is confidential. This hospital is a teaching facility, and the faculty will want the students to have access to observe the procedure. I can't have that. I do hope you understand. Although, if you can't agree then I will have to move on to another qualified candidate." Calvin worked to keep a smirk from his face. "I wish you and your family the best, Mrs. Stone," he said, turning to walk away.

"Wait. Doctor?" Calvin turned back to the grieving woman, making sure his face didn't show the pleasure that filled him. "We can't afford the transfer home or elsewhere, for that matter. If Terry's removed from the machines, he'll be gone almost immediately."

"Don't worry about any of the expenses. If you agree to the procedure, we'll cover everything, including the bill for his stay here at the hospital."

"Then, yes. If I could have the chance at just one more minute to tell my boy that I love him, I'd do anything. To have him hear and understand it, would all be worth it. The hope, alone, is worth it." Fresh tears spilled from the woman's eyes, causing Calvin to cringe internally.

"We'll check the records, and our private ambulance will bring Terry to your home this evening. If you could, please prepare a room for the set-up of the equipment needed—everything he is currently using: machines, bed, and so on—that would be extremely appreciated. It would save us time, as well. My colleague, Daphne Donovan, will be at your house by four this afternoon to verify everything's ready."

3. He Left

"Cal, do you seriously think you can transform someone who's brain dead? This Terry guy's brain probably looks like what an egg does if you shook it up inside the shell. Did you even read his chart?" Daphne said, pushing a lock of golden hair from in front of her left eye.

"Yes, I read the chart. I figure, why not start with a worst-case scenario? If we can transform *him*, nearly any condition should be possible." Calvin did nothing to hide the irritation in his voice.

"You told his mother that you could do this, but this guy's dead. The only reason his heart's beating is because a machine is beating it for him. The same for his lungs, Cal. Never mind the fact that his neck was shattered from the force of being thrown from his motorcycle and his head meeting a tree. He's completely paralyzed. Do you honestly think something like that will heal?"

"Actually, I do. Daphne, why do you have such little trust in me? Besides, he's human. What does it matter to you if he makes it or not? Don't you want to know just how much can be fixed by the transformation? This way, we'll know more about the limits of what we can do and what we can't," Calvin said through clenched teeth. "Now, enough with the questions!"

"Fine," Daphne said before plastering a fake smile on her face and knocking on the door.

Mrs. Stone opened the front door. Her eyes were bloodshot as she ran the back of her hand over her cheek, wiping fresh tears away. Daphne felt the uncomfortable tension as it pulsated off Calvin. She never understood his hatred for emotions, especially sadness. He seemed to lack the ability to empathize with anyone, which confused her on how he could be so tender when they were alone.

"Hello, Mrs. Stone. Sorry, I couldn't stay earlier and help set up Terry's room. I hope everything went smoothly," Daphne said, hoping not to sound too cheerful.

"Yes. Yes, everything went the best it could, considering," the woman informed them, stumbling over her words. "I hoped for you two to meet with my husband, but ... but—" Mrs. Stone collapsed into the doorframe, going into a fit of tears and sobbing.

"Ma'am? Are you okay?" Daphne asked, feigning concern.

Mrs. Stone fell forward, her arms wrapped around Daphne, and she buried her face into Daphne's shirt. Calvin stepped back and away from the women. Daphne watched him cringe in her peripheral, wishing she could get away from the woman as well.

Several minutes passed, and Mrs. Stone eventually pulled away. "I'm sorry. I'm okay. It's just when my husband came home from work and saw Terry here, he got angry—really angry—and he left. He said I was crazy. Said that Terry should be in the hospital. He just ... left."

"I'm sure he'll be back, Mrs. Stone. It's an emotional time, and he's handling it the best way he can. Now, Dr. Andrews and I are going to go check on Terry. Okay?"

"Yes, please do. The procedure, when do you plan on performing it?"

"We hope to start within the next hour or two," Calvin said while stepping forward, taking his spot next to Daphne again.

"Oh, so soon, Dr. Andrews? I thought it wouldn't be until tomorrow. Maybe later." Mrs. Stone wiped at the remaining wetness on her face before pulling a tissue from her pocket to blow her nose.

"The way I see it, the sooner the better. We just have to check a few things, and then I'll bring in my equipment." Calvin adjusted the watch on his wrist, avoiding eye contact with the woman as her eyes began to brim with tears all over again. He stepped through the doorway past her. "Where's Terry's room?"

"I forgot something in the car. I'll be right there," Daphne said, and Calvin nodded in response.

Daphne pulled her phone from her pocket as she walked to the car. After selecting the number she wanted, she typed out the text message, hesitating only a few seconds before hitting send.

We're in Prescott. I'll
give you the exact address
when you need it. If you
need it. Don't look for me
before I text back. I'll know.

4. Magic

"You brought the knife, right?" Calvin asked, knowing it was a bit late to find out she hadn't.

Daphne set a leather bag on the nightstand next to the bed Terry's body lay on, and she loosened the string that held it closed. She slipped her hand in the bag, withdrawing the black blade it held. The bright overhead light reflected off the obsidian knife's surface, helping to draw her attention away from the whirring sounds and beeping of machines.

"Do you have any idea what I had to do to get this?" Daphne said, holding the knife just out of Calvin's reach.

"Whatever it was, it was worth it. Actually, it probably wasn't enough. That blade gives us the power to create. It interacts with our blood to transform the human. I don't fully understand why. Whether it's the type of rock it's carved from or the spell that's been cast on it. Maybe, it's the combination of the two. However, I've seen the transformation attempted with an unspelled obsidian blade and with a steel blade that had been spelled, but neither worked. It must be obsidian, and it must be spellbound. It's all linked back to the ritual of The Thirteen." Calvin stopped reaching for the knife, and he watched as Daphne set it onto the leather bag that held its spot on the night stand.

"Magic," Daphne said and blew out a frustrated breath. "I've lived in this other-world nearly twenty years and still can't grip the concept that it was—is?—magic that brought me to join it and keeps me here."

"Daphne, I don't even think that witches completely understand the workings of their magic. So, do not fret because you don't." He shook his head before he reached across Terry's body to finally grab the knife.

He slipped the blade into the pocket of his white coat. It didn't go unnoticed by him that the sharp edge sliced through the skin of his palm, but the cut healed before he had the chance to wipe the blood away.

"I'll set up the tools. You go let Mrs. Stone know that we need her to stay out of the room. Tell her that we'll get her when she can see her son."

Daphne huffed, not wanting to deal with the woman. She understood the mother's grief. That didn't mean she had to feel comfortable with it. Defeated, she left the room to go speak with the other woman, realizing it was probably for the best that it wasn't Calvin doing so.

She walked into the living room where Mrs. Stone sat. "Okay, Mrs.—"

"Maddie. Please call me Maddie. Or Madeline if you feel the need to be formal," the woman told her.

To Daphne's surprise, the woman's face was dry and a weak smile played at her lips. "Well then, Maddie. We're about to start the procedure. Would you like to see Terry before we begin? If not, you won't be able to see him until Cal—I mean, Dr. Andrews is finished."

"No, no. If I go in now ... before, it'll be like I'm saying goodbye. Like I don't have faith that the doctor can do what he says. You come get me when you're done. Okay?" she said, tears springing back into her eyes, causing them to shine.

Oh, for the love of all that's dear, just stop it, woman. Daphne cringed at her lack of empathy, noting Calvin had rubbed off on her too much. It proved to her that she was making the right decision—well, if she chose to follow through.

"As long as you're sure." She waited for the woman to nod. "Okay, it shouldn't be too long. To be generous, an hour tops, but more than likely, less than half an hour."

Daphne returned to Terry's room to see that Calvin had set up a silver tray table. On it lay a small saw, much like a jigsaw with blade enclosed at the end. The blade measured two inches or so in length. Next to the saw lay a silver contraption that was made up of four sections—two extensions ending with curved lips, while the other ends connected to a toothed bar with a crank. One extension fixed to the end while the other could move back and forth when the crank was turned.

Daphne was unfamiliar with the tools with the exception of a scalpel that lay next to the silver contraption. *A rib-spreader?* Daphne guessed. She did notice the lack of sanitary supplies—alcohol, iodine, etc.

"I believe we're ready. Mrs. Stone, she still sniveling? You'd think humans would be less ... emotional? Death is their inevitable end. I don't understand why they are so affected by the course of life," Calvin said in disgust.

"You may want to keep it down, Cal. What if she hears you?"

"So what? If we as a species can control our emotions then they should be able to do so, too. We have far more time to develop lasting relationships. I have more right to emotional outbursts than a mere human who lives far too short a life to feel so deeply."

She didn't know what to think of his words. A reply sat on the end of her tongue. Something along the lines of the short lives of a human may very well be the reason they feel as deeply as they do. The lack of time forcing them to hold onto every little thing that much tighter, but she just shook her head, not wanting an argument. She took her place on the other side of Terry, across from Calvin and right next to the tray that had been set up in her absence.

"Now, hand me the scalpel," Calvin said.

"You're not going to use any antiseptic? No pain meds, either?" Daphne asked, but she complied with his request.

"If he transforms, he won't need it. If not, well, he'll be dead, and what good will it do him?" Calvin pressed the blade of the scalpel into the divot of Terry's collarbone.

Blood wept from the incision. Daphne restrained herself, refusing to bend down and lap at the pooling crimson. Calvin drew the blade downward, over the man's sternum, and Daphne saw when he'd gone too far. The blade losing contact with the bone as it slid deeper into the man's stomach.

Calvin removed the blade and handed it back to Daphne. "Bone saw."

She glanced at the two other tools, picking up the one that had the word 'Stryker' on it, the one that looked similar to a jigsaw. She flinched when Calvin tested the saw's battery juice; it made a loud whirring sound before he turned it back off. He inserted the tip of the saw in Terry's cavity just below the sternum, and then he brought the saw back to life.

The sound as the blade tore through bone made Daphne want to gag. It only took a matter of seconds, and then the noise stopped. She looked at the small gap that ran the length of Terry's chest. Blood ran down his sides, and the smell of it made her mouth water.

Daphne registered the alarms of the heart monitor before she did Calvin's voice.

"Aren't you listening? I need the retractor!" he bellowed, making her snap out of her daze.

She grabbed the saw, setting it on the tray, and she traded it for the silver contraption. "Retractor? I thought it was a rib-spreader."

"It is. Now, give it to me before his heart stops."

She handed it to him and watched as he put the lips on the extended arms where they pressed against either side of the opening. He turned the crank a few times, making each set of ribs start to slowly move away from each other.

"Turn this crank until I say to stop. Once I get the blood in his heart, you'll need to move it as quickly as possible." Calvin released the crank, allowing Daphne to take over, and he reached into his pocket for the obsidian knife.

She did as he said, watching in fascination as Terry's chest opened, revealing his pulsating heart and lungs. She stood in awe.

"Okay, that's good enough. You can stop," Calvin said.

Daphne looked up in time to see him bring the black blade forcefully across his palm and up his wrist, halfway to his elbow. She watched as the blood ran down the knife when he'd put it in the hand he'd maimed, but she knew that the cut had probably already healed. He held the blade above Terry's heart until the first drop fell upon it, sizzling. A small cloud puffed up from the contact.

"Interesting," Calvin said as he plunged the blade into the beating muscle.

The heart pumped erratically for a moment, and then it stopped abruptly, but Calvin's blood that had been running down the knife seemed to get sucked into the wounded muscle.

"On the count of three I will remove the blade, and you will then take out the retractor. Ready?" Daphne nodded. "One. Two. Three."

Calvin pulled the blade out, and Daphne turned the crank as quickly as she could. It obviously wasn't fast enough as Calvin pushed her hand away, grabbed hold of the contraption, and turned it sideways, nearly ripping the thing from Terry's chest.

Before the ribs fell back into place, Daphne saw the heart muscle beat once. She thought how odd it was to do so. Then the skin on Terry's chest began to weave itself back together. Instinctively, Daphne knew that the same was happening to the bone underneath.

"Amazing," she said under her breath.

"Indeed," Calvin responded.

5. Betrayal

Terry's chest had begun to expand outward as air rattled into his lungs, filling them. The growl leaving him became obvious upon his exhalation. It was low and deep as it grew stronger with each second that ticked by. Daphne took a step back, watching as Terry's eyes opened wide. The color of his irises was no longer that of a human, and though she didn't know what color they'd been before, she was sure they were far from the original, in that moment.

Burnt crimson, the color of dried blood, stared at her. All that they held was a need—a thirst—that when looking back on her own transition, she could almost remember the feeling. Something was off, though. That's all she could see in his eyes. There was nothing remotely tame within him, she just knew it.

"Boy, calm yourself!" Calvin said.

Daphne's head jerked up to look at Calvin, but not so quickly that she missed Terry's face turn in his direction, too. She heard the gnashing of teeth as the growling continued, and she glanced back in time to see him upright himself and jump to his feet, heading for Calvin.

"We should have restrained him, Cal!" Daphne shouted.

"Terry, you're safe. Calm down, young man." Calvin ignored her words and, instead, tried to vocally subdue his Newling, holding his hands out in front of him in submission.

Daphne could see the fear in Calvin's eyes as he dodged the blood-thirsty being and maneuvered behind him, grabbing his wrists and pulling his arms behind his back. He knocked Terry to the carpet, bumping the dresser with so much force a lamp fell and shattered on the floor.

Daphne's attention was taken from the quarrel in front of her when she heard the squeak of the doorknob as it turned. She rushed to keep the door closed, but Mrs. Stone stepped into the room.

"Terry! Oh, my goodness. What's going on? Why are you on the floor?" Silence fell upon the room for a moment, and Daphne slipped out the door, pulling her phone from her pocket. "What did they do to you? What happened to your beautiful blue eyes?"

"Mrs. Stone ... I must insist ... that you leave," Calvin said, obviously fighting to keep his grip on the out-of-control Newling.

Daphne pulled her cell from her pocket and hit send on the text message she'd prepared. The situation was now out of her hands as she sent their exact location to the hunters—the Wraiths. Her hands shook from her act of betrayal, but she didn't know what else to do. Calvin lacked empathy for anything. He was ruthless with little feeling and no regard for anything other than his own self-preservation. That was the thing, though, they had no reason to look over their shoulders. They kept to themselves, they fed cleanly, they didn't cause trouble, so neither Wraith nor Inborn would have sought them out. Calvin was a paranoid fool who'd managed to think of a way to put himself in a spotlight that would've never existed otherwise.

A scream and a loud banging noise had Daphne's feet moving back to the room. Even though, if she valued her life, she knew she should've left immediately after sending the text.

Upon entering the room, Daphne saw just how feral Terry was. The transformation fixed his brain, but just enough to move—just enough to feed. Calvin leaned against the far wall, his arm dangling by a small chunk of flesh. A huge gash decorated his forehead.

A sucking sound to her left made her turn her head in the direction, finding Terry on top of his mother. Nearly all the flesh had been ripped from her neck. Blood pooled around her head. Terry lacked any sense or else he'd have gone directly to the free-flowing blood instead of sucking at the loose meat that hung in clumps.

Such a waste, Daphne thought. The smell making her mouth water. *He's dangerous. I should keep my distance, but he's so distracted, and it's not like I want to stop him. I want to feed* with *him. Certainly, he won't mind one of his kind joining him.*

"Daphne? Resist! He's wild, unpredictable," Calvin said quietly.

"I don't think I can." She took her eyes off the woman's blood long enough to see Calvin's arm had nearly healed.

She crept closer toward Terry, watching Calvin shake his head before letting it fall. If she could show the Newling she meant him no harm—that she was the same as he—she'd be safe. A crash came from the front of the house.

"Shit!" Daphne shouted, so completely lost in her bloodlust that she didn't understand why she'd wanted to involve the Wraiths.

"What was that?" Calvin asked as Terry growled but continued to gnaw at his mother's neck.

"Wraiths! I'm so sorry, Cal!"

Calvin's eyes went wide, and he jumped to his feet. "Daphne, what did you do!"

Daphne flinched at the pain in his voice, truly realizing that the choice she made was wrong. Calvin cared, even if it wasn't for humans. He cared for her, and she didn't know how much until that moment. She opened her mouth, but nothing came out.

"Daphne, go. I'll be too slow. I'm still healing, and I'll never outrun them," he shouted, but she couldn't move. "GO! Please!"

Her body trembled; her head shook back and forth in quick, short twitches. Tears streamed from her eyes of their own will. She had no control over them. "I can't. Even if I could, there's only one exit to this room, Cal."

"We fight then," he demanded.

"I've little training, and you're wounded. We'd never make it. I'm so sorry!"

"DAPHNE!"

"I'm sor—" Her words were cut off by a cough; blood flew from between her lips.

Then Calvin saw the tip of the bone and metal stake break through the cloth of her shirt. She began to fall, and he saw the flame-red hair of the Wraith, then his silvery-blue marked brown eyes. Calvin watched as the hunter ripped the bone and metal blade from his love's decomposing body before it hit the ground.

He debated fighting. He readied himself for the attack, but Terry was quicker. The Newling impacted with the Wraith—snarling, gnashing, and snapping the entire way. They tumbled into the hallway, and Calvin took his chance. He ran from the room, not sparing Daphne a glance. He didn't want to see the pile of bones and goo she'd become.

He rounded the corner to the living room. The pain shot through his chest before he registered that someone stood in front of him. He froze. The stake had entered his chest, but it hadn't made contact with his heart.

"This was too easy. So easy, in fact, that it wasn't even fun." A man with jet black hair and light green eyes—which held the same pattern in the same color as his fiery red-haired cohort—stood in front of him.

"We've done nothing wrong. We merely wanted to save lives," Calvin said through gritted teeth.

"Really, saving lives? Is that why I smell two sets of stale blood? Is it why the female contacted us? I don't believe you," the hunter said.

"She was confused."

"Oh, yeah? Well, now she's dead." The hunter laughed, then he bellowed down the hallway, "Damien, you good?"

"Yeah," the other hunter replied as Calvin felt him approach from behind. "Man, that Newling was a wild cat, I tell ya. And, strong. Whoo. What's this one still standing for?"

"I was playing with him. Also, I wanted to keep him as leverage in case you got yourself in a mess."

"That thing wouldn't have cared you had him. The only thing it was worried about was its next meal." The one called Damien laughed and slapped Calvin hard on the back.

Calvin felt the tip of the stake puncture his heart. He'd known it would hurt, but he had no idea that he'd feel the effects of his body beginning to decay. He coughed up the rotting blood that filled his trachea as it began to collapse.

"You clean up. I'll wait for the husband." The words faded as they were spoken. Calvin didn't even know which one of the Wraiths had said them.

The End

You can connect Soleil Daniels at the following links:

Facebook: https://www.facebook.com/SoleilDanielsAuthor/

Twitter: https://twitter.com/Brokenlyfe

Amazon: https://www.amazon.com/Soleil-Daniels/e/B01MRA8STC

Cover by Sunni Seckinger

The Memories That Haunt Me

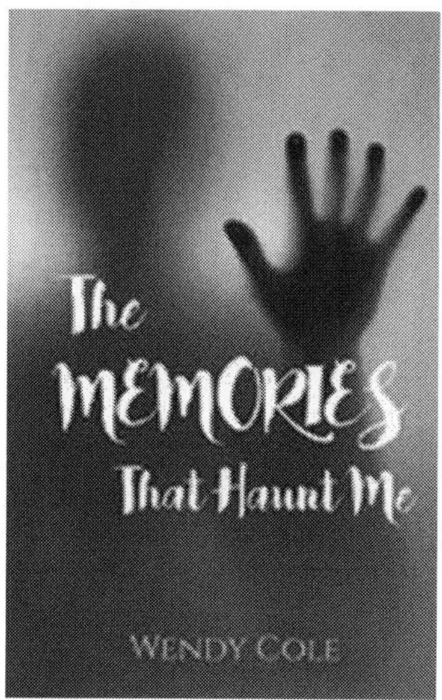

Wendy Cole

My name is Wendy Cole, and you'll find that most of my stories contain a bit of everything with a good deal of humor mixed in... This one not so much on humor...Well, unless you're evil...Which is okay! I totally dig my evil readers too.

The story you are about to read is based off of true events...

Kinda...Sorta...

Well, not really, but if it was I'd be terrified. I hope you enjoy.

Chapter 1

Something rough caresses my cheek. A hand. It pats me twice, administering soft slaps, before moving my head from side to side.

I open my eyes barely a fraction, and bright, blurry white fills the space between my lashes.

"Wake up, sweetheart," a deep male voice prompts. "Wake up."

My eyelids feel heavy, and my sight is unfocused. The blurred outline of his head looming above me comes into view first, then slowly his features begin to take form.

"That's my girl," he praises, running those rough hands down my shoulders. "You scared me."

I look around the room. Unfamiliar, everything: the man, the white walls, the silk sheets against my skin.

"Where am I?" I ask, more to myself.

"You're in our bed, honey." His eyes roam over my face in concern, settling down onto my head. "You hit your head in the shower."

I lift a hand to the spot and flinch at the raw pain that ricochets through my skull. I try to remember, and the more I fight to pull the information forward, the more I realize I don't know anything.

Who am I?

I have no idea. I don't know anything: my name, my age. It's all a fog. My brain is an empty bank. Memories linger in the distant cavities, just out of reach.

"I don't remember," I say to the man, my voice fearful.

He studies me. "You must have hit your head harder than I realized." He turns to the window, and I notice the rain hammering against the roof. Lightning flashes behind the floral curtain, followed by a loud crack of thunder. I recoil from the sound, burrowing myself further into the mattress.

"Shhh," the man coos. "There's a hurricane. We can't leave for a while, but I'm going to take good care of you." He runs a hand along my hair. "Do you know who I am?"

I shake my head no. "I don't remember." Tears pool into my eyes, stinging at the corners as I fight to hold them back. "I can't remember anything."

The man nods. "Amnesia. You must have gotten amnesia from the fall." He pulls me into him, holding me close against his chest. It feels unnatural, wrong. This man is a stranger to me. "I'm your husband, Tom," he says reassuringly, as if he can sense my reluctance. Tom pulls away and looks at me, his hands gripping my shoulders. "Everything is going to be okay." Soft lips press against my forehead in a tender show of affection.

I nod shakily, dragging a deep breath into my lungs.

Tom gently pushes me back down and pulls the cover back up to my chin. "Lay here. I'll go get you something to eat." His lips press against my head a second time before he stands and exits the room. I watch him go. He's tall with a sturdy build and wide set shoulders. Nothing about him is familiar, however.

I study the room next, fighting for a flicker of recognition, even the smallest of details, but I'm at a loss. The feeling is strange. I know I'm in a bed, but I don't know how I got here. I know other things as well, like there's a president, but I can't recall who it is. I know that this is Florida, but I can't for the life of me remember what city.

Little tidbits remain but not enough to get a clear picture, like a broken puzzle with too many missing pieces.

Thunder rolls, and a harsh gust of wind howls just outside the window. I pull the bedspread closer, gripping it into my fist as if it can shield me from the danger.

The bedroom door opens back up, and Tom comes walking in with a tray in his hands. "I made you some soup," he states, sitting the food down and helping me into a sitting position, propping a pillow behind my back for support. Once the tray is set in front of me, Tom smiles. "There you go. How's your head feel?"

"Okay, I guess." My voice is distant as I eye the meal in front of me. Chicken noodle. I know that the soup is chicken noodle, and the green bowl it's in came in a set of four, each a different color. Red, orange, yellow, and this one, green. How I know these things but not my own name, is a mystery.

"Eat up, sweetheart. The minute this storm passes, we'll get you to a doctor." Tom pats my hand. "I'm so happy you're awake. I was scared to death."

I lift the spoon to my lips and take in the familiar meal. I remember the flavor but not when I've ever tasted it before.

"The power's out," Tom continues, ignoring my silence. "It went out last night. That's probably why you fell."

I slowly sip the soup as I listen to him speak, fighting to remember anything he's saying, to recognize his voice.

Tom wanders the room, looking at the small mementos, touching a hand to the lamp shade. "This storm is a bad one. They're calling it a category four."

I let my gaze fall back to the bowl. For some reason, his presence makes me nervous. Something doesn't sit right with me. Maybe it's the lack of memory, but to me, he's still a stranger. "Tom," I start, looking up from my soup.

He turns his attention to me and moves back to the side of the bed. "What is it, Sarah?"

Sarah. My name is Sarah. "I don't remember you." My voice breaks.

Tom's eyes soften in understanding, but I also see hurt accompanied by an enormous amount of worry in their depths. "It's okay," he soothes. "You will. Get some rest. I'll go sleep on the couch to make you more comfortable." He caresses my cheek. "Just sit the tray on the side table when you're done. I'll come back for it in a little while."

I nod my head and watch as he once again exits the room.

A stranger.

Chapter 2

I finish the soup and sit the tray on the table. Tom hasn't returned, a fact I'm grateful of. I feel horrible for not remembering him. He's my husband. Surely, I should remember something, but it's as if my life has been erased.

On cue, a soft tap sounds against the bedroom door. I sit up, tucking the blanket around my waist. "Come in," I call out softly, but nothing happens. I wait, and after a few moments, the tapping sounds again. "Come in," I repeat, raising my voice, but once again there's no response.

Slowly, I climb out of the bed and approach the door. When I open it, an empty hallway greets me. I let my head turn, first left, then right, but there's nobody.

My gaze lands on the wall in front of me. An outline marks the wallpaper, a rectangle darker than the rest of the beige surface. A picture had hung there long enough to leave this spot behind as evidence of its disappearance.

My eyes travel as I journey, finding more marks, much the same: more missing photos, varying in sizes and positioning. Dozens of them. It seems strange, and my nerves become even more on edge.

A loud thud echoes out from somewhere behind me, and I squeak, whipping around as my heart rises up into my throat.

Nothing.

I stare, each breath shallow as I fight to remain silent, waiting for the sound to happen again.

Nothing.

Reluctantly, I continue forward. Three more doors line the hallway: one at the end and one on each side. I move to the closest and slowly turn the knob.

It's a guest room, decorated in pale pinks and the color of peaches. Floral curtains cover the window, billowing out in the wind pouring in through the opening. I rush over and pull it closed. This must have caused the noises, I rationalize.

The bedroom door suddenly swings shut, slamming so hard the hinges rattle.

I spin around on my heels, almost falling in my startled movement. The room is empty, but I can feel eyes upon me, watching me. I continue to try and remain rational. It was the air pressure that forced the door to close. I'm just stressed, nervous, paranoid, but still, I feel them, burning a hole into me.

Uneasiness settles down upon me like a hundred-pound weight, and my mind begins to play tricks. The more I strain my ears, the more I think I hear breathing, deep and ragged, coming from everywhere and nowhere. "Tom," I call out quietly, the sound echoing out in the terrifying silence.

A painting flies off the wall in response. As if thrown, it hurls its way across the room and into the opposite wall, shattering into a pile of sharp shards and pieces.

With another squeak, I stumble backwards, only stopping when my back meets the wooden dresser behind me.

The breathing starts again, louder, drawing closer. I hold my breath, my heart pounding like the bass of a tribal drum.

I close my eyes, clenching them, and as the sounds grow more and more pronounced, so does the beating drum that had once been my heart.

Cold fingers caress the side of my neck, and I collapse. A scream so loud my throat could bleed rips out of me, and the bedroom door flies open, revealing a panicked Tom.

"Hey! I got you," he insists as he rushes towards me.

I stay perfectly still, unable to do anything else. It's as if every muscle was frozen into place the minute that icy touch settled against my skin. It had been real—so, so real—and so terrifying. "Is our house haunted?" I rasp as Tom's arms circle me.

He leans back and studies my face. "Why do you ask that?"

"The picture." I point to the pile of glass. "It just flew off the wall and then..."

Tom looks to the mess then back to me, his brow furrowed. "Then what? What happened, sweetheart?" In a tender movement, he pushes a stray hair behind my ear.

"Something touched me," I whisper, my hand coming up to the

place where the icy fingers had lingered. I can still feel them there.

What scares me the most, however…more than the photo, more than the breathing, more than the touch itself…

It had been familiar.

My name, this house, the man who is meant to be my husband, all of it was strange and new, but the icy hand…

I know that touch. It lingers on my skin as if I've felt it a million times before.

"It's probably some ill effects from your head injury," Tom says, looking worried. "Let's get you back to bed. Hopefully the storm will pass soon."

He lifts me and begins carrying me back towards the bedroom.

My gaze lingers, once again, on the missing pictures. "Why are all the photos gone?"

Tom stiffens for a fraction of a second. "We were worried they'd become damaged, so we packed them all away."

I eye him but don't detect any sign of deceit.

Tom lays me down across the mattress and places a kiss against my mouth. I jerk away, and he pulls back quickly. "I'm sorry," he relents, taking another step back with his hands in the air in front of him. "Habit. I'm sorry, Sarah." He appears so torn, so upset, and worried.

Guilt gnaws at my gut. "It's all right," I softly say, swallowing the lump in my throat. "I'm sorry. I just…" I pause, eyeing the lightning still flashing outside the window. "I just don't remember."

Tom nods. "I know. It's going to be okay, Sarah. You will."

I smile at him, a soft smile that's forced, but it still seems to help ease him a bit.

"That's the spirit. Get some rest. Hopefully when you wake again, the storm will be gone, and we can get you to a doctor."

I watch him leave me once again, taking in his stiff posture. This must all be so terrible for him. His own wife doesn't remember who he is and is injured, and he's powerless to do anything to help her.

The air grows colder, and I touch my neck again, the icy fingers still fresh in my mind.

Chapter 3

When I wake again, darkness surrounds me. The unfamiliar furnishings are nothing more than black outlines, eerily calm in their stillness.

I can still feel the icy touch against my neck, and it makes the atmosphere even more unnerving. So real, it had felt so real, too real to be the effects of a head injury. Then again, what do I know? I don't even know my own husband.

I lay there for what feels like an eternity, each breath shallow, eyes darting back and forth around the room, repeatedly settling at the foot of the bed.

My knees are lifted, and my toes curl inwards as if something will reach out and snatch me away.

I feel ridiculous but can't shake the sensation. Something is wrong here. The missing photos, the picture flying off the wall, the heavy breathing.

And the touch...

Why had it felt so familiar?

A rattling noise sounds from somewhere within the room, pulling me away from my thoughts and back to my current situation. I strain my ears, listening intently, my pulse erratically throbbing, my heartbeat rivaling the sounds caused by the hurricane.

"Tom?" I call out tentatively. It's nothing. You hit your head. This is all your mind playing tricks on you.

It happens again. This time, louder and right beside the bed. My heart comes flying up into my throat, and I scramble in the opposite direction, landing into a heap on the floor. Each breath eludes me, and I have to fight to continue to drag the life-giving oxygen into my lungs.

"Laura..." A whispered voice filters through the air.

I squeak and move further back still, ultimately pressing myself firmly into the corner.

"Laura..." Again, louder this time, sounding eerily similar to the howling wind outside the window.

"What do you want?" I whisper, my voice hoarse and raw.

I wait, and once again the name reverberates through the empty room. "Laura..."

"What's happening to me!" I sob, burying my head into my knees. Do I have a mental illness? Am I insane and Tom is just hiding the fact from me?

The knees of my pajama pants grow damp with moisture, tears rolling out of the corners of my eyes and saturating the fabric.

Cold fingers caress the back of my neck. "Laura..."

My gaze jerks up and finds an empty space before me. I scramble to my feet, my legs like two limp noodles beneath me, barely able to support my weight as I rush for the bedroom door.

My hand shakes from excess adrenaline as I clasp the knob and pull.

It won't open. I fight it, turning, yanking, pressing a foot to the wall for leverage, but it's jammed.

"Laura..."

"Leave me alone!" I shout, banging a fist against the wooden barrier. "Tom!"

Something jerks me away, pulling me across the room and tossing me back to the mattress. "Get out! Get out! Get out!" Each word is a roar of distorted fury, like a scene from a horror movie I can't remember ever watching.

The handle twists, and a bang comes from the hallway. "Sarah!" Tom continues to beat against the door. "Sarah, honey? Open the door."

"Get out!" The window shatters, curtains billowing out, looking like a ghost in themselves. Debris begins to rush in, the sound of the wind like an approaching train, deafening in its fury.

The door releases, and Tom falls into the room in a heap. "Sarah!" He runs over, gathering me up. "What the hell happened?"

A dam I didn't know I'd built collapses the minute Tom's large arms engulf me, and sobs begin to rack my body. Tortured sounds exit my lungs, echoing out over the howling wind.

Tom gathers me closer, running his hand over my back in comforting circles. "It's okay," he soothes, his voice soft. "I've got you."

I force myself to calm and look at him. Tom gathers my hair into his hand and holds me in place, eyes searching, studying me, looking for injuries that can't be seen.

When his gaze settles down on my lips, I stiffen. Tom doesn't appear to notice my reaction and continues to lean closer, his mouth moving slowly towards mine. "It's okay," he murmurs again, his voice rougher than before.

"Tom?" I try to pull away, but his grip is too tight.

"Shhh..." His lips brush against mine, like a feather, so soft I barely feel it at all. "I love you, Sarah."

A roar sounds through the air, and Tom is suddenly jerked away, flying across the room like a doll cast aside by a bored child.

More screams threaten to destroy my lungs as I huddle back into the corner.

Tom crashes into the dresser with so much force it causes the wood to splinter. Mementos and trinkets fall to the floor. His head hits the corner on impact, the blow rendering him unconscious. As his body hits the floor in a heap, I scream again, terrified by the sight of him so still.

"Tom!"

"Laura!" the ghostly voice bellows out in return, sounding as if five people are shouting the word at once, each one tortured, each one desperate.

I bury my face into my knees once more, rocking, shaking, too afraid to run away, frozen in a ball of defenselessness.

The room falls silent, even the storm appearing to cease its rage, and after a few moments, the breathing starts.

Warm and soft, different from before. It caresses my ear, and a whimper escapes my lungs, my muscles tightening to the point of pain.

"Laura..." the voice whispers into my ear, soft, right beside me. "Get out..."

A shudder racks my frame, and I huddle down firmer, my eyes shut tightly in an attempt to simply disappear.

The breathing remains, and with each moment I sit here, it grows more ragged. "Get out!" it roars, loud enough to bust my ear drums, full of fury and rage.

My eyes fly open, a red flag going up at the sound of it, and in my attempt to get away, I see it.

An outline. A man, unclear and out of focus. Nothing more than a blur, kneeling down in the space I'd been huddled into only a moment before.

He looks like smoke, white and swirling, his facial features in constant motion, never pausing long enough to let me grasp a clear picture.

I scramble back further, crab walking towards the door. My eyes cut over to Tom, still motionless on the floor. Dark liquid pools surround his face, and I know it's blood. "Tom!" I call over, my eyes darting between him and the ghostly apparition. "Tom! Wake up!"

The apparition stares at me, what little I could make of its face forming into a snarl. "Get out! Get out! Get out!" It doesn't stop, each shout deafens me, drifting across the distance and searing my very soul with its fury.

I look at Tom one last time before scrambling to my feet and darting out the still open door.

Chapter 4

The hall light flickers as I push my way along the wall, leaning heavily onto the surface for support. The bedroom door slams shut, and I hear heavy footsteps stomping behind me in pursuit.

I increase my pace, desperate, almost stumbling multiple times in my frantic fight to escape.

When I finally reach a door and turn the knob, it won't open, and I kick it several times in panic.

"Go!" the voice shouts, so close I feel its breath against my neck.

I rush forward, moving to the next door in the hall. It, too, is jammed, and I want to give up.

"No! Go!" it rages, even louder, even more desperate, even deeper still.

I fall forward, landing on my hands and knees, immediately crawling in a desperate attempt to get away. Tears pour down my cheeks; my chest feels tight; my limbs are ready to give out completely.

When I reach the final door, it opens easily, but the victory doesn't last for more than the time it takes to look inside.

A scream rips through the air, and it only takes a moment to realize it's me that's making the sound.

Wide, lifeless eyes stare up at me, unseeing, blue as the sky on a perfect summer day.

Familiar.

Memories come rushing back. The puzzle pieces of my life reform inside my mind in a rush, one after the other.

My childhood.

My parents.

My wedding day.

All coming together to form one larger picture.

A picture of the lifeless man in front of me.

A picture of my husband, of him being murdered, of me trying to save him, of the man named Tom shoving me away and into the wall.

He'd broken in not long after the storm hit. He'd been following me for months. The police had been hunting him. They'd said to keep alert...

The report had said Tom had a history of mental illness; that he'd done this before.

"John!" I drop down to the ground and lift his head into my lap.

"John." A sob rips out of me. My life is gone. John is gone. It isn't real; it can't be real. He was the only thing I had in this world. "John!" I scream, clutching him tighter.

"Laura..." It's him. The ghostly mirage is him.

He's trying to save me. "Oh, John!" I cry, burrowing my face into his hair.

"Laura...Go!"

I look up and that's when I notice them. Footsteps heading down the hall.

Tom is coming for me.

"No," I choke out. "I won't leave you."

"Go!" the voice booms, startling me.

I look up just in time to see Tom step into the doorway. One look at the sight in front of him and the mask falls away, revealing the monster beneath. "He's gone now. We can be together."

"Never!" I scream. Rage at this man and what he'd taken from me fills me up to the point I feel like I might incinerate. Fire fuels my actions as I stand, grabbing the closest thing I can reach.

A lamp.

With a roar of outrage, I throw it as hard as I can, aiming for the man who ruined my life. "I'll kill you, you bastard!"

Tom deflects the blow and lunges for me.

He doesn't make it more than a couple steps, however, before more items begin to fly, not one of them coming from me. They come from any and every direction. Wall art, furniture, nothing in the room is left in its place. One by one each item lifts up and goes flying towards my husband's killer.

Tom's arms flail, attempting to bat the assault away, but he isn't fast enough to keep up. And as more items continue to pummel him, he becomes more and more defeated.

It's a chair that ultimately ends the struggle. It lifts up and something propels it forward. I watch in a mixture of horror and disgust as the leg imbeds itself right into the man's eye socket.

Tom stands stock still for a full minute, shock marring his features. A gurgling sound leaves his chest, and he falls backwards, crashing to the ground, his chest still and eyes just as wide and lifeless as the man he'd killed a few feet away.

I sink to my knees, shoulders heaving, chest tight, lungs deflated and unable to bring in any of the oxygen needed to fill them.

Icy fingers caress my cheek, and the apparition appears, more detailed than before.

John.

"Please, don't go!" I sob. "John!"

He kneels down closer, and his face becomes as clear as it was when he was still alive. "Laura..." Cool air caresses my flesh, sending an array of goosebumps across my skin. "I love you..."

"No! Don't go! I need you!"

"I'm sorry..." he says as his body slowly begins to fade.

I reach for him, but there's nothing tangible for me to hold onto, nothing for me to grasp to keep him with me. "No! Nonononono! John!"

But it's no use. He's gone, leaving me behind with nothing more than his lifeless body behind me and the body of his killer in front.

As I sit there, mourning the only man I'd ever loved, the only man I could ever love...

I wish more than anything that the memories would go away.

The End

Cover by Author.

The Ghosts of Blackwood

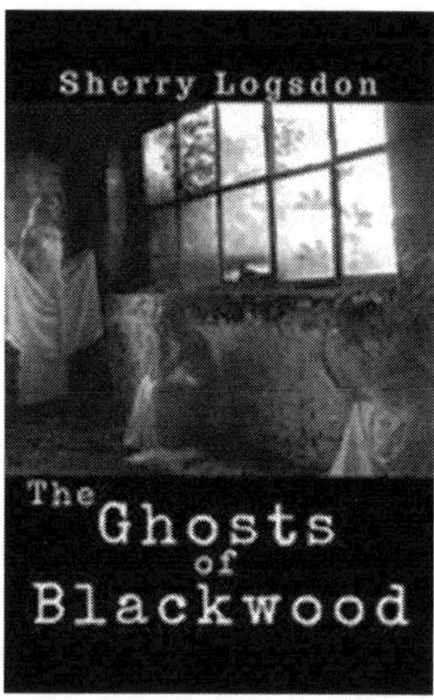

Sherry Logsdon

1896.

Sadie Connor found herself locked away within Blackwood Insane Asylum with no idea as to why she was there. Filled with secrets and lies, Sadie finds no woman there to be deranged or insane.

Sadie befriends two young women as they face the horrors of Blackwood together. The nightmare that awaits Sadie, as well as the other women at Blackwood, knows no boundaries.

Sherry Logsdon lives with her husband in Eastview, Kentucky. She is the mother of three and grandmother of four. Sherry earned a bachelor's degree in Exceptional Children and a master's degree in Counseling from Western Kentucky University. A retired, now substitute teacher, Sherry enjoys researching old insane asylums and the suffrage movement and writing both fiction and poetry.

"Where am I?" I asked two girls huddled close by in the corner. As I looked around the room, I saw the gray walls and metal beds filled with women.

Once again, I demanded to know where I was, but their sobbing was so pitiful that I began to worry more about them than myself. "Do you hear me? Where am I?" I asked with less harshness to my voice.

The girls looked up. "Blackwood," they answered in unison.

"Blackwood Hospital?" I asked.

"No. Blackwood Insane Asylum," they once again answered in unison.

It took me a minute to think of what an insane asylum was exactly. "Do you mean a place where people who have gone mad are taken?" Surely, I had misunderstood them. This made no sense to me. Why would I be in an insane asylum?

I looked around the room, confused. "But I was supposed to be here visiting my sick father. My uncle is tending to the horse. I explained to the woman at the front door that I was here to see my father, and she led me to this room. I think there has been a mistake."

"First, this is not a hospital, and second, there are no men here. This is Blackwood, an insane asylum for women," the taller girl replied. "Nurse Dunn told us that a new girl was coming today. And, oh, by the way, never, ever trust Nurse Dunn."

It was then I noticed the taller girl's dress. Not only was it dark and ugly but carried with it a bulge in the front. She looked down and placed her hand on her stomach. "Yes, I am with child," she said as she lowered her eyes. "That is why I am here. My father committed the most unholy of acts and brought me to this place to hide me away."

The other girl lowered her head into her hands and began to weep. I was not sure if she was weeping for the story that had just been told or for her own story, which I had yet to hear.

I thought the taller one to be no more than thirteen or fourteen. Her hair was dark, almost black, tightly pulled back from her forehead and wound into a bun on the top of her head with strands of loose hair hanging shabbily, whereas my hair was much lighter and covered my shoulders. Her eyes were hollow and echoed a sadness I had not seen before.

The taller one's hand remained upon her stomach. I did not know if her life had prepared her for what was to come. I hoped so. In my sixteen years, I had never even tended to a baby before. I was the only child my parents had. I was not exactly sure why, but I had overheard my parents talking about something that happened during my birth that had left my mother unable to bear another child. I could not imagine being in the girl's predicament.

"My name is Sadie, and yours?" I asked as I held out my hand to shake hers. I did not know if shaking hands was the appropriate thing to do, but I felt the need to touch her and soothe her in some way.

Hesitantly she offered her hand. As we touched, I could feel the calluses that had replaced what should have been soft and tender skin; I pulled a handkerchief from my pocket and wiped her cheeks. She was quite pitiful.

"I am Elizabeth," she answered, "and this is Sicily."

Sicily was quite beautiful. She was but a tiny thing with eyes that were sharp and piercing. Her hair was pulled back but not as severely as Elizabeth's. Her hair was closer to the color of mine.

I sensed Sicily to be the older of the two, perhaps a year or two my elder, even though she was much smaller than Elizabeth. There was an air about her that I felt came with age and life. Her eyes did not stray from my face as I looked at her. I did not know why Sicily was in this place, but she looked no more insane than I felt.

As I looked around the room, I could not understand any of what I gazed upon. "Am I to understand you correctly, that these women have been deemed insane?" I asked. By no means had I been granted a medical degree, but their eyes did not seem to be filled with madness; this looked to me to be nothing more than a large, drafty room filled with misery and despair. I could be wrong, being that I had never even met someone considered insane, but if one had fallen by the wayside and lost her mind, I could not see how this pitiful way of life could help.

I closed my eyes and thought as hard as I could about what my uncle had told me. Had I confused his words? No, there was absolutely no way. He had lied and deceived me, making me believe I was visiting my sick father. So, if my father was not here, then where was he?

I always obeyed and did what I was asked. I made good grades in school. I helped Mother do the household chores, and I even helped Father work in the barn. My parents loved me. This was purely my uncle's doing; I had always been leery of him but never believed him to be a liar or dangerous.

***

The weeks went by relatively fast. One would think, in such awful conditions, that time would creep; instead, working from dawn to dark made each day race by and sleep a welcome time.

Some of the women were so melancholic they never left their beds. And some who were quite alert upon my arrival had begun to just sit and stare. The women's frames of minds worsened with each day's passing. I saw no miraculous cures or women being set free. I saw only cruelty and inhumane treatment.

I had been correct in both Elizabeth's and Sicily's ages. Elizabeth was thirteen and Sicily seventeen. I honestly had thought Sicily to be older. I had also learned Sicily's story, and though Sicily's story was sad in itself, it was better than Elizabeth's.

Sicily's mother had remarried, and her stepfather had found Sicily to be in the way. He had money and wanted Sicily's mother to travel the world with him and without having a child tag along.

"It was not like I was a small child who needed to be fed and clothed," Sicily said as she held back the tears. "He was jealous of my mother's affections toward me, so he arranged for me to be committed to Blackwood, and my mother agreed to it." Sicily was heartbroken that her mother had betrayed her so. "How could she have discarded me in such a way, as if I was nothing more than rubbish?"

Elizabeth, Sicily, and I were lucky in one sense. Dr. Miller never called us to the basement for his so-called treatments. I was not sure if it was because of our age (we were the youngest in Blackwood) or if it was Elizabeth's condition, but I was thankful regardless. His treatments were no more than acts of torture. I had listened intently to the stories the women had told of what they had endured at the hands of Dr. Miller.

If nothing else, the women had found relief in sharing their stories and comforting one another. I tried to get as many women as I could to tell me their stories. I wanted to be of help to them the only way I knew, and that was by listening.

Caroline worked beside me making beds each morning. She was several years my elder, and I appreciated her wisdom and calm ways. Our last conversation had ended with her telling me the reason she was in Blackwood.

"Our preacher was wicked. I did not agree with his teachings, therefore I refused to attend the local church. He brainwashed my husband. One night while sleeping, my husband covered my head with a cloth and delivered me to Blackwood. I have been here ever since, nearly five years." Caroline spoke while watching the door, worried that Nurse Dunn would appear. Nurse Dunn did not want any of us talking about our past.

Not long after our conversation, Caroline was called to the basement for her weekly treatment. Since that morning, she has not spoken a word. She had talked before of the horrors she had endured by the hands of Dr. Miller: how she had been submerged in baths of iced water and had electrodes attached to her head in which electricity pulsated through.

Caroline no longer helped with the housekeeping but merely sat. She no longer laughed or cried. Dr. Miller had killed whatever emotions were within her. The wise and caring Caroline had ceased to exist. I had come to live in Blackwood filled with fear, both for the women and that I would be called next to the basement.

Elizabeth grew weary with each passing month. Her stomach grew larger, and she looked unwell. There was grayness to her color. I had seen that color on my grandmother before her passing. It worried me more than I would say. I was not sure how Elizabeth would do during childbirth.

I would find out sooner than I had thought. For, in two nights' time, it had come. I could hear screaming in the middle of the night. I knew right away it was Elizabeth. Had the time come already? She was not sure of the exact date but thought she had longer. I raced down the hallway praying that all would go well, even though my mind told me differently.

"Hold her down! Do you hear me? I said hold her down!" Nurse Dunn commanded. "The baby is coming!" No one questioned or rebuked Nurse Dunn. She was as evil as Dr. Miller and the place I had come to know as home.

Elizabeth no longer looked gray but a pale shade of white. If not for her screaming, I would have thought death had already fallen upon her. I wanted more than anything to run away. I did not want to know what the future held. I only wanted to forget this place and its horror. I knew there was no way I could help Elizabeth. I could not even help myself.

I looked around for a way out, but, as usual, there was none. The doors leading out were always bolted securely. Even if the doors were not bolted, I would not have tried to escape. I had seen plenty of women beaten for their attempts at freedom. Blackwood was built on the side of a cliff with water to one side and a dense forest on the other. The few women who had seized an opportunity to make it outside did not make it far before being hauled back, always in much worse shape than when they left.

The baby was coming. Again, I heard Elizabeth's screams. This time, instead of turning away, I craned my neck and stretched forward to try and get a glimpse of the baby as it was coming into the world. I had never witnessed the birth of a baby. I did not, however, see a baby making its way into the world; what I saw was a darkness that spread from between Elizabeth's legs. More blood than I had ever seen before. So much so that it was beginning to drip onto the floor. My worst fears were coming true.

"I cannot stop the blood," announced Dr. Miller. "She is a lost cause."

"She is in God's hands now," Nurse Dunn whispered to herself.

How dare she bring God into this! It was Satan she worked for, not God. Portraying herself to be a loving and caring soul to all, when in fact she was consumed with hatred, and how dare Dr. Miller refer to Elizabeth as a lost cause. To Hell with them both!

I had almost forgotten about the baby until I heard a whimper and saw Dr. Miller hand the baby to Nurse Dunn. I turned back toward Elizabeth. If not already dead, she was nearing the finality of her life. I could feel it. She would never get to see her sweet baby. She had come to terms with what had happened to her and was hoping to convince Dr. Miller to allow her to keep the baby. She had hopes that they both could flee from this place. I did not believe Dr. Miller would ever agree to it, but I would not tell that to Elizabeth. I could not dash what little hope she had in life. It was then I saw Elizabeth's head fall over to the side. She had passed.

The screaming now belonged to me. I could not bear to lose Elizabeth; she had become the sister I never had. I felt the hand of Nurse Dunn across my face. I tried to fight the darkness that was threatening to overtake me, but it was by far stronger.

I did not know how long I slept but awoke to a blur. Elizabeth, the baby! I leaped from my bed and shook Sicily from her sleep.

"Sicily, tell me. What has happened to Elizabeth, to the baby?" It was then my fears became reality, my dream a nightmare.

"She did not make it. She passed before even seeing her baby." Sicily spoke with trembling lips and tear-filled eyes. Her heart was as broken as mine. The three of us were now two.

"What about the baby?" I screamed. "Where is the baby?"

"I saw Nurse Dunn take her out of the room. The baby was barely making a sound. I never heard her cry. I pray she lived, but I am not sure. She was such a tiny thing and covered in blood. Perhaps Dr. Miller helped her and perhaps he did not. But something tells me he has done all he can for the baby. Not because he cares for her, but because I overheard Dr. Miller and Nurse Dunn talking about how babies bring a good amount of money from the right people."

I had heard the same. If Dr. Miller could find an advantage to saving the baby, then perhaps he would save her. Elizabeth had wanted a girl; she even had a name picked out: Liza. Elizabeth had talked about when she was a little girl and how her grandmother had called her "Liza" as a pet name.

It was still early, and the hallways were dark and empty. I could feel the ghosts of Blackwood all around me. My imagination was getting the better of me. I backed against the wall and became a part of it, easing myself toward Dr. Miller's office, praying no one would see me. I had to find out where they had taken the baby.

I had to find Liza and arrange to escape this place and take her far away. I did not carry the strength or the willpower to try for myself, but I would take whatever chance needed to get the baby out. I would not allow Dr. Miller to sell her to the highest bidder. I would find Elizabeth's mother. Elizabeth was positive her mother did not know of her father's doings. I would tell Elizabeth's mother what her father had done. I was not afraid of him. My anger made sure of that.

I waited around the corner until I could hear Dr. Miller and Nurse Dunn leaving. I let my eyes become accustomed to the darkness of the room, and then I saw that Dr. Miller had indeed saved Elizabeth's tiny baby. Liza had survived. She was lying in a makeshift bed within a bureau drawer. She was beautiful. Nurse Dunn had cleaned her up and wrapped her in a scarf. Liza had a head full of dark hair, just like Elizabeth's. She was sleeping soundly. I wanted to pick her up and hold her, but I was scared she would cry out.

I looked around the room and discovered that Sicily and I had been correct in what Dr. Miller was going to do with Liza. At six weeks of age, he was going to sell Liza. I found a paper with his intentions written on it. He had to keep her long enough to make sure she would live and he would not have to return the money, which in turn would be long enough for me to come up with a plan to escape with Liza.

I hurried back to share my plan with Sicily, but she did not agree. "Please do not try to leave," Sicily begged. "I cannot bear to lose you too. There is no way to escape from Blackwood. He will kill you if you try, especially with the baby."

I tried to no avail to ease Sicily's mind, but deep down I knew she was right, and I too knew Dr. Miller would be furious at not only losing a patient but also losing money for Liza. I had to try. I was doing this for myself almost as much as for Liza. I could not remain at Blackwood for the rest of my life without answers as to why I had been committed. I would rather be dead than live the rest of my days at Blackwood without knowing my uncle's intentions. Liza gave me the added strength to try.

Nearly two weeks had passed. It was early, still dark. I waited patiently for the morning light to come. I had overheard Dr. Miller making arrangements for the delivery wagon. Once a month, the delivery wagon brought in supplies; it was our only hope. Once the supplies were unloaded, Liza and I would slip into the wagon and leave Blackwood behind forever.

It had been easy enough to scoop Liza out of her bed and place her beneath my shawl. She did not make a sound. I hurried to the downstairs delivery door and waited in a doorway just an arm's length away. I watched as the delivery man carried the supplies inside. The door was large and closed slowly. Once he walked past me, I raced toward the door and grabbed it just before it closed. I then raced toward the wagon. "We are almost there, Liza. Please do not cry."

I swung one leg over the back of the wagon and just as I began to pull the other leg up, I felt it: a hand. "We almost made it, little baby," I cried out to Liza. And then all went black.

I closed and opened my eyes as I tried to focus. I looked around and tried to get my bearings. I looked beneath my shawl. Liza was gone. My fear mounted.

I looked around and realized I was still outside of Blackwood. I had all my wits about me, yet I could not remember what happened. The last I could recall was climbing into the wagon with Liza inside my shawl. Dr. Miller must have her. I had to go back in. I would not leave without Liza.

I crept along the wall and made way back inside. Something felt different. I made my way into the laundry room and was never so happy to see anyone in my whole life. It was Sicily, folding linen. I rushed toward her, but as I went to grab her, I fell. Something was wrong. She did not even look my way. I called her name over and over, yet she did not even acknowledge me. I once again tried to touch her; my hand went straight through her.

It was then I knew. I knew what had happened. I was dead. I took a deep breath; I could only smell air, thick and suffocating. Nothing felt as it had felt before. Death carried with it an emptiness of my soul, a feeling that there was no depth to my being.

Though I could not visualize my last moments alive, I could feel that it was not an easy death. I felt no sense of harmony or glory but, instead, was filled with dread and darkness. The angels with their tenderness and beauty were nowhere to be found.

The screams: Were they mine? Whose screams pierced my memories and sounded so horrible that I could not forget hearing them? It was the women of Blackwood. They were all around me.

The ghosts of Blackwood were real. The women who died within the walls of Blackwood were bound by those same walls even in death. Sicily had been correct in her premonition of my death. There was no escaping Blackwood.

The End

Connect with Sherry at the following links:

Blog: http:// sherrylogsdon.com/blog/

Facebook: https://www.facebook.com/asylum.sherrylogsdon

www.pintrest.com/sherry1331/

Twitter: https:// twitter.com/sherrylogsdon

e-mail: sherrylogson@live.com

Cover by T.E. Bradford.

The Image

Barbara Galvin

I am a novice writer having just joined the writing world about four years ago. I am currently working on my first novel. I was introduced to the writing community through WriteOn and then Wattpad where I have met some truly amazing, helpful people. I hail from Virginia and am a mother of three and a grandmother of seven. My favorite book has to be To Kill a Mockingbird. I am delighted to be part of the OMP community and am honored to be included in this anthology.

Jodie is a nature photographer by profession, captivated by the beauty of the natural world. An encounter with Monet's series on haystacks seen at the Museum of Fine Arts in Boston inspires her to find an object in nature that she can follow through the seasons with her photography, much like Monet did with his art. She finds the perfect subject, a worn bench on the side of the lake, and makes that the center of her project. Her year-long mission is almost at a close with her final season and final time of day when she is thwarted by an old man sitting on the bench. But she is so captivated by his aura that she begins photographing him, a contrast to her previous focus on solely inanimate objects.

What she finds later in her studio so baffles her that she sets out on a mission to prove that she is not crazy or imagining things. What results is so mysterious that the reader may never know the answer.

***

Click. Click. Click.

The familiar sound of the camera's shutter comforts Jodie as she continues her pursuit of the perfect photo. What she doesn't know is how one particular image, on this one particular day, will affect the rest of her life.

The old man sits on the bench, his tired silhouette framed against the glow of the setting sun. His tattered sleeves brush against the bag of nuts he is doling out to the squirrels. He glances out to the lake to watch the sun set, its orb like a saucer tipped on its side; just one more sundown added to the ones too many to count in his life. From behind, he is but a shadow. He is oblivious to any around him, preferring his aloneness to the stifling closeness of the crowds. He is unaware that he is being watched.

Jodie stays in the shadows slowly being extinguished by the darkness rapidly descending. In a matter of seconds, she has captured him, the weather-worn creases in the hollows of his cheeks etched in the waning light.

The clear autumn day was ripe for her photography: the multi-colored leaves still clinging tenaciously to the branches of the trees, the chilling breeze breaking the glass surface of the lake. All day Jodie walked along the lakeside, snapping the azure-blue sky with the clouds that seemed to float like swirls of whipped cream atop an ice cream sundae. She studied the boats on the lake, silhouetted like paper cut outs on a page. She captured the sun dappled patterns on the trees lining the shore.

Click. Click. Click.

Jodie was a nature photographer by profession and was undertaking a series called *Life on the Lake*, her inspiration taken from Monet's series on haystacks, which had so captivated her when she had seen the Impressionist Exhibit at the Museum of Fine Arts in Boston. It had sparked an idea of doing the same with her photography. She searched for months for the perfect subject and finally decided on the weather-worn bench, which stood by the side of the lake. The past year of changing seasons resonated with her quest for the perfect project.

She had already witnessed its simplicity during the winter, the dusting of snow sprinkled like powdered sugar in her lens. Spring had seen it coated with blossoms blown down from the tree it gently nestled under. And the summer had bleached its chipped paint to an unrecognizable hue. She now resisted the urge to dust off the ever-falling leaves threatening to cover it up entirely.

She had already captured the bench in the morning and at midday. The approaching evening would give her a perspective she did not yet have.

She approached her subject, time of the essence, to catch the light before it sank beneath the horizon. But this time the bench wasn't empty; an old man had neatly folded himself in its curves. The poignancy of his profile stunned her. Her bench had absorbed a living soul.

"Damn," she muttered under her breath, disappointed that she might not get her perfect shot before the sun set completely. But something about the intruder gave her pause. She continued pointing her lens in his direction.

Stealthily, she crept to the other side of the trees to get a different view and focused in on the sadness painted all around him. *Click. Click. Click.* She captured the toll the years had taken on him. Life had not been kind to this man. Not wanting to be discovered, she hid behind a tree and continued to watch his movements. She had been to this bench many times and never seen him before. She wanted to approach him, but something inside told her to let him be. His need for privacy leaked out of his pores.

She continued to snap away, capturing stark reality against a backdrop of breathtaking beauty. Humanity juxtaposed against nature. *Click. Click. Click.* Each picture was better than the last. Still life suddenly ceased to be her focus. Her heart beat rapidly with excitement for the slice of life that had swept into her lens.

Her entire career had focused on the inanimate. She, in fact, had avoided any human aspects associated with her subjects. She found great beauty in the serenity of nature—the trees, the lake, the pathways. There was a beauty in their stability, their unyielding grace, their permanence. And today was no exception. She had wanted to find the bench empty, but the old man had presented an opportunity so enticing she had stretched out of her comfort zone to capture him. His sheer simplicity was humbling.

She watched as he stood, unfolded his frail body, and slowly crept down the small path bordering the lake, his cane tapping away on the walkway. She kept him in her lens as long as she could without being seen.

She approached the bench after he left and saw the empty bag of nuts carelessly tossed to the ground. She muttered to herself as she picked it up and flung it into the nearby trash bin. She took one last photo of the bench with the setting sun stretched across the lake, her flash adding one more firefly to the waning daylight. *Click. Click. Click.* This last one would complete her series. It had taken her a year of seasons and days of daylight and dusk to finish her project.

Her idea was the culmination of years of study and experimentation to find the right nuances of light and shadow illuminating one single object. She had tried indoor still life: vases of flowers, vegetables on a cutting board, even the rocking chair in the corner of her living room. But they all lacked the changes she eventually discovered in her outdoor photography. There she could get not only the times of day but also the changing seasons to tell her story.

She first photographed a tree, with its obvious changes. But this, too, left her flat. It was too common. She tried the homes surrounding the lake, but they were uninteresting and often cluttered with people. It was when she discovered the old, weathered bench in the park that she knew she had found the right subject. And now she had the results she was so longing for.

But what of the old man? He had touched her with his pathos, and she couldn't bear not to use him in some way. Human portraiture clearly was not her forte. But his image was engraved on her brain like a negative. Clearly the human persona had resonated with her.

That evening she arrived at her studio and proceeded to process her work. She had hundreds of pictures from today alone. She was especially excited to see the old man, the only piece of humanity in hours of photography. Frame after frame came into view, a time-lapse portrait of the day. There were the clouds in all their wispy glory, the trees clinging desperately to the last vestiges of fall, and the slow-motion portraits of the ever-changing sky. The bench would be next, her last image in her year-long quest. And she was anxious to see the extra pictures she took of the old man.

Let's see. He should be here around the two-hundred mark.

Finally, she reached the last pictures. She had the late day sky, the lake, and the bench. And she had the final picture of the setting sun against her bench. But something was amiss. There were no squirrels, no bag of nuts—and no man. The bench stood empty, silhouetted against the sinking sun. Where was he?

These must be the ones I took after he left.

She went back over the prints; nothing. She could still envision his frail body so clearly, loneliness dangling from the shreds of his coat. Had she painted him into her lens, wishing him to be part of her vision? The memory of his image was burned in her brain. But the old man was gone.

Stunned and confused, Jodie sat down in her studio and reviewed the pictures once again. Her old man, in all his poignancy, had vanished. She checked the floor and her entire workspace, but nothing was amiss. She double checked her disk, and all the pictures came up devoid of the human touch she so needed to see. The pictures were missing. But her memory of them was vivid.

Jodie set out the next day for the lake, determined to find the man again to give herself a reality check. Part of her wished she had spoken to him yesterday, so she wouldn't think she had imagined him. A voice would clearly have stayed with her as much as his image.

She arrived early, prepared to spend the day if necessary; the bench was empty. She waited, concealing herself in the copse of trees across the way. Perhaps he would be there at sunset once again.

She stopped some joggers who frequented the path.

"Did you see an old man sitting on this bench yesterday?" she asked. "He was frail, wearing an old coat and feeding the squirrels."

"Never saw anyone like that," they answered.

She asked the daily dog walkers and the parents with children in strollers and received the same response. No one had seen such a man. In fact, they had never seen an old man around the bench. There had been the occasional young lovers or the people stopping to have lunch while taking in the beauty of the lake. But no one ever remembered seeing the man she described. And she knew he would be unforgettable to anyone who had seen him.

She began to question her sanity. Was he perhaps conjured up from a dream she had? What was her reality? And why a man? She had always avoided the human element in her photos, but this was no accident. He had been placed there for a reason.

Jodie grounded herself, came to her senses, and waited. He had to come. She passed the entire day watching the bench. Just when she was ready to lose her grip, a passerby took up the man's space on the bench. Could this be the one she was waiting for? Would she finally find some verification? But it was all wrong. This man was younger, better dressed, lacking the pathos that had so overcome her the day before. She needed him to leave—NOW. This bench was reserved. But it was too late. The darkness had already descended, and her man had not appeared.

That night, Jodie dreamt of "her" old man. She could so vividly see him in her subconscious. Images of sagging skin and hollow eyes began to haunt her. As day dawned, she began to see him everywhere. There he was on the street corner. No, here he was leaning up against a tree. No, this was him getting on the bus. But nothing about these visions was right. She even visited a homeless shelter hoping to find him there. But to no avail. She checked out all the other benches surrounding the lake, but he never appeared there either.

Jodie began to lose her grip on reality. She gave up her beloved profession and began focusing instead on scouring newspapers and magazines for pictures she began to think were just in her imagination. She relived that day a hundred times, like instant replay, and nothing changed. There WAS an old man on the bench, and she had captured his soul and him, hers. She was certain of that. Or was she?

Those around her worried. She was obsessed and depressed. Occasionally, she would pick up her camera and snap a few photos, always wondering what would turn up in her work room. She began taking people with her when she went out so that if she saw the old man she would have confirmation that she wasn't just seeing things. She was tumbling fast and couldn't stop the downward spiral.

She began seeing psychiatrists, all of whom tried to convince her that she had imagined the entire episode. Perhaps she was trying to recreate someone special from her past—a grandfather or uncle. She eventually gave up—no one would listen to her. She finally began to doubt herself.

Time passed, and Jodie began to accept the inevitable: The old man had just been a figment of her imagination. But his image never faded from her memory. She returned to the lake and its memories and, once again, began to pick up her camera. Her encounter, whether in her head or not, had attuned her to people instead of objects.

She began focusing her camera on the people passing by. There were the children feeding the ducks down by the shore. The young lovers sneaking a kiss. The elderly couple holding hands strolling along the path. *Click. Click. Click.* Stories she had never noticed before. Stories waiting to be told. But the one story she wished to tell was gone. The old man did not return. He had touched the innermost recesses of her soul like no still life ever had. She began to realize that the void he left had uncovered a void in her life. In her obsession with the inanimate, she had been neglecting the living.

Soon after, Jodie's photography began to change focus. She began to focus on life instead of still life. The beauty of the natural world now became merely a backdrop for human nature. The flamboyant rich to the abandoned homeless, the silky skin of babies to the wise wrinkles of old age filled her lens. Body and soul were imbued with passion into her work. She could no longer see a bench or a lake without a human caressing them. She began to have a passion for human nature and a connection with man which had been so lacking in her life.

And it was these candid snapshots of ordinary lives, inspired by her encounter with the solitary man on the bench, that were featured in many of the finest magazines. Her name became synonymous with human nature. But each time she captured the story of another human being, she always wondered if the image would appear in her proofs. Doubt became her companion.

Jodie's last picture that fateful day, the day her life changed, finished her *Life on the Lake* series. Each photo was a work of art, accomplishing what she had set out to do a year ago. But she could no longer look at her naked benches without a longing in her heart and soul for the human being she was convinced had once graced its worn slats.

Although her photos had now significantly changed focus, she was still proud of her original project. Her photos were so well received that she was the subject of a one-woman show in a local gallery.

At the artist's reception, she stood back and listened to the comments being made about her subject matter. She thrilled to the reference to Monet's *Haystacks.* She listened intently to the conversations about her ingenious portrayal of light and shadow. She accepted compliment after compliment about her work. Finally, her spirits began to lift as all around her there was a sense of awe at her accomplishments.

She moved through the crowd, studying all who had come to see her work. She saw faces young and old, rich and poor, some happy and some with the weight of the world on their shoulders. She began to file away the expressions for her next project that she would eventually call *Faces,* which would rock the photography world. But, for now, they simply filled her with immense satisfaction.

And now as she studied these people, she noticed, that to a person, all who saw her display paused and noticed a strange quality about her last picture in the series—the one taken on that fateful day, the day that changed her life forever. It seemed to speak more to everyone than any of the others. Crowds built up around it as the people lingered for one last look.

Jodie melded with the patrons and guests and studied it once again. Then she knew what was different about this one from all the rest. It seemed to breathe life. And, occasionally, a shadow crept across the vacant bench. *Where am I?* it said. And Jodie smiled.

The End

Connect with Barbara and see what else she's writing, at the following links:

Facebook: https://www. facebook.com/barb.galvin.585?fref=nf

Wattpad: https://www.wattpad.com/user/BarbaraGalvin

Cover by Author.

The Other Side

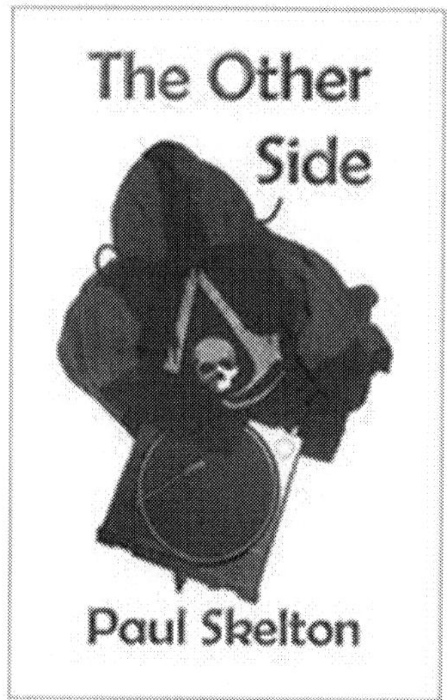

Paul Skelton

I'm Paul Skelton, otherwise known as Skelly. I make my living being a primary school caretaker, which is quite possibly the best job in the world. Writing is a hobby, which I hope, one day, will earn me a bit to top up my pension.

"The Other Side" was inspired by a Radio Four play from the Seventies. It's basically aimed at being a strange, chilling story of an elderly man who's out of touch with the times, full of indignation, belligerence and pride. However, as with all of us, he's really quite flawed, affected by an embarrassing incident in his military past. The incident catches up with him, when (finding himself on "the other side") his demons confront him. His reaction to some youths trying to assault him is a direct message to some of today's "hoodie rats" (as I call them): i.e. stop hiding in your hoodie, pull your trousers up and don't underestimate older, wiser people!! As with everything I write, all I care about is that it entertains the reader. I work on the premise if it entertains me, then it must (statistically) entertain others, and I hope YOU are one of those "others." Cheers. Skelly.

Part One: Mr. Bloomin' Jobsworth

"Well, Mr. Hampton, that's it. You move on Saturday the 26th. You will be picked up at six pm, from 9 Skellington Street. OK, Mr. Hampton?" asked the council official.

"It's blimmin' short notice, ain' it? I mean wot abart me stuff? Y'know all me furniture an' that?" countered the octogenarian, Ted Hampton.

"Your letter concerning re-accommodation was sent out six months ago, Mr. Hampton, and confirmation of arrangements was sent out three weeks ago. There were also three tenant meetings set up to discuss these matters, and you attended none of them. Now, all you're expected to take with you is the equivalent of erm" (light pause whilst checking something on his computer screen) "ah, yes. Ahem. The equivalent of two suitcases of luggage, as your new scheme is completely furnished and equipped with everything you will need. Yes," concluded the council official.

"I don't remember no letters or meetings. Look wot abart me radyo-gram an' me c'lection of records. They won' all fit in a blimmin' suitcase, I can tell you," said Mr. Hampton belligerently.

"What is a-a...*radio-gram* exactly?" queried the council official.

"It's a state of the art music centre: solid state electronics, twin cassette deck, belt-drive turntable, FM/AM tuner, yeh, an' it pushes art firty bloomin' watts per speaker. It's all housed in proper mahogany, yeh, wurf a MINT," answered Mr. Hampton emphatically.

"Hmmm," mused the official. "It sounds quite big. Would say you it's as big as my credenza here?"

"Yor wot?" said Ted Hampton and then, "Oh yeh, yor cupboard fing. Well yeh, it's easily as big as that an' yer can double it wiv me record cabinet an' all."

"I see, I see. Right. Well, you'll need to fill out a Form 476B for *Additional Removal Requirements.* Here," he replied, handing Ted a form.

"I carnt be fillin' art all this ole twaddle," raged Ted. "I mean orl the blimmin' forms I've filled in, I 'spect you got more info abart me on that compooter than I know abart meself. Orl I'm arskin' yer is for t' move me radyo-gram an' me records. I mean carnt yer jest pick up a phone an' arrange it for me?"

"It's not that simple, Mr. Hampton. We have to follow procedure. It's more than my jobs worth to—" The official was interrupted.

"Look, desk! Phone! Pick it up an' make a call, see? Orl yer needs is a flippin' van, innit? It IS that simple, Mr. bloomin' JobsWORTH," ranted Ted.

"Calm down, Mr. Hampton. Why can't you just fill out the—" The official was interrupted again.

"I ain't got me blimmin' glasses wiv me 'ave I. You fill art yer stupid form if it means so much to yer. I'm orf mate. 'Ad it up to 'ere wiv yor sort. Huh! Jus' sort art me gear for me, that's all!" Ted concluded and left the official with his head in his hands.

Ted stormed through the building, muttering obscenities loud enough to be heard by any passersby, and then he targeted a receptionist with his comments on his way out. "I'll fill summat in. Yeh. That Mister bloomin' Jobsworth upstairs, yeh, you tell 'im that! 'Cuz I boxed in the flippin' army, I did. Huh!" And Mr. Hampton was gone.

Part Two: Anything for You, Old Mate.

"So, Ted, yer movin' nex' Saturday then?" enquired Stan Gates, Ted Hampton's mate, who had popped round for coffee.

"Yep. That's abart the size of it, Stan. 'Ad a right go at the council tho' abart movin' me radyo-gram. Told 'em 'xactly wot he could do wiv 'is bloomin' forms. Yeh. Put 'im straight on that one."

"Good fer you, Ted. You don't like forms, do yer?" asked Stan.

"No, I bloomin' don't," affirmed Ted.

"I mean what with your difficulty with the old readin' an' writin' side of things—" Stan was interrupted.

"I've done all right over the years. Ken sorts art me forms for me ordinarily. I just didn't fink more forms were necessary in this case. Know wot I mean, Stan?"

"All I meant was these council people should make allowances, Ted. You know, we're not computer literate, are we? I mean, Ken, he's good at forms an' that, isn't he? On account of doin' all the admin for The Legion." Stan was attempting to keep the conversation calm, as he sensed he'd touched a nerve regarding Ted's inability to read and write.

"Well, Stan, talkin' of The Legion, the Friday an' Saturday nights ain't gonna work. See, my new gaff is right over the other side. A good four mile as the crow flies." Ted was fretting.

"That's not all that far, Ted, there'll be buses," Stan replied.

"Buses? Oh yeh, there's buses all right. But Jeff looked into it for me, an' I'd 'ave to get two buses each way. Which is Ok gettin' over 'ere, but on account of the blimmin' timetable, I'd 'ave to leave the club before nine to be sure of gettin' the buses back to me new gaff," Ted continued.

"Oh, I see. That would cut yer night short, wouldn't it? Wot about a cab 'ome, Ted?"

"That would use up all me beer money, Stan."

"I can't understand why they 'ave to move you so far. I mean, what about round here? Eh?" Stan reasoned.

"Not that simple, Stan. Not only are they pullin' my old 'ouse darn to make way for social 'ousing, but a-top of that, my GP reckons I need sheltered accommodation on accarnt of me age an' that."

"Anti-social 'ousing I call it, mate. I mean it's all single mums, flippin' hoodie rats an' migrants innit, Ted? Blimey, what's this world comin' to, eh? Tekkin' you out of your local area, away from yer mates. I mean, what is sheltered accommodation? Is that with a warden on call an' with a door entry system?"

"Yeh, that's abart the size of it," Ted replied.

"O' course if you'd bought your gaff when you had the chance to get it at a discount price you'd be in a position to choose where you move to, wouldn't you, Ted? I mean they'd 'ave to give you market rate for the place at least."

"Wot you on abart? All that mortgage malarkey? I'm council born an' bred, Stan. Served me country, paid me dues, but the way this country's goin' I don't reckon I'd be any better off whatever way you slice it. Anyway, I didn't buy the gaff an' wot's done's done." Ted was getting prickly again.

"'Ang on, Ted. Got an idea," Stan said soothingly. "If you bus it over here on the Friday, go to the club as normal, but instead of goin' back the same night, just kip over at mine. Then Jeff, Roger, Ken an' Ray can all take turns each week. That way we can all meet up for our Saturday coffee, lunch up the Vicky Café, down the club for six o'clock, play doms an' cards, kip over on the Saturday night an' head back at your leisure on the Sunday."

"That could work, Stan. Yeh. D'yer fink they'd all be up fer it?"

"Reckon so, Ted. I mean, we're all single or widowed, aren't we? We'll chat about it Friday night."

"Yeh, cuz I move on the Saturday. Yeh, even if some of 'em ain' up for it, at least you are, Stan."

"That's right, Ted. Anything for you, old mate," affirmed Stan.

Part Three: The Knowledge

"Wot time do you call this? I was meant to be picked up at six!" Ted barked accusingly.

"You Meester Hamp-ton?" asked the mini cab driver standing at Ted's front door.

"Tha's right."

"I late 'coz of traffic an' my sat-nav went off line twice," replied the cabby.

"TWAT-NAV I call it. Ain't you got 'The Knowledge,' son? Huh! It's quarter past six, mate. I've never been late fer anyfing in orl my eighty years, son. You gonna take my cases or wot?" spat Ted.

"Look, I sorry. OK? I no lift luggage, Meester Hamp-ton. Health and safety. I drive you, see?" The cabby gestured to his Mercedes.

"Wot's that? My radyo-gram won't fit in that fing." Ted pointed at the car.

"What is rad-yogram?" enquired the cabby.

"Come in 'ere I'll show you." The cabby followed Ted into the front room. "There." He pointed. "State o' the art music centre."

"That is furniture, Meester Hamp-ton. I no do removals. Come on, we must go. I running late."

"Ain't my fault yer late. Wot abart me radyo-gram?" insisted Ted Hampton.

"Do council know you want furniture removed?"

"Well, I went to see 'em an' I said abart it," replied Ted Hampton.

"Oh, OK then. Come on. We must go!"

Ted carried his cases to the Mercedes, and the cabby did help lift them into the trunk.

Once in the car, the cabby wanted information.

"OK, Meester Hamp-ton, wot is post-code of address you go to, please?"

"I dunno abart post-bloomin'-codes. Don't you know where you gotta take me?"

"Meester Hamp-ton, there is six schemes. I need post-code for sat-nav; it guide me."

"Blimey, if you had the blimmin' Knowledge you wouldn't need that fing. Huh. Orl I know is my new gaff's at a place called Farnham 'Ouse or sumink. It's right over the other side, parst all them flyovers an' that," Ted responded testily.

"Oh, ok. I check the map app on my phone, Meester Hamp-ton." Then after a short pause, he said, "Aah, here is place, I think. Eez it spell "F-A-R-E-H-A-M House?"

"Yeh. Sounds abart right."

They drove off and, around seven o'clock, pulled up at a large imposing, old building. There was a howling wind, and the rain was falling like stair rods.

"Is that it?" Ted was alarmed. "Don't look right to me."

"This address, Meester Hamp-ton. We here. You take cases now. I got another pick-up tonight."

"You sure? It looks old. My new gaff is meant to be NEW."

"This eez place. It on my GPS on smartphone. See? I sure the place eez new inside. Now come on, old man." The cabby was irritated.

"It's pissin' darn. Ain't you gonna 'elp me?" Ted was insistent.

"OK, OK. I help you to gates, that's all. OK, old man?" replied the cabby reluctantly.

Part Four: Rupert

"Huh! Wot kinda place is this? Better ring the bell," Ted Hampton muttered unhappily to himself.

There was no answer after several minutes and several attempts to ring the bell. Ted Hampton shuffled round the large building until he found an open door at the side. He went through the doorway: a store room. It appeared to be full of old medical and mobility apparatus. Ted Hampton put his cases down and, surveying the dimly lit room, called out.

"Allo! ALLO! **ALLO!"** His words echoed as a middle-aged, balding man appeared, quite agitated.

"Who are you? What choo doing here?" he asked in an effeminate nasal tone.

Ted stood to attention and replied.

"Edward Hampton. Here for my sheltered accommodation."

"Sheltered accommodation?" spluttered the middle-aged man. "I can't admit people. NO. If you think you can be admitted, well, think again."

"Wot d'yer mean? I was brought here by the council, to be moved into me own flat. WIV," continued Ted Hampton, "WIV a warden. Now where's my flat?"

"Council? Flat? Warden? I've no knowledge of that stuff. Look, Mr. Hampton, I don't know where you think you are, but this is not your accommodation, I can assure you of that!" The reply was emphatic.

"This is Farnham House, ain' it?" Ted Hampton was getting worried.

"This, Mr. Hampton, is Fareham House, the old asylum. We were shut down, but they...er...kept me on as...er...caretaker, you see. That's why I can't admit people: we're shut DOWN. You're in the wrong place."

"Wrong place? Asylum? Wot's goin' on? The cabby said this was the place. 'E did." Ted Hampton was virtually sobbing with emotion. "I'm cold, soakin' wet, an' I'm in the wrong place. Wot am I gonna do?" he wailed.

"Look, calm down, Mr. Hampton. I'm sure we can sort this out. Yes, umm. Look, come through to my boiler room; you'll dry off in there. And I can make us a jolly cup o' tea, yes, Mr. Hampton? And then we'll find out where you should have been taken to, yes?"

"Yeh, ta very much."

"You must understand though," the middle-aged man continued, "that I'm not admitting you. OR, issuing things. My name's Rupert, by the way."

"'Ello, Rupert," said Ted.

"Come through..." sang Rupert. "There. You sit on that armchair there, by the boilers. I'll be Mother, shall I? Sugar? Milk?" Ted nodded.

"Ta very much for the tea." Ted was starting to feel better.

"Right, Mr. Hampton, have you got some kind of paperwork? You must have a letter or something with the address of your new place?"

"'Ere." Ted fished out a crumpled letter from the inside pocket of his old duffle coat.

Rupert regarded the letter carefully and then showed it to Ted.

"Look, Mr. Hampton. See the error? Look. There."

"Ain't got me glasses," Ted replied.

"Well, you're supposed to be at FARNHAM House with an 'N' not an 'R.' See this place is the asylum, FAREHAM House with an 'R.' See? Look, the post-code's different, see? You don't see, do you? You can't read, can you?"

"Ain't got me glasses, 'ave I? I told yer I—" Ted was cut off.

"Look, Mr. Hampton, I wasn't born yesterday. You're moving to a new place, and those suitcases contain all your stuff, right?" Rupert asked bluntly.

"Well, yeh...erm..."

"Well, if that's all your stuff, Mr. Hampton, where would your flippin' glasses be? Eh? They'd be there, wouldn't they? In your luggage, you silly old man. You can't read, can you?" Rupert was ranting.

"I've done all right...served in the army...boxed for 'em. I jest struggle a bit wiv the old paperwork, that's all," an embarrassed Ted replied.

"You served in the army? Didn't you have trouble with, erm, written things and so on?" Rupert enquired.

"Well, yeh, some trouble I 'spose, but I was exonerated by the Agitant, yeh, discharged wiv full honours," Ted lied. "There was a court martial o' course, but I was exonerated. 'Mix up over sign-age' they said."

"Really? So you're the one. Ran over two personnel. I vaguely remember a newspaper report some years back. Fatalities weren't there?" asked Rupert.

"A mix up over sign-age. I wuz drivin' the troop carrier darn the shootin' range, an' hit a Major an' a private. They shouldn'a bin there. Like I say, I was exonerated of all blame."

"Fatalities. There were three fatalities," insisted Rupert.

"Well, yeh, fatalities. But I was exonerated, and interestingly enough, the sign-age was replaced later on wiv pictoral signs, yeh. So I fink that sez it orl. An' my bit o' trouble wiv writin' an' that ain't 'eld me back. Judge me as you will, but I know wot's wot. It was a mix up over sign-age."

"Oh, it's OK. I'm not judging you, Mr. Hampton. Some would tho', oh yes." Rupert's voice rose in pitch, and he spoke with real feeling. "Oh yes, if you're dyslexic they label you as *thick*. Oh my gawd, and if you're dyspraxic, well then, you're *retarded*. And God help you if you're left handed like me. Oh, yes. They hate you if you're a bit...different, you know, if you're a bit sensitive. Yes, the taunts, the shame, and, oh, the cruelty. If it wasn't for Major Washford a-a-a-and this place, heaven only knows where I'd end up."

"Wot d'yer mean?" Ted was curious.

"I had my own bit o' trouble, Mr. Hampton. Misunderstanding at the swimming baths. Yes, it was horrible. I was NOT exposing myself, Mr. Hampton. Just a slight wardrobe malfunction. I tried to stop the kid screaming. They didn't like that, did they? No! Oh, the shame, the humiliation. Just 'coz I'm a bit different. That's why I like it here in the facility, you see. Hidden away, safe, warm. No one to judge you. Know what I mean?" ranted Rupert.

Rupert would have gone on in this impassioned ranting fashion, and he was starting to foam at the mouth. Ted felt very uncomfortable in Rupert's company, sensing that he was a seriously disturbed man, and so he cut him short.

"Yeh-yeh, I know wotcha mean. Look, I fink I'd better get off, mate. Find me new place. You any idea which way I should go?"

Rupert didn't appear to have heard him and carried on.

"Oh, Major Washford, he understood. Not like the others. He knew it was a misunderstanding in those changing rooms...he knew about the voices, the urges, the—"

"WHICH WAY OUT OF 'ERE?" Ted shouted as he stood up, shaking.

"OK, OK, no need to shout, Mr. Hampton. It's the other side of the canal. Shall I draw you a map?"

"Nah, I'll be all right. Served me time in the army. Just tell me the directions, OK?"

"It's raining out there. Shouldn't we call you a taxi?" asked Rupert.

"Just tell me the way. It's only like a route march. I'll be fine."

Rupert gave Ted detailed directions.

"You got all that, Mr. Hampton?" Rupert concluded.

"Yeh, got it. I'm off. Ta very much," Ted called as he exited hastily.

"Good luck, Mr. Hampton," called Rupert with an eerie chirp.

It was nearly eight o'clock.

Part Five: The Major

Ted Hampton passed the mosque but could not see the underpass. There were two youths in hooded tops sheltering from the rain in a doorway. Ted approached them.

"Scuse me," he said. "Where's the underpass?"

"You wot, old man? You want directions? It'll cost yer," said one youth.

Then the other one spoke, producing a knife, which he waved in Ted's face. "Yeh, give us some change, innit? Come on, old man, empty dem pockets an' cough up an' we'll take yer down de underpass, innit?"

Ted responded instinctively. He dropped one suitcase and karate chopped the smaller youth on the side of his neck; the youth passed out. The larger one tried to stab Ted, but the blade punctured Ted's other suitcase, which he was holding defensively.

"You stupid boy. You don't pull a blade on an old soldier," hissed Ted and pushed the youth back with the suitcase. As the youth fell, he kicked him in the head as hard as he could and then brought the suitcase down on him. The youth was now sobbing as Ted took the knife from him and hurried away nearly bumping into a tall man in a greatcoat.

"What ho? Steady on, old chap," barked the man in the greatcoat. "I say, are you all right, old chap, you look a bit shaken."

Ted was shaken and bruised from his skirmish and replied breathlessly, "I'll live, just 'ad a bit of bovver wiv acouple of kids. Fort they'd try it on wiv an old soldier. I got the better of 'em tho'."

"Down, Rufus! That's my dawg, Rufus. Soldier, eh? Well, pleased to meet you, soldier. Major T. J. Washford, retired, at your service."

"Oh, yessir, Private 'Ampton, retired, member of the British Legion, sir!" Ted saluted.

"At ease that, man," commanded the Major. "So hoodie rats, were they? You did well, Hampton, yes-yes-yes. Down, Rufus! I say, look at those contusions."

"Wot's contusions?" Ted asked.

"Bruises, old chap. Yes, bruises," answered the Major and continued. "Where you tryin' to get to with that luggage at this time of night?"

"Well, I'm off to the marina on the uvver side, to me sheltered accommodation, the council fixed me up," Ted replied.

"In this weather? Well, I can help you get over to the canal. Goin' that way mesself, doncha know. Down, Rufus! I say, Rufus likes you; he won't bite. Yes-yes-yes, you take Rufus, I'll carry your luggage, and we'll cross the common together. Soon be at the canal. I've got me narrow boat moored there. We'll fix you up a bite to eat, a mug of tea and get you on your way. Steady now, soldier," the Major said, leading Ted across the common, over the dual carriageway, and down the steps to his narrow boat.

"Ta very much, Major. I'll get on me way now," a very grateful Ted said as they reached the Major's boat.

"Nonsense. You need some char. Come onto the boat, that's it, what-what."

After a hot tea cake and tea on the Major's boat, Ted got up to leave.

"Fanks, Major, you're a lifesaver. 'Ow far is it to the marina?"

"Not far. I'd offer to take you over in me rowin' boat, but some of those hoodie rats scuppered her the other night. Need to get her out of the drink and fix the bally hole. Look, just carry on down the towpath; you'll soon come to it, barely half a mile."

"And then I cross at the marina bridge, don' I?"

"What? Oh no-no-no, it's not finished yet. Was supposed to be finished last month, doncha know, but they're behind schedule. You'll have go down to the Sainsburys further on; there's another bridge there. Just cross there and then come back this way on the other side. Well, good luck, Private Hampton, what? See you anon." The Major helped Ted onto the towpath, and Ted set off.

Part Six: The Passing Over

"Just a route march, 'Ampton. Quick march. Left-right. Left-right," Ted muttered to himself as he walked along the towpath.

Eventually Ted reached the Sainsburys' bridge and crossed over. There was no towpath on the other side, so Ted asked a lady walking her dog for directions.

"Just follow that road there," she said, gesturing. "Barnham Lane takes you straight to the marina, and you'll see Farnham House left of the Old Mill Pub."

"Ta very much," replied an exhausted Ted.

As he lumbered on down Barnham Lane, huffing and puffing, he encountered a loiterer.

"Hey, old soldier. You done my blood. Gonna make you pay, innit?" squeaked the hoodie rat.

"Yor wot?" asked an exhausted Ted.

"My blood, my bruv. Earlier. Well, this where you get yours." The youth lunged at Ted with a small flick knife. Ted wasn't so quick this time, and as he felt the blade puncture his belly, he went down heavily. The hoodie rat made his escape, shrieking in delight.

After what seemed like an eternity, Ted recovered himself and took a look at the wound. There was less blood than he imagined.

"Fank gawd," he muttered, "jest a flesh wound. Right, 'Ampton, fish art the old first aid kit...ah, that's it. Jest patch it up wiv this 'ere plaster. That's it. Now, let's see if I can stand." Ted shook as he clambered to his feet, just as a late-night jogger came running up.

"Hoi, are you all right, mate? Had a fall? Come on. I'll give you a hand." The jogger helped Ted to his feet.

"Ta, son. 'Ad a bit o' bovver wiv one o' them hoodie rats, but I'll be ok now, I fink," Ted grunted. He was experiencing some pain.

"You've got luggage!" exclaimed the jogger in surprise. "Where on Earth are you off to at this time of night?"

"The marina, Farnham 'Ouse," gasped Ted. "Carnt be far, can it?"

"Not at all. You're practically there. Come on. I'll take your luggage and help you. It's only fifty yards. Come on," the jogger reassured Ted.

They got to Farnham House, which was modern and well lit. The jogger took Ted into the reception area and deposited his suitcases. Ted sat down, and a warden appeared at the reception desk.

"What in Heaven's name is all this?" He sounded alarmed.

The jogger approached the reception desk and gesturing at Ted said, "He was coming here, but some kid knocked him over, he's a bit shaken and..."

"Private Edward 'Ampton, all present and correct!" Ted stood to attention and saluted. "I've come fer me accommodation," he concluded.

"You gonna be OK now?" enquired the jogger.

"Yup! I'll be fine. Now you jest get on yer way, and fanks fer yer 'elp," replied Ted.

With that the jogger left, and the warden started looking at a list on a clipboard and then looked up at Ted and asked, "Hampton, did you say Hampton?"

"Yup!" replied Ted.

"Mmm, yes, um, flat eleven it says here. Mmmm, you were supposed to be here before seven pm. It's ten thirty now," stated the warden.

"Yeh, well...'ad a bit o' bovver, didn' I? Flippin' cabby didn' 'ave the blimmin' Knowledge, di' 'e? Didn' seem t'know 'is way abart. You gonna sort art me accommodation now or wot?"

"Well, I can't admit you, if that's what you mean," the warden said firmly. "The admissions officer went off at quarter past seven, you see. I'm locked out of the computer. Yes, locked out."

"Ain't there anyfing you can do?" retorted Ted angrily.

"Well, I don't know who you are. I mean, you could be anyone," the warden insisted.

"I've gotta letter on me, look. And I got me pension book an'—" Ted was cut short.

"Look, Mr. Hampton, I'm sure you're genuine, but there are procedures. Yes, there's a system, and I'm locked out of it because I'm just a night warden, not an admissions officer. Therefore I can't admit you. Or issue things, like keys, etcetera," the warden said officiously.

"But I'm tired. 'An cold. I need to lie darn. Just let me in me flat for tonight, would yer? An' then tomorra, if I'm not 'oo I say I am, you can frow me art onto the street, CARNT YER?" Ted ranted, rising very unsteadily to his feet.

"OK, OK. Calm down," said the warden, starting to panic as he could see Ted was not in a good way. "Look, let's get you a cup of tea, eh? Then I'll contact the out-of-hours team, they may be able to…er…do something. OK, Mr. Hampton?"

"Look 'ere, I got taken to the wrong place, bin set upon by thugs, walked best part o' three mile in pourin' rain, and then—and THEN stabbed by a kid…"

"STABBED?" squealed the warden, clearly alarmed as Ted was showing him the site of the wound with blood seeping through the dressing Ted had applied. "Oh my god, OH MY GOD…oh…don't panic—don't panic. Right, er come through here, er, this is our emergency room, we'll clean up the wound and get help."

The warden helped Ted through to his emergency room, cleaned Ted's wound, and applied a fresh dressing. True to his word, he made Ted a cup of tea.

"There," the warden said soothingly. "You stay in here and rest up while I get help, yes? And I'll contact the out-of-hours team. I'm sure when I explain the facts of your case, they'll sort this mess out. Back soon."

Time passed, and Ted dozed off. When he came to, he was lying on a couch in a sterile-looking, white room with very bright lighting. Two faces stared down at him.

"I say, Rupert, look at those contusions. What-what?"

"Oi, wos goin' on? Where am I? Wos 'appening? I know you, don' I?" blurted Ted.

"You're on the other side, old chap," the Major stated matter-of-factly.

"The other side," repeated Rupert.

"Wasn't your fault, Hampton, what? Mix up over signage, wasn't it, Rupert?"

"Mix up. Signage," agreed Rupert in a spooky voice.

"You were exonerated, Hampton. Honourable discharge. Clean slate and all that blah-de-blah," the Major intoned.

"Exonerated," raved Rupert.

"You're with us now, on the other side: the hereafter, with me and Rupert."

"With us. Remember us?" ranted Rupert.

Ted was trying to speak but couldn't get any words out.

"Yes-yes-yes. Remember us?" the Major asked. "We're the two bods you ran over, Hampton. And Rufus? He likes you, but then he would, wouldn't he? He was your dawg for eleven years when your wife was still alive, wasn't he? Remember Rufus?"

The Major and Rupert were howling insanely.

"Oh my gawd. I recognise you. Yeh, both of yer,"' Ted managed to murmur. "An' I do remember, oh gawd. I've…I've passed over. Wot 'appens now?"

The howling stopped, and the Major spoke soothingly. "You stay here, Private Edward Hampton, with us. You're safe and sound here," said the Major.

"Safe and sound, in the asylum," Rupert shrieked.

"With us," said the Major. "For all eternity."

"Eternity, in the asylum. Let's have a jolly cup o' tea shall we, Mr. Hampton?"

"Jolly good idea, Rupert. What-what-what?" enthused the Major.

Ted felt strangely relaxed and calm. He looked round the padded, sterile, white room and asked, "Is this my sheltered accommodation?"

"I do believe it is," shrilled Rupert in an enthusiastic manner.

"Abso-bloody-lutely, old chap. What-what-what?" affirmed the Major.

"Well…in–that–case—gentlemen." Ted spoke slowly. "I want my bloomin' radyo-gram." He then shouted, **"MY BLOOMIN' RADYO-GRAM AND MY BLIMMIN' RECORD CABINET!"**

The End

How to contact Paul:

Paul is a notorious luddite who avoids the internet when he can, but if you really want to comment on his story and ask him about his other writing, you can do so care of:
https://www. facebook.com/TheJasonGreenfield/ and I'll pass on any messages.

Cover by D. J. Meyers.

Dawkins and Booth

John A. Riley

At an old funeral parlour and quell any curiosity that it is abandoned and deserted, a visitor allowed to enter this late hour. A stranger now sitting at the side of a closed coffin, paying his respects while inside it a corpse sleeps, and upon the closed eyelids, a request for pennies to lay on them. In the darkness, a floorboard creaks, and there appears Mr Dawkins emerging from a dark corner of his sanctuary. So begins the revelation of a truth this night...and a ghost story best read during the hours of darkness.

The moment you meet John A. Riley, the co-creator of the Ghostly World, you'll sense his otherworldly presence. As he confidently reaches to shake a hand, a wide smile shows a disconcerting set of vampiric canines. There is something enigmatic and a magnetism that draws curiosity. He publishes stories under a variety of personas, and at each mention, there's the impression we are not sitting alone anymore. Although you cannot see them, you know they are in the room. A creator of fictional ghost stories for readers of all ages, his short tales to chill and scare can be comic, sad, dark and weird, revealing the eccentricities of lost characters set in their own ghostly realities: A world that may be contemporary or back to a Victorian era or beyond into the future, no doubt with hooded phantoms gliding towards you upon a spectral mist. This earthbound soul is striving to work off karma and express all splinters from source in one lifetime. It leads me to think is the man here John A. Riley or Jonathan Harker, Valentine Heart, Silas Crowley, Thomas Flyte, Victor or Victoria? I sense each one, but who is really sitting with me?

***

The old funeral parlour of Messrs. Dawkins and Booth is not a building able to hide. Built during the Victorian era, replacing the former house on the site, its location is along a scuffy back street heading out of the town. A forbidding, shadowy establishment throughout its long service, tainted with an aged reputation, it possesses a fearful history over the town's collective, visibly affecting people when passing it, attention shifting to other matters while hurrying to take a shortcut and avoid Melrose Street.

The town, Sabden Heights, falls under the shadow of its neighbouring villages as well as the hill. An area already cursed with superstition and notoriety because of its association with the witch trials and the Craft during the sixteen hundreds. So of no surprise that an atmosphere draped and drawn over the place lingers across the years. There's even a tale long ago of finding a grave on unconsecrated ground beneath the funeral parlour. Perhaps souls are trapped or that something residual remains and exists throughout eternity. Rumours, then, of witchcraft and trapped souls bound by a curse and haunting the house prevail throughout the generations. Dawkins and Booth will hear none, citing it as mere superstition and gossip put about by rivals challenging their independence.

If brave enough to look upon this house and stare because one's curiosity seeks answers, you might well question what took place, knowing half a tale and the rumours. There're boarded shutters, presenting a barrier from staring in, says the elusive homeless man bedded in with cardboard and newsprint. Knowing as he does, he'll 'end up inside one of these freezing nights! Laid in narrow bed for sure!' He can tell you, you've to climb up nine stone steps and cross the threshold through the heavy double doors. It's the way the living enter while others access and leave from the back in wooden boxes.

It is a fact the duties of an undertaker will need calling upon; death is an inevitable and yielding profit for Messrs. Dawkins and Booth. Death holds no discrimination over the poor or the wealthy. Mr Dawkins and Mr Booth collect money from both and plenty more in establishing their reputation. So, troubled souls enter this shadowy inner sanctum and, in their anxious states, take note of things lurking. The house is imposing with a sinister side to its grim front face; gossip spreads whether anyone lives on the premises and stories of ghosts haunting. For the record and seen on occasions, a dim, yellowy glow resembling a flickering lantern, as though something is entering through an opened back door when, in truth, there is nobody there. At the upper floor windows, shadows appear on the glass. People have heard the pounding of nails rising in a crescendo, banging into wood from the workshop out back during the late hours of night. The hammering stops—suddenly—as if the source knows when you're listening. As for ghosts, well, children on their way to school talk of it, believe many spooky tales according to their teachers. On grey and rainy days, the younger ones say dead people stand at the upstairs windows.

There will invariably be hearsay after the incident. This site is old enough to bear its terrible history forward through time, attracting fiction upon fact. It soon becomes a pointless task to isolate the two, for an urban myth slithered and coiled its way around the idle talk and actual reports. Assumption and surmise, as well as old wives' gossip, poisoned any hope to unearth the truth.

What is true, according to individuals, is an odour, predominating in the public rooms. The nearest description one can offer is of over-ripened oranges ready to turn. Such is the smell it survives after visiting the place. A phantom sensory perception, tainting clothes and skin. For those describing such an experience, they remark on seeking washrooms to purge themselves of the sickly stench.

If tuning into the stillness, it aligns the thoughts with wandering impressions. How many sit, waiting, recalling that unhappy event taking place here, finding its way to one's perceptions when not wanting reminding? Inside this mausoleum, it is cool, gloomy, morbid and full of death. A place wherein the murk and shadow anticipation grows, that around you and possibly in the room next to you, coffins stacked and, within them, endure the dead sleeping in repose. Would you, if passing, keep a distance so as not to look at what lies in deathly sleep?

To dispel any curiosity of this funeral parlour deserted, a visitor, allowed to enter at this late hour, is sitting at the side of a closed coffin. A man with worker's hands, clasped together while he is immersed in contemplation. His journey to this point not without its trials. Inside the oak coffin, a corpse sleeps, and upon the closed eyelids, a request for pennies to lay on them.

In the darkness, a floorboard creaks.

"We uphold the duty of ritual," a voice speaks somewhere from outside the room, addressing the visitor with a dismal tone, grave and woeful.

The stranger knows of the presence but not yet acknowledges the undertaker.

He appears from a dark corner of his sanctuary, a hidden private abode, his temple of the dead. He stands, observing and waiting before approaching.

A weasel-thin creature, whether Dawkins or Booth one was not at all sure on first meeting. But all would know of either man dressed permanently in black and a countenance, pale and looking ghostly. A wordsmith might characterise this man as cadaverous, one resembling a corpse. He stands looming with hands closed, casting a look around the room before declaring: "It is our way to turn the mirrors towards the wall, drape black cloth upon them and stop the clocks while we make final adjustments for the interment." He tips his head, bowing and holding a forward stare.

It is as though he is expressing his opinion at the coffin. This shady, lank man peering again towards the reversed wall mirrors, squinting at the ceremonial detail, and grinning his sinister smirk. The undertaker seeks out one of the rare and expensive clocks. Time stopped; silence lingers in this place. Who is this stranger? A familiar rounded shape, hunched over caught in a moment of deep reflection.

"Let me offer my condolences at this time of loss." The undertaker is unsure whether the visitor heard. After a short break and with trained quiet discretion, he speaks again in a low whisper: "I am Mr Dawkins. I don't recall if we've met. Might I be of help?"

The stranger, alerted, makes no reply.

The undertaker respectfully coughs.

"Oh, sorry, yes, thank you." The stranger, turning to encounter Mr Dawkins and captured by shock when setting sight of the figure, stooped and hovering above him with milky white-skinned eyes, reaching out to locate him. His attention, one could say, scary to a child and to an adult.

"Forgive me, are you a relative of the deceased?"

"Er, no." Backing away from the scary leering. "I'm passing through and fulfilling a wish for an old friend. Bit of a wandering lost soul, in limbo at the moment."

The undertaker thinks on the second, considering a delicate matter.

"I'm sorry, but I was anticipating...someone...who could aid with instruction."

A lingering silence and unseen across the stranger's face, his eyes narrowing.

"I'm not sure about that. I'm here on behalf of a request," answers the stranger, his voice noticeably broad tuned to the local dialect. He returns to gaze at the coffin.

The undertaker continues:

"Might I inquire, in case you can help in a modest way? It appears the arrangements are on hold, and one is accustomed to dealing with the deceased and afford it dignity and eternal rest...If I may state, you remain the sole person visiting the departed in our care...I was hopeful of an opportunity. I'm not clear if you have a few memories to serve the dedicatory composition. Facts are all we dispense; we are not here to compose romantic prose. Please, let no qualms prevent such a restraint." Mr Dawkins gestures with his open hands. "If one might...say...grant me a confidence, the requirements can proceed." He waits. "You might deliberate upon something that comes to mind. Take whatever time you need."

Undetected by the stranger was the following thin smile, whether it conveyed sincerity or the expression on a face fixing its scary eyes on him, better not to know; either way, both looked menacing.

***

How still a room becomes without the constant ticking clock or sounds seeping from outside. Silence can grow to a height where it implies no other place exists beyond the confines of where one remains. It is strange how a person, incapable, cannot stir or think through mental blocks that act on consciousness. What is it maintaining a cataleptic state at such times? What is it? This building? Its grip upon the senses? No surprise it attracts gossip for its presence within, by occult force, stretches out, manifesting a mood upon the structure's outward aspect. And no wonder that in its abandonment, this place soon attracts talk of ghosts and the undead.

The stranger breaks from the reverie. "Do you not wonder on matters relating to the afterlife?"

His voice telling of a man who engaged in manual labour, thinks the undertaker, yet a man with studious and thoughtful ways. One might further say troubled by a cramp in his mind.

The stranger speculates:

"Reality prompts questions. Whether we are judged by our deeds and actions? I've considered other ideas, as in the matter is this it—birth, life, death! We shall never understand until confronted with the reaper? What say you? I've been a man who serves, buried away in a black hole. The name's Burton, Samuel Burton; I'd answer to Sam…or worse!"

Mr Dawkins, taken by the man and his question, roused an interest in him, thereupon thinking over the query, whether he might have answers.

"May I?" The undertaker now offering to consider matters over at the writing desk and inviting his guest to accompany him. He pulls the client's chair before it, then glides around, feeling his way to take his place. He makes a signal for Mr Burton to sit when doing, so he sat down.

"I imagine it disheartening to observe details of death. Oh, I'm sorry, I didn't mean to imply…"

"I agree, a profession to which all not suited. One needs a disposition to carry out the honourable duties attending to the dead."

Samuel could better hear the inflection of his voice when not whispering. It reverberates deep.

"I might recall a memory suitable for you, if I talk." Dawkins' eyes are scary.

He was ready to take questions, offer answers on subjects he may have knowledge when speaking his mind. To do so, as well, while the clocks stopped and having the space to collect thoughts.

Samuel looks to his clasped hands. "I need to recall, as if something…"

"Ask me what you want to ask. Your time is my time."

"I have few friends. A loner, I suppose."

Mr Dawkins sits upright in his chair, observing and pensive, bringing his bony finger points to his lips as if in prayer. He appears like an old judge, ready to pronounce sentence.

"I can identify a similar predicament. Our profession can quickly see you struck from social circles. We are stigmatised as if we are in league with the Grim Reaper and clearly not welcome at society and trade functions."

For the first time, Samuel Burton feels able to hold the undertaker's stare, and those skinned eyes seem to smile. There contained within a presence not of this world. Samuel breaks the contact, looking at the desk.

Mr Dawkins returns to an earlier question: "Let me ask you—if I may?—before commenting on my beliefs. Do you believe in an afterlife?"

"I didn't. I never thought there was one...Although, if faced with Heaven and Hell and the judgement befalling, I might prefer to stay earthbound."

A silence grew while each rested on different thoughts.

What is it that causes Samuel to glance upon an object on the desk? As if he sees a bloodied quill. On second view, it is just a paper knife, unsoiled. He must have noticeably reacted.

"Mr Burton, are you okay?"

"...Yes...I'm sorry..."

He peers towards the artwork on the wall between the shadows and behind Mr Dawkins.

"You have fine pieces of art around the room."

The undertaker remains pensive, taking a sideways glance to look at a picture on the wall. "A collection spanning generations, you might say."

"Your business established over many years?"

"It has sustained, no doubt by our attention and delivery; we are held in the highest regard." Mr Dawkins broadly smiles, frightening and sinister.

Samuel thinks upon the casket.

"There's something..."

"In...good...time..." Mr Dawkins replies in that way a mesmerist spoke when inducing a subject.

To move things along, Samuel's next enquiry brings the outcome partly expected. For he feels that, at such time of asking, others are listening at the edge of their reality and waiting for a precise moment.

"You have new business competition in the town?"

It changes the mood: The shadows in the room become darker, and an atmosphere prevails.

Mr Dawkins stares hard before answering.

"True...There are others who claim to attend to the dead!"

Had he touched a nerve? Dawkins is fixing his eyes upon him in a way that probes his motives for asking.

"I'm sorry. I meant no offence by the question."

"We are, always will be, a long-serving establishment of the parish. Since you raise the matter, let me tell you something of our value as opposed to those who try to perform this role."

"I'm sure," replies Samuel. "I'm sure, just by your time in service. I can see you are an established and well-respected firm."

"Yes," comes the guarded reply.

There is something to Dawkins, and it can raise dread when aware and exchanging points of discussion.

"I thought I might have something to remember, but it has slipped my mind. It is strange. When you are not considering a matter, it lies within grasp. Yet the moment you try to remember, you cannot. How odd!"

Mr Dawkins does not react, his face stony, set hard and unemotional. He returns to a point.

"It is true. Rivals, who one could describe as envious, no doubt, consider us as birds of prey, on the scent for death, hovering like vultures ready to swoop and profit from grieving."

"Really! I had no idea the profession thinks in such ways."

"It is unfortunately true." Mr Dawkins reaches out to return to its proper place the letter knife he had nudged when explaining himself.

"We carry the highest respect to those we give and service. Their bills always paid at once, politely so, and never any suggestion of it being over what they can afford." Mr Dawkins reflects, thoughtful of times that were an age ago. He smiles that thin and dark grin. "I know of no one trying to drive a bargain at the edge of the grave."

Samuel feels exposed as if the point aimed at him.

Dawkins continues:

"Considerations of economy are the farthest thing from the mind of a grieving soul. When a heart deep as a well, burdened with sadness, take it as read, even if not spoken, provide what is fitting. All true and just, all you could need, be at your disposal. Surely thoughts of penny pinching are likely banished as out of place and disrespectful, not appropriate. I'd say somewhat vulgar to the memory of the departed." He stops and switches his sights to the coffin, bathed in a soft candlelight. "Consider, to a grieving and sorrowful patron of my respected establishment, that such material matters of pounds, shillings and pence are the most distant thought from their minds."

The darkness to his tone is revealing.

"Mr Booth and your good self have built up a reputation to live up to, by keeping your ways. Are suitable people coming forward to be apprentice? Death inevitable, wouldn't you want the business to continue?"

Dawkins seems to pick up on something, attention drawn to a point beyond the room, as if something requires his presence.

"Forgive me, please; I have digressed at this time of loss. Allow me a moment to attend to circumstances?"

Samuel, left alone, immediately becomes aware that the room is becoming darker. What little light there is, succumbing to a greater darkness, and Samuel caught, paralysed, as prey to unseen predators gathering en masse. Something is about to happen.

In the darkness, a floorboard creaks. Samuel is alerted, lifting his head. He is aware of the presence of a man. A fear takes a grip, that its face looking at him set grim, eyes full of determination born of anger. A fearful creature, chilling the flesh, and he unable to turn and confront it. But if he should, without turning to face it, it appeared in his mind. A spectral and grey entity with dead eyes, wild and staring.

"Samuel Burton...Samuel Burton...Look upon me..." The voice booming, commanding, not knowing if it speaks within his mind or fills the room with its frightening utterance. He froze on hearing the order. Fear never far a companion in the darkest recesses, stalling the mind of reason and the body of movement when casting its rigor. Samuel gripped by the throat as if a rope tightened. He knows the name, a Mr Booth, haunting his terrified thoughts.

Samuel senses that a nightmarish creature, stalking in the shadows of a dream; a dread is advancing closer. He can see him in strange, intangible ways. See him, Mr Booth, attired in garments that were decaying, not becoming of a man in profession. A spectral figure, sharing the room with him, risen from the grave. His fearsome expression, skin drawn and pale with the appearance of a chalky dusting. He raises his arm, pointing with a long gnarled finger towards the coffin. "Samuel Burton should now remember."

An evil gathering to encircle its prey.

The coffin, waiting and prepared. A casket to entomb him. One in which to bury him deep underground.

Mr Booth says nothing more, his face a terror to all who would dare to contemplate, as if another looked back through the eyes and again that bony finger gestures at the coffin...

Then darkness.

A grogginess.

Then, like breaking too quick out of a heavy slumber...

"Can you hear me? Sir! Can you hear me?" Mr Dawkins is calling for an answer.

Samuel slumps in the chair for a time before able to gain consciousness.

Dawkins sits opposite.

"I'm sorry...For an instant...I must have..." Samuel is declining the glass of water and quick to glance around the room.

"You were lost in the moment," points out Dawkins.

"I had the most terrible..."

Dawkins face solemn.

Samuel turns, facing the coffin bathed in a low light. The candlelight flickers and produces soft shadows that dance and sway on the underside. He searches beyond silently, questioning what had happened. There is no Mr Booth, no phantom, bemoaning its lot, trapped in limbo and seeking eternal rest. What is this place Samuel has come to, a place of wandering souls dispossessed and earthbound? It is minutes before he feels able to draw himself back to an earlier thought, still wary of what had occurred.

"Mr Dawkins...may I ask you a personal question? Are you afraid of dying?"

His face expressionless and anticipated the point before answering.

"It is the manner in which one dies, I suppose. I should not wish to suffer a painful death." His milky eyes switch to the coffin.

"Might I ask and return to my question, querying the afterlife?" Samuel enquires.

"As for death and what comes after, well, there are those sustained by a belief and faith in an afterlife. Can I bring evidence to dismiss such belief or can I prove it to them that there exists something beyond? I see to the physical remains when death pronounced." He is prepared to go further. "If I may speak frankly, I carry out the rituals of death, hoping the dead are ready for whatever happens next. I have faith in what I do but only that."

It is, without doubt, when you are not trying to think upon a matter that the issue flashes into your mind. Samuel remembers.

"Mr Dawkins, might we continue our conversation over by the coffin?"

The question sits with him a moment.

"Why, of course."

The two of them walk, standing head and foot at the coffin. To Mr Dawkins, Samuel has newfound confidence.

"I have to be here this evening. Take my part in the rituals of death."

Mr Dawkins remains quiet.

Between them is the coffin and beyond the room, darkness. A darkness that swallows as a void, so that no edge defines what form it embraces. If in the dark, are others waiting, then they hide.

Mr Booth's name draws attention whether if spoken in thought or said aloud, difficult to ascertain. Maybe one can imagine hearing a name called out when it remains in the imagination.

A floorboard creaks just the way it would when something walks over it, trying to pass by unseen and unnoticed. Someone is there and with familiar presence.

"Mr Dawkins, a confidence I should like to share."

His milky white eyes staring at Samuel, he is trying to force a memory and remember. Mr Dawkins draws upon a breath, saying nothing.

Samuel turns to look at the coffin.

"Been a long time to arrive at this moment. Sometimes you think you're mindful of going around in circles until something happens to make you realise that might be the case."

Mr Dawkins carefully studies Samuel's face, sure he knows of him but not able to place. "You have me at an advantage should I know you. I was expecting..."

"Expecting...waiting on a person or event that seems to take an age to arrive? Well, that moment is here, always been here. Actions lead to consequences. Maybe only one of us is allowed to remember."

"Who are you?" Dawkins asks.

"Someone once..."

Dawkins feels a chill uncommon for him. There is a silence, thinking time, Samuel studying him with an unblinking stare.

"Why don't the dead stop screaming, Mr Dawkins? Not like the living can hear them."

"I am not sure I understand to what you are referring...Why are you addressing me in such a way?"

"I'm here on behalf of a mutual friend. To settle a debt," Samuel mocks.

"What friend? What debt?"

"A friend that brings suffering; they bring sorrow..."

"Who's they?"

Samuel doesn't answer but continues to stare to a distant point.

"Come, come. Much of common knowledge, how you operated the business. There're those who'd said you'd give anything to get even." Samuel points out the gossip.

"I'm sorry?" Asked in puzzlement.

"I know things...what you've said outside these walls over Mr Booth. I'll not need others to tell me."

"Just tittle tickle tackle. Mr Booth!" Dawkins exclaims, close to temper and about to reveal more than appropriate to his client. A sudden anger gets the better.

"I'll tell you what you've not heard. It was common knowledge, all except for me, until too late! Destroyed what I'd built up over the years with that Halls and Son outfit. That's what they'd say if they knew! Robbing me! It was only...well...that ended it, death couldn't come quick enough!"

"Mr Dawkins, we shouldn't speak ill of the dead."

"The dead are dead! Life is for the living. I told you, I handle facts not romantic prose. When you're dead, you're dead!" Then he turns. "I know you, don't I? Something about you, familiar..."

"Please, Mr Dawkins, let's not raise a voice. Remember where we are, and afford a dignity to the dead. You know the rules. Not me who's forgotten, eh. Have you forgotten?"

Dawkins feels threatened and firmly instructs, "How dare you address me in my establishment with such a condescending manner? I shall ask you to leave!"

Mr Dawkins turns with a thought and the paper knife in his mind, quick to his desk. He surreptitiously palms the knife, turning back to face Samuel.

Samuel grabs the coffin lid and lifts it away, setting it against the chairs. He stands by the open casket.

Dawkins plots and maintains a dignity at Samuel's summons. His stately presence gliding, he stops short of being able to see into the open coffin.

"Come, what is there to be worried of? Study your workmanship." Samuel is taunting him, his hand gesturing over the subject within the coffin.

For the first time, the undertaker's manner registers apprehension as he moves nearer to the corpse.

"There, life after death. How can you dismiss what your own eyes see?"

Dawkins says nothing.

"I'll allow you a confidence. When you sold your soul with such an intentional remark, to profit by the death and rid yourself of Mr Booth, you did just that...Sold your soul!"

Samuel continues mockingly:

"You're dead, Mr Dawkins, as I am. Both ghosts haunting your abandoned funeral parlour. You never treated me right for what I accomplished for you, gave me to the gallows!" Samuel reveals the rope marks burnt into his neck.

"I made your coffins, Mr Dawkins, around the back there, surviving on a pittance and you never once setting sights on my face, never once seeing that hell hole! Neither of you cared. And I, grasping for a freedom, grasping as you for your profit. I, the one to rid you of Mr Booth to obtain favour! Doomed I was, except now!

"I'm here to settle, Mr Dawkins. On behalf of my new Master. Check in that coffin, made by these hands from your own wood in your yard. Take the pennies from your corpse because old age caught up with you, and you'll need them where you're going, to pay the ferryman on your voyage to Hell!"

***

The homeless man didn't care for his chances sleeping rough while this arctic blast of icy air pierced the night. He went around to the back of the abandoned funeral parlour, and the back door easily forced. He'd a lantern to allay some fear of the dark. There was a smell; he noticed it straight away; over-ripe smelt funny in here, old corruption. Fear found its way into his guts. He'd planned on sheltering overnight in the cellar than be taking a chance in the upstairs rooms. He weren't resting in them. It had taken courage to convince himself of entering in the first place.

The funeral parlour was dark; a shuttered-up, classic, haunted house appearance that loomed stately, guarded from intruders of the physical kind. "Sure is a creepy place," he'd murmured to himself when approaching. He hadn't to believe in ghosts.

There was a small door under the staircase, and opening it revealed the cellar steps. The house was icy cold, enough to see his quickening breath escape, but nevertheless a shelter from the openness of the street. The steps were stone, precarious and narrow cut. Throwing the lantern light ahead, he checked the way forward.

Slowly, he descended, noticing the long shadows play across the walls. He stopped on the stairs when seeing the open coffin lying on the stone-flagged floor. His heart beating faster, he noticed.

He moved on down to the ground floor. The ceiling was low above, and, scanning the cellar, he saw more coffins stacked. He'd a bag slung over his shoulder and dropped it in the casket on the floor as he passed. In another he found a pile of lining enough to make a blanket to keep the worst of the frost away.

The thought of sleeping in a coffin was not his first idea of choice, but other than that, the frozen stone floor no better than outside. He weren't going upstairs, not yet. His heart thudding heavily in his chest, he fumbled twice, shifting the coffin over to a bit of matting on the ground. He drew in breath, audibly wheezing at the exertion.

He'd set himself in as best he could, seeking the widest one he could find. Bulked up in his layers of clothes and a blanket covered with the musty smelling lining cloth, he'll sleep warm tonight at least.

He'd only given it a passing look, groundwork long abandoned over at the narrow end of the cellar. The stone broken and roughly patched up, one of the coffins lying over it. The lantern had caught some odd markings etched into the broken stones. He was tired so hadn't bothered checking them, sleep close and calling.

***

He'd awoken and in a panic. The cellar, pitch black. His whole body crawled into gooseflesh. He listened again. He was breathing in small, whistling gasps. He heard a murmuring then the sound of a floorboard creaking up above.

There were voices, enough proof he'd need to step sharp and prepare to scarper. He wouldn't risk lighting the lantern and ended up fumbling to gather his possessions together in the dark. He began to shake badly.

The cellar steps were hard to sneak up, and at the top, pressing his ear to the door, he waited and listened over his thumping heartbeat and wheezing breath. The voices sounded muffled.

He'd have to ease the door enough of a crack to see the way out was clear. He could hear the voices, both male. There was no light in the hallway and the place icy cold. He took a chance, looking out from the door, then to the other closed door across the way where he heard them talking. He had to take his chance now, step out and get clear of the place.

What possessed him to lend an ear to the closed door, listening into a conversation?

"Mr Booth and your good self have built up a reputation to live up to by keeping your ways. Are suitable people coming forward to be apprentice? Death inevitable, wouldn't you want the business to continue?"

There was a silence. The homeless man pulled away from the door and listened.

"Forgive me, please; I have digressed at this time of loss. Allow me a moment to attend to circumstances?"

He felt he was coming out; he slipped into the room next door and waited, holding his breath, hiding in the darkness. Giving enough time, he'd risk an escape. He heard voices from the room; fear had a grip of him. He moved, passing the room, horrified that the door opened and voices coming from inside. He'd to pass and not be seen. The murmuring from a room dark, without light, and for the moment, suggesting it empty. The homeless man was drawn by a curiosity without any sense. He faced what urged him with apprehension of the consequences; he stepped into the room. It was pitch black; instantly the voices stopped. The room abandoned, empty and silent but carrying an atmosphere that of ghostly presences. When a floorboard creaked just the way it would when something walks over it, trying to pass by unseen and unnoticed, the homeless man ran, shaking badly, getting clear of the place, never wanting to see it or return ever again.

***

But in this place of limbo, memory is short-lived, and all will continue to play their part over and over again, giving rise to rumours that the old, abandoned funeral parlour of Dawkins and Booth is haunted and continues to be throughout the years and that Hell already exists here and now.

The End

For more stories by The Ghostly World and further details, the following links are provided:

For more stories by The Ghostly World and further details, the following links are provided:

The Official Author's Website: http://www.jonathanharker.co.uk

Facebook: https://en-gb.facebook.com/theghostlyworld/

Youtube: https://www.youtube.com/user/theghostlyworld

Publisher: http://www.lulu.com/spotlight/theghostlyworld

Cover by Author.

The Catwalk

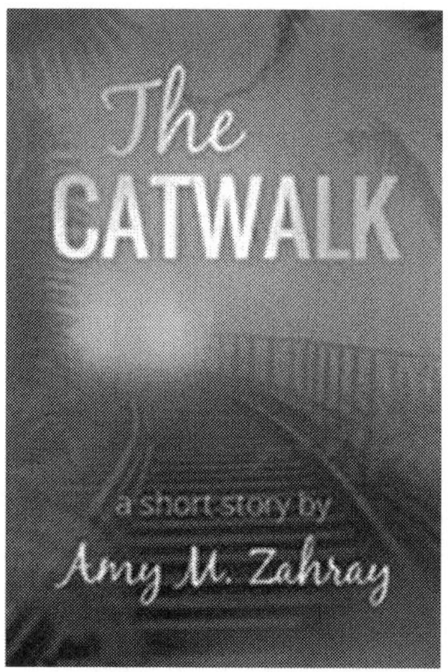

Amy M. Zahray

Zoey knew there were stories about the catwalk. Everyone had stories about it. Things like that—dark, old, abandoned things like that—collected stories. They collected ghosts like a child collects baseball cards. Everyone you talked to could tell you a different ghost story about the old train bridge. But the only stories Zoey knew to be true were the girls. The jumpers.

But what other stories about the catwalk were true? What really happens when you walk out on the bridge at night?

Maybe it's something Zoey would be better off not finding out.

Amy Zahray currently lives and works as a Naval Architect in Houston, TX. The short story "The Catwalk" was inspired by the wooded areas of New Jersey where she grew up.

***

Zoey checked her phone for the seventh time in the past fifteen minutes. This was the place Gia had said they were meeting. This was it.

She slipped her phone back into the not quite big enough pocket of her jean shorts, sighing heavily to herself. It was already 8:43. Gia had told her that they were all meeting here at 8:30.

Where were they?

She felt a mosquito bite at her ankle and swatted at it, flinching at the delicate but just slightly painful tickle. She knew her legs would be absolutely covered in itchy red splotches tomorrow morning and regretted not allowing her mother to coat her arms and legs in bug spray like she had when Zoey was little. "Turn around and cover your eyes!" her mom had always instructed. And Zoey would place both hands over her face and do a clumsy pirouette as her mother sprayed every surface of her skin and clothes with the chemical smell of summer—paying special attention to get the back of her neck under her ponytail.

Fireflies flickered and danced around the beach in the humid July evening, and Zoey could hear the bullfrogs croaking to each other on the lake in the last glimpses of twilight. Just past that, she could faintly make out the sounds of laughter and shouting echoing from across the lake.

It was the 4th of July, and everyone in town was out for the night. The popular spot to watch the fireworks from was on the other side of the lake—the side that wasn't completely covered in nearly impassible underbrush and vines. That was where families took their children and laid out picnic blankets and beach chairs and bought snow cones and ice cream sandwiches from the Ice Cream Truck and wore glow bracelets and necklaces.

But Zoey was too old for all of that now. Fifteen—a sophomore in high school. Way too old.

This side of the lake was where the high schoolers watched the show from—or at least the cool high schoolers. And Gia had invited *her* to join them this year—*Zoey*!

Zoey had told herself: "If they offer me a cigarette, I'll take it. If they offer me a beer, I'll take it. Even pot, even that. I'd try that." This was her chance. Her chance to finally get in with the cool kids. The cool kids...and Zack. (Their names even started with the same letter—Zack and Zoey, they were meant to be! She could sing it in her head. *Zack and Zoey, Zack and Zoey, Zack and Zoey*. Just thinking about him made her feel giddy! *Giddy!*)

Zoey had been so excited to get Gia's text inviting her to watch the show with them that she hadn't even really thought about it. Had she ever really heard from anyone other than Gia that *this* spot was where the cool kids came to watch the fireworks? Had she ever even heard of people going to "the other side of the lake" before Gia started texting her about it?

She couldn't remember.

She pushed her humidity-and-sweat-soaked hair out of her face and back behind her ears and checked her phone one more time. It was already 8:50. She had texted Gia at 8:40:

Where are you guys?

Still no response. She ground her teeth together, trying to fight back the tears she could feel welling up hot under her eyelids.

They weren't coming. They weren't coming. They had tricked her. How had she not seen this coming?

She should be on the other side of the lake right now—the other side with her mom and her dad and her little brother, Chris. She should be sitting on the picnic blanket with them and eating ice cream and letting the vanilla and chocolate swirl with rainbow sprinkles drip down her hands, laughing with her family.

But no—she had stood them up. Told her mom she was too old for that now. Too old for *family.* She could almost laugh at how silly she felt now. Stood them up for *this*? To be left alone on the buggy side of the lake for the Fourth of July fireworks show? And for what? *Gia?* And some stupid boy named *Zack?*

No. Not stupid. Zack wasn't stupid. He was...he was...*perfect*...He was probably making out with Gia behind some tree on the other side of the lake and making fun of how stupid Zoey was.

She hated Gia. She hated her. But she didn't hate Zack. She couldn't hate Zack. No matter what. No matter...

"Hey," a voice suddenly called from behind her, the sound of it almost getting lost in the heavy night air and the dull hum of mosquitoes.

Zoey swiveled around, startled, half expecting to see Zack standing there.

But it wasn't Zack. The boy who stood behind her was around her age, but she had never seen him before.

"Oh, hi," Zoey said, her voice shaking just a little from nerves.

"What are you doing down here?" The boy navigated his way through the thick undergrowth down towards the lake until he was right in front of her. He flashed her a smile, and she couldn't help but smile back. He was gorgeous—his bright blue eyes twinkling in the moonlight, the sharp angles of his face shadowing his cheeks in just the right way, the softness of his pale skin, the way his dark hair fell so gently over his forehead—everything.

Gorgeous.

"I-I was supposed to be meeting some friends down here," Zoey finally answered his question, stuttering slightly after a pause that was just a little too long. "But I got..."

"Stood up?" the boy finished the sentence for her. "I know the feeling." He smiled at her again, and Zoey thanked God it was dark enough out that he wouldn't see her blush. "What's your name?" he asked her.

"I'm Zoey."

"Zoey," he mused. She loved the way he said her name. No one had said it like that before. *Zoey.*

"I'm Nick," he finally said.

"Nick," Zoey repeated his name. "Where are you from? I don't think I've ever seen you at school before."

"I live one town over," Nick replied. "But my family comes down to the lake every year to see the fireworks show. They're on the other side over there." He gestured to the other side of the lake. "But I snuck off. I was supposed to meet my girlfriend here to watch the show, but I haven't been able to find her."

"Oh," Zoey said, suddenly feeling remarkably embarrassed about how much she had been lusting after him. He had a girlfriend. Of course he did. Fifteen-year-old boys who looked like him didn't not have a girlfriend. "I'm sorry," she apologized.

He shrugged. "It's fine," he said, grabbing on to a smooth, barkless tree branch and swinging on it a bit. "I'd only gone on one date with her anyway. I was kind of expecting she might do this."

"Oh" was all Zoey could manage to say.

"But hey, since we're both stood up tonight, maybe we could watch the show together."

"Sure," Zoey said distantly, unable to fathom the sudden sway in luck she'd just had. "Sure, yeah. That would be great."

He smiled at her, looking directly into her eyes. "Hey, hold still for a second," he said. Then, he reached to her face with his hand, and Zoey was near certain he was about to kiss her, and she was ready for it, practically puckering her lips. But he didn't kiss her. Instead, he just wiped his thumb gently under her eyelid.

"You had a little mosquito under your eye." He smiled at her. "Got it for you."

Zoey blushed again, embarrassed by what she had just been

thinking. It was just a mosquito, of course. Of course he hadn't been trying to kiss her. Of course. Things like that didn't happen to *Zoey.*

"Thank you," she nearly whispered.

"Come on," Nick said, placing his hand on her lower back and leading her toward the sandy bank of the lake. "I think the fireworks are about to start."

***

Halfway through the finale, Nick placed his arm around her shoulder, and after that, Zoey didn't hear any of the fireworks. The loud booming explosions were all drowned out by the hotness behind her ears and the light fluttering in her chest. She could feel herself beginning to sweat, slick and cool.

"Beautiful, don't you think?" Nick whispered to her when it was over. She could feel his warm breath against her face, ruffling her hair just a little.

"Hmm," Zoey mused, still lost in the moment.

"I bet you have to get back to your folks now," Nick sighed. "I know mine are probably looking for me by now."

Zoey didn't answer him. She didn't know what to say. She didn't want him to leave. She didn't want the moment to end.

"I wish we could stay out a bit longer," he continued. "It's such a nice evening."

"I don't have to go back just yet," Zoey replied.

Nick smiled at her and took her hand in his. "I like that," he said.

They sat quietly together for a minute or two, and then Nick spoke up again. "Have you ever heard the story of the catwalk bridge, Zoey?" he asked her.

"What?"

"The catwalk," Nick replied. "You know, the old abandoned train bridge running over the ravine."

"Oh, *Jumper's Bridge*?" Zoey asked, finally realizing what he was talking about. "Yeah, I've heard the stories. The ones about the girls. Every couple of years or so. *Jumping.*" It gave her the shivers just thinking about it. *Jumper's Bridge. The Suicide Spot.* Just the idea of jumping from the old, rotten train bridge gave her the creeps.

Jumping. Falling. What a way to go.

Nick nodded. "I've heard another story about it, though," he said.

Zoey shivered a little, and Nick pulled her in a bit closer to him. A bit of a chill was starting to blow in from the lake—cutting into the thick humidity left behind by the long summer day.

Zoey knew there were other stories about that bridge. Everyone had stories about it. Things like that—dark, old, abandoned things like that—collected stories. They collected ghosts like a child collects baseball cards. Everyone you talked to could tell you a different ghost story about the old train bridge. But the only stories she knew to be true were the girls. *The jumpers*. Those were the only ones she had seen in the papers. The only ones that were fact. The only ones that were true for *sure.*

"The story I've heard is an old story," the boy began. "It happened back before the bridge was closed, even. Back when the trains still ran on it."

Zoey watched him as he spoke, completely hypnotized by his voice.

"Back then, back in the 80s, the high schoolers used to play a game called *Catwalk*. How the game worked was, you waited in the shrubs beside the bridge for a train to go by. And then once it had passed, you would get on the catwalk and try to run across it before the next train came.

"Of course, there were usually at least fifteen or twenty minutes between trains, so you had plenty of time to get across. It was just a silly game. No one had ever gotten hurt before. But then one night, and I think it was the Fourth of July, actually..." He smiled at Zoey and winked as he said it, and she could tell he was trying to freak her out just a little. Just a little though— not too much—he was still trying to be flirty.

"It was the Fourth of July, and a boy and a girl went out to the train bridge to play Catwalk after watching the fireworks show. They waited for the train to cross the tracks like the kids always did, and then they went out onto the bridge, laughing and giggling to each other as they went. The boy thought the girl was beautiful, and he wanted to show off, so he ran ahead. And little did he know, she was attracted to him too, so she went chasing after him. They were halfway across the bridge when suddenly the boy's foot broke through an old, rotten board.

"He cried out, and the girl ran to him to help. They tried to get his foot out, but they just couldn't seem to get it to budge. His leg was stuck past his knee, and the old, splintered board had cut him up badly. The girl tried to help him, but they just couldn't get his leg out. And then in the distance, they heard the whistle of a train coming. Getting closer. *Toooghhhh Tooooogghhhh*!"

Nick mimicked the sound of a train whistle, and Zoey shivered as she watched him, wide-eyed, completely captured by the story.

"And the train got closer, but still the foot wouldn't budge. And when they could almost see the light of the train approaching from the distance, with tears in her eyes, the girl kissed the boy goodbye and ran across to the other side of the catwalk, leaving him behind as the train got closer and closer until..." Nick stopped talking and just held up one hand in the air. Then he made a fist with his other hand and slowly inched it towards the first hand—miming a train edging down the catwalk towards the boy.

Zoey covered her eyes as his fist met his hand, feeling silly for getting freaked out by just the gesture of it. But for some reason, the story had made her stomach do somersaults and sent goosebumps down every inch of her skin.

But then Nick put his arm around her shoulder again, and he kissed her on the cheek.

"It's just a story, Zoey," he calmed her, rubbing her back. "Just a story."

Zoey smiled at him shyly, wanting to kiss him back. Wanting to kiss him on the cheek. On the lips. *Wanting* him.

"Come on," he said, standing up. He gave Zoey his hand and helped her to her feet. "I want to take you somewhere."

***

"It's fine, see?"

Zoey watched as Nick bravely walked out onto the old bridge. Unafraid and so sure—standing up straight and walking like a gymnast on a balance beam down the old, rotten wooden boards.

"I can't!" Zoey called from about twenty feet behind him, crawling on all fours along the bridge and trying not to look down. Trying not to think about how far below them the bottom of the deep ravine really was. Trying not to notice that every time the wind blew, the bridge swayed and shook just a little, making a deep groaning noise like an old grandfather getting up from his easy chair.

"Stand up!" Nick shouted at her. "You'll be fine, Zoey! See look, it's easy!" He walked along the rusted metal rail back towards her, arms stretched to his sides for balance, only wobbling a little as he went—showing off.

The wind blew, and the bridge shifted and creaked, moaning loudly. Zoey shivered, and she could feel her stomach dropping. She couldn't be afraid though. She needed to impress Nick.

After a deep breath, Zoey finally pushed herself up from her hands and knees and slowly inched forward half a step at a time—still squatting down as she went, her hands right in front of her, ready to catch herself if she faltered.

"It'll be a lot easier if you just stand up!" Nick called to her, the wind carrying his voice away, creating a ghostly echo in the ravine.

Zoey took a deep breath and stood up straight, keeping her eyes pinched shut in fear.

"See, you're fine," Nick called to her. "Now just open your eyes and walk towards me!"

Hesitantly, Zoey opened one eye and then the other. She picked up her foot and took a step towards Nick.

"There you go!" He smiled at her. "You're doing it!"

A sudden gust of wind screamed through the ravine. Zoey faltered once, but then she regained her balance and began to slowly walk towards Nick, like a child taking her first steps.

"See, it's easy!" Nick exclaimed. "No different than walking on the ground!"

"Yeah, except for the fact that we're, like, one hundred feet up in the air!" Zoey exclaimed, trying to make herself sound confident. Trying to joke with him and have fun with it. But meanwhile the only thought that kept going through her head was: *Don't look down, don't look down, don't look down.*

She couldn't help herself and peaked over the edge of the bridge. She felt her head do a backflip and a sick feeling rise in her stomach. *One hundred feet up. One hundred feet up.*

One hundred feet down.

"Keep walking," Nick encouraged her on. "We've got to make it across."

He started to walk away from her, towards the far side of the bridge. Zoey tried to keep up with him, but her feet would only allow her to go so fast. "Wait up, Nick!" she called. "Why are you going so fast? Slow down!"

But Nick only just sped up more, and the wind carried Zoey's voice away from him. She wasn't sure if he was even able to hear her calling.

And then, caught in the wind, she thought she could hear something else.

"Nick!" she shouted as loud as she could, over the now nearly gusting wind. A storm was blowing in. A summer thunderstorm, it must have been. That could be the only explanation for how windy it had suddenly gotten.

"Nick!" Zoey yelled. "Is that a train whistle?! Do you hear that?"

But he couldn't hear her. He was too far along the bridge now. And as Zoey watched him go, still trying to keep up with him, she started to notice a warm burning sensation in her throat, and a deep feeling of unease settled in her stomach. There was something off about him. Something off, but she couldn't quite place it. Maybe it was his clothes. Maybe his hair. Maybe something in the way he spoke. Something just seemed...off.

And for some reason, she just couldn't seem to shake the feeling that she was watching an old movie.

"Nick!" she called one more time, one last attempt to get him to hear her and slow down and wait for her.

And then she heard the whistle again.

Toooghhhh Toooooghhhh!

It was much clearer this time. *Closer*. There was no way she could be imagining it.

It was getting closer.

Zoey turned to look behind her, half expecting to see a train light coming up the track, but there was nothing. Of course there was nothing. She was being silly. Trains didn't run on these tracks. The old bridge wasn't even connected into the system anymore. Trains *couldn't* run on these tracks. She must have just been hearing a whistle from a train at the station—carried in the wind somehow. She was just being silly. Being up on this bridge, the sudden gusts of wind. She was just freaked out a bit. That was all.

She turned back around to face forward, but something was wrong. Where was Nick? He hadn't been that far ahead of her, had he? But now...now he was...where?

He was gone! Had he already made it across the bridge? But there was no way he would have been able to get across that quickly. They had only been halfway across the bridge when he had...*disappeared.*

"Nick!" Zoey shouted into the wind.

But it was useless.

Nick was *gone.*

Suddenly, the train whistle came again, and this time it sounded like it was right behind her. Zoey flipped her head around to look behind herself, and this time she did see a light. A train light, trundling down the tracks toward the bridge!

Toooghhhh Toooooghhhh!

No! It couldn't be! It wasn't possible. Trains didn't run on these tracks. They couldn't. They couldn't. They...

Toooghhhh Toooooghhhh!

But there it was, an old steam train—tons and tons of metal and fuel and rage—barreling furiously towards the bridge.

"No," Zoey whispered in disbelief.

But there it was.

She broke into a run, sprinting down the tracks. Away from the light. Away from the whistle.

Away from the train.

It was *coming* for her.

The whole bridge started to shake beneath her as she ran, her feet slipping on the wet, rusty rails and damp, rotten boards as she went. She couldn't fall. She couldn't slip. She had to get across.

She took a fearful peak over her shoulder, and light blared in her eyes, blinding her.

She wasn't going to make it. The other side was still too far.

Toooghhhh Toooooghhhh!

The train was right behind her now; no tracks left between the two of them.

She couldn't outrun it.

It was too fast. It was too close. She could *feel* the heat radiating from the engine and sinking into her body.

"Oh, God," Zoey whispered to herself, taking one last deep breath of the hot July air.

And then she jumped.

The End

To connect with Amy, visit the following links:

Follow Amy on Wattpad:

https://www.wattpap.com/user/AmyMartinez

Cover by Karen Zahray.

Who I Am

Alicia J. Britton

Nick can't win. He has money, but someone wants it. He can't seem to outrun his mistakes...or his worst fears. He's falling in love, and someone is out to destroy it. To find her. Haunt her. To make her pay.

As a hacker, he came to her rescue. But there may be someone better than him out there... watching.

In a sick game of "Who Am I?", Nick is trapped and at the mercy of a computer screen and the "Freak of Nature" who's taunting him. He's forced to tell all, his only way to figure out who did what, if he ever hopes to see Kendal again...alive.

Though she despises snow, Alicia lives in upstate New York and wouldn't have it any other way. When she's not speeding around Suburbia in an SUV that's too large, coaching her kids through site words, long division, science projects, etc., and counting down her days of "freedom" before her family of five gets a puppy. She enjoys writing "high-stakes" romance stories. It's been a genre journey that began with her Fairy Tale series (Amazon/Fantasy) and has progressed through Teen Fiction, Horror/Dystopian, and

Mystery/Thriller (among others), most of which are available for free on Wattpad.

Her stories are known for their dark themes, lots of steam, strong characterization, and unapologetic rule-breaking. Since she loves movies almost as much as books, her dream is to have James McAvoy play Law in the movie version of her book The Fallow or Taylor Kitsch agree to the role of Christopher MacRae in Fairy Tale: Winter's Bite. But she would happily settle for Dylan O'Brien and Lily Collins in Songs of the Season (because that would be adorable).

< 1 >

The computer was my beacon of hope…until it wasn't.

Freak of Nature: You know what I want.

The screen provides enough light for me to realize how fucked I am.

I have a horrific upper leg wound, patched up by someone who clearly doesn't give a shit.

After limping around for a while, I came across a desk and rusty folding chair.

Never have I been more grateful for my tetanus shot.

There's a blocky screen on the desk and a keyboard. Both look like they are from the Computer Stone Age.

Weird. There are no wires attached, and all the code I've typed did absolutely nothing when I pressed enter. The cursor just continued blinking below my short back-and-forth with whoever is on the other end of this inexplicable connection.

Freak of Nature: Sorry, Nick. Your Jedi computer tricks won't work on THIS computer.

I slam my fist on the keyboard. It's the only weapon I know how to use, and it's useless to me.

Freak of Nature: Temper, temper!

Someone is watching me, but there are no cameras that I can see. Just white walls and a locked door that contains the room's only window. I can't make anything out behind the wires running through it.

> I'm not going to tell you my story.

Freak of Nature: Oh, c'mon, Nick. If you ever want to taste Kendal's sweet lips again, you better cough up the dirty details.

>I already offered you the money.

Freak of Nature: For YOUR life. Hers is another story. And that's what I want, Nicky Boy. Tell me how you did it. I'm in awe. Truly! How could a freak show like you could score with Miss Tight Ass?

>What do you want from me? I'm not a fucking romance novelist.

Freak of Nature: I want to know exactly what it feels like to be you. What a girl will do for a big bank account and even bigger cock. So...which did she prefer? Was it the tongue ring or the Prince Albert?

>You're a sick bastard.

Freak of Nature: Says the man who pierced his genitals.

>Fuck you.

Freak of Nature: Testy, testy! Ouch. I can understand why! But, you probably like the pain. She does too. A little, right? And, well, I'm a romantic at heart. So convince me that you and Kendal were made for each other, and I may refrain from letting Teeth Marks over here have his way with her.

>Don't touch her!

Freak of Nature: Well then, you have a job to do. And who knows? Maybe it'll help. Maybe you'll actually be able to figure it out.

>Figure what out?

Freak of Nature: Who I am.

>My father was your typical multi-millionaire asshole. Is that what you want to hear?

Freak of Nature: I'm not your fucking shrink, Nick. But whatever gets you through the day.

>Fine. It's as good of a place as any. Picture this. Napa, California. I was supposed to be the heir to a wine-country fortune. But when he said jump, I said go to hell. And once I was of age, he offered me a handsome chunk to get out of his life.

I took it and ran.

Running has always been a thing for me. I'm a snowboarder in the off-season. I was lucky to land my first System Analyst job in Park City, Utah, at SkyHigh. It *was* one of my favorite "up and coming" snowboard companies. But by day two of fixing printers and phones and setting up emails, I was bored out of my fucking mind.

I guess it's not so bad. I can do the job in my sleep, and I'm usually home by 4:30. It leaves plenty of time for leisure activities.

Freak of Nature: Drinking to excess, fucking around, hacking into other people's business.

>I was going to say marathon training, hiking, biking, and snowboarding. I do have legitimate hobbies.

Freak of Nature: Whatever. I don't want to know what marathons you run, Nick. Or DID run, I should say. I can't say that leg will ever be the same, eh?

So tell me more about the hacking. Did it lead you to Kendal and her little problem?

>For the record, I don't dig up dirt on everyone. I usually reserve it for people I don't like.

Freak of Nature: Like your boss.

>No comment.

Freak of Nature: Oh, c'mon, Nick. Dicky McBean is no friend of mine.

>Fine. He spends more on Oxy and kiddie porn a month than I do on gadgets and booze combined.

Freak of Nature: And that's saying something! And what about Damien?

>I told you, I don't snoop on friends.

Freak of Nature: Be honest, Nick.

>All right. He's a waste of space. I do his job and mine. But I don't complain because I usually have time to take a nap at 3:00 regardless. I didn't look him up because I never found him that interesting. And lately, I've kept my distance.

Freak of Nature: Out of guilt?

>Because of Kendal? No, not really. Because I know he never had a shot with her. Truth be told, she didn't give much of anyone a second glance. She kept to herself. Though she did surprisingly come to our last office Christmas party. Her little black dress was probably the least slutty in the room, but still, it gave us a glimpse of legs with nice muscle contour. I never took her to be the working-out type. Asking about the workout routine was an icebreaker I never had with her before. Thought I might as well go for it.

Just after I swallowed a much-needed shot of liquid courage, I turned around and she was gone. She bailed after one cookie and glass of cheap red wine.

Kendal didn't want attention. As hot as she was, she didn't abuse the privilege. Why make a fuss? Especially when she made it her goal to disappear in every room she's in.

After she left, the Christmas party was an opportunity for my eye to wander. It unfortunately landed on Rayna. By the way, she has a profile on every online dating site and pretty much never eats...or sleeps alone.

Unbeknownst to me at the time, we hit the town together after the party, danced, got sloppy drunk, and I got a blowjob out of it sometime after last call and before dawn in some piss alley. The details are fuzzy. All I know, it was rough on the piercing and mostly teeth.

Christmas Day turned out to be fucking godawful. Rayna whined until I broke down and bought her the diamond bracelet she had dropped hints for. Which, silly me, I apparently ignored.

That was the beginning of our rather tumultuous end. I knew all along it wasn't meant to be. Then I found out she was seeing other people the whole time. And she can't keep a damn secret. People from the company I barely knew would ask about every tattoo, every piercing, every "technique." And somehow, I'm the asshole!

Rayna couldn't stop at that, either. She often finds a way to park her piece-of-shit next to my new Xterra. When it comes to cars, I'm not that OCD or ostentatious. But for God's sake, new dents and scratches every time I leave it alone for a few hours?

Okay. Back to Kendal. After finding a cracked headlight, I was ready to swear off women for a while. First project of the day and I ran out of printer paper too. I popped into the copy room just as Rayna took the last pack.

Cunt.

Her spiked heels had me almost instinctively shielding my manhood, and her short pleather skirt reminded me to get a blood test. Not in the mood for her bullshit, I walked away unseen and took the back stairs to the basement.

Kendal was facing the spare copier, her back to me. As I was checking out her ass, it became clear to me that I couldn't write off women for very long and quickly concluded, before I was snagged, that it was the pants and not her ass that left much to be desired.

"Coming in behind you," I said, reaching for the paper over her head and almost smirking over how dirty that sounded.

Her blue eyes usually have this sparkle of innocence to them. But this time, I saw fear. Her phone shook right out of her hand. It hit the cement floor at a bad angle and of course, the screen shattered, making a bad morning worse...for us both, it seemed.

We both went for it and the ream of paper slipped out of my hand. It landed on her head, she went down, while I had her phone bobbling in my grip first.

"I'm really sorry. I know a guy..." I was going to offer to pay and give up my lunch break so that I could get it fixed and back to her by the end of the day. But behind the crack, there were a few too many words that caught my eye.

The Philadelphia Tribune...Out on Parole.

As I looked up, she snatched the phone out of my hand. "I got it. Don't worry about it."

Then she bolted out of the room like she was being chased.

When I got home that evening, I stared at my computer screen for a small forever. Kendal wasn't on my shit list. I'd be invading her privacy and breaking my rule. But...I couldn't let it go. It was such strange reading material for someone who lived seven states away.

So I began a large-scale excavation mission.

I knew from her work file that she was born in Maryland and was twenty-seven years old. Apparently, she moved around quite a bit. Her dad was in the army. I found a few old addresses but not all of them. So I didn't immediately find a Philadelphia connection.

Her computer didn't help me all that much. She didn't even have a Facebook or Instagram account. Barely did any internet searches. If she had any old friends, she wasn't curious. She had one douchey looking ex-fiancé, a David Wayland—the type of guy my dad would slap on the back and call "son"—but there was no hard evidence that it ever got freaky or violent. But she did move from Boston to Park City two years ago, not long after the breakup...

Her pictures told me a little more. The only man in her life since she moved here was a German Shepherd named Tecumseh, but she calls him Tuck. He's practically as big as she is. That's a lot of dog for a single girl in a small apartment.

It was the dog that helped me make an alarming connection. The victim was never mentioned by name in the article I read, but about ten years ago in Avondale, PA, there was an attempted abduction of a seventeen-year-old girl.

The ages lined up.

This girl was an honors student, a star athlete—track and field—and a neighborhood dog walker. Allegedly, she was jogging by a stretch of woods when Julian Miller, the troubled nephew of a neighbor, tried to pull her into the back of a minivan.

She somehow made it to the edge of the property of one of her clients. The German Shepherd they had plowed over the electric fence and tore into the guy. The injuries were life-threatening. But he survived, and thanks to his clean record, hotshot lawyer uncle, and claims that the girl had been "teasing" him for months (which I find very hard to believe), and because of a lack of eyewitnesses until after the dog attacked, Julian Miller got only ten years.

The dog wasn't nearly so lucky.

Ten short years despite the zip ties and duct tape, a shotgun, and a nice sized shovel.

Ten years that ended in April. What day was it then? March 27th.

I really had no idea. And every dirty or unkind thought I ever had about her, I regretted and atoned for it not in tears but in sweat. After pacing around, feeling like an asshole to the nth degree, I went for a long run.

On the way back to my condo, I picked up a gourmet dog biscuit at a local shop and found my way over to Kendal's place, hoping a good excuse for dropping by would come to me.

Tuck wasn't thrilled with me at first, but we came to a tentative truce thanks to firm commands, plus a treat and affection for being a "good boy," which, like all men, he loved hearing.

I was in a squat, rubbing his ears when Kendal noted, "He's not like that with most people."

He's a handsome dog, friendly and well-groomed, and had a collar that resembled a red bandana. It looked sharp against his dark coat.

"I have a down-to-earth aunt who has a farm in Napa. She breeds Bernese Mountain Dogs. I used to help out."

Not a lie.

"And you typically carry treats around when you go running? Do you have a dog?"

"No, but I knew you had one."

"That's not something I've ever mentioned to anyone...You *know*, don't you?"

"I'm sorry..." Snagged. What else could I say? "The way you were acting earlier. What I saw on your phone. I wanted to make sure you were okay. And you are, so...I'll leave you to it, then. I'll see you tomorrow, I guess. Holler if you ever need anything."

I turned to go, not expecting a reply or the change in tone. "Funny. Most men run in the *other* direction when they find out."

"I'm not most men," I said...and instantly wished I hadn't. It was my worst line yet!

"I'm actually glad you're here, Nick. Out of all the IT guys, you seem like you know what you're doing."

"Knowing who you're comparing me to, I'm not sure I should take that as a compliment."

Better. And I even said that one with a smile that made her cave into one as well.

"I bought this security system. And I have no idea how to set it up. Do you have a minute?"

"Um...yeah," I said a beat later, trying not to sound overeager. "I can take a look."

She opened her door a little wider and pulled Tuck to the side by the collar.

And just like that, I took my first step into her life.

< 3 >

Freak of Nature: Aw, that's sweet. The techie gets to be the hero for once. But what I want to know is when you started fucking her.

>It wasn't that first night if that's what you're thinking. Or anywhere close to it!

We became friendly associates—one step above where we were before that. I didn't finish what I needed to at a decent hour and offered to come back the next day, which she accepted.

By the end of the second night, I made her apartment—hopefully—safer than the Kremlin.

After I packed up and declined letting her pay for any of the extra gadgets I added, she offered me a glass of wine.

"You call this a Cabernet?"

I got a light smack on the arm for that.

The wine and moment of levity had me rambling out the abridged version of my sob story. It's nothing compared to hers, but still, it earned me a couple of sympathy points. Plus, another "date," and the next time, I brought the wine. And I spared no expense.

Since it was a warm night, I saw her in track shorts for the first time. "Do you still run?"

"I take Tuck out for short jogs, but he gets joint pain sometimes. So I mostly use my treadmill."

"You live in Park City, and you use a treadmill?"

As a proud resident and dedicated outdoorsman, I was honestly offended...until I saw her disheartened shrug.

Her attempted abduction happened while she was running alone outside.

"Let me guess. You 'know people,'" she mocked while I was attempting to find a way around her dilemma.

"Well, sure. Plenty of running groups around here. I know a girl—"

"Of course you do." The twinkle in her eyes brightened.

"Let me finish," I quipped back. "A friend of mine. A lesbian, for the record, has a runner's club for just women. But I have a better idea."

"Which is?"

"You go with me."

So we started running together. And somewhere in our getting-to-know-each-other phase, we worked in our first kiss. It was after a run, dinner, and another bottle of good wine. She made the first move—a kiss on the cheek and a genuine "Thank you" on my way out the door. I took a moment to kiss her back, a little tongue ring action, to let her know how I felt and to plant the notion further in mind. And it seemed to work. Her eyes lingered on my mouth. And she didn't quite make the smirk disappear before I had a chance to ask.

"What is it?"

"Nothing. I'll see you tomorrow?"

My jaw clenched. "Sure thing."

Spring became summer. As more and more clothing disappeared, it'd be an understatement to say I was chomping at the bit. But after all she'd been through—even the ex-fiancé WAS a douche, and it DID get scary when she broke it off—it wasn't as if I could push an agenda.

Then one warm Friday afternoon, we both left work early and took a road trip to Lake Blanche, a hiking site outside of Salt Lake City.

I'm not sure how it happened or why. But one minute, we stepped into the woods and I was on the ground, massaging the cramp in her leg. And the next minute, I was trailing my mouth below her sports bra and down her abs. The taste of salt, the scent of her, raw but still pleasing, like pure pheromones. Add in our mutual "runner's high," and soon her shorts were around her ankles.

Since there was absolutely no one around, I parted her cleft with my tongue and tugged the remnant of my post-adolescent rebellious phase lightly through her.

I don't want to brag or anything but had a feeling she'd call me the next day.

After some heavy petting on the ride back, I didn't shy away when she invited me inside and offered me a shower. The words were unspoken, but a couple minutes in, she joined me in there.

In her presence, I was humbled. Her skin was as smooth and unmarred as the day she was born. She's so different from me in that way, but there we were. Indulging on the unfamiliar...

As eager as I was, I didn't know where to start. But she had a system. As hard as it was to hold back, I gave her free rein.

She grazed her fingers over every tattoo. Mouthed each piercing. She absorbed the details, the flaws, the entirety of who I am with such delicacy and attention.

Then, in her bed, under sheets that smelled slightly tropical, like her hair, with a hint of vanilla that I could taste on her skin, we shed light on our last bodily mystery.

The only weirdness was when Kendal climbed on top and took control of the riding. As she was really getting into it, Tuck took that as a call of distress. He trotted into the room, and though he refrained from launching into full-attack mode—we had more respect for each other than that—he let out a grunt of disapproval when he collapsed on the floor next to us.

We made brief eye contact. The message was clear. *You hurt her, I break you.*

Duly noted. But, undeterred, Kendal climaxed; I rolled her onto her back and finished strong, reveling in every one of her aftershocks...and mine, so pronounced and excessive that they seemed to quiver and carry on to next Tuesday.

We fell asleep not more than a few minutes after I kissed her shoulder and told her how lucky I was to have her in my life.

In the weeks that followed, we were just sort of a normal couple. But what the hell do I know about "normal"? My relationships have always been mind-numbingly casual or intense and reckless. This one felt right, but because of our histories, I knew where it was heading. And I was scared shitless.

Freak of Nature: Is that all?

>Yes, that's all! I gave you every fucking detail of a story that probably isn't even all that interesting to a whack job like you!

Freak of Nature: That's not very nice, Nick.

>I'm sorry. I don't know what else to tell you. I love her. All right? And I'd like her back in one piece!

Freak of Nature: Funny you should mention that.

< 4 >

>What did you do to her? If you so much as harmed a single hair on her head, I'll—

Freak of Nature: Relax, Nick. You'll get your kiss soon enough.

>I'm not going to relax! Where is she? I gave you everything you asked for. Now let me see her!

Freak of Nature: All right. You win. But first, and this is important, you'll get one guess. Who am I?

>How should I know?

Freak of Nature: I'll even help you out. Am I Teeth Marks...toying with you? What about your perverted, drug-addicted boss? You always knew he was unstable. And he's onto you. He knows what you can do to him.

Moving on, am I your vengeful ex? You pretty much called her a filthy whore, am I right? And let's not forget Kendal's ex-fiancé. She moved across the country to avoid being his doormat...and punching bag. Then there's your jealous coworker. He's lazy as hell, but he can hack like the best of them. He's supposedly your "friend," but did you bother to notice?

Let's be honest, Nick. You have more enemies than you know what to do with. But surely you have some hunch.

>?????????????????????????????????????

Freak of Nature: Not to confuse you even more, but did you ever consider that your precious Kendal is manipulating you?

>No. That's not it!

Freak of Nature: She's got some debt, Nick, and this could be a play for the money. Or heck. Maybe this is all in your head.

I look down at the wound on my leg. For some reason, it doesn't hurt anymore.

Freak of Nature: Well, I'm getting bored with this, so...out of the goodness of my heart, I'll try to help you out, Nick. What's the last thing you remember?

>Kendal and I were out for a run.

Freak of Nature: And?

How did I get to where I am? It's all so hazy...nightmarish...

>The only tipoff that something was wrong was when we passed a neighbor's house. Its annoying-as-hell terrier usually barks at us like we're about to kill it. But this time, the silence was...eerie.

Kendal didn't seem to notice. And I tried to forget about it.

But couldn't.

When we got back to her place, the stench of death didn't shock me as much as it should have.

Kendal flew past me. I restrained her. Told her to RUN. But she wouldn't leave. She squirmed free. And burst through the bathroom door. Where Tuck was...

Dead. Strung up. Dripping.

And...there was a gunshot. My leg. I was hit. I searched for a face and saw?

Nothing...

I squeeze my eyes shut. It makes my current reality fade and the memory...or the *delusion*...filter in through the clutter.

>Wait! There was a car that stopped in front.

Freak of Nature: That's right, Nick. What else?

>It was one I recognized. Or thought I did. It was one of those unremarkable sedans that a lot of people have.

I was limping. No idea where Kendal was, but we needed help. I didn't care who was driving the car. It stopped, and I was getting in. But...

Freak of Nature: Now you're getting somewhere! Where did that someone take you?

>Here?

I stare at the screen. It's the first time the person on the other end doesn't immediately reply.

>Damien? Was it you? Did you do this???

The cursor blinks out more torment.

At the point I'm ready to bash the computer against the floor, an ominous knock squishes that rage to a flimsy gulp. An outline of a head appears in the door's window.

The person who enters has a man's build, a hooded sweatshirt, and a limp. He's carrying what looks like a dog bowl in his scarred hands. His face at a glance is, to put it kindly...he's the one-and-only Teeth Marks.

As he approaches the desk, I scoot my chair out of his way. The leg wound certainly punishes me for that. The pain's...blinding again.

He sets the bowl down.

While he hobbles away, I peer into it through watery eyes. "What the fuck is this?"

Teeth Marks stops mid-limp to face me. He brings a piece of grisly meat to his mouth. At first bite, blood squirts out and runs down his deformed chin. "Careful what you wish for..."

Next to the blinking cursor, words finally appear.

Freak of Nature: Enjoy your kiss goodbye.

What?

My uncooperative eyes bobble back toward the bowl. Muscle, fatty tissue, tufts of skin and hair. I pull one out. Long and blonde.

At the peak of the pile of gore, I focus in on two thin, strategically placed strips of flesh. Are they...lips?

Out of nowhere, a booming whisper slices into my ear and shoots through my soul.

Nice try.

< 5 >

I know that voice...

And I'm awake with a head-splitting jolt.

The nightmare was so real. Most of it was true. Fact and memory processing. Except the part where my worst fears played out in real flesh and blood.

Kendal rolls over and places her head and hand on my chest. "You okay?"

"Yeah, I think so," I lie.

She nods and falls back to sleep.

Meanwhile, I stare at the ceiling. Without even realizing I'm doing it at first, I drag a finger back and forth over the ring she has on her right hand. It's the only piece of jewelry she wears regularly—a simple silver band with a braid-like pattern.

The reason I bring this up? Someone's trying to extort me. One million dollars. I have a chunk of change saved up, but not *that* much. And if I don't cough it up by...today...there's a *you will pay dearly* hanging over my head.

It's impossible to skim through every minute of the surveillance footage and still have a life, but as far as I can tell, it's been clean. Last I checked, the biggest potential threats—Teeth Marks and Le Douche—are still on the East Coast where they belong.

Kendal and I may have people in our current lives who aren't our biggest fans. Maybe they'd be enemies if they knew we were together. But we've been careful, and we've never bumped into any mutual companions while out and about.

And, really, why should we have to keep it a secret? It's not like either of us were officially bound to other people at the time we started seeing each other.

I know a gold digger when I see one, too. My mother made me an expert, and so did my parents' pompous, boring, golf-course-and-dinner-party friends.

Kendal…she may have some debt. But her problems are a mere decimal point compared to what the *Freak of Nature* is demanding.

Despite the doubt that must be at the back of my mind somewhere, this can't be some massive ploy of hers to get at the money.

Right?

"What's the matter?" she asks when I try to sneak out from beneath her arm.

"I have to go back to my place." I grab my jeans from the floor and throw on my T-shirt. "Something's come up."

She tries to pull me back into bed by the waistband of my boxers. "We work at a snowboard company. And it's September."

"I know."

When I don't smile back at her, she releases me and her angelic face goes dark with dread. "So that must mean…?"

"It's probably nothing. But…just to be sure, I need my computer."

"Be careful," she says after a kiss goodbye.

And I get a flash of her lips from the grisly nightmare.

"You too. I mean it. Break routine today. Go in early. Or late. Whatever you do, though, let me know."

"I will."

And I know she means it.

On my way out, Tuck lifts his broad chest from his favorite spot on the couch.

"Keep an eye on her for me."

He cocks his head, and his gaze bores into me as I leave her apartment at what even he seems to know is an ungodly hour.

Once I'm home, I slink into the seat at my desk, slap some life into my face, and boot up.

First, I access the surveillance footage. Kendal went back to sleep, and Tuck is in the warm spot I left for him on the bed.

I crack a smile. *Jerk.*

Then I pull up the email that's been haunting my every sleeping and waking moment.

A crudely drawn cartoon figure of Teeth Marks appears. He bobs along and bites the head off the German Shepherd that wobbles onto the screen. Cartoon blood spurts out, and a matching red message fades in.

Three days. . .

The request, the threat, and an untraceable bank account number appear at the bottom.

After massaging my eyes, I chase down four Excedrin with a cup of black coffee. And I begin a search I should have done a long time ago.

>Damien Warner

< 6 >

I check my phone for the umpteenth time on my way into SkyHigh.

Kendal's car isn't in the lot. Her desk is empty. If she took my advice and was coming in late, she should have texted me by now.

I take my seat in the cube I share with Damien and stare at him...livid. It's just as infuriating that my tormentor is most likely *not* him.

His habits are completely textbook. He lives in his parents' basement. They don't ask him to pay a cent, so he has plenty of spending money...and not much to buy.

"What's with you?"

His question spurs me to my feet like I was cattle prodded or something.

"Nothing," I grumble on my way out, pulling out my phone.

No texts. No messages.

Kendal's cubicle? Still empty. Her laptop's closed.

Doing a poor job of masking my anxiety, I ask around the marketing department. No one has seen or heard from her.

Back at my desk, Damien's spot is empty. It gives me a chance to call her.

Goes to voicemail. I text her...again.

Glancing over my shoulder, I bring up the surveillance. Not something I typically do at work, but...

No Kendal and no Tuck, either. I find little comfort in the notion that she may be taking him for his morning walk. She'd undoubtedly have her phone with her if that were the case.

I look for signs of a struggle. Every room. Carefully...

"Kendal still not here?" I can hear the smirk in Damien's voice.

It launches me to feet...and over the edge. My forearm is against his throat in an instant.

"Where the hell is she?"

"How the fuck should I know? You're the one who's banging her!"

There's a resentful edge to his tone. That's to be expected. But is it...pathological?

"Who told you that?"

My arm retreats slightly. I let him breathe.

"Like there's anyone who doesn't know."

I jam the arm back against his throat.

"All right!" he sputters and I ease up. "It was Rayna!"

I stagger over to my desk. The blow brings about a chill and a hot flash. I collapse in my seat, the back of my hand to my mouth to sequester the gag.

I'm about a second away from calling my father. I doubt he'd give me the money even if it was to save *my* life. I'm dead to him already.

The squeak of Damien's chair is quieter than usual. "Anything I can do?" he mutters, reasonably sincere.

Got a quarter of a million dollars?

"No," I puff out.

Then, due to my resolve, my newfound hatred for someone else, and the morbid hunch I have, I find myself in a race to the parking garage.

My phone rings as I push open the door. I get a foul whiff of exhaust fumes...and my own fear.

I glance down. I don't recognize the number.

Should I answer it?

While I'm deciding, I catch a glimpse of my Xterra.

Every window is shattered. There's a crater on the hood. And like it was made for just that purpose, it contains...Tuck's red bandana and Kendal's silver ring.

My phone is still chiming. The shock compels me to answer it.

"Yeah?" I answer, turning around in a full circle.

"Time's up."

I hear the breathy, subtle static of an active line.

They—*she*—is waiting for my response.

< 7 >

"If you laid a finger on her…or that dog, I swear to God, I'll…"

Rayna struts over and ends the call with dramatic flair. "You'll what, Nick?"

"Kill you with my bare hands."

"Aw, you must *wuv* her." She pouts her blood red lips. "And yet for me, you wouldn't have killed a spider…even if I asked nicely."

I feel a presence sneak up behind me. The cold muzzle of a gun gets pressed into the back of my neck before I even have a chance to check who it is.

"Drop it," the dude gurgles, like he's foaming at the mouth.

I lift my hands and make sure the phone hits my foot on its way down.

The man circles in front of me, keeping the handgun aimed at my head.

Teeth Marks.

He kicks the phone out of reach. My eyes follow it to its new location.

His trigger finger gets twitchy at that error in judgement. "Don't even think about it."

He backs me between my SUV and the one next to me. I can't say I blame him. He's holding a gun at someone in Park City of all places and during business hours. And that dog way back when, who I'll call a *hero*, really did a number on his whole face.

With a flick of the gun downward, I sink to my knees, careful not to make any sudden movements.

He has the control, and yet his hands are shaking. He may be dangerous and unstable, but I don't get the sense he's the brains…or the nerve of this operation.

"Keep him there…and quiet," Rayna says dismissively. "I'll go get my car."

Her clicking heels gradually fade away.

"If Kendal's dead, you may as well just shoot me. Save yourself the trouble later."

The gun goes to my forehead. Wobbles, I should say.

He's almost all gone.

"With Kendal…every emotion reflects in her eyes. But Rayna? I don't think she's capable of *feeling*. Doesn't matter what she says. She just wants the money! The rest of us are expendable. You know it too, don't you?"

"Shut. Your. Mouth!"

"Man, I get it. I fell for her lies, too. You and I? Are we really all that different?"

His exhale is scathing.

"C'mon, Julian. Hear me out. Abusive, impossible to please father. And my mother, well…she didn't do anything illegal like yours did, but she had her vices."

He glances over his shoulder when a distant car engine comes to life.

"And man! The medicine cabinet on her! Her doctors made sure she never felt any pain…or remorse or empathy or…*love*."

Rayna's car pulls in front of us.

She opens the backseat door closest to us and clomps her way over.

"Well? Get him in the car!"

The gun is still pointed at me, but the fragments of his perception land on her.

"What are you waiting for? Don't tell me you now *like* the guy!"

His wild eyes return to me. His fist clenches around the gun…almost pressing that trigger. But it slackens with uncertainty again.

"This isn't the time for some stupid prison fantasy…"

I blink my eyes and nearly miss the *snap*.

Rayna must have crushed her stiletto on his last lucid nerve. Because the gun rounds on her. It fires.

I don't think he expected to hit her on the first shot. But he did. She goes down immediately. Bullet wound to the chest.

He's shaking. More than ever. She was his leader, maybe like both his parent and conquest, and his only way out of this mess.

When he whirls back toward me, I close my eyes, bracing myself for another shot. One with my name on it.

The bullet rattles me. It's so fucking loud. But I don't sense anything other than the rumble of collapse.

Julian "Teeth Marks" Miller took his own life…a bullet to the mouth.

I take a moment to subdue my own shakes. As much as I feel incapable, it's something I have to do.

I find my phone. 911. "There's been a murder-suicide..."

And I don't give a shit about "evidence." I dig through everything.

I come across another set of car keys. I run toward the sound of locks clicking open, experiencing an even mix of relief and dread.

Sliding the minivan door open, Tuck's tail starts wagging...sluggishly. Kendal is covered in duct tape, but her eyes flutter with tears and pure gratitude.

She clearly put up a fight—and lost—but it looks like she'll be okay. Tuck, however, struggles to get to his feet. He manages somehow, despite what appears to be a gunshot wound to the shoulder.

"Took one for the team," I say, stroking both of his ears. Then I help him lie back down. "It's all right. We'll get you help, buddy."

After climbing in, I peel Kendal free of her restraints. She doesn't say anything. And she doesn't have to. I just know.

She immediately buries herself in my arms.

About me, she never had any doubt. I was always the good guy in her eyes. Something I've never really been before.

And I have to admit...

There's no better feeling.

The End

For more information about Alicia's life and work, visit the following links:

Since her ideas are usually too vast to be confined within a "short" story, there is an EXTENDED VERSION of "Who I Am" (for Mature audiences only) available on Wattpad as well. It includes extended scenes, an extra chapter, visual media, and story casting: https://www.wattpad.com/story/117528679-who-I-am

Wattpad: https://wattpad.com/user/Fairy Fabler

Amazon/*Fairy Tale: Winter's Bite*
https://www. amazon.com/Fairy-Tale-Winters-Alicia-Britton-ebook/dp/B00L88NNFC

Facebook: Alicia Britton – Author

https://www. facebook.com/Cassiopeia4queen

Goodreads:
https://www.goodreads.com/author/show/8338870.Alicia Britton

Twitter: @alicia_britton

Admin for the @onemillionproject page on Wattpad and OMP SPOTLIGHT blogger/creator.

Cover by Author.

Writer's Block

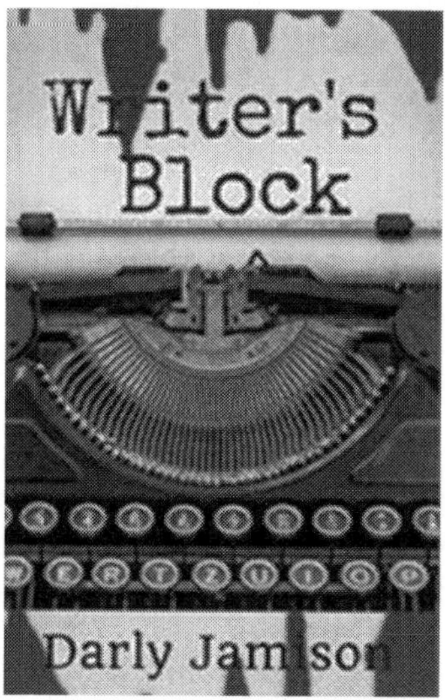

Darly Jamison

Darly Jamison is a Midwestern girl who lived as a Southern Belle in a previous life. She's an award-winning author of contemporary romance and was once fired from the library for continuously reading on the job.

When not writing, Darly can be found hanging out with her husband and children or trying to perfect her chocolate cheesecake recipe.

Darly's debut novel, *Strawberry Wine,* was released through Kensington Publishing January 31st, 2017. She would like to dedicate "Writer's Block," her short story for the OMP anthology, to her cousin, Jeff, who recently passed away after a long battle with cancer.

***

Matilda Bloom stood at the back door, admiring her new husband as he trimmed hydrangea shrubs in the yard. He wasn't overly tall, just about six feet, with wide shoulders and muscular arms that came from years of hard work. Somehow sensing her presence, Colin glanced up from the lavender blossoms and blew a quick kiss, his blacker than black hair curling around a perfect face.

A heated blush rose to her cheeks. Some found the newlyweds to be an odd pair. Matilda couldn't deny that her corpulent and homely appearance in comparison to Colin's sturdy and striking one did seem a bit mismatched, but every day he made her feel eminently beautiful, both inside and out. From the moment they'd met, he'd swept her off her feet and never shied away from declaring his adoration, using words like "alluring" and "soulmates" while in the company of others. If ever there were a man in love, it was Colin Bloom.

Her mother disagreed, as mothers often do. "You've only known each other for a few short months," she'd said when Matilda announced their engagement. "He's a complete stranger to you!"

"I know we're in love," Matilda stubbornly insisted. "Colin promised we're going to be married. He's going to buy us a house in the country where we can grow our own vegetables and raise a small family. Where we can play all day in the sun and relax by a roaring bonfire at night. We're going to be together forever. And *that*, Mother, is all that matters to me."

"Oh, *he's* going to buy you a house?" Mother snorted with disapproval. "I'll believe that when I see it."

Four weeks later, at her fiancé's urgent request — he couldn't stand to be apart from her another moment longer — they married at the courthouse, a quiet ceremony witnessed by her thin-lipped mother and Colin's only living relative, a sister just as physically dazzling as him. Neither guest seemed pleased.

Matilda studied her husband now, beads of sweat dotting his forehead, taut muscles moving effortlessly beneath a clinging black T-shirt, and a sudden shadow crossed her face. They'd been married exactly six weeks, and six times now she'd had the same dream. A nightmare, really. Colin lying dead on the bathroom floor, a long shard of glass protruding from his bloodied chest. More disturbing still was the severed reflection staring back from the walnut framed mirror—a satisfied sneer spread wide across her own face. Matilda shuddered at the memory. She decided it best to not mention the dreaded dreams, especially to Colin, but they bothered her more than she cared to admit.

Shaking off the unease, Matilda's gaze roamed, taking in the sumptuous green acreage and endless jewel-blue sky. It had always been her wish to own a secluded parcel of property, far-removed from the chaos of the only city she'd ever known. A turn of the century Colonial with a broad gambrel roof and a porch that stretched far along either side.

Once upon a time, she believed herself doomed to her mother's home forever, but when her manuscript sold to the highest bidder, her wildest fantasies came true. The advances alone were enough to secure a comfortable future, and sales from her psychological thriller were exploding. Rumors of a movie adaptation were even beginning to circulate. Unexpected, to say the least. But her sudden success paled in comparison to meeting Colin, the great love of her life. Of course, she'd never been in love before and therefore had nothing to compare it to. But she knew it was fate.

Since her current net worth far outweighed his, Colin suggested a prenup, much to her doubting mother's surprise. But Matilda declined. She trusted her future husband inexplicably. His offer was just one more way he'd proven his undying and selfless devotion.

The oven alarmed behind her, dragging Matilda from her thoughts. She rushed to remove the steaming hot contents: a deep-dish homemade chicken artichoke pizza. Lunch fit for a king, and one her hardworking husband would surely appreciate. She set the table quickly and called him in to eat.

"Good afternoon, my beauty," Colin greeted, using the pet name he'd so lovingly christened her with. No one had ever called her beautiful before. "The afternoon sunlight does wonders for your eyes. Have I ever mentioned that before? They're more magnificent than a thousand emeralds." He smoothed back a lock of mousy brown hair and planted a kiss on her broad cheek.

"I think you may have mentioned it yesterday." A girlish giggle escaped from her lips. "And every day before that."

"Well, I hope you've not grown tired of hearing it, because I plan to remind you every day of your life."

Matilda's stomach did a slow somersault. Colin Bloom was like a popsicle on the Fourth of July. He quenched a thirst she hadn't even realized she'd had. A deep desire burned inside of her to understand every last thing about him: what he was like as a child; the aspirations he'd had growing up. On many occasions, when she'd tried to acquire the details of his past, he'd always shied away. Some people just didn't prefer talking about themselves. But she hungered for more and knew just the person who would be able to answer her questions.

"What do you think about inviting Savannah over for dinner?" she asked as they settled into their seats. "I'd love to get to know your sister."

Colin paused and then took a healthy bite of his lunch. The melted white cheese stretched in long strands from the thick slice of pie to his mouth. "I don't think she'd be able to make it," he said between chews. "She's awfully busy."

"Too busy to visit her only relative?"

He swallowed his bite and leaned forward in his seat, his dark chocolate eyes twinkling as they collided with hers. "To be perfectly honest, my beauty, we're not very close."

"But you're her brother." Matilda winced. "How can she not want to see you? To see *us*? We're family."

A slow smile worked its way across his face. "There, there." Colin set down his pizza and cupped a calloused hand over hers. "If it means that much to you, I'll give her a call."

Matilda nursed a long, shaky breath. "I really think you should. She's your only sibling, after all. I can make a special dinner. Her favorite meal perhaps?"

"I'm sure she'd like that very much. I'll get in touch with her soon." His eyebrows raised. "Does that please you?"

"It pleases me very much. Thank you." She stared at him through her lashes. "Your family is my family now, too. And I want my sister-in-law to feel welcome in our home."

Colin held her gaze for just a moment longer before returning to his lunch.

***

The next morning, after her husband busied himself in the yard, Matilda sifted through a steep pile of laundry. Ever since Colin had begun numerous projects about the property, the hamper typically spilled over with clothing soiled from the efforts of his labor. She didn't mind the extra chores—she'd always fancied herself a homemaker—and now that she was caring for more than just herself, keeping busy around the house gave her a satisfying sense of purpose.

As she put away a stack of boxer shorts, a slender pine box at the bottom of the dresser drawer caught her eye. Fiddling with the latch, Matilda lifted the lid. Inside, a credit card-sized booklet stared back at her. She picked it up and flipped opened the cover. A passport issued to Colin only two months before glinted in the brilliant beams of afternoon sunlight. How odd. Her husband had told her once that he'd never left the country and, according to him, never intended to. The mere thought of boarding a plane made him queasy.

Why on earth would he need such a thing?

The troublesome words of her mother suddenly sliced through her. "You've only known each other a few short months," she'd warned. "He's a complete stranger to you!"

Matilda's teeth grazed her bottom lip. So what if they'd only known each other a short while? How well did a person ever really know another? Still, the teensiest shred of uncertainty nagged at her conscience. What else could Colin be hiding inside that wooden compartment? Her fingers fumbled quickly through a stack of irrelevant papers until they met a thin booklet lying at the bottom of the pile. **Moving to Mexico**, it read in bold white font. An image of palm trees swayed invitingly in the background.

Who was moving to Mexico? Certainly not them! They'd just spent a small fortune on their historic home in the country. Matilda lifted the book and a small slip of paper fluttered from between the pages and onto the floor.

In big bubbly letters, the single word *SOON* perched in the center of a carefully hand-drawn heart, along with that very day's date. Undeniably a female's writing. But what did it mean?

Matilda swallowed against the dryness of her throat. She went to the bedroom window and peered outside, placing a hand on the wall to steady herself. Two stories below, slaving away in the scorching summer sun, Colin glanced up and gave her a wave.

Watchful as ever. Just like a hawk.

Had he always been so vigilant? Unnerved, Matilda gestured back before turning away.

***

The unsettling note, Colin's passport and the book about Mexico plagued Matilda, all the while she finished the laundry and shopped for groceries in the next town over. If she told her husband what she'd found, he may accuse her of snooping. Which, of course, she had been—but purely by accident.

If only she could confide in her mother, maybe they could work through the possible explanations of why her husband might own such items. But that option wasn't feasible. Mother prided herself on being a good judge of character, and Matilda couldn't bear to hear another "I told you so." Bringing the matter to her circle of persnickety friends was also out of the question. They were already stunned Matilda had landed such a man, and the thought of them gloating behind her back—as jealous women often do—did not sit well. She'd just have to lay low and pay careful attention to Colin's behavior. Maybe that would give her a clue as to where his thoughts might lie.

When she finally arrived home after a long afternoon of errands, Colin met her at the front door, showered and well-coiffed.

"What's the occasion?" Matilda asked, handing over a bag of groceries.

"I'd like to take my beauty out for a nice dinner." He flashed an innocent smile. "Why don't you get showered up? I'll take care of the groceries."

Several moments later, Matilda stood in the master bath, a plush beige towel fastened tight around her considerable chest. She leaned against the gleaming white countertop and stared into the walnut framed mirror. Shame swelled in her throat. The only thing Colin Bloom was guilty of was trying to keep her happy. How could she have ever doubted the man she loved?

Squelching her remorse, she turned to the tub and stopped short. Funny. It was bone dry even though Colin had clearly cleaned himself up. Reaching down, she adjusted the knobs on the shower, careful to get the hot and cold temperatures just right. Without warning, a razor-sharp jolt threw her back. Matilda stumbled and fell bottom-first onto the tile.

She let out a mighty scream. "Colin!"

Rushing through the door, her husband stooped over top of her, a concerned expression fixed to his handsome face. "My beauty! Are you all right?" Carefully, he helped Matilda to her feet.

"I don't know. When I tried to turn on the water, I received a huge shock! It tossed me to the floor like a rag doll." Matilda held trembling hands before her, still tingly and numb. "What do you think it was?"

Colin scratched his head. "I'm not sure. Probably just a buildup of static electricity."

"But that's never happened before! And I've been showering for the past 34 years."

"Only not in this house," he firmly reminded her. "Sometimes older structures have unexplainable quirks." He brushed a wisp of dark hair from his forehead then tenderly cupped her chin in his hand. "Those eyes," he said smoothly. "They're more magnificent than a thousand emeralds." He parked a tender kiss on the very tip of her nose. "Why don't you shower in the guest bathroom tonight? I'll take a look at this tomorrow."

Matilda nodded and glanced back at the tub. Her husband cradled a protective arm around her waist and ushered her from the room.

***

Sitting across from one another at an upscale ocean-side restaurant, Matilda fought to focus on her husband's idle chatter, but the curious events of the afternoon had her whole self on edge. She sat rigid in her seat, forcing the occasional nod in response to the conversation. Not only were the items she'd found in the drawer reeling through her thoughts but now the peculiar accident in the master bath as well. Perhaps more bizarre still was Colin's cavalier reply. *"Probably just a buildup of static electricity,"* he'd offered nonchalantly. She'd been electrocuted by water, for goodness sake! Nothing nonchalant about that.

She expected more from him than that. After all, her husband was a former electrician by trade, having recently given up the profession after minimum coaxing from her. He should have offered her a more knowledgeable explanation. Watching him now, a wave of restlessness rolled through her. She fidgeted uncomfortably in her chair.

"Earth to Matilda," Colin teased, an amused smirk tugging the corner of his kissable lips. "Have you heard a word I've said?"

Matilda shook her head, shooing away the nagging thoughts. "I'm sorry, darling. I must have missed that last part."

Something flashed across his face, but in her preoccupied state, she couldn't make sense of it.

"I said, how's the next book coming?"

Matilda sucked in a breath then let it out slowly. "It's not," she replied honestly. That very question had been weighing heavily on her mind. She'd been racking her brain for months, but nothing new came to her. Not that she needed the money, but her publisher expected another bestseller. So did her fans. "Would you still love me if I was a one-hit wonder?"

"Of course I'd love you," Colin said without a breath of hesitation. "With the smart investments we've made, what you've earned so far would easily last us two lifetimes each. Imagine what our bank accounts will look like next year!"

She gave a distracted nod. There was only one bank account to speak of, recently put in both of their names. Matilda suspected her new husband had meager means before, but now that he had a fair amount of wealth to play around with, he proved to be a whiz with financial transactions and the stock market, a subject of interest he said he'd studied for fun.

"I'm sure you're right," she relented. "Still, I hope inspiration strikes soon. I do love to write, and my fingers absolutely ache to touch the keyboard again."

"And I'm certain they will. You'll just have to be patient." Colin rolled up his sleeves as the waiter delivered their meals. Puffs of steam rose from the crab legs and lobster tails and swirled high above their plates. "But rest assured, even if we'd met before your novel came out, I'd love you all the same." Colin glanced up at the waiter. "Matilda's my beauty. How could I not adore her?"

The server gave a polite nod then scurried off. As Colin forked a tender hunk of meat into his mouth, a drop of garlic butter dribbled down his chin and onto his white shirt. Matilda turned away, perturbed by the sight.

"Have you gotten a hold of Savannah yet?" she asked, pushing food around her plate with her fork. With all of the uncertainties that had recently arose, her appetite had evaded her, and the thought of getting to know Colin's sister felt more important than ever.

"Not yet, my beauty." Annoyance tinged his tone. "We only discussed the matter yesterday, and I believe I did mention, she's a very busy woman."

Matilda took a slow sip of ice water, barely noticing the cool liquid as it slid down her throat. She focused on keeping the edge from her voice. "I'm sorry, I'd just like to have her over as soon as possible. She's family, after all. And there's nothing more important than that." Questions about what she'd found earlier tempted her tongue. She bit them back.

Colin tilted his head. "Is something wrong?" he asked. "You're not acting yourself."

Matilda forced a smile. "I'm fine. Just anxious to get to know my sister-in-law."

"Patience is not simply the ability to wait—it's how we behave while we're waiting," Colin pompously announced through another forkful of food. "I heard that on television last week. A very wise proverb, don't you think?"

And curiosity killed the cat, she thought wryly. But didn't dare say it out loud.

***

The next afternoon, Matilda sat alone at her computer while Colin tended, as usual, to the many tasks around the yard. Hands hovering over the keyboard, she prayed inspiration might come. How was it that she could write a ninety-five-thousand-word manuscript and the sentences had flowed from her fingertips like drops of rain in a downpour? They'd come so quickly at times, she could barely keep up. And now—nothing.

What if she didn't have it in her? What if that one story was the only story she'd ever tell?

From somewhere in the distance, a familiar noise caught her attention. A text message, perhaps. But not from her phone. Hers sat right beside her. Matilda ignored it at first, but a moment later, it sounded again. And then again. Colin must have forgotten his cell, which was always tucked into his back pocket.

Standing from her chair, Matilda began to search. When the phone beeped again, she found it underneath an overstuffed pillow on the couch. *It must have slipped out from his jeans.* She pressed her finger to a button, and his phone illuminated. Four text messages appeared on the screen, each one from his sister.

Savannah: *Colin, are you there?*

Savannah: *Colin?*

Savannah: *Why aren't you answering me? We need to speak ASAP.*

Savannah: *It's about Costa Alegre.*

Had Colin finally gotten a hold of his sister? And if so, why did she want to talk to him about Costa Alegre? Wasn't that in Mexico?

The book hidden at the bottom of his dresser!

Perhaps Savannah was the one moving? But why hadn't Colin mentioned it before? Matilda wanted desperately to ask, only then she'd have to confess she'd been snooping through his box. And if there was one thing she knew about her husband, it was that he appreciated his privacy. Even if it were his sister moving away, that still didn't explain why he owned a passport. Shivers of apprehension crawled up her spine as she returned the phone to the couch.

A sudden noise sounded behind her. "You found my phone! I thought I'd lost it."

Colin reached for his cell and stuffed it into his back pocket, then gathered her in a tight embrace.

"Colin!" The scent of sweat and moistened earth offended her nose. "What are you doing?"

Matilda wiggled from his grasp and stepped back, her eyes widening. Her husband stood before her smothered in mud from head to toe.

"Just needed a little hug from my beauty." His lips tugged up playfully. "Is that all right with you?"

Matilda's mouth gaped open. What in the world had gotten into him? She looked down at her sundress, now smeared with black soil. "But now I need to shower."

His eyebrows shimmied suggestively. "Well then, why don't I join you?"

Despite herself, a wave of desire flooded through her. How was it he could have such an effect on her? Even now, with all of the strange questions that had surfaced. It was maddening.

"Why don't you hop in first?" he suggested. "Get it nice and steamy hot. I'll join you in a moment, just as soon as I slide out of these dirty clothes."

Matilda's eyes traveled over her husband's toned physique, and she felt herself weaken. "Don't be long," she told him. "I'm trying to write."

Colin leaned forward and brushed his lips to hers. "I promise not to keep you waiting." He gave her a slow kiss.

Anticipation spiraled low in her stomach. She wished she could fight it, but the innate need she had for her husband was no match. Colin Bloom was addictive—and he knew it.

"Let's shower in the guest bath," she said after their embrace. "I'm afraid to get another shock."

"Sorry, we can't." In one velvety motion, Colin pulled his shirt up and over his head. The muscles along his torso made her mouth water with longing. "I investigated the situation this morning. Something's off with the plumbing in the guest shower, not ours.

With the wires and whatnot. Look, it's difficult to explain, but an electrical current from there somehow transferred into ours. Some screwball set up from the previous owners, I suppose. I had to shut the water off in the guest bath for now, just until I can fix it." He flashed a pearly-white smile. "Don't worry, my beauty. We'll be fine. I'll meet you there in a few minutes, okay?"

Matilda's gaze dropped to the floor. Her husband had no reason to lie, but unease moved through her all the same. "You promise not to be long?"

Colin moved two fingers over his chest. "Cross my heart."

Matilda made her way upstairs, trying to rationalize her anxiety. Over the past twenty-four hours, there were numerous things not adding up. Yet her husband's behavior was just as charming as ever. Maybe she was just paranoid from worrying about her next novel? As she passed the guest bath, she had a strong urge to peek inside.

With a quick glance over her shoulder, she stepped closer to the shower. If Colin had turned off the water as he'd said, there should be no danger of receiving another shock. Her fingers inched forward until they were touching the knob and very carefully she gave it a twist.

Nothing.

She twisted further.

Still, nothing.

Colin had shut the water valve off, just as he'd promised.

***

Matilda paced in front of the tub, a towel fastened tight to her chest. What was taking her husband so long? If he was so sure the master shower would be fine, *he* could turn the knobs himself. She had no intention of getting shocked again. Once was more than enough. She peeked into the empty hall. Colin's hushed voice drifted up the stairs. Who in the world was he talking to? Matilda tiptoed closer, ducking when he moved past the stairs.

"You think I don't know that?" Colin hissed into his phone. "I dealt with this shit for almost twenty years. I'm pretty sure I have a better grasp of what's going on than you. The wires are hooked up to the plumbing in the shower, just like I said. It's foolproof. In another five minutes, she'll be halfway to the moon!"

Colin paused, listening to the person on the other end. He rolled his eyes.

"I'm telling you, Savannah, it'll work this time. I fixed it. The last shock wasn't strong enough. And if this one doesn't take that heifer down, nothing will. It'll be strong enough to break the bones of an elephant! By this time next week, wifey-poo will be six feet under, and I'll be on my way to Mexico—the grieving widower, escaping the pain of his loss. And a few weeks later, I'll send for you. Then we can get married on the beach, just like I promised."

Matilda leaned forward, disbelief clouding her eyes.

"We both agreed this was the best plan." Colin let out an exaggerated sigh. "Why are you so upset? I already told you, baby. While I lie in bed next to her every night, I'm only thinking of you. You're the one I'm in love with, Savannah. Not her. She's just a means to an end. Once Matilda's out of the picture and I have sole access to the bank account, we'll have it made for the rest of our lives. Do you understand that? Just hang in there for a few more weeks. We're almost in the clear. Then we can start making all of *our* dreams come true."

Matilda's lips parted. So the shock in the shower had been no accident after all? Colin had plans to kill her and run away with her money! He didn't love her; he loved her bank account.

And Savannah. She wasn't Colin's sister. She was his *lover*. The pieces were all falling into place.

Matilda's blood boiled over but only for a moment. A new thought embraced her. Her husband expected sparks to fly...literally. And if something didn't happen soon, he'd be upstairs to investigate. What would happen then? If he wanted her gone so badly, would he try to kill her himself?

"Matilda, my beauty? Is the shower ready yet?"

At the sound of his voice, Matilda's eyes shifted from the tub to the door. Colin stood staring, a shadow of confusion moving over his face.

"Why aren't you in the shower? I thought you were getting it ready for me."

She bit down on her lower lip. A metallic taste tickled her tongue. "I overheard you on the phone," she whispered, her gaze steady on his. "Savannah's not your sister. And you're not really in love with me. You want my money." Her gaze diverted back to the tub. "You're trying to electrocute me. That's what that shock was yesterday. Wasn't it?"

Colin laughed easily, never missing a beat. He stepped into the bathroom. "You have an excellent imagination. It's no wonder you're a world-famous writer." He cupped her chin in his hand, his mouth curling into a sexy half-smile. "Those eyes, they're more magnificent than a thousand emeralds."

Matilda jerked away. "Cut the crap, Colin. I said I heard you on the phone. You can't deny it."

Perplexed, his lips pursed. "Well, shoot. This didn't work out quite as I'd hoped. You're a smart cookie, Matilda. I'll give you that. Must be the mystery writer in you. You've foiled my evil plot twist!" Her husband took a step closer. "It may be too late for my original plan, but I'm still going to kill you. And then yes, I'll drain the bank account and run off with Savannah, my *real* beauty. Maybe to Mexico," he said thoughtfully. "Or perhaps Chile or New Zealand. We'll start over, just her and me. We'll sip piña coladas by the seashore and make love underneath the stars. Maybe we'll even have that baby you and I discussed—as if that was actually going to happen! I'm *so far* out of your league. Didn't you realize that?" Colin tipped his head back and let out a long laugh. "And when Savannah and I look around us, we'll have *you* to thank. So thank you, Matilda. In advance. I sure would hate knowing you went to your grave without understanding just how much I appreciate everything you've done."

Colin took a slow step forward. And then another.

Matilda swallowed hard against the drought devouring her throat.

"Now, don't make this difficult, my beauty," he mocked. "It can be easy; pleasant even. Did you know that just before a person passes out from strangulation they feel deeply euphoric? What a way to go. Right? Riding waves of delight? I can think of worse ways to die. But I certainly would hate to see you suffer. Especially after the hospitality you've shown. And after all, you *are* my loving wife."

Colin reached for her throat.

Using her considerable bulk, Matilda lunged forward, driving her shoulder into his chest. Colin slammed into the sink, his head smashing against the mirror. Shards of glass broke away and fell into the porcelain bowl. He rubbed the back of his head, stunned.

She needed to act quickly. If she didn't, she'd die. With an intake of breath, Matilda bolted toward the door slamming into Colin's leg as he blocked her path.

He launched himself forward, his hands grasping her shoulders. "You didn't think you'd get away that easily, did you? Aren't all authors supposed to know things can never be *simple* for the protagonist? There needs to be obstacles. The damsel in distress needs to be in the wrong place at the wrong time so the handsome hero can save her. But guess what?" He gave her a devilish grin. "There's no hero in this story."

Matilda shook her head. "You won't get away with this, Colin. The police will know what you've done."

Her husband chuckled. "By the time they find out, I'll be long gone. A good villain always has a backup plan. Didn't they teach you that in Creative Writing 101?"

Sneaky like a fox, Matilda slid a hand behind her, searching for a remnant from the mirror.

"They did." Her voice broke. "But they also taught us that a real hero always saves the day. And I plan to be my own hero."

Before he could respond, Matilda buried the shard of glass deep into his chest.

For a long moment, Colin stared at her, a grimace contorting his face. Finally, his gaze staggered downward in disbelief, his hand spreading around the crude impalement. A torrent of blood gushed between his fingers.

Colin's eyes met hers again before rolling upward. He stumbled back, first smashing into the door, then hitting the ceramic tile with a thud.

Matilda's stomach clenched as she took in the scene.

All this time, the man she thought she loved had been the devil in disguise. Charming yet deceitful as he and his lover plotted her demise. Matilda knelt down and fished the cell phone from his back pocket. With trembling fingers, she called for help.

"9-1-1," the operator said from the other end. "What is your emergency?"

Matilda sucked in a breath. "Please come quickly." Her voice sounded unusually calm. "I've just killed my husband."

Matilda's hand dropped to her side, and the phone clattered to the floor.

Fragments of the dream she'd been having suddenly flashed through her mind. Colin lying dead in the bathroom. A shard of glass protruding from his chest. Finally, it all made sense.

Relief flooded through her. If she hadn't lived through the ordeal herself, she never would have believed such a tale. This was the kind of thing you just couldn't make up. But it *had* happened, and it happened to her. She'd need therapy for sure. But on the other hand, she had a fantastic idea for her next novel. And this one promised to be far greater than the last. The publishing house would be thrilled!

Matilda's gaze fastened on Colin's dead body and the long shard of glass protruding from his bloodied chest. Then very slowly, her eyes rose, connecting with her severed reflection in the walnut-framed mirror.

And she smiled.

The End

Connect with Darly at the following links:

Amazon: https://www.amazon.com/dp/1420141643

Facebook: https://www.facebook.com/Darly-Jamison-author-384509295086507/
Twitter: https://twitter.com/darlyjamison

Website: https://darlyjamison.com/books/

Cover by T.E. Bradford.

The Girl with Her Face

Jenni Clarke

Jenni Clarke lives in the beautiful Jura Mountains of France, where the fresh air and peaceful surroundings inspire many stories. She has several nonfiction books published, both traditionally and self-published, and many fiction books in a variety of genres as works-in-progress.

Patricia is a recovering alcoholic who returns to the town where she had been a wife and, briefly, a mother. She seeks lost memories around the trauma of losing her child but, instead, sees a girl with her face. Strong emotions lead her to follow the girl, and she discovers more about her past than she expects.

Part One

'Hello. My name is Patricia, and I'm an alcoholic. It's been two years, seven months and four days since I last had a drink.'

'Hello, Patricia.' A chorus of voices welcomes her. Sweat gathers at her temples and the nape of her neck. She snaps a blue elastic band off her wrist, pulls her brittle hair into a rough ponytail, and twists the band as tight as she can. Un-trapped hairs stick to her face.

'Have you anything else you wish to share?'

Patricia shakes her head and stares at her legs, willing them to stay still. She frowns; it was a bad idea coming back to this town. She hears other people talking through the curtain of her thoughts, raising her head at a familiar name. The man's jaundiced eyes are swallowed by grey bags of skin; his fingers twitch. She doesn't remember him.

Patricia coughs to cover a snort of black humour. It would take a miracle to remember an old neighbour, or maybe he was a shopkeeper or postman. Her therapist said the memories of her brief marriage and briefer experience of being a mum could return if she stopped drinking. But after being dry for over two and a half years, she couldn't remember what her baby had looked like. She only saw the empty cot.

She waits for the prickling behind her eyes to change to a pressure in her nose, then rummages in her coat pocket for a tissue.

***

Leaving the community centre, she averts her eyes and hurries down the road, not stopping until the do-gooders are shadows behind her. The smears of light from the streetlights pull her through the town, further than her legs want to go.

She stops and sits on a bench near a play park. There are echoes of children's laughter in the gloom. She stumbles through the fog in her head. Did she sit here before? She turns her clenched hand over and opens it. Her palm bleeds, and there is red under her short nails. Memories hurt, and she has no alcohol to deaden the pain.

A bus trundles by, the number thirty-four. She knows that bus. Patricia stands and watches it slow at the traffic lights.

A memory flutters into her head. Once, she ran up this road, hand supporting her swelling belly, and the bus driver took pity on her smiling face. He opened the door although the lights had changed to green and cars behind beeped their rush-hour frustration.

She should smile at the happy memory, but her face doesn't remember how.

Placing one foot in front of the other, she walks past the grey, shuttered shops and a derelict pub. The flap on her shoe catches on the edge of a cracked paving slab, and her hands slap the red brick wall. Had these bricks watched her stumble before? Frustration lends her the strength to push her body upright and continue up the street to the hostel.

***

Patricia closes her eyes and pulls the thin sheet over her head to block out the harsh light filtering through the mismatched curtains. She pushes fingers into her ears, but the rhythm of the town taunts her: the revving of an engine, sirens in the distance, laughter walking past the hostel with a group of young voices—slurred, alcohol-lightened voices. Her stomach clenches, and she licks her dry lips.

Her dreams are fragmented: a man's firm hands guiding her, a hospital bed, tears and accusations, a baby's cry. She follows the baby's cry, walks on soft carpet and pushes open a door. There is a cot against the wall, a star mobile swaying above...an empty cot. A man's hands on her back. Falling...she is falling.

Patricia falls awake, the sheet twisted around her legs, trapping her, holding her down. Kicking it away, anger swells in her veins like a tidal wave; her breath is short and rapid. Fumbling for the brown paper bag on the bedside table, she holds it to her mouth and counts air in and out. Panic fading and her breathing slowing, she puts the bag down and grimaces. A new use for an old friend. Lying back down, she waits for her alarm to tell her to get up and get ready for work.

***

Streetlights flicker off as she leaves the office building. Like her, they had finished work for the day. A memory nudges her.

Hands pushing a pram, her footsteps loud in the quiet of early morning.

Her eyes widen, and she leans against a window for strength. It wasn't here, not this street.

Her therapist had told her not to chase the memories. To let them come. Breathe gently and be patient.

How long does she have to be patient? She scratches her arms, dry skin and scabs fall to the pavement, revealing a thin scar from her elbow to her wrist.

Patricia breathes and waits.

She remembers the ache in her calf muscles, pushing the pram up a hill, birds singing, a car going by, a drop of water on her arm.

She shakes her head, feeling weariness in her bones and the rain. It is raining today. It wasn't raining eighteen years ago. The alcohol-induced amnesia is fading but not the rain; it soaks into her clothes and splashes at her feet.

She peers through the steamed-up window. Other early morning workers release damp into the warm café. She opens the door; the coffee aroma entices her in. The café feels familiar. New owners, new décor. Not a memory but a knowing. Progress.

***

Nursing a coffee, she watches the crowd change. The weary workers are diluted and replaced. People in suits with clean hands, hurrying for morning doses of caffeine in takeaway cups. No time and no umbrellas. The rain has stopped.

A group of yawning students tumble into the café, bags slung over their shoulders. One of the students is wearing her face. Her heart beats double time, and she shivers. Is this a memory of her student days? She shakes her head. No. Here she was a wife and a mother, not a student.

Patricia stands and walks towards the group, willing the girl to turn her head, and she does. It was not a memory. The girl is real. Patricia gasps and bends over, pain slashes through her stomach. Her shaking arms grasp the edge of a table.

She lifts her head at a giggled whisper; the students move away. What do they see? A broken woman? A woman in pain? And yet they laugh. The girl with her face glances back, her lips curled in disgust.

Part Two

There is a pattern to her days. She works and then finds places to sit while broken memories skitter through her head and a gritty anger grows in her stomach.

She sits in the café, nursing her coffee. Every day for five days, the girl with her face buys drinks with her friends. Who is she? How is she possible? Patricia spits out her mouthful of coffee. She needs a stronger drink.

'Euh. Gross!' The girl with her face speaks with a nasally voice. Patricia shudders; she knows that voice. She gropes her way from the seat and staggers out into the street. Her thin scarf is whipped away by the bitter wind. She pulls her coat tight and crosses the road to stand in the shelter of a doorway.

The students leave the café and catch the number seventeen bus. An hour later, Patricia catches the same bus. It smells of smoke, but there are no smoking signs. When the bus passes the local college, Patricia stands, getting off at the next stop and walking back to the college entrance. She sits on a wall, waiting.

At four-fifteen, the girl with her face walks to the bus stop. She is texting someone. Patricia steps closer with hands fisted in her coat pockets. The girl lifts her head; Patricia walks past, counts ten shaking steps, and glances over her shoulder. The girl's eyes flick away, her fingers dance on the screen in her hand.

What is she telling her friends? The crazy drunk from the café is outside the college? How dare she judge. Patricia bites her tongue. The warm, salty taste eases her anger. She walks on.

The number thirty-four bus passes by. The face she wore as a teenager stares out from the back window.

***

On Saturday, her pattern changes. She doesn't walk to the café but catches the number thirty-four bus instead. It leaves the main town behind and takes her to where the cars are shiny and each house has a private drive.

Her heart thumps. She knows this part of town. This is where she pushed a pram. Down these leafy roads. She stands up and walks to the front of the bus. She alights and allows her feet to take her home.

The house looks the same, but there is a double garage, and a drive has replaced the small front garden and white fence.

She sniffs her fingers, remembering him wiping them with white spirit before he'd let her back in the house. She smiles, but it twists her face into a grimace. White spirit burns if you swallow it.

The trees, reclaiming the pavement, are larger than she recalls. Choosing one, she stands in its shadow, watching the house. The garage doors lift silently as a silver car turns off the road. A man with her husband's face stops the car in the safety of the garage. She grabs the tree, fingernails scraping the bark as her legs turn to dust. The garage door closes. It was not a memory. It was now.

Searing anger and shivering fear fight for control of her body.

A door slams, and the girl with her face—and his voice—shouts something about being back for tea, while her hands and eyes chat on her phone.

Patricia stares. A car pulls into the curb; music abuses the air as the girl opens the passenger door and climbs in.

'Can I help you?' A woman's voice startles Patricia. She flinches and steps out into the sunshine. The girl turns her head, and their eyes lock as the car drives away.

'Are you lost?' The woman steps closer.

Patricia looks up; she sees sympathy in the woman's eyes. 'No. I'm fine.' She walks away, straightening her posture, needing no one's pity.

***

'Hello. My name is Patricia, and I'm an alcoholic. It's been two years, seven months and eleven days since I last had a drink.'

'Thank you, Patricia. Do you want to share anything?'

She opens her mouth then closes it and shakes her head, leaving the meeting early and hurrying to catch the last bus to the better side of town.

Her chosen tree creates a deep pool of blackness in contrast to the light from a nearby lamppost. She looks at the house and watches the window on the left.

She remembers the dusty pink walls with a border of fairies. Her arm aches with the memory. He didn't like the border. There was a changing table. She smells the baby powder and sees the white tube of baby cream. Her fingers tingle at the softness of the tiny baby. But the cot is empty.

A movement at the window pulls her back from the past. The girl with her face is peering out into the darkness. Patricia steps into the puddle of light. The girl flinches and pulls the curtains together, shutting her out.

Patricia's shoulders shake; she cries out with the sudden pain of her cracked memories. As she staggers away, her cries soften to a kitten's mewl before fading into silence. Silence is better. Silence does not hurt.

As she walks back through the town, people and laughter spill from the pubs and clubs. She stops her limping progress and inhales the scent of forgetfulness. It takes a mountain's strength to drag her body past the welcoming doors. Two years, seven months and eleven days.

***

Dressed as a Sunday morning jogger in her hoodie, trainers and loose-fitting trousers, she leans on the tree. Her ex-husband walks out of the door. He is a mirror image of her, except his jogging clothes are new and his trainers do not flap like a gasping mouth, and he has a large dog on a lead. He stretches and jumps on the spot, while the dog yawns, before leaving the safety of his drive. When he sweats his way home an hour later, she crosses the road and stands in his way.

'What the—?' He tries to dodge past, but she steps in front.

'Hello, Simon.'

He freezes, wide-eyed, like a startled animal. 'Patricia?'

'Simon.'

His eyes darken. 'What are you doing here?' The dog sniffs her feet.

She stiffens. 'Remembering.'

He grabs her arm and pulls her away from the house. 'You can't be here. Go away.' He pushes her, and she stumbles into a wooden fence. He sneers in disgust, turns his back and walks away, pulling hard on the dog's lead. 'Drunken sot.'

'No. I'm not.' She rubs her arm; a memory shivers through her body, but the slamming of a door pushes it away.

***

There is a new pattern to her days, and memories elbow each other for space, none of them complete. A seething anger builds as she walks to the pleasant side of town, a takeaway coffee cup in her hand. Leaning against the tree, she gulps the lukewarm drink and watches Simon drive to work.

Patricia crushes the empty cup in her hands, drops it, and grinds it to a papery mush under her damp shoes. She walks across the road and up the drive to the quiet house.

The girl with her face opens the door with a smile before her face pales, and she tries to push the door shut, but Patricia is quicker. She kicks it with a strength born from anger, and the girl stumbles back against a table. She stifles a cry of pain. Patricia remembers the sound, and red hate flashes through her body.

The girl whimpers.

Patricia sighs. 'I won't hurt you. I want to see the house.' The girl is trembling, but her hand slips into her pocket. Patricia grabs the girl's arms, pinning them against her body. 'Give me your phone. I won't hurt you.' She releases the girl.

Tears in her eyes, the girl hands her a phone. Patricia slams it on the hall table, and the girl winces.

'Walk in front of me, and keep your hands where I can see them. Go to the kitchen first.'

The girl's steps are hesitant, her shoulders hunched. Patricia follows her. Her eyes skimming the room. Everything is different. Her shoes squeak on the tiled floor.

She gasps and stares down. A blurred memory of nails scraping the floor buzzes through her head.

'What do you want?' The girl stifles a sob.

'Memories.' Patricia points to the lounge. Photos of the girl growing up and Simon cover the walls, but there are none of a baby. Patricia bites her lip, and they walk the house in silence. It has been redecorated and refurnished, except the upstairs bathroom.

Patricia sees the memory of blood and smells vomit; she sways against the doorframe and gags.

The girl steps away, eyes wide. Patricia shakes her head and points to the bedrooms, leaving the baby's room for last. The bedrooms stir no thoughts or feelings.

Patricia stares at the two plaques on the door in front of her: *Samantha's Room* and *Knock before entering*.

The name echoes deep in her heart. 'Your name is Samantha?' Her voice a mere whisper.

The girl nods and opens the door. Patricia hesitates; her legs weaken. She leans on a wooden table outside the room. It wobbles and a painted pebble tumbles to the floor.

She picks it up, remembering the smell of salty water, the fresh wind in her hair, ice cream and laughter. A stark contrast to the life she knows now.

Her fingers curl around the comforting weight, and she steps into Samantha's room. Dusky pink has been replaced with a cool green. Posters and pictures cover two of the walls. There is a desk strewn with paper, pens and books. More books on shelving. A large wardrobe, its door open, revealing colourful clothes. A single bed with an open laptop and more books. A teenager's room.

An anger swells. 'Where is my baby?' Patricia steps towards Samantha.

Samantha backs into the wall. She cries out as her shoulder catches on the corner of a wood-framed photo.

Patricia steps closer, her lips twitch as she pulls back her arm, raising the pebble above her head.

'No. Please don't hurt me.' Samantha drops to a crouch, covering her face with her hands.

Patricia releases her anger and smashes the pebble into the framed photo. Glass rains down on the terrified teenager. The pebble thumps to the carpeted floor as Patricia pulls the baby photo from the broken frame.

She turns and closes her eyes.

Seeing the dusky pink walls and her baby's cot, she steps towards it and grunts as her shin hits a bedside cupboard.

The memory is shattered.

Patricia takes a breath, and the memory returns.

In the cot is a baby. Wisps of fine hair cover her perfect head. Her tiny eyes are closed, and she suckles on her thumb.

A door slams, and the memory is lost again. Patricia looks out the window and sees Samantha running across the street with her phone to her ear.

Patricia closes her eyes again, willing the memory to return, but an ache in her hand and sirens in the distance force her into reality. She runs from the house, clutching the crumpled photo in her fist.

Part Three

Patricia returns in the evening. Curtains twitch, and a patrol car prowls. Bedroom lights switch on. She leans against the tree, safe in its shadow, and picks at the plaster on her hand. It wasn't until she reached her room that she noticed the cut. She pats her pocket where the blood-stained photo nestles.

Patricia breathes in the cold night air, but the smouldering anger in her stomach keeps her warm. The front door opens. Simon stands in the light, his body a dark silhouette. The dog at his feet growls and stares through the darkness. Patricia sees the glint of its eyes.

Simon takes one step forward and looks across the street. 'You went too far, Patricia.' He pats the dog's head. 'But you were careless, and now he knows your smell.'

The hairs on her neck prickle as if she is the dog with hackles raised.

'Forgetting is healthier.' He clicks his fingers; the dog trembles, muscles bunching.

Patricia runs. His laughter chases her, but there is no mirth in the sound. Her breath catches in her throat. Her feet pound the pavement. She turns a corner, heading for busier roads. Her pulse thumps in her ears, too loud to hear her pursuer. Muscles tensing in anticipation of the first, tearing bite, she stumbles off the pavement. A horn blares, but she runs across the street, ignoring the screech of brakes, and heads for the light of an all-night café.

The door protests her violent entry. She slams it shut, leaning back against it, gasping. Stunned faces stare, then turn away. She blinks and stumbles to the counter.

'Coffee, milk, sugar.'

'Takeout?' The server doesn't meet her eyes.

'No.' Patricia uses the counter to keep upright. She aims for the furthest table from the door, but her legs stop supporting her body before she reaches it. Any seat will do. She rests her head on her shaking hands, and her breathing slows, only to increase in speed when someone stands beside her.

'Your coffee.'

Patricia takes the mug. 'Thanks.'

The server grunts in reply.

Patricia pulls the photo from her pocket and smooths the creases. A baby in its mother's arms. Is that a crease or a scar? She peers closer, wiping off the smears of blood and pushing up her sleeve to compare the thin line. Her neck prickles, and she glances at the window. Simon is staring at her, his face creased with anger. The dog is by his side. She stares back, and small black spots swirl in the air. He nods, a cruel smile growing; he waggles goodbye with his fingers, turns, walks past the door and down the street.

Patricia shivers as if ice cubes slide down her spine.

***

Her coffee is cold. The server wipes the table with a grey cloth and pries the mug from Patricia's fingers.

'There are plenty of homeless shelters.' She sighs. 'You can't stay here all night.'

Patricia frowns. 'I have a place to stay.'

The server shrugs and moves on to the next table.

Patricia gathers strands of courage and walks to the door, opening it with care and peering both ways. There are no men with dogs outside. She shrugs up her hood and walks, hesitating at every junction, stiffening when a dog barks. An off-license beckons.

One drink will stop the ache. One bottle will blur the pain.

She recognises these as Simon's words and dashes away from temptation and back to the hostel. Empty-handed.

***

The light in the hallway outside her room is broken; the glass crunches under her feet. She fumbles for the lock and forces the key in, looking over her shoulder at the shadowy corners and doors. Her cold fingers are as stiff as the key. She leans on the door, and it moves inwards. Frowning, she pushes the door open and reaches for the light switch. Light flickers on. The room is empty. She tugs the key but has to turn it to pull it out. Shaking her head, she slams the door behind her. Leaning against its flimsy protection, she rubs life back into her fingers.

Three steps from the door and she is in the kitchen. The dishcloth is on the floor, a spoon in the sink. Her stomach clenches. Paranoia. She flicks on the kettle, and the everyday action settles her anxiety until she opens the fridge to grab the milk. It's the wrong side of the juice bottle. Her hands tremble, and white drops spit onto the floor. She places the milk carton next to the kettle, and with a mounting fear, forces herself to open the bathroom door. It is empty. She whimpers with relief, adrenaline draining her body of its last speck of energy.

***

Patricia wraps her tingling fingers around the hot mug and allows the coffee aroma to seep into her soul. It was stupid to come here to remember. She sips the scalding drink, and her body relaxes. She sips more, enjoying a euphoric moment, a lifting of the darkness. Who needs alcohol? Who needs the past? She stares into the empty mug. More coffee would be good. She stands, but the room spins, and Patricia slumps to the floor.

She remembers Simon's voice: 'Special milk to help you with feeding her, special K. Drink it all. And take these.' His arms around her shoulders, coaxing her to drink, watching as she swallows vitamin pills. 'They will make you feel better. It's just the baby blues.'

Her eyes snap open. She drags her wavering body to the fridge and pulls open the door. On the shelf. Smeared in jam. A message: 'Goodbye.'

A floodgate opens and memories drown her. Depression, tears, pills, pain. She remembers shouting, throwing things, being hit.

She crouches, wraps her arms around her legs, and rocks.

It was all lies. Simon made her feel this way. Simon drugged her, abused her, and stole her memories.

Patricia crawls for miles and reaches the bathroom. She rams her fingers in her mouth. Vomit burns her throat, and tears pour from her body. Her hands slip on the edge of the toilet, and her knees hit the floor. It doesn't hurt.

It won't hurt until the morning, when she won't remember what happened. When she will believe his story and take more tonics and pills. No. She shakes her head, and the room spins; that was her past.

Another memory bursts in her brain. Simon leaving her at a clinic, telling someone she had turned to alcohol when their baby died, his voice cracking with tears.

She sobs. A baby, soft and innocent, changes into an eighteen-year-old with her face. Her baby never died. He lied.

Anger gives her the strength to pull herself up on the sink and turn the tap on full. She opens her mouth and gulps water until her stomach sloshes. Her fingers know what to do. Yellow bile splashes on the lino floor. Her stomach cramps, begging her to stop remembering.

She sees his smile through the café window, his waving, his message in the fridge. Had he meant for her to forget permanently?

Her mind clears. The lock on her front door. It was not stiff; it was broken. Fear crashes back through her in ever-increasing waves. She drags her leaden body to the kitchen, pulls a dining room chair by its scratched leg and wedges it under the handle.

Curling into a foetal position on the sofa, her lips remember how to smile. It is weak but will become stronger now she knows her baby is alive, and she is not to blame.

The End

Go to the following links to connect with Jenni:

Facebook: www.facebook.com/J-Clarke-Author-481692291932909/

Website: www.Jenniclarke.com

Cover Designer: Martin Clarke.

Cover Artist: Jeff Haines.

Website: http://www.jeffhsainesart.com

Psycho Dynamics

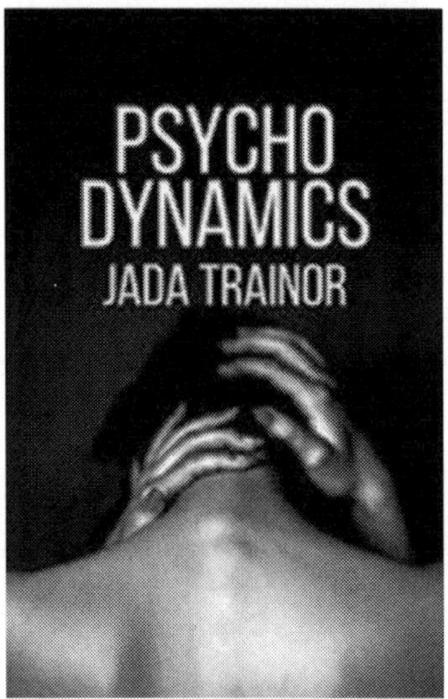

Jada Trainor

"Psycho Dynamics" is a story about a young woman who discovers that nothing is more dangerous than the power of one's own mind.

My name is Jada Trainor, but on Wattpad, I am better known as letmelivetonight. I am the very proud recipient of a Watty Award, and some of my works have also been featured on Wattpad. I enjoy genre-hopping, and "Psycho Dynamics" is my first venture into the Mystery/Thriller scene.

Part One

Melanie Rivera grabbed the ends of her wedding dress, rushing after the beautiful man who was very close to leaving her at the altar. "It was an accident! It had to be! I-I don't even remember what happened! Please!"

"Samantha's dress caught on *fire,* Mel! Fire! You knocked the candle off the table—that has to be some kinda sign!" But there must have been something in the way Melanie fell at his feet, in a puddle of Vera Wang, begging his forgiveness for the *accident.* Because it worked—Tom changed his mind about the wedding. Samantha was booted from the dress rehearsal, for her safety, and the following day the wedding proceeded as planned. Tom was never more handsome. Minus the funeral.

Not long after the newlyweds returned from their honeymoon in Ibiza, Samantha moved out of her brother's apartment as Melanie moved her belongings in. I remember helping Mel unpack her boxes, hearing Tom and Sam arguing on the other side.

"C'mon, Tom, you hardly know her!"

"I know that we love each other. That should be enough."

"If that was really enough, then maybe Mom and Dad would have been at the wedding."

"That's not fair, Sam. You know I've never seen eye-to-eye with Dad on anything. That's not Melanie's fault."

"Whatever, dude. I just hope she signed that prenup."

Of course, my best friend was crushed. Tom loved her, but his family didn't exactly share their enthusiasm for Melanie. Her parents were dead; she had no siblings, had fallen out of contact with all of her living relatives, and presented absolutely no savings to speak of. In the eyes of a tight-knit family running a very profitable business in the canned-food industry, either Melanie was a gold digger or luckier than she deserved.

Her friends told her it was useless: Melanie would achieve world peace before she ever changed their minds. But she was determined to try. Melanie spent hours on her wedding invitations, signing each one by hand, hoping the invited would see the card as an extension of her, the real her. The her who belonged with Tom and Tom's family—but the invite she sent to Tom's mother and father was returned with no forwarding address. And despite the huge stack of envelopes Tom watched Melanie lick and stamp, her side of the chapel was nearly empty at the wedding.

But it wasn't his family's reaction to his marriage nor the odd emptiness to his wife's vague background that troubled him the most. It was the fear that his friends and family were right. He didn't know his wife at all. He would gaze at her sometimes and see nothing more than a pretty picture: a beautiful girl smiling in a sundress, cutting tomatoes for their dinner as she mused over the weather and whether he had a chance to add her to his will. For the future sake of their children, of course.

"Don't you think it's a little soon? For kids, I mean?" Tom pecked her cheek as he passed, snagging a grape on his way to the cabinet. He wanted to drain the lettuce, but he never did it right.

Tom never seemed to notice when I came around. He ignored me. I pulled my little baggie of grapes closer, rolling my eyes at him for not ever considering my feelings. Or boundaries.

Melanie cleared her throat. "Having a family is incredibly important to me. I'd hate to be lonely when you're gone."

Tom froze. "What do you mean, '*when I'm gone*'?"

Melanie smiled, licking the tip of her knife. "Hon, at the rate you keep scarfing down these 'homemade burgers,' what do you *think* is gonna happen?"

Tom relaxed. Melanie giggled. He took a leap of faith and invited her to monthly Sunday dinner with his family. Sunday dinners were always perfect, and so was Melanie. She deserved her spot at the table.

Tom was so confident that night after their lovemaking, he didn't even care he'd been scratched to ribbons and pieces by the wild animal that became his wife. But the next morning, as he searched for the condom and found the waist bucket empty, he remembered the sting.

***

From what I can say about Sunday dinner, it went smoothly—up until Tom's father had a little too much wine and made some very crude remarks about Melanie's expenses. She had all this money to spend on herself and not so much as a W-2 to show for it. It was *insulting*. Who did Melanie think she was?

"I'm just saying, I paid a half-mill for a wedding *no one came to.* Not even me! Who the hell are you?" He slapped the dinner table, and two greyhounds took off, running from their pillows by the fire.

"Dad, you're being ridiculous!"

"No, Tom, it's fine." She sneezed, suffering through her allergies because Tom's family had staunchly refused to be one second from the dogs. "Your parents have every right to be upset. I should leave."

Only Tom objected, but Melanie knew better. She went home and erased the note I left in pink lipstick on the mirror.

Be a good girl, Melanie.

As always, I was there the next morning to help her through the process. She rose fresh as a daisy and served Tom the breakfast I made. I stayed out of his way. He was recovering from the most awful voicemail.

Tom pushed his plate away and hung his head. "How can I eat? They weren't just dogs, they were family. I can't believe Laa-Laa and Dipsy are dead."

Melanie pressed a hand to her heart. "Oh my goodness, that's *awful*, sweetheart. French toast?"

Part Two

Tom's family threw a wake in honor of Dipsy and Laa-Laa. Needless to say, I was not invited. When they returned home, Tom tossed his jacket in the closet, loosening his tie as he stormed down the hall.

Melanie had embarrassed him at the wake, laughing out loud in the middle of his father's pompous speech about—

"Wow, he is mad. At. You." I shook my head, pretending to jump in fright when he slammed the front door.

"Why are you here? *I didn't call you*, get out!"

"I came because you needed me, duh." I followed her into the kitchen, where she furiously tackled the dishes left behind from lunch. "What's his deal, anyway?"

"I *embarrassed* him at the wake." Bitter, Melanie scrubbed furiously at dishes that were better off soaking. "His father made that *ridiculous* speech about constructing statues for Dipsy and Laa-Laa—and I *laughed*!" She released the dishes, which clattered against the sink before disappearing in the soapy water. "We've only been married a month. I thought this relationship was going so well..."

"Babe, Tom's a total catch, but let's face it, his family is *never* going to accept you. At this point, all you can really do is cross your fingers and hope for the best."

"You're *toxic*."

"No, I'm a realist." I bumped Melanie out of the way to take over the dishes, jamming my hands in her bright yellow gloves. She sat down at the kitchen table, completely zoned out as I brainstormed. "You really do wanna fit in here, don't you?"

"It's a new town, a fresh start. I can try, can't I?"

"Uh-huh." I raised the plate I was drying, one eye cracked to measure the shine. "But Becky's already caught up with you how many times now? You can hide from Tom's family, but you can't run from her."

Running from Becky was never a good idea. In fact, it was damn near impossible. But, for whatever crazy reason, Melanie thought Tom was worth the risk.

"You don't deserve to be alone, Mel. Tom's not safe." I stacked one dish on the next. *"Now that you've dragged that poor man into our mess, things are getting ugly."* I glanced towards the kitchen doorway, lowering my voice to whisper. "*Becky don't play*. Which is why Laa-Laa and Dipsy had closed casket funerals."

"You're right." Melanie got to her feet with a sigh, pushing back her hair with both hands. "Maybe I should be honest, tell Tom what really happened."

"No!" I waved my rubber-gloved hands through the air like a mad woman. "If you do that then he'll make Becky leave, which means I'll get the boot too!"

"Well, you *are* a bad influence."

"I'm the best influence you got, sister. If you wanna keep Becky off our tail, ditch that beautiful idiot you married and empty his bank accounts so we can hit the road."

"I'm not. Leaving. Tom. I'm pregnant."

"You did *what*?" I sagged against the kitchen sink, legs buckling. Not only did babies ruin clothes, babies ruined figures.

"Oh, don't be so dramatic."

"Well, I guess it is *somewhat* reassuring. When you mentioned Tom's will the other day I was worried you might pull a Becky and…" I drew a slicing motion across my neck.

"I would never hurt Tom—"

"But—"

"Becky would, I know—I know." She sighed. "That's why the will is so important. It's for our family…" She touched her stomach. "I can handle Becky. She won't be a problem anymore, I promise. Thanks for always being here for me. You're the only one I can trust."

"Of course I am. Get some rest. I'll finish up the dishes."

Before I left the house that night, I left another message on the bathroom mirror for Melanie to find the next morning:

Woosah.

Some people don't know this but stress kills.

***

Melanie and I were beginning to sense a pattern with Becky. Like a shark chasing blood, Becky always seemed to show at Melanie's lowest moments, disaster following her like it had since we were all kids on the playground. I lost count of all the times Becky's bad behavior was blamed on Melanie. How many people Becky pushed away over the years, how many relationships Becky ruined. We lost count, and we didn't talk about it. Just to be safe, I kept an eye on the news.

But preparing for Becky is like preparing for a storm. There's only so much preparation you can do. The girl could strike anytime, anywhere—but the news about Melanie's baby placed a delay on the inevitable. Despite his earlier reservations, Tom was excited about the baby. Even Tom's parents were less glacial, sparing time to color their excuses colorful and sympathetic each week they dis-invited her to Sunday dinner.

Things were going well.

To show my grudging acceptance of Tom, I turned their guest bedroom into a nursery that Melanie, Tom, and I assembled together. Four months into her pregnancy and as the baby bump was growing, so was Melanie's hope that Becky had finally fallen from the face of the Earth. Melanie and I never said a word as we took turns peering through the curtains at night, searching out strangers in the lamplit darkness for fear of what lurked beyond our control.

Melanie was terrified, but still she kept silent. I think she worried if she caved and told Tom the truth, her nightmares about Becky would start coming true. Tom was struck by the change in Melanie. He didn't understand the mood swings and sullenness and made an appointment with a skillful O.B., who chalked it up to pregnancy hormones. Neither Tom nor Melanie could muster the energy to laugh at the O.B.'s joke about pregnancy and how it made women crazy. The doctor recommended sleep and lots of water, but confining Melanie to her bed only made things worse.

One day, she snuck out of the apartment while Tom was away at work, returning with a new mobile for the baby. She opened the nursery door, saw the wreckage of what used to be a sanctuary for her child, and knew at once that Becky had returned.

Part Three

After the nursery incident, Tom called the police. And since Melanie couldn't admit the truth about Becky, she let Tom believe the break-in really was a random home invasion. But within a few weeks, heat for the investigation died down. The only prints the police ever found belonged to people familiar to the apartment. So Tom took matters into his own hands. He bought a gun, showed Melanie how to use it, and gave her the combination to the safe. I reminded her we didn't need a gun. The house was full of knives.

But the more Becky threatened Melanie, the more unhappy Tom became. Maybe his parents were right about Melanie after all. Maybe they had rushed the marriage. They had certainly rushed the pregnancy. As Tom began to drift away, Becky drew ever closer.

Melanie came home to sinister voicemails from Becky, who's unestablished presence threatened to end her relationship with Tom at every given moment. One night, the two fought over the dwindling finances as I flicked through pages in *Vogue*, drowning out the arguments with my new Beats.

"I *told* you not to marry him. But you just had to settle down and ruin all our fun..." I rolled my eyes, feet propped on the couch as I strolled through the television channels.

"Oh, god! Why do I *listen* to you!" Melanie paced back and forth, her path sending her in and out of the way of the television. "This is partly your fault, y'know! What were you thinking, taking Tom's credit card?!"

"Hey, if you get a baby, I get a fur coat." I sat up, rubbing the lapels of my jacket as if they might grow ears and suddenly be insulted. I had seen it happen. "Don't play coy. You know what has to be done. You can keep the baby, but you can't have *him*. Becky won't let you. So sad." I inspected my manicured nails for blemishes as Melanie bit hers to the quick.

As evidence for my case, I picked up her phone and pressed play on the newest voicemail from Becky. By the end of the recording, Melanie was as pale as a ghost. I couldn't help but cackle at our poor misfortune. Becky had really nailed us this time.

Tom came home twenty minutes later with a manila envelope of newspaper clippings from obits in three different parts of the country. The men in these obits all left behind a grieving, nameless widow, they all had the same first name as each of Melanie's ex-boyfriends, and they all died the same way. They also looked a helluva lot like Tom. Tom wanted to know how this was possible, but Melanie couldn't explain it. So he did what any sane man would do. He asked for a divorce.

By midnight, he was dead.

***

The struggle didn't last long. They never did. When it was over, I took Melanie by the hand and led her to the couch. I used a tissue from the coffee table to blot her forehead, but that didn't begin to a put a dent in the mess. She was covered in Tom's blood head-to-toe. I draped my fur coat over her shoulders, taking my place beside my shuddering friend.

"You knew it would happen. It always happens." I rubbed her back in slow, soothing circles. "Tom's parents were wrong. Tom's the one who didn't belong."

Her eyes were red with tears and anguish. "He was different. He wasn't getting in the way—"

"They *always* get in the way. Becky understood that, but you didn't listen. You never do." I clucked my tongue between my teeth, exhaling as I rose. "Welp, better start packing. We gotta hit the road, toots."

Sirens wailed in the distance. I froze. *"What the hell?"* I sprang to the window, stomach curling as I peered through the blinds at the blue and red lights flashing in the distance.

"I figured it out." Melanie was standing, my fur coat on the floor at her feet. "Becky's not real. That's why I've never seen her. You made her up like I made you up. It's only ever been me and you, and you want it to stay that way."

I took a bow. The set changed, but the players never did. It really was the performance of a lifetime.

***

Dr. Welson sat back in her chair, the only person unperturbed by my story or the fact that the jury had decided a hospital was better than prison, despite the outrage of Tom's family.

I watched the dawn outside the window, brighter than all the colors in the hospital combined. I missed the fresh air. And my fur coat.

"Melanie—"

"Allison—" I sighed, flicking the ashes on my cigarette.

"I apologize. *Allison,* would you mind putting that out? For the sake of the baby?"

"My body, my choice, Doc." Regardless, I stubbed the cigarette, glancing at the bump in distaste. Two months and counting. Then

Tom's parents would come, and I would be rid of the very last memory of Melanie's betrayal. First Tom, then the baby. Never again.

"Please, help me understand. You said when Melanie takes over..."

"She has full control over my body. Yeah, it's horrible, Doc. Honestly, I don't know what she was thinking when she thought it was a good idea to kill my one true love."

Or call the police and turn us both in.

"Well, that's what we're here to find out." The doctor pressed the end button on her recorder and called for the security guards to lead me back to my cell, where Melanie was waiting. She sat on the edge of our cot, scuffing our government tennis shoes on the linoleum floor. The fur coat didn't look right on her at all.

Melanie hung her head in defeat. "So, when can I come out again?"

I flopped on the cot, plucking the *Vogue* from her hands. "It's simple, Melanie. You can come out again when you can be a good girl.

The End

Connect with Jada at the following links:

Wattpad: https://www.wattpad.com/user/letmelivetonight

Twitter: https://www.twitter.com/letmelivetonight

Cover by Author.

Candlelight Secrets

Ruby Julian

Editor's Introduction

Ruby Julian is a writer/photographer residing in the Lone Star state. Ruby began her writing journey in the 4th grade when, dissatisfied with the ending of a favorite book, she took it upon herself to compose a rewrite. She's been writing ever since. Through the past thirty years, she has had non-fiction and fiction pieces published in various magazines, newspapers and Christian resources. Ruby's interests include photography, spirituality, perusing thrift

There is a fantastic site for writers I discovered earlier in the year, full of talented and supportive people. It's called Write-On. Ruby is just one of many talented authors I have interacted with there and this particular story has its genesis in something called the Weekend Write-In Challenge.

Every weekend the site admin gives participating writers a prompt (such as 'Falsetto - In 500 words, imagine what happens when a character breaks out into song at a bad time.') and some wonderfully creative stories are produced. Ruby wrote a brilliant entry for the prompt Macabre Menagerie and to my delight created a second part for the prompt Meddle.

Hers is a unique, subtle and creepy entry to the horror/thriller genre with a brilliant twist ending that wouldn't be out of place as an episode or two of American Horror Story.

Write on Prompts: The Task.

Macabre Menagerie - With no word limit, tell a story that includes at least three of these elements: Witchcraft, face paint, candy corn, ducks, a candle, a mirror, chanting, dread.

Meddle - In 500 words, tell the tale of an unwanted interference.

Candlelight Secrets

"No! No!"

Her hand flew to the screen, as if that could do any good.

It was too late. Her message was Sending ... Sending ... Sending ... Your message has been sent!

Glad her email carrier was excited about it - she certainly wasn't. She would pay for her impulsiveness. There was nothing left to do now but wait.

Two minutes later, email alert beep.

Garrison Robinson has sent you a message.

Uh oh. Click.

Jessica, WTH? Why are you emailing me? I told you to NEVER contact me by email!

G xx

Her temples began to pound as an ache gripped her chest. The two kisses were the only thing that stopped her from throwing the laptop across the room.

Garrison, stop being so anal, you

(Backspace, reluctantly)

Garrison, I'm sorry. Let's just forget tonight. You seem to be in a grumpy

(Backspace)

Garrison, I'm sorry – I forgot. I just saw that funny link and wanted you to see it. I'm tired. Let's just forget about tonight.

Liar. She was so hungry for his arms, his lips, that she would have walked barefoot across broken glass to see him. She didn't sign off with anything. Nada. Not even an "x." She was so tired of his crap.

Less than a minute later, he responded, just like she knew he would.

Jessie, I'm sorry, babe. I want to see you. Tonight? Same time, same place?

Her heart was already halfway to their little isolated cabin in the woods. But things that irritated her in the beginning about Garrison had escalated, slightly dulling her passion. No, it wasn't his occasional bad breath or a tendency to get whiny when he was ill. It was the rather bizarre relationship he had with his teenage daughter, Danielle.

When they first started seeing one another, Garrison explained that after his wife died several years ago, Danielle would get hysterical if she saw him with another woman. And as a teenager, her behavior had only worsened. Therefore, Jessica was not allowed to call his home phone, visit him at home, or even email for some strange reason. Their only mode of communication was by cell phone – but no texting! She had been compliant with his requests until this morning. But she was growing weary of the stipulations - the secret meetings at the cabin, the fact that he would never spend an entire night with her, his refusal to email, text, etc. It was almost as if he didn't want any proof that their relationship even existed ...

However, by all accounts, Garrison was a well-respected member of the small town, seemingly devoting night and day to the care of his daughter after his wife's death. He also had a reputation for hosting the biggest, scariest haunted house each Halloween. Since she had just moved to town in August, she hadn't seen it herself, but she had heard it was terrifying, as well as realistic.

Her friends were convinced Garrison was a player, and the daughter story was just that - a story to keep Jessica away from his love nest. Jessica wondered if Garrison was just embarrassed about Danielle's appearance, which some gossiped as being rather grotesque in nature.

Jessica knew she was too trusting, too easily swayed by a handsome smile. They had met online. Once they met at her home, she ignored the warning bells when he instructed her to never call him on his home phone and always insisted they meet at her place, or the cabin. The more she thought about it, the more she began to fume. She'd had enough, and it was time to get some answers.

Of course, Garrison. Will see you later tonight. xo

She pushed "Send" and smiled.

She was going to break all his stupid rules and just show up at his door this afternoon. It was the week of Halloween – hopefully she would find him in a good mood, excited about the upcoming haunted house. People came from far and wide to attend. According to Garrison, the ticket sales helped support them financially, along with Danielle's disability checks and the inheritance left by his wife.

Finding his home address was not difficult, at least, not as difficult as finding the courage to turn down the dark, unlit gravel driveway and face his wrath for breaking his "rules." Shaking, she pushed the gas pedal and drove cautiously up the driveway, wondering if the tires crunching on gravel would alert him and spoil the surprise...

"Damn it!"

The car's headlights illuminated a heavy, single chain link running across the drive, elevated just enough to block a vehicle from accessing the rest of the driveway.

Flustered, she parked in the grass, stepped over the chain barrier and made her way to a dimly lit front porch. The two story home was old and unkempt – perfect for a haunted house. White paint peeled off the wood like a bad sunburn; the porch steps resembled a rickety accordion. With a deep breath, she pushed the doorbell, embarrassed to find herself trembling. What would he say?

The door moaned in protest as it opened slowly to reveal a young girl in a wheelchair. Before Jessica collected herself, a gasp slipped from her lips. Half of the girl's face was severely disfigured. One eye was shut tight, while the other rolled aimlessly in its socket. Half her nose was missing – both lips gathered in a permanent snarl. The roaming eye stopped and fixated on Jessica's head.

"You my new black hair friend? Yay! Daddy got Danni black hair friend!"

Jessica retreated a few steps as Danielle's crooked fingers stretched out for a fistful of Jessica's long hair. Black hair friend? What a strange thing to say ...

"Hi, Danielle. Is your Daddy home?" Surely to goodness he would not leave her alone.

"Daddy got Danni black hair friend!" the girl repeated with a smile full of missing teeth.

Jessica fought the alarms going off in her gut, squeezed past Danielle and walked into a shadow-filled, sparsely furnished room - no sign of Garrison. A giggle broke the silence. Jessica turned to see

Danielle staring in a nearby mirror, admiring the face looking back at her with a lopsided grin. Jessica froze when a hoarse female voice drifted like smoke from underneath a door a few feet away.

That bastard! He did have someone else, and apparently, she was good enough to be welcomed into his home! With clenched teeth, she quietly opened the door, pausing for a moment to let her eyes adjust to the darkness. What was waiting for her downstairs? Would she find him in bed with another woman?

A moan cut through the darkness. Shaking, Jessica reached out to grasp the handrail and continued to descend the stairs as violent fantasies of revenge consumed her. A gagging stench assaulted her– what was that smell? A few lanterns clung to wooden beams, and candles were scattered about the room, yet she could barely see two feet ahead of her.

"Help me! Help me!" a woman shrieked - other high-pitched voices soon joined her. The hair on Jessica's arms snapped to attention. What was going on? Peering through the darkness, she could see what appeared to be a jail cell. A yellowish, thin arm poked through the bars; its bony hand clawed at the concrete floor relentlessly. Jessica's eyes slowly adjusted to the lack of light. Her vision was still impaired, but it looked like there were three women behind the bars.

Ah ha! Jessica's face broke into an embarrassed, relieved grin. How could she have forgotten the Haunted House was opening tomorrow?

"Oh, sorry - didn't mean to disturb your practice. You're doing a great job! I about pooped in my pants!"

At the sound of her voice, all three women began begging for help. Jessica smiled approvingly as she noticed they were dressed like Barbie dolls, albeit bloody ones. This really was one creepy haunted house. One girl was a platinum blonde, another a fiery redhead, and the one moaning the loudest was brunette. Jessica fingered her raven-black hair. Daddy got Danni a black hair friend ... Ah, now it was making sense. Danielle must see these girls as her very own play dolls, and thought Jessica had arrived to play the "black-hair" girl in the collection.

"You girls are doing a great job, but seriously, save your voice for the performance."

"Get us out of here! HE'S GOING TO KILL US!"

Boy, they sure were dedicated to their performance. She hoped Garrison was paying them enough.

"Here, let me see if I can find the lights. I'd love to get a better look at your costumes before I leave."

It didn't take long for her exploring fingertips to come across a light switch on the nearest wall.

***

Oh God, no ... OH MY GOD!!! Jessica's mouth opened, but the bile clogging her throat silenced her scream. The women were lying in pools of urine, their lips painted as red as the blood splattered across various parts of their bodies. Rusty chains connected to ankle shackles ran haphazardly across the floor, embedded in the piles of feces dotting one side of the cell. A trickle of urine raced down Jessica's leg as she watched the blonde woman tear out clumps of her own hair, moaning repeatedly, "He loves me, he loves me not." The scene became even more bizarre when she noticed a white duck with 666 painted in red across its back pacing nervously, jerking its chained leg frantically. The scream in Jessica's gut finally made it to her voice box just as the women's mouths snapped shut in mousetrap fashion, their eyes widening in terror. What were they looking at?

"You stupid bitch, I told you not to come here," a familiar voice whispered, before something hit her head and everything went black.

***

Millie James and her husband Hilton timidly made their way down the stairs as Millie trembled with anticipation. This was her favorite part each year – the torture chamber in the basement. Millie didn't care for her standoffish neighbor, but she always looked forward to the Haunted House. Sure, it bothered her to see all the cars packed like sardines up and down the street, leaving tire ruts in manicured lawns as they came and went. The noise that came with the crowds was horrific too, keeping them awake well past midnight during the three-night performances. But Millie bit her tongue – she didn't want to do anything to upset that poor little girl.

"Millie, would you take a look at that! A painted duck – have you ever seen such a thing in all your days?" Hilton exclaimed. Millie knew he was just trying to pretend he wasn't looking at the half-naked girls screaming their heads off. That is, three of them. One, a black haired girl dressed like a gypsy Barbie, just rocked back and forth on the floor, laughing hysterically whenever her head hit the concrete wall.

Where in the world Garrison found these crazy actresses was beyond her. She took a long look at the duck and became spitting mad. Garrison had apparently forgotten she was President of the local PETA chapter. She was willing to overlook the traffic, the noise, and everything else that came along with living behind a haunted house the last few days of October. But abusing an animal for entertainment? The nerve of that man!

"We're leaving, Hilton. I'm reporting this to Animal Control the minute we get home! They'll have an officer over here first thing in the morning to investigate exactly what's going on in that basement. Putting chains on that poor duck – just who does Garrison think he is!"

"And you wonder why they call you "Meddlesome Millie?" Hilton muttered underneath his breath as he shuffled behind the angry rhythm of her footsteps marching home.

The End

Learn more about Ruby's other published works and her photography with the links below:

https://www.amazon.com/Ruby-Julian/e/B073RQ4LS1

http://rubyjulianphotography.zenfolio.com/

Cover by D.J. Meyers.

Forlorn

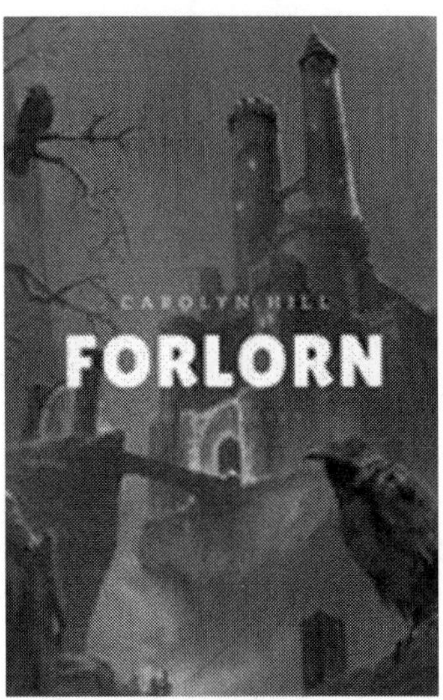

Carolyn Hill

The evil kingdom of Gatál conquered the peaceful kingdom of Halcía and has governed the land with an iron fist for almost two decades. Under their rule, Helena de Grazia and her Halcían family must serve the Gatál as part of the hardworking peasant class.

On her sixteenth birthday, Helena must choose which peasant occupation to follow. But her mundane life soon comes to an abrupt end when an unexpected summons arrives, changing her life forever.

***

My sixteenth birthday would stay with me like no other—it was the last day I'd see Mama and Papa alive.

Had I known what Fate had in store for me, I would have made every second count in those upcoming days before they met their demise. Instead, I wasted time whipping my wooden sword through the air and pretending to rescue political prisoners from our Gatál oppressors.

"Take that!" I shouted in a hushed whisper as I thrust my sword forward. "And this! Death to tyrants!"

At that, Mama knocked on the door, and I scurried to hide my fake weapon under my pillow.

"Are you decent?" she asked.

Ha! Never! I thought with a sly smile.

Grabbing my brush, I pretended to style my hair like a *lady*. Never mind that my dark auburn mane could never be tamed by a mere utensil made of boar bristles.

"Come in," I said as I attempted to still my breathing from my imaginary tussle.

The floorboards creaked as Mama walked into my room, dressed in traditional Halcían garb in preparation for her daily foraging. Her blue surcoat matched her sapphire eyes. She wore it every day she didn't face the public as a silent protest against the Gatál occupation.

"You're finally reaching the Age of Knowledge," Mama said with a broad smile. She tucked a stray strand of my hair behind my ear. "Are you ready for the big day?"

I nodded. "I hope the Gatál choose me for the Adventurers' Guild."

"Because you want to explore the world or because your friend Marlena has been chosen?"

"Both."

Mama gave me a pensive look as she sat down on my bed and patted the space beside her. I rolled my eyes and sat down heavily on the mattress.

"Please don't try to change my mind, Mama."

"They choose only a handful of people every year," she said. "I want what's best for you, but you should assume that you'll have to choose either your father's profession or mine."

"Okay, what *exactly* would you teach me?" I asked, tossing the brush with a callous flip as I furrowed my brow.

"I'd teach you how to scavenge for wildflowers and herbs and show you how to use them to concoct herbal remedies."

"Sounds boring," I said with a grunt.

"Maybe, but here's something I never told you before," she said with a twinkle in her eye. "I make potions and sell them to the Gatál directly. I'm one of the few Halcíans with that privilege."

"Really?"

She gestured at the fine wooden furniture in my room. "That's how we can afford all this. It's also how we can justify all of the restricted research equipment we have."

Mama lifted my chin with her index finger until her gaze fixed upon mine. "I can show you how to win the hearts and minds of men. I can teach you how to tame the inner beast of evil creatures and how to make potent warriors. I can show you how to give life and how to take it away."

I gaped at Mama with wonder. Never in my wildest dreams did I believe she could do all that.

"I don't get it. How can you do all that by walking around in the forest and picking stuff?"

"Things are not always what they seem."

"If I go with you, will I be able to hunt or fish with Papa, too?" I asked. "Can he teach me about his special inventions?"

Mama shook her head, and my heart sank. I'd wanted to learn Papa's science secrets ever since I was a little girl. Picking flowers seemed a poor replacement even if that meant learning how to make fancy potions.

My shoulders slumped a little. "Oh, Mama, I don't know."

"Toil in the fields if you will," she said. She tightened her grip around my shoulders. "You seem adamant on choosing your father's profession."

"I can still read at night just like you. The Gatál will never find out."

She smiled and eased her grip. "If you decide to change your mind, come and find me. Just remember that once you make your final decision, it'll be your profession for life."

I scoffed as I shrugged away from her touch. *You just don't think I can manage.*

"Enjoy your first day, my little hawk."

Mama chuckled with a knowing smile and gathered her ankle-length skirts. After she'd fetched her wicker basket, she strolled along the gravel path towards Papa with a happy hum.

"Andreas, my love," she said to him, "I'll be home before sunset."

Papa wiped the sweat from his brow and waved as he approached her. "Helena hasn't chosen *your* path?" he asked. "Wonders will never cease."

"No," Mama replied. "Not *yet*. She has until her birthday to change her mind. Remember, her Gatál assessment results still haven't arrived. We'll just have to wait and see."

"Go on, Aurora," he said with a chuckle as he kissed her. "Don't worry. She'll see reason soon enough. Helena's a bright child. After all, she takes after you."

Mama deepened the kiss, and Papa wrapped his hands in her strawberry-blonde hair. With a grimace, I turned away from the window and put on my leather boots in the foyer. "Enough already," I muttered under my breath. "I'm never getting married as long as I live."

A few moments later, I ran out to meet my father just as my mother disappeared into the thick green. Papa waved at me to come nearer, and his dark eyes twinkled when they saw me.

"There you are, my little dreamer," he said with a chuckle.

"Hi, Papa!"

The golden waves of grain rustled in the breeze as my father prepared his sickle for the autumn harvest. "You'll be helping me in the fields today gathering the harvested wheat."

My face fell. "What? Can't we spend time in your science lab instead?"

"Shh," Papa said, furrowing his brow. "That's a secret. You promised not to speak of it."

I rolled my eyes. "Who's going to hear?"

"You never know."

***

For hours we toiled under the morning sun, and the blistering rays burned my skin. I heaved bundle after bundle onto the cart, and sweat poured down my back and face. Papa gathered the golden grain into bunches that I tied up and threw onto a wooden cart.

"Where is this going after we're finished?" I asked.

"To the Gatál marketplace in the center of Halcía," he growled as he used the scythe to slice through the wheat. "They'll buy it from us for pennies and sell it for gold."

"Why can't we sell our own grain?" I asked as I heaved another bundle. "And cut out the middleman? Like Mama?"

"That's illegal, Helena," Papa replied. "They make a special exception for Mama because of her skills. But Halcían farmers live to serve the Gatál Crown. It's our duty—they rule over us now."

"This is so boring," I muttered. "When can we go hunting and do more exciting things?"

He chuckled and swept his thick, dark hair out of his eyes. "If you want to follow in my footsteps, there's more to farming than grand adventure."

"You're kidding?" I asked in a skeptical tone, scrunching up my face in disdain.

"No," he replied, "farming is fifty percent toil, forty-five percent patience, five percent adventure, and five percent knowledge and wisdom."

"But, Papa," I said, rolling my eyes, "that makes one hundred and five percent."

He gave me a wry smile and ruffled my hair. "You don't miss a thing, do you?"

"It's just that you always seemed so happy. I thought farming would be amazing."

Papa stopped scything grain and leaned against the wooden handle of his sickle. "When your back's against the wall, you do what's necessary to survive."

"But you hate the Gatál, Papa. How can you do their bidding so easily?"

He took a deep breath. "Perhaps one day when you have a family, you'll understand. If I didn't farm the land, they'd search our house and find the lab and your mother's potions."

My eyes widened. "You do it to protect us."

"I protest in silence, like your mother. Knowledge is power, Helena."

"So, I can follow in your footsteps—work my body and my mind."

"Of course," he replied with a shrug. "Just remember that you have other options, though. If you follow your mother, you can make something of yourself."

"Why do people always think that I can only do *her* work?" I asked, my voice terse. "Just give me a chance. Please? Show me how to use a bow or a dagger."

"Foraging and potion-making aren't women's work," he replied in a solemn tone as he reached out and touched the top of my head. "It's the work of a keen mind like yours."

I batted his hand away playfully. "Come on, Papa," I exclaimed. "You wouldn't be caught dead picking flowers—don't lie."

He chuckled. "I'd change places with your mother any day, but I don't have the skills." He shrugged. "Besides, I wouldn't do that to her—she loves her job too much."

"Well, someone has to tend the fields, and that's going to be me," I said with a defiant glare. "So, let's get this done so that we can get to the good stuff!"

"Yes, Your Ladyship," he said in a playful tone with a deep bow.

I raised an eyebrow at him, shook my head, and lifted heavy bundles of wheat with a grunt. He gave me a broad grin, and I laughed. Never would I be a lady, and we both knew it.

Just when I thought I'd lose my mind from boredom, the cruelty of life turned my world upside down. Fate would give me more adventure and excitement than anyone needed in a lifetime.

And not in a good way.

***

On the following day, horse hooves thundered along the gravel path towards our farm. I gazed up from my toil to see the village messenger deliver a scroll. When I squinted to get a closer look, I gasped.

He didn't carry just any document—the message was tied with a red ribbon. It was an official decree from the Gatál Crown.

My father wiped the sweat from his brow as he approached the messenger, took the scroll, and nodded his thanks. My mother stopped tending to the corn and raced up the road to meet them. When Papa handed her the document, she glanced at it and pointed towards me.

My heart raced, and my stomach sank as I dropped the bundle of grain in my arms. Good gods! What did the Gatál want?

If the Gatál issued a decree, it often resulted in punishment or death. Sweat beaded on my brow as I wracked my brain to think of any wrongdoing I could have committed.

Yesterday, things got a little heated between my best friend, Lena, and me. Our fight escalated until we almost dueled over whether she made an illegal move during a board game. Otherwise, I hadn't done anything wrong. Certainly nothing deserving of a summons.

Mama and Papa called me over to them. I tried to detect any sign of agitation or anger, but their voices seemed pleasant. Lowering my scythe, I took a deep breath and faced them.

"Yes?" I tried to sound innocent, but my voice came out as a squeak.

My parents raised their eyebrows. "Why do you look like the fox who stole the chickens, my little hawk?" Mama asked with a chuckle. She ruffled my hair and smiled.

With a sigh of relief, I relaxed. Mama would never joke if the decree meant something serious. She knew when to play and when to get down to business.

"No, I'm just surprised is all."

Then Papa broke into a grin. "You forgot, didn't you?" His laughter boomed across the field. "It's your results from the aptitude tests to determine whether you're best suited for your mother's profession or mine."

"Or the Guild," I said as a rush of adrenaline surged through me from head to toe.

My heart raced when I saw the letter that would determine my future. Even though I had very little chance of being chosen, I was dying to find out my results.

"Go ahead," Papa said with a smile as he handed over the document to me. "Open it."

Full of excitement, I took the parchment and slid off the red ribbon without untying it. *Please choose me! Please choose me!* With great care, I released the red wax seal with the official emblem of the Gatál monarchy.

When I saw the results, my face fell.

It didn't matter how many times my eyes scoured the page. The answer remained the same.

Name: Helena de Grazia

Status: Gatál noble

Suggested profession: to be determined

Please report to Castle Halcía at the sixteenth bell on Midweek, the 3rd of Fall to discuss your assignment.

I groaned and handed the document back to my parents. "They've put me in the wrong category. Look! I have to appear at the castle in three days' time."

"What?" Papa asked in an incredulous tone. He took one look at it and balked. "Good gods, this can't be right!"

"What is it, dear?" Mama asked as she glanced at the document. "Oh, my word! Andreas, I'm sure it's just a mistake."

Even though Mama didn't express her concern with words, I could tell. She shifted on her feet and pursed her lips. Papa ran a hand through his hair, his face turning bright red.

"Aurora, come with me," Papa said in a firm tone. "Helena, wash up and go to the study."

"But I have to finish—"

"No buts," he growled. "Aurora, follow me, please."

Both of my parents walked deep into the amber fields, which undulated in sweeping, rippling patterns. After I traipsed back towards the house, I turned around and saw my father gesticulating with wild motions, the wind swallowing up his words.

I'd never seen Papa so livid.

Papa probably couldn't bear the thought that I'd work for them. To be honest, neither could I. Even if it meant my family and I would have a better life, I could never torture innocent people who rejected Gatál rule.

Working for the Gatál didn't mean I'd support that kind of brutality, though. Gatál civil servants also taught in the schools, worked in the offices, sold goods at the official markets, and worked as engineers on civil projects. Why did Papa assume my work would be evil?

After several minutes, my mother returned to the study, and I lowered my book. She sat down next to me with a deep sigh.

"You are blessed with a great mind, Helena," she said. "Perhaps the Gatál have noticed your skill and made an exception in your case."

"Mama, I'm not that smart," I insisted. "And the law says Halcíans can't rise above peasant status unless they're chosen for the Adventurers' Guild."

"The Gatál ignore the laws when it suits them," she muttered in reply.

"Yeah, but never in *our* favor."

She forced a smile. "Think of this as a possibility to undermine the system from within its walls. You could even help free your people."

My parents thought I was destined for greatness. If only that were true...

I'd be lying if I said I hadn't imagined a life of freedom. Beholden to no one, not even the Gatál, Lena and I could fight as independent women in the Adventurers' Guild.

However, I knew it was merely a fantasy to make me feel better about scything grain or picking berries. Nothing more. Tomorrow I'd turn sixteen, and I had to journey to the so-called "Castle of Screams" where a group of Gatál nobles would discuss my fate. They'd force me to pick a side.

I shivered at the thought.

"Mama, we need to focus on reality. You have to admit that the summons makes no sense."

"Be that as it may, perhaps you should take advantage of this opportunity. The Gatál can take on any profession they choose."

"I'm a Halcían peasant," I said, holding up the summons. "They made a mistake here. If I played along, I'd be living a lie."

My mother stared at her hands in silence.

"You both raised me to believe in truth and science," I said with a scoff.

"They have selected you, my little hawk, no matter what race you are." She gave my hand a reassuring squeeze. "You deserve more than a peasant's life. I know you will fight for justice no matter what profession you choose."

I nodded and tried to ignore my unease.

Later that evening, I knew something was wrong when my parents hardly spoke as they prepared and ate dinner. Papa and Mama always talked about local politics around the table. They avoided my gaze and shifted in their seats whenever I mentioned the results.

"Just eat your supper, and we'll discuss it later," Papa said in a terse voice.

After dinner, Papa descended into his private lab and Mama retreated to her study. One thing I knew for certain: My parents wouldn't have reacted that way if the Gatál had made a simple mistake.

***

When I woke the next morning, adrenaline rushed through me. My sixteenth birthday should have been a joyous occasion with family and friends. But my heart pounded at the thought of appearing at Castle Halcía, which the Gatál had transformed into a fortress of evil covered in perpetual darkness.

With a deep sigh, I suppressed my dark thoughts. *I won't let them win and spoil the most important day of my life.*

That morning when I entered the kitchen for breakfast, three presents lay on the kitchen table, wrapped in parchment that Mama had painted by hand. The room was decorated with flax ribbons my mother had dyed purple and frayed until they coiled in tight curls.

It almost made me forget about the ominous appointment.

"Happy birthday, my little hawk," Mama exclaimed as she gave me a warm hug.

Papa wrapped his arms around me too. "Happy birthday, Helena." His voice sounded happy, but his eyes betrayed his worry.

"Thank you," I said as I looked around the kitchen. "It's beautiful."

"You can open your presents this evening at your party," Mama said. "Lena said she's coming, and she's bringing friends with her."

"I can't wait!"

"Until your appointment, you can help me in the field," Papa said. "And if you manage twenty bundles per hour, I have a special surprise for you tomorrow."

"Really? What?"

He ruffled my hair. "I can't tell you, or it wouldn't be a surprise. But let's just say it has something to do with my..." He lowered his voice to a faint whisper. "Lab."

My eyes widened, and I clasped my hands over my mouth. "Oh, that'd be amazing, Papa!"

"Andreas, we talked about this," Mama said, putting her hands on her hips.

"Just a little experiment," he said to her with a wink. "Careful in the forest, my lovely starlight."

Mama gave Papa a critical look before her face broke out into a smile, and she gave him a peck on the lips. "Don't forget the cart is picking Helena up at the thirteenth bell."

Forget? Not likely.

***

As time droned on, I picked up the heavy bundles of wheat and tossed them onto our wooden cart. I felt like an achy animal; flies buzzed around me, and I swatted at them in aggravation. Cicadas sang in the early afternoon heat.

With a casual glance, I noticed that Papa was hacking down the grain on the far end of the field.

He won't notice if I just take a little break.

Bending down to the ground, I picked up an imaginary sickle and twirled it in my hand. In my mind's eye, a Shadow Rider appeared before me with a frightened Halcían family in his grasp.

Let go of them—they're innocent, I hissed at the dark lord.

The dark knight turned to me, a metal mask obscuring his entire face—even his eyes. *None of you are innocent.*

You have one last chance, I growled as I brandished my fake weapon. *Hand them over or face your end.*

With a mirthless chuckle, the dark lord drew his broadsword. *My, my, aren't you a feisty one?* He pointed the tip of his weapon towards me. *Leave now, and I shall spare your miserable life.*

I narrowed my eyes at him. *Never!*

With all my might, I lunged myself at my attacker, wielding my airy sickle to and fro. In a fury of lunges and parries, I dueled the dark lord until he breathed his last.

Filled with gratitude, the little Halcían child grasped my leg. *Thank you, Helena!* she cried. *You saved us!*

How can my family ever repay you? the father asked.

"The fight for justice is reward enough," I whispered to myself.

A broad smile swept across my face as I imagined telling Lena about my tales of glory and adventure. She listened, enthralled by my heroic feats.

Damn, we'll save the world together, Lena said as she gave my shoulder a playful punch.

My fantasy soon came to an abrupt end.

Without warning, several strands of black fog rose from the field like the mists on the Bogman Moors. The wispy fibers weaved and meshed into each other until a ghastly Shadow Rider emerged from the darkness.

The Rider's deep, eerie voice slithered towards me like an eel and burrowed itself into my mind as he savored each syllable of my name.

He-le-na...

Unable to breathe, I simply gaped at the monstrous creature. A metal mask covered his entire face and even cast a dark shadow over his eyes. Dressed in black, the evil creature sauntered towards me as his cape fluttered in the breeze.

Desperately trying to keep calm, I tried to get Papa's attention, but he simply waved at me with a smile as though nothing was wrong.

When I turned back, the Shadow Rider reached out to touch me. He dwarfed me in both size and strength, and my courage failed me as I retreated from his grasp. A gale whipped across the plain, and I shivered in fear.

The Gatál have discovered your father's secret. Run!

Who are you? I asked, my eyes wide with fear. Suddenly, a raven descended and landed on the Rider's shoulder, and I gasped. *My gods, he's real!* I thought with a shudder.

There's no time. Find your mother and hide!

A muffled voice pulled me back to reality. "Helena!" Papa shouted as he shook my shoulder. "What's the matter?"

My voice trembled as I pointed at the Rider. "Can't you see him?"

"See what?" Papa shielded his eyes from the sun. "I don't see anything."

When I whipped around to face the Rider, he'd disappeared, and the raven croaked as it flew across the field.

My heart pounding, I scrambled to gather more grain into bundles. Even though I ignored the vision at first, it itched at me and made cold tingles crawl down my spine.

I'm not crazy. I'm not.

Despite my best efforts, I couldn't forget what I'd seen—it looked so real. The next bundle of wheat tumbled from my arms when I stumbled over a rock.

My father sighed as he approached me.

"Try to focus, Helena. You only have two hours before you have to get ready to leave."

"Sorry, Papa."

"Remember the surprise," he said with a twinkle in his eye.

I gave my father a weak smile, but I couldn't muster any real enthusiasm. Thinking about the dark apparition made me feel like someone had dunked my head into a bucket of ice water.

"Hey, what's the matter?" Papa asked. "You look like you've seen a wraith."

I have.

"Why don't you get a bite to eat?" he said. "You can start again after lunch."

Words tumbled from my lips before I could restrain them. "Papa, does Mama have visions?"

My father furrowed his brow. "Visions? What kind of visions?"

"Just now, I was pretending to fight a Shadow Rider, and then one appeared right in front of me."

With a faint chuckle, Papa placed his calloused hand on my shoulder. "I've always admired your creativity and imagination."

"No, Papa," I insisted, shrugging away from his touch. "I know what's real and what isn't." I took a deep breath. "The Rider told me he knew our secret. *Your* secret."

At that, my father dropped his sickle to the ground, and it landed with a thud. "What did you say?"

"He was scary—he wore a mask and their black leather uniform, and he told us to run."

"Helena, if you're bored, you can go into the forest with your mother. But you should never joke about..."

My face flushed with anger. "I'm not kidding, Papa," I said, my voice terse. "He looked wispy like the fog on the moors. The mists congealed into the form of a Shadow Rider."

At that, Papa's eyes widened. "You're serious, aren't you?"

Suddenly, black clouds swept across the sunny autumn sky as though some force had covered the heavens with a blanket of darkness. Papa blanched as he watched the unnatural patterns swirl like a whirlpool above us.

Skeletal fingers traced down my spine, leaving an icy chill in their wake. My teeth chattered as a wintery gale rushed across the field.

As I clutched my upper arms in fear and cold, a voice echoed across the field.

Why didn't you listen? I told you to run!

Lightning struck the great oak at the far end of the field with a deafening crash of thunder. Gray clouds twisted in the sky, spiraling closer and closer to the earth until they touched the ground.

"Is it another tornado?" I asked, my heart pounding in my ears.

"No," he murmured. "This is no natural occurrence. Perhaps you did see a vision, Helena."

My heart leaped into my throat as a terrifying boom resounded as the funnel collided with the neighboring fields. A furious gale blew across the plain, and I grasped Papa's arm to steady myself.

"What is it, Papa?" I asked. "What do you see?"

Papa covered my mouth to silence me.

Twelve galloping horses emerged from the raging storm and raced towards our farm. My father squinted in the distance with a perplexed expression before his eyes widened with shock.

The ground trembled under our feet as the frightening steeds approached. An otherworldly whinny pierced through the air, one that struck awe into even the bravest men. I cowered in shock behind my father's strong frame and shivered as ice crawled down my spine.

It was *them*—the cursed Shadow Riders of Gatál.

To my shock, Papa stood his ground. Was he going to *fight* them?

The Riders advanced on us, bringing unsettling darkness with each gallop until the sky above us turned obsidian. A howling wind swept through the plains and whipped dust into the air, blinding us and making it impossible to breathe. Electric pulses coursed through every nerve.

A deep voice rolled through the air like distant thunder, chilling my soul to the very core.

"I...see...you," the voice boomed with an angry hiss. "We've found you, at last, child of Gatál."

"Papa!" I screamed. "They've come for the *Falcon*!"

Papa turned to me. "Go, Helena. Disappear into the corn fields. They'll never find you there."

"I'm not leaving you," I insisted as I tried to take his dagger from his side scabbard. "Give me a weapon! Let me fight with you!"

"Run, Helena!" he said in a frantic whisper as he gave me a shove towards the fields. When I looked back, he'd snatched his sickle with one hand and drawn a broadsword with the other.

As quickly as my short legs could carry me, I raced into the tall stalks of corn and hid behind the giant plants. I peeked in between the husks and watched the Shadow Riders gallop through the front gate towards my father.

I didn't even dare to breathe.

"Stay back, Lord Hesse von Gatál," Papa demanded as he wielded his broadsword. "What business do you have here?"

The dark noble's voice boomed across the plain, augmented by some unknown dark magic. "Where is the device, Andreas de Grazia?" he growled in reply.

"What device?" my father growled.

Clad in dark armor from his black metal helmet to his black leather boots, Lord Hesse exuded authority and strength. As Protector of Halcia, Lord Hesse wore black ceremonial robes that billowed in the breeze behind him. Bile rose in my throat as I watched him.

Lord Hesse looked like the devil himself.

His voice crept into my mind in a clash of guttural, harsh consonants and hisses. *Come...to...me, Helena.*

To a casual observer, it would seem Lord Hesse simply sat upon his black stallion in silence. His dark magic urged me towards him like a magnet towards metal—compelling me to follow his command.

Squeezing my eyes shut, I resisted his power. *Don't listen,* I told myself. *Fight him.*

"We have heard about your killing machine," Lord Hesse said to my father. "Master de Moravia betrayed you last night to save himself during a raid."

"You are both mistaken as you can see." My father gestured around the farmland. "I'm but a simple farmer who serves you in accordance with Gatál law."

"Lies!" Lord Hesse's voice boomed with such a deep, ominous

rumble that my eardrums hurt. "Give us the machine, and I'll let your family live. Fail and I'll kill them before your eyes."

"Leave them out of this," Papa sneered as he brandished his weapons. "They know nothing."

"You can keep your wife if you follow my orders," Lord Hesse said, "but the girl belongs to us."

"My blood may not run through her veins, but Helena is *my* daughter," Papa roared. "We raised her as our own. You have no right to take her."

I stifled a gasp. What did Papa say?! And what did these riders want with *me*?

"I'm your lord and master, so I have every right," Lord Hesse hissed. "The law decrees that no Gatál blood shall reside among Halcían filth. Either give me the child and the device, or we will take them by force."

The evil Rider whipped his gaze in my direction, and I stifled a gasp. He extended a long, skeletal hand clad in a black leather glove, and his voice tempted me as it curled and twisted through the air like a serpent.

"Come to me, Helena."

An invisible force prodded me, nudging me towards the dark lord. Clenching my jaw, I willed myself to stay hidden. At that, the dark noble leapt from his steed and hit the ground with a thump. Lord Hesse towered over my father by at least a foot and brandished his sword.

"Bring her to me, peasant."

"Never!"

Papa took advantage of Lord Hesse's proximity and whirled his broadsword to slit Lord Hesse's throat. To my astonishment, the blade didn't even bite the dark lord's skin.

"A valiant attempt," the dark noble hissed. He drew a second sword and spread his arms wide. "Would you like to try again?"

My father groaned as he stumbled to his feet and slashed at his opponent's midsection. Papa damaged Lord Hesse's leather armor, but the man hadn't shed even a drop of blood.

With an evil cackle, the sinister Rider slashed my father's leg, and he dropped to the ground. My blood curdled in my veins—at that moment, I realized that my father could never defeat them.

Papa was just fighting for time.

Adrenaline coursed through me, and I tried to run.

Tearing through my resolve, Lord Hesse reached his hand out to me. His spell gripped my body like an invisible hand and tried to draw me nearer. Although I could fight his power, I couldn't run.

"I can feel your presence, Helena," he hissed. "Do not resist me."

"You see," Papa said in a defiant tone as he rose to his feet with a grimace. "She's stronger than you think. And she hasn't even been trained yet."

The dark lord roared in frustration and lowered his hand. Advancing towards my father with slow, deliberate steps, the Rider whipped his sword up to Papa's neck.

"Helena, you have one last chance to save your father. Come out now."

Papa shook his head as though he could see me watching him. "Never give in, Helena."

My father took a metallic device out of his pocket, pressed a button, and our house exploded in a huge fireball. Lord Hesse ducked and whipped around towards the conflagration.

Stifling a yell behind my hand, I stared at the wreckage. Smoke billowed from the smoldering ruins as though a giant fire drake had destroyed it within seconds.

The black stallions shrieked with terror and reared up on their hind legs as the Riders struggled to control them. A nearby Rider grasped the reins of his master's frightened steed. With a single touch of his hand, the steed stood as calm as a statue.

I wished I could calm myself like that. My heart was racing, and my insides turned to liquid jelly.

"You fool!" Lord Hesse roared once he'd regained his composure. "What have you done?"

"You'll never get the plans or the machine now," Papa said with a wry smile.

"You're so naive." Lord Hesse cocked his head and observed my father as one would a wayward pet. "And to think you used to be the pride and joy of the Halcían monarchy."

Papa scoffed. "To think we used to work together at the science academy," he retorted.

"My, how far you've fallen, you filthy peasant. Just admit that you supported the wrong side."

"Has the darkness corrupted you that much?"

"I've tolerated your betrayal long enough," the dark lord sneered. "This time, you've gone too far. As for the plans, we'll get them from Master de Moravia. Now give us the girl!"

"If you want to get to Helena," my father said, "you'll have to kill me first."

"As you wish."

Without another word, Lord Hesse crossed both of his blades and chopped off Papa's head in one deft swing. His head fell to the ground, and his body collapsed with a sickening thud.

"Traitor!" the dark lord hissed as he spat on my father's body.

"No, Papa!" I screamed. I covered my hand over my mouth, but it was too late.

The Shadow Riders whipped their heads toward me. To my surprise, the dark lord's iron grip over me faded, and I ran for my life...

The End

Connect with Carolyn Hill at the following sites:

Twitter: @lively_linguist

Wattpad: @Carolyn_Hill

Cover by Wattpad artist @amazewrites (permission obtained from the artist), Ama from Am's Gallery.

Valentine's Day

Rosie Dean

Although Rosie Dean has been writing stories and plays since she was big enough to type, she came to fiction writing after teaching art in high schools and writing marketing materials for the corporate world.

Now, happily inhabiting the imaginary world of her characters, Rosie loves to write sassy, romantic fiction with a sense of humour and, sometimes, a sense of the ridiculous—because we all know life and love aren't exactly how we'd like them to be.

Rosie has four romantic comedies available on Amazon: *Millie's Game Plan, Vicki's Work of Heart, Chloe's Rescue Mission,* and *Gigi's Island Dream.*

The short story "Valentine's Day" was originally written in response to a homework set at a writing group. Rosie's novels are not as dark as this.

***

Kate thought the cranberry lip sheen added an air of dark eroticism to her countenance. Tonight, she would give Seb an experience he wouldn't forget. She shimmied in her satin skirt as she smoothed it over her hips. Shame the suspenders ruined the line of it, but they would drive Seb wild.

There was a small Post-It note stuck to the mirror. "Love you, honey-pie," it said with a large, curly "B" from Bernie at the bottom. Tearing it off, she scrunched it up and dropped it into the bin. On second thoughts, she retrieved it and pushed it into her handbag. Her husband might be wetter than a bath sponge on Sunday nights, but she didn't have to rub his face in her callousness. Far better he continue in his delusion that she still loved him.

A smile lifted one corner of her mouth. Scrabbling around for a scrap of paper, she wrote "Love you too, sweet cheeks" and slipped it onto his pillow. Downstairs, she placed his favourite supper—chili con carne—on the kitchen table with another note giving reheating instructions.

Thirty minutes later, she was ten miles away and stepping into Seb's blue Audi TT. He smelled of citrus and cedarwood.

Once she had bestowed a soft, moist and probing kiss, she settled back into the seat and re-applied her cranberry lip sheen, as he drove the short distance to his apartment in the next town. They had a system: He always picked her up from a different pub so she didn't have to pay for parking and could hope for some anonymity—he was considerate that way.

Seb handled the car with confidence—maybe even a little recklessness. Kate stirred in her seat as she looked at his strong, square hands curling sensuously around the steering wheel. Her gaze traced the line of his wrist and arm until she focused on his handsome face—the intense blue eyes watching the road. His blond hair was unruly from driving to meet her with the top of the sports car down. He turned towards her, his lips slowly lifting into a smile that warmed Kate in places she'd forgotten she had.

Her la Perla underwear certainly did the trick. Seb was hot, eager and unbelievably willing to satisfy. That was the beauty of a younger man; he had more stamina than Bernie and certainly a more vivid imagination. He made love to her like it was his last day on Earth. Kate revelled in the resurgence of her own sexuality—which had lain dormant for years. Yes, Bernie had always found her attractive, and, since the children had gone to university, they had fallen into a Saturday morning ritual of sex before the supermarket shop. Well, most Saturdays. Recently, she had taken to jogging round the park in an effort to tighten up her thighs—for Seb's benefit, naturally.

"Tonight was superb," Seb told her, running a finger down her cheek. "It must be so distressing for your husband not to be able to make love to you anymore."

Kate dropped her head slightly. "It's not easy for him. But he must never find out about us—it would break his heart. He has enough on his plate with..." She didn't continue but closed her eyes and took a deep breath.

Seb squeezed her hand and said quietly, "People don't appreciate good health till it's gone."

She smiled back at him. "Thanks for understanding."

"Hey," he said softly. "Life's for living—that includes you, too."

A tingle ran up Kate's arm. She had struck gold with Seb, and soon they would be together forever. What bliss.

***

Bernie had left the kitchen looking immaculate. All trace of his meal had been cleared away, and she could hear the TV running. She took a deep breath and walked through to the sitting room. As she expected, his head was back on the cushion, his mouth slack, and he was snoring softly. Kate looked at him for a moment. *So typical of Bernie,* she thought, a slight curl on her lip. He would never snore noisily for fear of offending anyone.

Holding both his hands, she said, "Come on now, Bernie. Time for bed." He was heavy with sleep, but eventually, she managed to rouse him enough that she could guide him up the stairs. In the bedroom, he dropped onto the bed and didn't argue as she helped him out of his clothes and into his pyjamas. In the early days, she had thought Bernie looked deliciously vulnerable in pyjamas. Not anymore.

"Don't go back to sleep, Bernie! You need to go to the bathroom."

He peeled open an eye and looked at her. "Hello, gorgeous," he mumbled. "Had a nice time with the girls?"

Kate managed to manoeuvre him to the top of the stairs where the bathroom door stood ajar. With her back to it, she pushed.

Bernie let out a surprised whimper as he teetered over the top step, grabbed for the banister and missed. For the first time since Kate had come home, his eyes fully opened and almost saw her before he toppled backwards and tumbled like a bulky package down the stairs.

She watched. She waited. She listened to the thumping of her heart as it rocked her chest. Finally, she made her way down to check on him. His neck was bent awkwardly, and there was a slight glimmer in his eyes, but his breathing had stopped.

She picked up the phone, dialled 999 and gave the performance of her life.

Waiting for the ambulance to arrive, she stepped over Bernie and returned to the bedroom, hanging his trousers up as he always did and putting his dirty clothes in the linen basket. She lifted the duvet, revealing the note she had left earlier, and placed it back down again. If the police were called, she wanted them to find it in situ. She checked his bedside drawer. Yes, there was a small square package wrapped in pink paper and a pink envelope containing, no doubt, a cutesy Valentine card. Her card for him was sitting in her bedside drawer, along with a wine-tasting voucher for two. Good.

She looked up and gazed at the portrait of herself, which Bernie had commissioned for her fortieth birthday. How she hated it. He had given the artist one of her least favourite photos, and the result was worse than the original—but Bernie had loved it. He had loved her, she knew that. Why hadn't it been enough? She thought back to the first time they had met, in the school library: Bernie studying for his physics A-level and she looking for a copy of *Frenchman's Creek*. He'd seemed so desirable—a sixth former and captain of the basketball team. She remembered their first kiss outside her parents' house when he'd walked her home from school. He had been handsome before the basketball had stopped, the love of food had taken over and testosterone had absorbed his hair.

She cried, at last. Thank God. She sobbed and gulped, allowing the tears to run down through her nose and over her cheeks, so much so, she barely heard the ambulance man ringing the doorbell.

***

The verdict was accidental death. After a couple of glasses of wine and a long day at work, Bernie had lost his footing and fallen. His doctor knew he was overdoing it. Kate had persuaded her husband to visit the surgery the day before to report palpitations and a heavy feeling in the chest. She had told him to ask to be booked in for a day wearing a heart monitor. After all, she had told him, she didn't want her lovely hubby dying of a heart attack if it could be avoided—and too many people died unnecessarily because they didn't do a MOT on their bodies. Bernie had liked her concern. And she'd had a point. The doctor couldn't prove he hadn't had palpitations and would be obliged to comply. "Yes," Bernie had said. "Better safe than sorry."

Kate felt somehow more guilty for getting away with it so easily than she did for committing murder in the first place. She should have done it months ago. Now, she had a whole future ahead with Seb. Smugness and elation combined to dilute the guilt, and she struggled to maintain the appropriate level of self-composure essential for a grieving widow. But she'd pulled it off and wasn't about to destroy the future she'd planned by dropping her guard too soon. Oh no. Her future was lying before her, like a tropical beach where she could languish and fill her senses with pleasure. And Seb would be there to enjoy it with her.

***

The church was surprisingly warm and bright, with sunshine flooding in through the chancel window and onto the oak coffin. Kate sat, chilled and tense on the edge of the pew; she was surrounded by people she didn't recognise. Every row had filled with friends and family come to pay their last respects. She had really known so little about him.

Nothing could have prepared her for the emptiness, the pain and the sickness she was feeling now as she clutched Seb's letter in her hand. *Dear Kate,* it had begun.

Why? It was senseless and so bloody cruel.

The coffin was ornate with floral tributes. So many of them, it was almost shocking. But then, there *were* so many of them. Women—all here to mourn his passing, all clutching notes of explanation and farewell.

Seb, the sexy, life-loving hunk was no more. Terminal cancer—the real murderer—had driven him to suicide. He hadn't wanted to tell any of them, of course, especially Kate, who had been struggling with her own husband's illness. No, he had wanted to wring every last drop of pleasure from his last few, healthy months on Earth and then bow out gracefully. He hoped he had given them a good time and would understand and forgive him.

He wished every one of them long and healthy lives. After all, life was for living, wasn't it?

The End

Connect with Rosie Dean at the following links:

Website/blog: http://www.rosie-dean.com

Facebook: http://www.facebook.com/RosieDeanWriter

Twitter: http://twitter.com/RosieDeanAuthor

Goodreads: www.goodreads.com/RosieDean

Cover by Susan K. Saltos.

Headlines and Deadlines

Lauren O'Neill

I'm a journalist, and like a lot of professions, my job success is measured in numbers—specifically, in trying to make the numbers go up: sell more papers; get more people reading; get more people looking at the website; keep them there for longer. The bigger the numbers are, as far as my employers are concerned, the better I am at my job.

But what happens when someone whose job it is to make numbers go up has to rely on someone whose job it is to make the numbers go down?

***

"Hey," Jess Loxton squeezed herself into the office, looking as apologetic as always. Her dark brown hair was swept up and clipped behind her head in a lazy, messy ponytail. Anxious green eyes framed with black glasses distracted somewhat from her pale complexion and the dark shadows beneath her eyes. A spray of freckles marked her cheeks and nose, and a security pass dangled on a cord around her neck.

She was dressed entirely in black, a well-worn notepad clutched in one hand, a pen jammed into the spiral at the top. She stood a little awkwardly, making eye contact almost maniacally, as if to say, "Yes, you have left the intelligence sheets up on the wall, and I'm not going to look at them."

Sergeant Sam Edgware offered a smile that didn't reach his eyes, wheeling away from the computer and reaching almost lazily to pull down the shades on the notes tacked to the wall: a drug dealer believed to be in the area; someone suspicious who'd been lurking around a primary school; Crimestoppers intelligence about who might or might not be dealing drugs.

Information for his officers' eyes.

Not for the reporter on the local rag.

Sam was around six-foot-three-inches tall, lean and wiry compared to some of his shorter, but wider, colleagues.

Dressed in his uniform, he had intelligent brown eyes on a handsome face, which was only just beginning to lose its edge.

Beneath his white shirt, one could see the outline of a tattoo on his bicep: some sort of spiked, tribal thing that had seemed like a good idea at the time. His hair was brown, short and neat, and he carried the weight of the law on his shoulder: a friendly confidence that only just fell short of cocky arrogance. He was personable enough but gave the impression he was just breezing through the area on his quest for promotion.

These briefings had become something of a joke.

The idea was, once a week, he'd meet with one of the local reporters to tell them what they'd been doing. About the good work the police had been doing in the community.

She'd report it in the paper, filling valuable space and helping to assure the good citizens of Little Uppington and the surrounding areas that the police were, in fact, doing their jobs and preventing the area turning into an inner-city nightmare where hordes of hoodie-wearing youths rampaged through the streets, hopped up on the latest designer drug and snatching babies out of prams to sacrifice them to the dark lord.

Fortunately, for the residents of Little Uppington—but not for Jess—the village was a world of dog shows, fêtes and jumble sales. It did not have a bank to rob. Its sole drug dealer was a man known as "Jack Weed," who everyone knew grew cannabis in his loft and sold it to the handful of bored teenagers who lived in the village.

Six months back, a storm ripped through, tearing down trees and blowing down fences. A handful of tiles had fallen off the village shop, smashing on the main road. It had made the front page of the newspaper. *That* was the sort of place Little Uppington was.

A good place to live. A bad place to try and fill a newspaper.

Jess perched on the edge of her chair, some sort of relic from 1983. Sam stood, reaching to turn down the volume of the radio, settling into an equally decrepit plastic chair that looked as if it had escaped from the nearby comprehensive school. A small, white coffee table, the perfect height for bashing your shins on if you weren't paying attention, sat between them. Wendy, the support officer, had left a small plate stacked with Tesco Value biscuits in the centre of it. He waved a hand at them, already knowing what Jess was going to say.

"Not for me, thanks."

He nodded and offered her a cup of tea or coffee, already knowing she'd turn him down. She couldn't balance the cup and write down what he was saying, she explained, for the umpteenth time. He nodded, standing briefly to head back to the computer desk and grab his own half-empty, lukewarm coffee.

"Anything exciting happen?" she wanted to know, a slight edge of pleading to her voice. It was hard to blame her, really. Writing the *Little Uppington and Marstock Gazette* couldn't be easy.

Every Thursday it appeared on the shelf; every week there were eighty odd pages full of news from the area—14 pages devoted entirely to Little Uppington and Marstock and the dozen or so villages between them.

God only knew how they found it all—it wasn't as if anything much happened around here.

Last week's front page had been about plans to build a new housing estate near the village. The week before that, it had been about some kids who'd been using a hedgehog as a football. It wasn't exactly groundbreaking stuff.

And as much as he wanted to help her out, the fact was that, no, nothing exciting had happened.

There'd been the usual antisocial complaints, generally at around 11:30 pm on Friday and Saturday nights, after kicking-out time at the pub. A few minor car crashes—shunts, mostly. People—with their minds on things other than the road—who'd suddenly found their bumper pressed up against the car in front when it'd braked to avoid an oncoming badger or to make a turn.

A domestic disturbance, but they never made it into the paper; not until it went to court, anyway. Someone had been caught trying to steal a £1 roll of tin foil from the shop; a few under-aged kids drinking in the park at 2:37 am. A bag being taken from the back seat of someone's car. Shoplifting. More shoplifting.

He reeled them off. She wrote them down. But they both knew none of them were going to make front page this week.

"...Anything on there you can't tell me?" she asked, looking up from her shorthand. The lines might as well have been hieroglyphics, and he stared at them for a moment. Jess claimed to use shorthand because it meant no one could look over her shoulder and see what she'd been writing.

"Uh..." Sam said, flipping through his own notebook.

"No drug raids coming up? Be great to get a photo of you dramatically kicking someone's front door in."

No, no drug raids planned. No weapons confiscated. No, he assured her, there hadn't been a serial killer or mass rapist or bomb threat in the last seven days. No suspicious deaths. As always, things had pottered along much as they always had.

"Well. We'll be running our spring drink-driving campaign soon," Sam said, feeling a little sorry for her. She glanced up, but he could see she'd already written it off. It'd be squeezed into a corner on page thirty-four, somewhere.

"Oh. Really? Cool." Another squiggle on the page, but he knew her heart wasn't in it. They ran the campaign every year, after all. There was something about lighter mornings and the promise of summer that seemed to make people go crazy on the roads.

Well, except it didn't. They drove like they always did, really: too fast, in cars that hadn't been maintained properly, while trying to overtake on blind corners.

He gave her the spiel, anyway: driving tips, maintenance suggestions, and the obvious lines about not drinking and driving. As if people didn't know that already. Urging people to contact them if they suspected someone of being under the influence, as if they ever would.

Jess nodded and kept scribbling, but they both knew they were wasting their time.

"So..." he said, standing to show her the way out. She flipped the notebook closed and picked her handbag up from the floor. "Are you finding these things productive?"

"Sure," she said, not entirely convincingly. "I mean, you know. Responsible reporting and all. We want the residents of Little Uppington to feel safe knowing you're all on the case."

The corporate line like the one he'd fed her.

She couldn't afford not to come because the week she didn't would be the week he'd be planning to storm a £10 million cannabis farm or rugby tackled a knifeman to the floor.

And for all her niceness and friendliness, he knew she wouldn't fail to splash his station all over the front page the moment they didn't make it to the house of some pensioner who thought she'd heard a noise in her back garden within ten minutes.

They made their way to the stairs in a semi-awkward silence. Two people who met once a week to talk about work but didn't know what to say when there was no work to talk about.

"Things all right down your place?" he asked, rounding the staircase.

"What?" Jess hadn't been paying attention. Or she had been. It was hard to tell. She gave the impression she never really was, but it was the things you thought she hadn't been listening to that she ended up quoting you on.

"Things all right down your place?" he repeated as if he hadn't said it in the first place.

"Oh. Yeah. You know." She waved a hand absently. He didn't know but nodded as if he did.

For someone in the communications industry, Jess wasn't much on it. She stood opposite him, next to the door.

Sam nodded. "Will you be at the parish council meeting on Friday?"

She glanced off to the left. "Yeah. Can't wait. Another exciting evening with the council talking about dog sh—mess in the park."

Sam grinned. "Dog mess and parking," he said with an easy shrug. "If it's all people have to have for the police to do, at least you know you're living in a safe area."

"Mmm," she conceded the point, shrugging a little. "There is that. Well, I should let you get back to your day. See you Friday. Don't forget to call me if you get a bomb threat called in or Al Qaeda blow up the High Street."

"You'll be the first to know. Take care, Jess."

"See you."

***

She went with the antisocial behaviour in the end. He didn't blame her. It looked like it had been slim pickings this week: a woman planning her first skydive for charity on page two and something about a school on page three. The rest of it was so generic, it barely registered with him.

Jess had managed to round up a few residents who'd told her how the antisocial behaviour was making their life hell. A photographer had been out to get photos of smashed bottles of Smirnoff Ice and empty cider cans, while the remains of a few joints had also been photographed to bring in a drugs element.

She'd added in his comments about increasing patrols and having sympathy with those living nearby and a rent-a-quote parish councillors had got in on the act, saying it was all the fault of the county council, who had cut grants to the youth clubs so kids had nowhere to go in the evenings.

His week didn't get any more exciting. A shoplifter, a drink-driver, a few minor accidents. An ex-boyfriend who wouldn't leave his girlfriend alone, a car-stereo theft, and the usual nonsense from Paul Granger—a man who was tactfully described as "having issues"—dialing 999 because he thought his next-door neighbour had been kidnapped by aliens and replaced with a doppelgänger.

It was just one of those sorts of weeks.

***

There was a distinctly nervous atmosphere in the newsroom. They weren't walking on eggshells as much as dragging their wrists over them.

With two reporters out with stress and one on holiday, the current newsroom was run by a tired-looking Jess and her colleague, James, as well as an equally frazzled looking news editor, Ed, who had been there for longer than anyone cared to admit and would likely die of a heart attack at his desk. There was the freelance photographer called Mike with the patience needed to press a button for a living. The rest of the staff was currently made up of a small, blonde girl, Claire, on work experience from University and two terrified looking fifteen-year-olds from All Hallow's School.

It was not a good time to be a journalist, Jess knew. Times were tight, sales were sliding, and the current parent company had decided it was all about the internet and insisted everything was uploaded to the website before it hit the papers.

Give away the content for free and people would buy the paper, they surmised. It was a decision they had all railed against but ultimately been ignored about.

But, apparently, the future was digital, and print had become something of a side project. If she couldn't make sure five hundred people would read her story on the website, she wasn't supposed to publish it.

Never mind that Little Uppington and Marstock had a population of just under 7,000 between them, and roughly seventy-five percent of them were over the age of seventy-five and probably didn't even know how to turn a computer on.

"Jess, a word?"

Paul Webb had been the editor for longer than anyone could remember but somehow never really seemed to age. He radiated the aura of a mildly disappointed grandfather at all times—grey hair, thick glasses, and a predisposition towards blue shirts with white collars and red ties. It wasn't that he wasn't supportive; it was just somehow, no matter what you did, it was never good enough.

Heart sinking, she followed him into his office, noting without much surprise that he'd closed the door so no one else could hear what was being said. Mind whirling, she tried to think about what she'd done. Complaint? Something she was meant to have done but hadn't?

There was a thick, heavy silence that filled the space between them, Paul taking the time to consider his words before he freed them. The uncertainty doing little to help Jess' nerves.

"As I'm sure you know, the industry in a state of flux."

Oh, *God*. Of course she knew. Everyone knew: Papers were selling less copies; advertisers were buying less adverts; and since the advent of online auction sites, they didn't even get the money from classifieds anymore. The industry hadn't adapted well—journalists were being made redundant left, right and centre.

She nodded dutifully, wondering where this was going and trying to ignore the sick feeling in the base of her stomach.

"Well, newspaper sales are a bit concerning. Sales of *The Gazette* are starting to slip. The general feeling is some of the stories recently haven't been strong enough."

Her fingers flexed, nails pressing into the palms of her hands, trying to control her temper. Paul reached behind him, pulling out the last three editions of the paper. Antisocial behaviour, new housing estate, hedgehog football. She caught the headlines as he flipped through the pages: church fêtes, council meetings, residents unhappy because their bins weren't being collected on time.

She had to admit, there wasn't anything particularly earth-shattering in there.

Paul huffed out a long, slow breath, disapproval hanging in the air between them.

"Sales are down by...nearly thirty percent compared to last year. They probably wouldn't worry so much, but you're not getting the web hits, either."

Dread settling into her stomach, Jess kept her eyes trained on the pages in front of her.

"Look," Paul said, throwing her a lifeline or maybe just needing to fill up her defensive silence with words. "I've gone through the figures from last year. We can see what did well—that's the sort of stuff you need to be finding."

He slid a sheet across the table towards her, tilting it at an angle so they could both read it.

"This was your highest selling edition last year, shifting 6,432 copies."

Her eyes flicked across the sheet. "'Four Killed in Tragic Crash,'" she said, her voice flat. She remembered the edition well: four teenagers coming home from a night out, taking a corner too fast in the early hours of the morning. Their Citroen Saxo flipping and finally coming to a stop, embedded in the wall of a farmhouse.

She wondered what she was supposed to do. The crash had happened where it had happened—it could easily have been anywhere else in the country. Sadly, it was a scene repeated on roads everywhere with depressing regularity. She'd just been...lucky. If that was the right word, which it really wasn't.

"All right, let's look at number two," Paul said, conceding a point she hadn't actually made. She could smell coffee on his breath as he spoke. "'We'll Never Forget Our Beautiful Rosie.'"

A story she'd broken her heart over. A baby, only three-days old, dying in the middle of the night. She'd never been able to shake off the cold, flat sound of the child's father as he described finding her lifeless body in her cot. He wanted to raise awareness so it wouldn't happen to anyone else, he'd told her.

"Paul, I...I don't know what you want me to do. These aren't stories I can...chase. They're just...horrible things that happened here."

He tutted, as if she was being idiotic, running his hand through his hair.

"I'm not suggesting you replicate them," he said. "It's just...these are the sorts of stories that make people buy papers."

"Horrible deaths?" She arched an eyebrow. Her temper and sarcasm were trying to bubble to the surface. A flat, dull anger made her feel exasperated, hot and cold all at once.

"*Strong* stories," he said patiently. "People don't care about...housing estates and church fêtes."

"I can't write about things that aren't happening, Paul."

"I'm not asking you to." He sounded a tad peevish now, leaning back in his chair, stomach nudging at his shirt, pale pink skin visible as the buttons strained against an encroaching pot belly.

"Everyone's got a story, Jess. You need to work harder at finding them."

***

To: Edgwell, Samuel. [Edgwell.samuel@ruralcounties.police.uk]

From: Catherine Hope [pcc@ruralcounties.police.uk]

Subject: Concerns

Samuel,

My apologies for contacting you by email, but I know that you are on lates for the next three days.

I understand your local paper has run a piece about a spike in antisocial behaviour, with the reporter claiming a group of teenagers are terrorising residents in our rural communities. I also understand that you are quoted at length in the article.

While I believe the press have an important role to play in local politics and holding us to account, I am concerned about some of the quotes you have given this particular reporter, and you appear to be the source of the story. As I'm sure you are aware on being elected to the role of police and crime commissioner, one of my promises was to stamp down hard on antisocial behaviour in our communities.

I'm sure you are aware the perception of crime is far higher in our communities. Last year's Crime and Order survey revealed that 23% of people believed crime had risen in our region over the last two years when actually it had fallen by seven percent.

Although I admire the work you have done with your community and the rapport you have built up with the local paper, I believe these things might be best left to the press office in the future.

Please call me to discuss.

Kind regards,

Catherine

Catherine Hope
Police and Crime Commissioner—Rural Counties
"Safer and stronger together."

***

The atmosphere in Sam's office was tired and awkward. Jess had practically bitten through her pen while Sam, Catherine's words—"I'm disappointed, not angry."—still ringing in his ears, glanced over this week's callouts.

Domestic abuse. Drugs overdose. Pædophile spotted taking photographs of children outside the primary school. A mentally ill teenager who had tried to stab his mother.

"Burglary?" he offered, trying to ignore the pained look on Jess' face.

"...How many?" she asked, pen poised over her pad.

"Just one."

"What was taken?"

"Uh..." He clicked his mouse a couple of times. "Games console. £14 in cash and a mobile phone."

She scrawled on her pad, trying to find a way to make the story work. He could see it in her face. Terminally ill kid? Mentally ill man? Hundred-year-old victim?

"Isn't there anything else?" she pleaded.

A woman half beaten to death by her husband. A man who'd been sending his ex-girlfriend decapitated animals.

"...Handbag taken out of a car? Sorry, Jess. It's been a bit quiet this week. Crime's down seven percent, year-on-year." He tried hard to inject some enthusiasm into his voice. She was quiet, and when he looked over, he thought he saw tears. For the first time, he noticed the dark shadows beneath her eyes, the bitten fingernails. Her gaze was downcast and desperate.

He wanted to help.

"Sorry, Jess. You could try the press office, maybe?"

She gave him a thin smile. "Don't worry. Thanks for your help."

She was getting to her feet, the pad disappearing into her bag, pushing a lock of hair behind her ear. He stood, his hands finding his way into his back pockets, his spine cracking as he rose.

"What's going on the front this week?" he asked, more for something to say than any real interest. She shrugged, looking desolate.

"I...don't know. I guess I'm just going to have to take matters into my own hands. Run amok with a sword. Kill some randoms. Least I'd get a front page out of it." The ghost of a smile on her lips, she tossed her hair. "...Sorry. Joking. Probably not what you should say to a policeman. I'll see you next week, Sam."

***

"Jess, do you have a minute?"

Jess did not have a minute. She had four pages to fill and nothing to fill them with, which was the exact opposite of a minute.

She had a dozen press releases masquerading as news, which were thinly disguised adverts she already knew she wouldn't get away with using. She'd had a long phone conversation with a slightly confused elderly woman about the weather and bunions. She'd had an argument with the manager of a shop who couldn't understand why she wouldn't be getting a front-page story about the fact she was selling a new range of ceramic frogs.

Shop sells things. Hold the front bloody page.

She could feel the panic in the pit of her stomach. The machine of the paper churning her up. And it wasn't going to end. She'd struggle to fill these pages; she'd work until ten pm tonight and pull news out of nowhere just to fill the pages. She'd sit through meetings while members of the public sat at home and watched TV, while democracy happened around them and planning decisions were waved through. She'd get stroppy calls from parents because they hadn't used the photograph of their little darling with their sunflowers; she'd get abuse for running court stories. There would be emails from local politicians accusing her of bias and from residents accusing her of being corrupt. And on social media she'd get berated: lazy journalist; fake news; slow news day; biased; lying; misquoted; "I don't buy the paper anymore. This is why I stopped reading this rag. So called journalist."

And it would never stop. It was a machine that needed feeding—it didn't stop. It never stopped. The moment the paper was off the printer, being delivered to the shops, it was already out-of-date. The next edition needed to be filled. Put in words and stories. Put in your heart, your soul. Feed it your personal life, your social life. *Your soul.* And for what? To receive nothing but abuse and hatred. Open yourself to threats, to ridicule, to trolling, to complaints and hatred.

Then Paul would tell her it wasn't good enough, wasn't strong enough. Wasn't selling enough. Wasn't getting enough views online. He'd talk about people "upstairs" asking questions. He'd talk about it being tough times and difficult decisions having to be made.

She stood slowly, feeling the eyes of the office upon her as she followed him into his office.

"Just wanting to touch base," he said before she'd even sat down. "What are you looking at for your front page this week?"

And she had nothing. Literally nothing. And she was in here talking to him about what she was supposed to be doing instead of actually finding something.

Jess forced herself to take in a slow breath, to calm herself and push down on the anger bubbling inside her.

"...Nothing," she admitted.

Paul's face creased, annoyance flitting across his eyes. "There must be *something*," he said.

She wanted to cry. "I don't know. Nothing feels strong enough. Nothing's going on. Nothing's happened. I've got four pages, and...I'm really struggling."

"Something will come up," he told her, stretching back in his chair, linking his hands behind his head. "We've never yet gone to press with blank pages."

"That's not..." She bit back on her anger, her heart pounding and her head throbbing. She could feel her anger rising again. It felt like wire in her veins, her jaw tight with stress, teeth clenched together. It took every ounce of effort to pry them apart so she could speak.

"That's...not really helpful. I don't have any stories. I don't know what to do. There isn't anything happening. I don't have anything for a page seven, let alone a front page."

He shrugged his shoulders in the universal gesture for "not my problem."

"Something will come up," he repeated, his tone of voice suggesting he'd somehow solve the problem. It made her breath boil in her lungs, even as she tried to slow her breathing. "You'll think of something—just make sure it's strong."

Jess leaned forward, resting her head in her hands, trying to ignore a tsunami of anger boiling just beneath her flesh, making her bones feel too hot, and her heart hammering erratically against her ribcage.

You'll think of something.

And that was the problem. She had.

***

Sam shuffled the papers from one side of his desk to the next, trying to drum up the enthusiasm to reply to a letter of complaint. Paula Rickman—known as something of a...character.

Character. A pain in the ass, more like. A 40-something yoga teacher and Reiki therapist who had been inexplicably convinced the police had been trying to kill her since she was handed a caution for cannabis possession three years ago.

Apparently this week, PC Ashcroft had tried to cut the brakes on her car.

At this point, Sam wouldn't have minded if she actually had.

On his uniform, his radio crackled and beeped with conversation. Ashcroft and Pearce were on foot patrol in the High Street. Carter was escorting a shoplifter to the custody suite fourteen miles away. King and Ellis were at the scene of a shed burglary, trying to find out exactly what had gone missing from the owner.

Just another day.

***

"Hello, emergency service operator, which service do you require? Fire, police, or ambulance?" Lisa Compton's fingers were paused above the keyboard, ready to type.

Around her, the office was buzzing with her colleagues taking call after call after call. Fights breaking out, wives being beaten by husbands. Husbands being beaten by wives. Car crashes. The occasional drunk person who couldn't find their remote control.

On the whiteboard on the wall opposite her desk, written in red marker in her boss' spidery handwriting:

Target: answer at least 90% of 999 calls within 10 seconds.

April: Total calls received: 14,960. % calls answered in Target: 89.7

She could hear screaming in the background, something that made the hairs on the back of her neck rise. The sound of something being smashed. Someone screaming.

"She's got a knife. You have to help."

The voice sounded young, terrified, out of breath as if he'd been running. The muffled sounds of a phone being pressed against skin, a mobile phone signal fading in and out, crackling and hissing.

Going from no calls in her queue to five, red lights flashing dangerously. She exchanged an anxious glance with her colleague.

"What is the nature of your emergency?" Her voice was calm, in control, even as the adrenaline surged through her, her blood turning to ice. "Can you tell me your name? Where you are? What's happening?"

"Paul. Paul Sant. I'm on work experience at the...at the paper. She just...she just went crazy...she's got a knife. There was...there's blood everywhere. Oh my God..."

"A knife?"

Police. Ambulance.

"Paul, the first thing I need you to do is get somewhere safe. Are you safe?"

There was a heart-stopping moment of silence, and for a moment, she thought she'd lost him. Seconds that seemed like hours. When he spoke again, she felt herself release a breath she hadn't known she'd been holding in.

"I—yes. I'm outside. I—"

"Can you tell me what's happening? Who's got a knife?"

"...I don't know. One of the reporters. A reporter. A girl. Look, can you just g-get here?"

He was sobbing now, the sound of traffic and wind picked up by his phone. His words punctuated by gasps for air.

"I think she killed him. Jesus, I think she fucking killed him."

The End

Cover by Anthony Mihovich.

Knock Three Times

Susan O'Reilly

This flash fiction piece shows us every action has its consequences. Beware who you decide to mistreat...

It's rare to see Susan's pen visit the horror/thriller genre. She's a poet at heart but decided, like any good writer, to stretch herself with this foray into the dark parts of the human experience. She hopes you enjoy it very much!

***

It's a well-established routine now. One which I will forever dread. It's not made any easier now that I know what's ahead for me. It used to be called Knock the Dolly; after a while, it became Knock the Dolly Up. I was too young at first to have a clue what was going on. I just was happy my big brother gave me some of his time and played with my Dolly. As I got older, he started getting me to prepare Dolly for the game. Knickers were already removed; we'd already gone past the tickling-Dolly-into-submission stage.

Oh, how I wish we were back to playing with Dolly. Days now, I'm his latest craze. It's been renamed simply The Knocking Game. Its rules are simple and to be obeyed at all times:

Rule No. 1: I tell no one or everyone, including me, is dead.

Rule No. 2: When games are being played, I tell him I love him, convincingly, at least three times.

Rule No. 3: I know the sequence of knocks and what they mean.

He hasn't played in a while; I think he's busy with college. I hope he meets someone who keeps him away from me. I've been feeling a bit of security lately; it's been so long. That feeling falls on top of me with a resounding bang when I'm awoken with the knock.

One knock means he's cased the house, and we're okay; no one will interrupt our game.

Two knocks mean I have to get ready. Knickers are removed.

Three knocks: He's in. I leave the building spiritually, but my body remains.

As time went on and I got older, he got rougher and more demanding. He complains it's taken too long for him to reach the desired ending and he doesn't like my new curves. He's started to turn me around now, and I want to scream with pain, but I won't give him the satisfaction. I feel like I'm going to snap in two, but at least it's over quicker.

With each thrust, a plan is forming. I'm creating my own game. I've formed a group in the school of other girls and boys just like me with brothers/uncles/fathers just like him. We meet regularly to form a plan and get our routines down just so.

We've already sorted out two; the police are still looking for them. They'll never find their bodies. My dear brother is number three.

I smile at the first knock; it means they tell no one and he's going to be dead. The second: they're in and we let him know how much we hate him, convincingly, at least three times. The third he's dead and I'm tied up, crying.

Another break-in, just like with the other men. There's been so many of them lately. When are the police going to do their job and catch them?

I listen to my mother for the third week in a row wail and howl over her precious son. I had told her at least three times about his little games. She never believed me; I'm going to have to start counting. I can't listen to her anymore. In his room she's built a shrine; I knock on the door with glee. Ready or not. 1, 2, 3. She and he are reunited forever.

The End

Connect with Susan:

Wattpad: https://wattpad.com/user/bubblysue

Tumbler: https://tumbler.com/writersstuffbuddyor

https://tablo.io/susan-oreilly

Amazon: https://www.amazon.co.uk/Susan-OReilly/e/B01EGFHDJ0

Cover by Author.

Mummy's Torchlight

Sebnem E. Sanders

Toby waited for Mummy, but she never came back. Uncle Jim and Aunt Doris told him she was in Heaven. Why did Mummy go there without him? Why couldn't he go to see her?

He kept Mummy's torchlight safe, to guide him through the darkness, knowing she'd watch over him…

Sebnem E. Sanders is a native of Istanbul, Turkey. She currently lives on the eastern shores of the Southern Aegean where she dreams and writes Flash Fiction and Flash Poesy, as well as longer works of fiction. Her flash stories have been published on the Harper Collins *Authonomy Blog, The Drabble, Sick Lit Magazine, Twisted Sister Lit Mag,* and *Spelkfiction.* She has a completed manuscript, *The Child of Heaven,* and two works in progress, *The Child of Passion* and *The Lost Child*. Her collection of short and flash fiction stories, *Ripples on the Pond,* will be published this year.

***

Desolation

The child crawled between the stacks of old furniture in the basement and stood in front of a sofa, the back of which supported the plywood sheets piled up against the wall. The night before, he found the safe place, a nest where Mummy made a bed for him. She'd said, "Go hide, I'll be with you soon" and turned off the light as soon as he disappeared behind the panels.

He stayed put, as warned. Eyes adjusted to the darkness, he turned on Mummy's small torchlight to look for the wicker chest she had shown him many times when they played the game. "This is a safe tunnel," she said. He could hear voices and the noise of shifting furniture coming from upstairs but didn't understand the meaning. She'd also said, "Switch off the torch when you find the basket and only use it when you need to."

Through the small window, a pale stream of moonlight dissipated the darkness. He closed his eyes and slept, seeking to find comfort in his Mummy's arms again.

As daylight broke in, he awoke hungry. It was all quiet upstairs. He crept up the wooden stairs, creak by silent step, and placed his ear against the door. No sound. Turning the doorknob, he opened the exit with care and tiptoed to the kitchen to see if Mummy was there.

She was there, on the tiles, in a pool of red, asleep. He crawled across the floor and poked at her.

"Mummy, wake up. Wake up, please!"

She did not budge. Her floral dress was red around her belly. He snuggled up to her, wrapping her limp arm around him. It slapped to the floor as soon as he let go. Cuddling her, he rested his head on her bosom and sobbed, his tears mixing with the stains on her dress. He closed his eyes, holding onto his only true love.

***

Jim unlocked the front door, holding it open for his brother. Jack crept along the hallway, halted by the kitchen door, and froze. Their eyes met briefly as Jim entered the room and took in the scene. He covered a gasp with the back of his hand and turned to Jack. "Call the police, ask for Tom!"

He stepped slowly toward the child and, kneeling, stroked the boy's face. Warm. He was asleep, breathing deeply. Jim lifted the mother's arm and checked her pulse. Nothing.

Gently, he shook the boy. "Toby, wake up, it's Uncle Jim. Let's go play ball."

The boy opened his swollen eyes and looked at him. Gaze drifting to his mother, he said, "Mummy's sleeping. I can't wake her up."

"I know. Let's go outside."

Jim lifted the boy, the child's face and clothes stained with dried blood. Carrying him away from the kitchen, he stepped through the front entrance and into the garden. Time stopped. He paced the lawn with the child in his arms until he heard an ambulance approach. He stood in the driveway and put a finger to his lips, directing them to the kitchen. "My brother Jack's inside. I must stay with the boy."

The hot summer sun sent twinkling beams over the lawn and the creek at the bottom of the garden. Jim's eyes welled as he held the four-year-old tight against his chest. He kissed the top of the boy's head and whispered, "I think we both need a dip in the creek before we play ball."

As Jim stripped off Toby's clothes, something fell from the pocket of the boy's trousers.

"Mummy's torchlight," the boy said. "I must keep it safe."

"You will, Toby, you will."

Jim washed the blood from the child's face and body, leaving his own shirt till last.

"I'm hungry, Uncle Jim."

"Let's go have breakfast with Danny and Robin. Would you like that?"

"Yes, and Mummy will come, too?"

"Later. She'll come by later."

***

Seeing Jim and Toby getting out of the Rover, Doris came to greet them. Eyes swollen and bloodshot, Jim's look warned her something was wrong.

Jim sighed, pointing to Toby. "He's hungry, Doris."

Thirteen-year-old Robin dashed through the door with Danny at her tail and came to their rescue. She hugged the child, her favourite cousin. "Hiya, Toby. I missed you."

She lifted Toby up in the air and carried him to the kitchen. Jim and Doris followed.

"What'll you have, guys?" Doris asked. "Almond Oates, Shreddies, or Muesli?"

"Oates," Danny and Toby shouted in unison.

Children fed, the parents stole into their bedroom, where Jim put his head on his wife's shoulder and wept the torrent he'd held back. "What do we do now? She's gone. My baby sister's gone. How do I tell the boy? I told her the restraining order wouldn't protect either of them. She should have gone away, somewhere remote. I knew he'd kill her."

"Hush," Doris said, stroking his head. "I'm so sorry, my love, but you don't know for sure. We'll find a way. Toby can stay here. Danny is only a year older. He'll be fine. We'll give him all the love he needs."

The house phone rang. Jim reached over and lifted the receiver to his ear. "Hello?"

"Jim?"

He recognized the voice of his police inspector friend from high school. "Hey, Tom."

"I'm so sorry. If it's any consolation, we've already arrested the bastard. Delusional. I know he was under surveillance, but he managed to disappear last night. Our teams are searching the grounds for the murder weapon. His fingerprints are all over the knife-block in the kitchen, and one's missing." The inspector paused, his breath heavy across the line. "How's the boy?"

"He doesn't know...and I don't know how to tell him. He's only four, for God's sake." Jim broke down and Doris took the phone.

"Thank you for everything, Tom. We'll be all right. Toby will be all right. Just make sure that psycho is locked up for good."

"Social services are on their way. I've filled them in. They'll ask all the right questions. Be patient with the process, and the boy will be kept safe."

***

Toby waited for Mummy, but she never came back. Uncle Jim and Aunt Doris told him she was in Heaven. Why did Mummy go there without him? Why couldn't he go to see her?

He kept Mummy's torchlight safe to guide him through the darkness, knowing she'd watch over him.

***

Jim and Doris adopted him after the formalities were completed.

Redemption

It wasn't until Toby celebrated his eighteenth birthday that Uncle Jim and Aunt Doris told him the story behind his mother's death.

At the age of four, he had come to live with them after they said Mummy had gone to Heaven. Though Toby never understood why she'd gone away and left him with the torchlight, he liked his new family, especially Cousin Danny and his big sister, Robin. When Toby started school, he discovered they all had the same surname: Nelson.

Mummy came to visit him at night in his dreams. She told him the torchlight would keep him safe and Uncle Jim and Aunt Doris loved him as much as she did.

After beginning school, each night before he went to sleep he pulled the duvet over his body like a tent, supported by his knees. In the comfort of the cosy den, he read his books using the torchlight. He remembered the safe tunnel Mummy made for him in the basement of their house and the kitchen floor where she lay asleep in a pool of red. He recalled the words of a song she sang to him and repeated them, trying to capture her voice in his head. *Three Blind Mice.*

The music coming from Robin's piano fascinated him. The instrument, capable of creating sounds that flowed in a quaint pattern, reminded him of the water from the fall that gushed into the creek. He stood by Robin, watching her fingers glide along the white keys, forming melodies that spread out like the ripples on the pond.

When Robin asked if he'd like to try, he was overjoyed. She guided his fingers along the keys and taught him to play *Three Blind Mice*. His legs, too short to reach the pedals, and his mind unable to understand their function, he could only cope with the black keys as his fingers gained agility. A piano teacher continued his tuition as he grew up, until he could perform classical pieces by heart. He knew what he wanted to study in his teenage years. The Conservatory accepted his application at the age of eighteen.

This coincided with his Uncle Jim and Aunt Doris disclosing the facts about his mother's death. They also told him about his father, whom he thought had run away after he was born. Having loved Uncle Jim as his father, thoughts about this missing parent did not disturb him until they filled in the details.

His biological father, Richard Willsteed, had fallen in love with his mother as a teenager. As flower children in the mid-sixties, they travelled everywhere hippies gathered, encouraging peace. Drugs and hallucinogens being an important part of the culture, they sometimes disappeared for long periods. In the end, his mother returned home with Toby in her belly, saying to her parents, "I'm back for good and through with Richard, but I want this baby."

Richard followed her and refused to grant her the divorce she wanted, claiming ownership of their unborn child. This was when she told her family about his psychosis and hallucinations, which were not only related to the drugs he took. His schizophrenic condition had deteriorated over time, and he often threatened her life. She turned to the courts and obtained a restraining order while she spent her pregnancy at her parents' home, safe from his abuse.

She stayed with her family until she gained independence as a sculptor and began to sell her work. The cottage by the creek became her home when Toby was two, an idyllic setting to give free rein to her creative ability, yet its isolation provided the path for a threat she misread.

Despite the restraining order, Richard discovered the cottage location and demanded to see Toby. He had just finished serving a three-month jail sentence when he turned up at their door.

Toby remembered the basement and the noises coming from upstairs. He also recalled the kitchen.

"It was blood, wasn't it?" His eyes misted and tears rolled down his face. "The bastard killed my Mummy." He clenched his fists. "Where is he now?"

"Locked away," Jim said.

"Why couldn't they just hang him?"

His uncle hesitated and turned to his wife, Doris. She held Jim's hand. "He has the right to know. You must tell him everything. He's old enough to understand."

He nodded and turned to Toby. "He's being held at an institution for the mentally disturbed. I understand your anger. We both tried to shelter you from him, but we also thought you should know the truth one day. If you want to confront him, do so, but please let it stay there. Don't let this ruin your life. A bright future awaits you."

***

Torn between sense and revenge, Toby struggled with this news over the next few months. His heart, full of hatred for the man the law would call his father, wanted retribution. He knew he couldn't bring back his mother, but maybe he could do something for her.

Waking in a lather one night, he hatched a plan to bury his nightmares once and for all.

***

That summer Toby volunteered to play the piano once a week for the inmates of said institution but under the alias Alex Smith. He drove there on Saturdays, observing the audience as he performed. A tall man with long, dark hair walked into the room during his second concert. He settled on a chair. Tapping his fingers on its arms, he listened with his eyes closed as Toby played Chopin's *Impromtu No.4*.

Toby knew it was him, though he double-checked with the nurse at the reception on his way out. "Who's the tall man who came in late? He seems too peaceful to be in here? Is he a doctor?"

"No," she said. "That's Richard, one of our inmates and an artist. He has wonderful paintings. Some of them are in the lounge, others in the corridor. He donates the funds from the ones he sells to an orphanage."

Toby examined the paintings signed "R." All the women he depicted in his pictures had something in common: his mother's face.

***

After several performances, Richard approached Toby with a request. "Could I ask you to play Beethoven's *Moonlight Sonata* next time?"

The following Saturday, Toby accommodated his wish. Richard applauded and thanked him. "You're a very talented pianist, Alex."

"Thank you. And you're a good artist. I've seen some of your paintings."

They continued to talk, Richard filling in the details of the paintings along the corridor.

Unable to contain his yearning for knowledge, yet remaining calm, Toby asked, "Who's the woman in the paintings?"

"Ah," Richard sighed. "She's Angela, the woman I loved."

"What happened to her?"

"She died."

The time had come for Toby to drop his mask. He took the torchlight from his pocket and shone it in his father's face. "You killed her, didn't you?"

Richard froze, his eyes drifting away.

"Why did you—how could you?"

"I...I've been waiting for this moment all my life." He fell back against the wall and tilted a painting of Angela. She sat in a glade by a creek with a ring of flowers over her golden locks, which flowed down to an exposed and burgeoning belly. "I don't remember. I thought I was better and dumped the drugs my doctor prescribed." His voice broke and he wept. "I'm guilty. I've been carrying the burden of her...death...ever since. I'm not asking you to absolve me. You can kill me right here, and I won't say a word. I deserve it. I'm so sorry for depriving you of your beautiful mother."

Toby's eyes filled with tears. "So, you knew it was me all the time."

"How could I not? You look so much like her."

Toby raised the torch, almost crushing it in his rage, its plastic splintering across the handle, yet he lowered the weapon and dropped it into his pocket. "I'm too much like my mother. I couldn't kill a fly if I wanted to."

Their voices echoed through the hall. A nurse approached them and asked, "Richard, is everything all right? Do you wish to go to your room?"

"Everything is fine, Nurse Jane. As right as can be. We were discussing music and art, which often brings out the passion in us all."

Toby bowed, turned around, and left the building, his head bursting with thoughts.

***

His hatred and vengeance had dissolved into sadness and pity, but mostly sadness...a feeling of loss. Something he'd have to live with for the rest of his life. He knew one thing for certain. He'd never return.

Before he drove away from the Acacia Retreat, Toby held the torch tight in his hand. "I have confronted him, Mummy. I've done it for you and me. Rest in peace."

On the way home, he stopped on an old wooden bridge and threw the torch into the mirror-surfaced creek. He waited as the ripples extended outward and disappeared.

The End

Connect with Sebnem E. Sanders:

Blog: https://sebnemsanders.wordpress.com

Twitter: https://twitter.com/sebnemsanders

Cover by D.J. Meyers.

The Fall

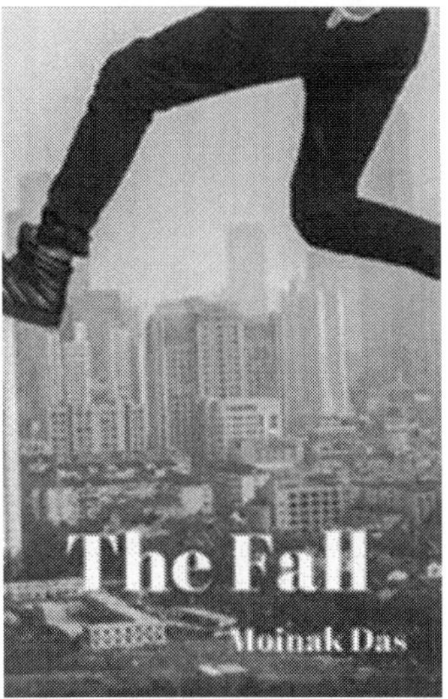

Moinak Das

Sometimes, it is wise not to run away from the things you fear. In fact, sometimes, running towards the things you fear is the only way to conquer them.

***

Sitting above, he was eighty-three meters away from life. Rishikesh, the land of tranquility, saw a commotion from thousands of visitors each day. Bhairav was sitting quietly on the edge of the cantilever of an old structure that stood tall, offering a picturesque panorama of Mohan-Chatti village, fifteen kilometers away from Lakshman Jhula, the heart of Rishikesh.

Though Bhairav was an acrophobic thirty-year-old, today his senses were too numb from a December morning chill to experience the phobia. As he sat on the metallic edge, deeply contemplating his life, the distant ripples of the river—eighty-three meters below—

weren't loud enough to disturb him. When he looked down the cantilever, everything was so small that he could actually see the entire Mohan-Chatti village from up there. In this village, there stood thousands of people, spread around like ants. The people below him and the fuss they created about their trivial problems, everything seemed just vague from up there.

"Sir, may I help you with anything? You seem so depressed about something."

His contemplations drew end as he was jolted back to reality by a stern voice behind him.

"Stay back!" He sprung up. "I said stay back. Give me some time. I am not going anywhere. And, I am warning you, do not dare come near me." He turned his back to the man once again. And he continued with his introspection, which brought tears to his eyes. He fought hard as he tried to hold them back.

He looked down from the cantilever again. Maybe his friend, Shahid, was somewhere down there in that crowd of ant-sized people. Maybe he was frenzied by now. Maybe he was searching for him. Maybe he had even filed a missing person case for Bhairav with the local police.

He suddenly started crying out loud, almost involuntarily. He thought of all those times he had failed to make his parents proud. Times when he failed to be a good son, a good friend, a good boyfriend and a good person all sprung up in his mind. Everyone he knew had almost called him a coward at some point of his life. And why not? He had been a coward up until now.

He didn't know the reason why he was suddenly crying out so loud. Was it the jolting from his deep contemplations? Was it the remorse of an ordinary life that he had spent all these years? Or was it just his phobia taking over him, as always, with his numbness finally drawing aside?

He couldn't take a chance again. He had to finish this fast, for once and for all. He needed to free himself forever, and this was his last chance. The bells of a distant Mahadev Mandir sounded different today, more like the death knells. Yes, he was afraid.

He looked down one more time, heaved himself up on his heels, and tilted forward. The gravity was about to do the rest.

There was again that same voice from behind: "Sir! Shall I help you with something?"

But it was already too late. Gravity isn't as indolent as human beings.

Soon after the fall, Bhairav began to descend like a frenzied missile. Shearing through a gushing stream of wind, he was falling down each moment with an acceleration of about ten meters per second squared. His speed increased every second with the fall. Such was the beauty of acceleration. With his head down and feet up and the wind ripping through his hair, he saw the ground approaching him, getting bigger each second.

After having fallen for a good few seconds, all his anxieties had now subsided. All his phobia and nervousness disappeared eventually, very much like the calm before a storm!

And suddenly, he came to a halt!

The bungee had finally stretched to its limit as Bhairav felt a pull on his stomach. He was now ready to move up once again and prepare for another adrenaline rush.

As the session finally ended with Bhairav riding his way back up to the cantilever one last time, he looked down, he looked up, and, then, looking all around, he shouted at the top of his voice, the sounds of which echoed far and wide in the valley: "WOOOOO HOOOOO! I did it. I am not a coward. YAAAAAAAAY!"

Sometimes, it is wise not to run away from the things you fear. In fact, sometimes, running towards the things you fear is the only way to conquer them.

And Bhairav didn't just run. He accelerated towards his fears.

The End

To connect with Moinak, follow the links below:

Blog: https://theculturalbridge.wordpress.com/

Cover by S. L. Baron.

Inconvenient

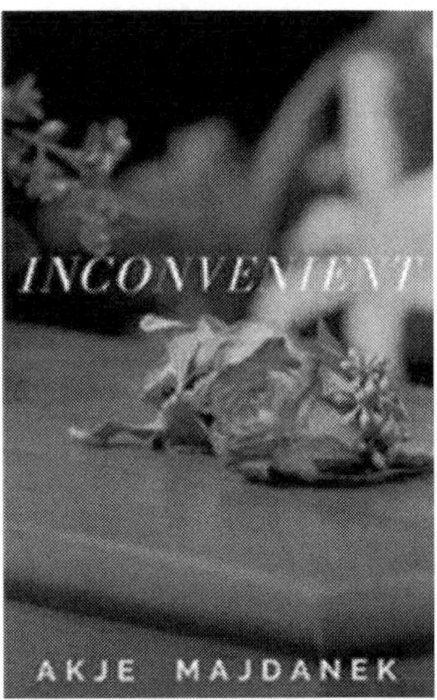

Akje Majdanek

After a funeral, a mortician discovers the dearly departed isn't quite dead yet. This wasn't murder.

Akje Majdanek began her writing journey in 2003 after reading a book that made her say, "For the love of God, I could write better than that!" She decided to take the advice of Benjamin Disraeli (or whoever the hell it was): "Whenever I want to read a good book, I have to write it my damn self." Akje loves books that say something meaningful about the world we live in. Therefore, in her own writing, she strives to address issues facing people and the world today.

***

He was a God-fearing man and it was a sin to kill. A mortal sin. Anyway, there was a death certificate. Officially the dearly departed was already dead. Dead and eulogized. The funeral had taken place that afternoon. All that remained to do was to bury it.

If only he hadn't noticed warmth while moving the corpse from the decorative display casket to a plain pine box, he wouldn't be suffering this crisis of conscience now. Okay, so the family had paid for the fancy casket. Well, they'd seen it. There was no reason to put such an expensive coffin in the ground. For all they knew, he was doing that right now while they drove home from the funeral. No one had stayed to watch the interment. He could sell that casket to the next family.

Family was everything.

This shouldn't be so hard. I have four kids to feed. That alone justifies it. I'm doing this for them.

Four kids, and a mortgage payment due on their $300,000 home. Was it so wrong to...to do his job? He wasn't killing her. He was simply going to bury her. Like he was paid to do. Had already *been* paid to do. Oxygen deprivation would kill her...if she didn't go mad and kill herself first somehow.

Could they kill themselves? He couldn't imagine how, but he'd heard the stories. He was a mortician. Of *course* he'd heard stories of bodies being exhumed for legal reasons, only to find they hadn't been quite dead when buried. Gashes in the wood, torn clothes and shredded casket lining where they'd tried to claw their way out.

Maybe we should bury them with bells like they did in the Middle Ages, he thought. But he couldn't afford to pay a gravedigger to dig them up again, and no one would do that kind of work for free, even when a person's life depended on it. Everything was so expensive these days.

If he hadn't noticed the warmth, this wouldn't be an issue. How many others had been buried alive? Before today, he'd insist it was none. Everyone knew the five stages of death. It wasn't his job to determine mortality. What had the doctor been smoking when he'd signed that certificate?

It's not my fault. It's the doctor's. I'm just a mortician.

Last week, he'd buried a three-year-old who'd choked to death and a teenager who'd overdosed the week before that. They were both dead, weren't they? He had to wonder. No one wanted embalming anymore due to environmental concerns. If he'd drained them like in the old days, he'd at least know they were deceased.

Brain dead, cell death, vegetative...who knew anymore?

It wasn't like he was the worst undertaker in history. Lizzie Borden's father had cut the feet off corpses so they'd fit into smaller boxes and he'd save money on the cost of wood.

At least his victims would've bled to death, if nothing else.

Maybe I should kill her so she doesn't suffer? It's not like I'd go to jail. There's a death certificate. She's already dead, even though she isn't.

But he couldn't bring himself to do it. No one else would know, but God would know, and *he* would know. Murder was a sin. He'd never killed anything before in his life. How could he hug his kids with hands that had killed someone? A woman, for Christ's sake. Even though the woman was a stranger, he couldn't do it.

Why did I ever try to move her from one box to another? If I'd just locked the lid and buried the damn thing, I'd be none the wiser now. She'd be just as traumatized when she awoke, but I'd never know it.

When she awoke. How long would that be? He was running out of time; he'd have to make a decision soon. Maybe someone would step into the parlor and make the decision for him. They'd walk right in here and ask if he needed any help, and he'd say no, he was just making sure all the paperwork was in order, and then he'd walk over to the casket and pretend he was arranging the hands more gracefully; he didn't want her to enter Heaven with her hands looking sloppy, and oooh, her hand feels warm. She doesn't have rigor mortis at all, he'd say. She must be still alive; what a good thing we noticed before the interment, eh?

If someone came in here right now, he'd say all that. Maybe it would look better if she were back in the expensive casket. They'd surely ask why she was in a pine box when her family had paid ten grand. Fine, he'd do that. He'd sacrifice the fancy casket. She deserved to go first class. With the lining, it was more comfortable. Maybe so comfortable she'd never wake up and simply expire without regaining consciousness. There was more room in the casket—at least two inches between her face and the lid. No room to raise her hands or push against it, not that it'd matter. There'd be six feet of dirt over her. How much would that weigh? Far too much for a human to lift the lid. And it had a lock anyhow. Expensive, fancy lock. Family members didn't like it when the lid of a coffin flew open while lowering it into a grave.

Family was everything.

Her family was already mourning, going through the process of letting go of her. It'd be months, maybe years before they'd work through their grief, but it had already started. A funeral was about closure so they could begin that process. Wouldn't it traumatize them more to have her come back now?

Maybe they'd sue me.

Everyone was so litigious these days. Well, who could blame them? The cost of living was so high, especially with four kids. His wife wanted a new car, but ten grand was barely a down payment. And now this woman—this stranger—was going to take that away from him? If he didn't bury the body, he wouldn't get paid. He'd have to cancel the credit card transaction. How did you even do that? He'd never had to before. Probably a complicated process. Everything was.

No, not everything. There was one thing that was very simple. He'd returned the departed to the casket, and she'd remain unconscious. Wasn't that a sign from God this was okay? It was in God's hands now. Surely God wouldn't allow one of his children to be traumatized by being buried alive. God would end her life and take her up to Heaven before she was even aware of where she was. All those reports of living people being interred were nothing but ghost stories conjured up around a campfire. Surely this was the first time it had ever happened for real. How could anyone these days not know the five signs of death?

He could name them all himself: pallor mortis; algor mortis; rigor mortis; livor mortis; decomposition.

The patient had none of these signs. It was the doctor's fault. Just who were they conferring medical degrees to these days? Frat boys from *Animal House*? This was what came of rewarding medical students who cared more about money than about people. Too many students majored in medicine solely because of the pay. The cost of living was so high. Seven hundred for an iPad; forty dollars a month for WiFi. Not to mention all those apps. Smartphones. Game consoles. Satellite TV. A college education. Thirty grand for a new car, and three hundred thousand for a house.

So many mouths to feed.

The cost of living was so high, the cost of dying could barely keep up. Ten grand for a single funeral was scarcely a down payment. Human life was measured in dollars, and this woman was worth more dead than alive.

She hadn't woken yet. Maybe she was in a coma. Probably in a coma. Surely God would put her in a coma so she wouldn't suffer. Must be awful to wake up in a coffin. He could never stand it himself, but he was a lot more claustrophobic than other people. Couldn't even bear to get in crowded elevators.

Maybe he should put a knife in her hands so she'd have some way to end the trauma, but suicide was a sin. He'd never contribute to the damning of another's immortal soul. Hell was so much worse than being trapped in a box; he was sure of it.

She didn't need a knife anyhow; she was probably in a coma. God would never let someone suffer so horribly unless they were truly evil. Things like this never happened to the just. Whatever happened now was God's will.

Yes, God's will.

God was responsible. The undertaker was no killer. If he hadn't noticed the warmth, there'd be no issue. Well, he'd learned his lesson. This was a warning from God that he shouldn't cheat the clients by replacing the expensive casket with a cheap pine box. He'd never do that again, but he'd only been thinking of his family. Four mouths to feed were so expensive. Six, actually. God said to be fruitful and multiply, and He'd make you prosperous if you did. Surely this was a sign that they deserved prosperity.

It's in God's hands. He'll have to do what I cannot.

He was no killer; he was an undertaker. He followed all the rules: prayed every night before bed, went to church every Sunday. If he killed, he'd never get to Heaven. His family and friends would go to the Promised Land, and he'd go to Hell just for showing a stranger some mercy.

It was in God's hands. Taking the smartphone from his pocket, he called the gravedigger and locked the casket.

The End

Akje Majdanek's books are available from Amazon at:

http://amazon.com/author/akjemajdanek

Photo Credit:
https://visualhunt.com/f2/photo/4068696971/9f216d4a5a/

Cover by Susan K. Saltos.

Mister Sandman

J. Robin Whitley

Mister Sandman is a story from a collection I'm writing called *Jukebox Stories*. As a musician who has lived half a century, I know a lot of music. As a result, my mind drives me crazy at times with earworms. Other times, I awaken to a lovely song playing in my mind that I forgot I had known. I had been pondering a thriller called *Jukebox Mind* when approached for OMP. "Mister Sandman" was a story started for my writers' group. My collection is still being formed as songs continue to haunt me. Each story will be based upon a song that comes to mind when I awaken or one that becomes an earworm.

While I am a lifelong musician, I am also a lifelong writer. Most of my life I spent teaching or leading music in some way as well as singing gigs when possible. My free time was often spent writing poetry or short stories. *In A Southern Closet* is a memoir first published by Regal Crest Books in 2011. *More Than Knowing* is my first collection of poetry published by Regal Crest in 2014. My debut novel is due out this fall under the pseudonym J.R. Frank. Another work in progress is a different collection of short stories based upon dreams and nightmares.

I would like to say my writing is influenced by Alice Walker, Rilke and Barbara Kingsolver. Yet, I know that my first novel has more of a Jan Karon influence. O'Henry is also a favorite of mine, and he is from my region. As a US Southerner, I know there will always be a hint of the South in my stories. From rural settings to dialect, I write stories that live or were born in my area. I love to read and hope that the great writers sink into my being enough that when I tell the stories in me, they resonate with the stories in you.

***

She woke up at two a.m., her head feeling like the Sandman had added a bag of sand to her nose and eyes. She stumbled through the dark to find the eucalyptus ointment near the greenish night light. Oh, how she missed using Sudafed. She loved the energy it gave her as well as keeping her head clear. She mumbled under her breath as she rummaged in her medicine cabinet, "Dang meth-heads mess up ever thang."

It wasn't only the meth-heads that kept her from using the Sudafed but the fact that she had heart problems. Sudafed made her heart feel like a voodoo daddy drummer after years of perpetual use. After getting the eucalyptus, she placed some on her nose and went back to bed. Her heart beat fast just from the short walk to the bathroom and back. She decided she could sing to the rhythm. Suddenly, the old Harry Nilsson song "Put the Lime in the Coconut" began threading through her mind. How annoying to have that earworm start up.

She turned over and began to sing "Jesus Loves Me" to get the earworm out of her mind. That never became an earworm for her. It was more like a lullaby. Then she thought of Brahms tune for "Rock-a-Bye and Lullaby." Slowly she began to drift off just as her husband began to snore like a dragon. The garlic toast he had eaten at dinner must have been real garlic too. He rolled over, snoring in her face. She was sure her eyebrows were singed. She turned her back to him and put a pillow over her head.

Dean had been so tired from work, she didn't want to risk waking him to tell him to turn back the other way. He hadn't slept well in ages. Now he slept soundly...or rather resoundingly. She held the pillow tighter over her ears. "...Put the lime in the coconut..." The tune went around and round in her mind.

Lordamercy, she thought. *Might as well get up and read.* Between the earworm and Dean's snores, she wasn't returning to sleep. Besides, the eucalyptus had not worked, and it was still hard for her to breathe. The pillow over her head didn't help cushion the sound of the snores. She got up again and threw the pillow on the bed, not thinking about how hard pillows pound until she heard its *poompf.* Dean's snores didn't miss a beat though. *Well good. Let him rest,* she thought. She closed the door gently behind her and walked through the loft to the desk.

Tap, tap. The touch lamp brightened the stairway. The tabby cat ran to the top of the stairs, greeting Martha with a chirp. "Don't you even thank about getting on me, you old cat. I cain't take any more allergic reactions!" The cat swirled at Martha's feet, almost tripping her down the stairs. "Put the lime in the coconut...call the doctor woke him up." Martha sang "Doctor!" out softly as she reached the bottom of the stairs.

She crept quietly to the kitchen, trying not to awaken the little chihuahuas. *Dean loves them noisy animals,* she thought. She flipped the light on over the kitchen sink and reached for the kettle. As she stood waiting for water to boil, she thought about how true some idioms and clichés were. The Nilsson song continued to wind through her mind. She began to think if she couldn't get the tune to change, it would unravel her. She began to sing a different old tune. "Mister Sandman, bring me a dream..." She hummed the rest of the tune. She didn't need another man or a different man. After thirty years of marriage, she had just gotten used to this one. While waiting, she turned to the sink window to grab her teacup and rinse it out. Her mind began again: "Ain't nothin' I can take, I said, doctor..."

Suddenly, she thought she saw something move outside the kitchen window, and it caused her to jump. She dropped the cup, and it shattered in the sink. The chihuahuas began to bark and howl. Martha moved quickly away from the window to the back door. She had to be careful because if it was a human, she would be seen. If it was a bear, which was more likely, maybe she would scare it. She was thankful now for the noise the chihuahuas were making. As she moved to the door, she ducked below the glass windowpane and then flipped the back-porch light on. Her heart and mind were racing. Now she needed her husband to awaken.

"Dean!" she shouted. "Bring yer shotgun down."

Dean didn't have a shotgun, but no one knew that. Everyone thought Dean was a gun collector like his dad, but he was as tame as a kitten. Tamer really. Martha saw the movement again and thought, *That ain't no bear*. Now she was so mad at Dean for not waking up, she didn't care who saw her. She hollered some more at him then began to stomp heavily to every porch-light switch, hoping she could sound like a man walking. "Dean! Dammit! Get down here!" she shouted above the small dogs. She turned on every light inside the house too but still tried to stay away from any open windows.

Finally, she worked her way around the first floor to the stairway. Just as she was about to start up the stairs, Dean appeared. His shadow looked frightening so she screamed. Then Dean turned on the upstairs light, squinting down at her.

"What in the world is all this racket about?" He began to make his way down the stairs.

"Dean, somebody is outside our window. I thought it was a bear the first time, but that ain't no bear out there."

"Well, whatta ya want me to do about it?" he asked grumpily, but he opened the hall closet and put on his coat and hat. He reached in the closet again and brought out his old baseball bat. Then he mumbled to the bat, "Louisville Slugger, don't fail me now." Dean was a big man and a strong man. If he swung a bat, he didn't miss.

"See if you can calm 'em dogs down and git the phone." He went out the back door. Going out the back, he could sneak behind the azaleas and could hide better while making his way around the house.

Martha went to the crate and got the small dogs out. Each of them ran to a different door before she could stop them. She had to admit, they were fearless for their size...or just plain stupid. She picked the smallest one up at the back door. As she hurried to pick up the other one, she petted Sylvie and told her it was okay. "Deddy's going to take care of the problem." She shushed and cooed after picking up Rufus. They didn't settle down until Dean came to the front door.

"Did you unlock this door?" he asked, poking his head in. He sounded angry but was really alarmed.

"No. Now why would I do that when I am afraid?" She could tell that she snapped at him, but she really was afraid.

She sat on the couch, soothing the small dogs until Dean finally came back in the house through the back door. "Well, there ain't nothin' out there. Turn some of them lights off!" He tromped to the hall closet to put everything back in its place.

"Dean, I swear I saw a human figure out there." Martha was breathless as she began turning lights off in a reverse pattern.

"Hon, I think it's just your imagination. Did you have another wild dream?"

"I couldn't even get to sleep, much less dream." Now she was annoyed. She wanted to tick him off for being so insensitive. "Between your snoring and garlic breath, it's a miracle I wasn't burned alive up there."

"See. Too much imagination." He spoke in a loving way as he kissed her forehead. "I'm goin' back to bed."

"Fine." She spat it out. He chuckled at her as he walked up the stairs. She shook her head in annoyance and moved to clean up the mess in the kitchen. Much to her exasperation, her mind began to sing the tune "Just my imagination." She sighed heavily and wondered yet how people ever slept listening to the radio. She began to sing aloud, hoping Dean would hear.

"Mister Sandman, bring me a dream. Make him the cutest that I've ever seen."

Then the chihuahuas began to bark at her. She hushed them from the kitchen. She picked up the shards of her favorite porcelain cup as she sighed and puffed. Cleaning up the cup pieces helped her to get her mind off what she was confident she saw. She was puzzled as to its nature, but since Dean was alive and back on his way to Dreamland, she knew they were safe.

She took down a coffee mug, put a tea bag in and poured the hot water. The act of making a cup of tea was soothing too. As she carefully made her way back to the couch, she decided she would make up her own lyrics to the Sandman tune. She softly began trying them out as she checked each door to assure that it was locked.

"Mister Sandman, send me a dream. Give me the best sleep that I've ever seen. Let me go walking through the beautiful dream world. And if you don't mind, teach me a beautiful dance twirl..."

She laughed to herself. The dogs sniffed at the air as she sat down on the couch, hoping for a snack. When they realized she had no food, both dogs moved to the opposite end of the couch where Dean sat. Martha watched them as they curled up tight together and soon were sleeping. She wished it was that easy for her to sleep. She sipped on her tea and then picked up the latest book by her favorite author. She loved murder mysteries. Perhaps it was her imagination, she thought, but she really didn't believe that there was nothing outside the house. She had to let it go though. Everything was fine.

Before she had read a page, Martha fell asleep on the couch. She was taken into a dreamland full of dunes of sand. The wind was blowing, and it was hot, but not so hot that she was uncomfortable. She looked down, expecting exotic attire, that of a Bedouin or perhaps a member of a harem. Instead, she was in her nightgown and walking in bare feet.

"So much for that fantasy."

Someone spoke.

She turned, but there was no one there. Just miles and miles of sand and blue sky. She stood still in the sand, wondering if she was in the Middle East or somewhere in the US, Africa, or Mongolia. She waited for the voice to speak again but nothing. She shrugged her shoulders and began to walk. *Might as well,* she thought. Maybe something was over the highest dune. However, as soon as she started walking, the scenery began to change.

She moved from a desert to an oasis to a seashore. Stopping on the shore, she wondered if she could walk back to her starting point. But turning around there was a deep darkness. In the darkness was a frightening void, frightening to the point she wanted to run. She turned to run to her right and ran directly into a brick wall. She fell back onto hard concrete instead of sand. Somehow, she was suddenly in an alleyway. She stood up and touched the scrape on her cheek where the roughness of the brick had skinned her.

What a dream, she thought. She put her hands on her hips and tried to remember how to wake herself up. She began telling herself to wake up. She was still in the alleyway. She was afraid to move now, not knowing what would happen. Then around the corner came three struggling figures. One man threw another to the ground, then both began to kick him. She was afraid to call out to them because everything seemed so real, and she didn't want to be killed in her own dream. She had always heard that if you dreamed you died, you really died. She wasn't ready to die.

Instead, she remained still, watching, waiting, holding her breath. She was also furiously chanting "wake up, wake up" inside her head. She watched as one of the men took out a gun and shot the helpless man in the head. It all happened so fast that she could not have intervened or turned her head. She was terrified and began frantically whispering to herself, "Wakeupwakeupwakeup!"

The man with the gun then yelled, "WHO'S that?" and began walking towards her. She thought if she could turn around, she could run to another scene, but she was frozen in place. The man drew nearer and nearer, coming into the light with the gun extended.

She felt something clawing at her and soon awakened from a blood-curdling scream. Sylvie was standing on Martha's hip, pawing at her arm and looking into her face. She had never been so thankful for that chihuahua. She carefully picked Sylvie up and gingerly sat upright. She thanked the dog, who leaned her head into Martha's cheek. She could hear Dean in the shower, so it was time to get up anyway. She didn't want to return to that dream for sure. She put the dog on the couch, slipped her feet into her slippers and stood.

"Come on, pups. Time to go outside." She smiled at the way they raced to the back door. Still she remembered the events of the previous night and guessed she had been more spooked than she originally thought. After letting the dogs out, she went into the kitchen to start breakfast.

She mixed up some biscuits and put them into the oven. While they were baking, she got out Dean's sausage. She wondered if he really liked sausage that good or just liked that he was named after Jimmy Dean. As she opened the sausage roll, the red meat reminded her of the shooting in her dream...no, nightmare. *What a horrible nightmare.* She shuddered at it and then was sad that there were those who lived such scenes. As she thought about those suffering through nightmares, she was suddenly surprised.

"Good morning, sunshine!" Dean boomed. She jumped. He was a morning person. She was not.

"Lord," she gasped. "You scared me."

"Aww, don't be so jumpy. You are all right because you're with me." He wrapped his arms around her waist and bent to kiss her cheek.

"Ow!" She pulled her head away. "Didn't you shave?" Her skin was stinging where he had kissed the left cheek.

"Smooth as a baby's—"

"Don't finish that sentence! I don't want to be kissed by a baby's butt. I have cleaned enough of those to know that's not a compliment."

"Maybe some grease popped up from the sausage. Here, let me see." He stepped to her left, and she lifted the stinging cheek so he could inspect. He squinted and made an odd face then gently touched the place. "Hon, looks like you scraped your cheek."

"What? I couldn't have scraped my cheek." She pushed him away. *Men. What do they know?* She was grumpy from the nightmare. He chuckled and lifted his hands in mock surrender. Then he went to let the chihuahuas in. While he was feeding the dogs, she lifted her hand to her cheek, trying to remember if grease had popped up and burned her. The place on her face felt like a burn, but to her fingers, it did indeed feel like a scrape. *No. It can't be,* she thought to herself. She shook her head in disbelief, then focused on cooking breakfast.

She decided she was going to look at her cheek after Dean left for work. It was stinging as they ate breakfast. She stood to pick up her plate. She couldn't eat. The nightmare made her sick. Dean soon finished and came to kiss her goodbye. He was only outside the front door for a few minutes when he returned.

"Um, hon, come look at this." He was scratching his head, and he looked puzzled.

She was wiping her hands on a dry towel from the kitchen as she followed him out the front door. "What?" She was aggravated because she wanted him to leave.

"Look." Dean pointed at the ground. There was a trail of sand going around the front of the house.

"See, I told you there was someone out here!" Martha exclaimed with satisfaction.

"I know. The thing is, when I came out last night, that sand wasn't there. I know because I looked for footprints around the doors and windows. Nothing seemed amiss."

For a moment they both stood stunned, staring at each other. Then, as her heart began to race, Martha began to follow the path of sand, going counterclockwise around the porch. Dean followed close behind, looking to the woods and at the house. The sand made a perfect path all around the house. After they had returned to the front steps. They stopped and looked at each other.

"I think we should call the sheriff," Dean said.

"Probably just a prank by some teenager, but won't hurt. Some of 'em teens are mean. I'll call as soon as I go back inside the house."

"Maybe I should stay with you today."

Martha looked at the beauty of the day. She felt okay. She was sure it was a prank. As she reached to gently touch her cheek, she said, "No. I think I will be okay. It's daylight, and I'm calling the sheriff. He'll come out here for a while. If I feel unsafe, I'll call Jillian."

"Shouldn't you call her anyway? She will want to know before hearing it on her scanner."

"Lord, I guess I should call her first."

Jillian, their only daughter, was a police officer for the town. She had been an officer for years. Once, when they didn't call her after an accident, she was pissed for months at them.

"Well, I'm gonna go on," Dean put both hands on Martha's shoulders and made sure she looked him in the eyes. "You're sure you gonna be okay?"

"Yeah. This is just some kid."

Dean pulled her into a hug. "I don't want nothin' happening to the only person who put up with me for these past thirty years. See you later, dear."

Martha swatted him with her drying towel and stood on the porch until he had backed his Ford F-150 out of the driveway. After he drove away, she turned and looked at the sand path again. She put her hands on her hips, wondering what in heaven's name was going on. Walking back into the house, she made sure she locked the front door, then walked quickly to the back door to make sure it was locked. Before she called Jillian or anybody else, she was going to look at her cheek.

She went into the guest bathroom and flipped on the light. Leaning into the mirror, she discovered it was true. Her cheek looked skinned like she had run into a brick wall. When she reached up to touch it, the skinned place appeared to have sand on it. She automatically reached up to brush it off. The sand was fine like sand on a beach. Shaking her head, she said aloud, "This doesn't make sense."

Puzzled, she walked back into the living room. She decided she was going to check the path that Dean found around the house. She also needed to remember to call the police. As she followed the path around the house, she only became more puzzled because the path was a lot of sand. From her left, she continued to stop and then pace the circle counterclockwise, trying to figure out who had done this and its purpose. Why so much sand and a ring around their house? She had walked around the house enough times that she began to walk as though in a trance. Only the *BEEP BEEP* of Jillian's Jeep brought her to the time and place at hand. Dean must have called her on his way into work. Sometimes she hated cell phones.

"Mom, what are you doing?" Jillian walked with purpose and strength as she strode towards her mother. "Haven't you called the police yet?"

"Well, no. Not yet." Martha was tentative. "I just got caught up in this path of sand and why it's here. Don't you think it strange?"

"Of course, it's strange. That's why you need to call the police."

Jillian pulled the radio off of her heavy black belt, clicking the transmit button. She turned away from her mother to talk to her office. Martha couldn't understand what was being said because Jillian talked so low. When Jillian turned back, she tried to be less official toward her mother. "Come on, Mom. Let's go in the house. Headquarters is going to send the police out here so we can figure out what is going on."

***

The police came and went. Jillian did the same. They were going to be the talk of the town, and everybody was going to have an opinion of what happened when she went to the grocery store. She would become a pariah if she told them what she thought really happened. The song kept trying to seep back into her consciousness. "Mister Sandman…" She hadn't slept much, and with all the hoopla at the house, she was tired.

Most afternoons she could nap, but she was afraid to sleep after all her ordeals. She decided to clean. That would awaken her and also help her get her mind off of strange things. Maybe Dean had made a good point about her imagination. Maybe she was too curious and liked reading the sci-fi and fantasy thrillers where something extraordinary happened to people too much. Her life was so ordinary, but she didn't want to have a thriller life. She didn't know what she did want, however.

As the vacuum hummed, she began to relax a bit. Nothing like taking action and living the ordinary life. She vacuumed every inch of the second floor like her life depended on it. She stopped the vacuum to dust the den and could hear that a wind had blown up outside. There was a hurricane off the coast of South Carolina, but they weren't supposed to get any wind that close to Charlotte. She looked out the window and saw the sand was rising with the wind. She looked to the trees, and their leaves didn't seem to be moving.

She moved to the door to the screened-in porch to see if it was just her imagination. By the time she went on the porch, the sand had risen up to half of her height, making a small wall of sand, blowing counterclockwise like she had walked. She was terrified and ran back into the house. She hurriedly turned on the vacuum to drown out the sound of the wind. She was still for a moment, and then, in the blowing sand, she saw a grinning figure. She began to focus on the floor and hurriedly returned to work. She continued to vacuum until Dean came home two hours later.

Dean sensed something was wrong immediately. He spoke to her, and when she looked up, he thought she was not herself. "Honey, what have you been doing? You look awful. Will you turn that damn thing off and talk to me?"

She just stared at him, but she had stopped the mad vacuuming. He reached for the off switch and noticed a look of fear in her eyes. "What is wrong with you? Here, come sit down." He took her gently by the elbow and led her to the couch. "What did the police say today?"

She shook her head absently.

"Nothing?" Dean asked, trying to get her to speak. She only shook her head no. "I'm gonna get you some water. Is Jillian coming back over?"

There was total quiet as Dean waited for the cool tap water to fill the cup. "You must've scared them dogs to death with that monster machine for them to be so quiet." Dean joked about the vacuum, trying to get Martha to talk. She only sat on the couch like a pillar of salt. He became concerned. "Listen, honey, we'll find out who's up to this."

He knelt in front of her and lifted the glass to her lips as though she were a child. She gulped down the water as though perishing. Her eyes grew as large as saucers, and she looked pleadingly at Dean but would not say a word. A look of terror came onto her face, and she pointed over Dean's shoulder. He turned to see what she was pointing at, and when he turned back to her, she had turned to sand.

The End

To learn more about J. Robin Whitley, visit the following links:

Facebook:
https://facebook.com/RobinWhitelyartist/?ref=bookmarks

Website: http://www.robinwhitely.com

Twitter: https://twitter.com/JoyRobin

Cover by Susan K. Saltos.

The Lighthouse

Seb Jenkins

Thompson had been working at Bishop Rock lighthouse for years, and many partners had come and gone in that time. As he shows new boy David Wells around the isolated island, items begin to go missing and strange voices whisper through the cold night's breeze. Thompson must try to figure out if it's all in his head or if Well's wants him to think it is.

Seb Jenkins is a 20-year-old student from Bedfordshire, England. His recent works are described as dark, gritty, and atmospheric, which he attributes to a lifetime of immersing himself in endless horror books and gore-fuelled TV shows/films. When he isn't writing, you can find him banging his head slowly against a brick wall or desperately trying to think of that best-selling idea he came up with at 3am last night. As of 2015, Seb is currently attending the University of Kent to study journalism and hopes to carve a career out of his passion for writing.

***

1801-Smalls Lighthouse—just off the coast of Pembrokeshire

In the early 1800s, British lighthouses made the switch from two-man crews to three-man, following a disturbing incident in 1801.

The Smalls Lighthouse team of Thomas Howell and Thomas Griffith were famously known to argue intensely. During one long shift together, Griffith fell ill and died of natural causes. Howell was so petrified of being blamed for the death of his colleague that he kept the body as evidence, rather than throwing it over into the sea. Worried that the corpse would soon start to rot and smell, Howell built a makeshift wooden coffin and lashed it to the outside of the lighthouse. Before long, the wind and waves tore the coffin apart, and the decaying arm of Griffith fell from its wooden cage. As the wind bellowed, it is said that the swaying hand almost looked as if it was beckoning Howell to come outside. The violent storms continued for a horrifying three weeks, at which point Howell was eventually relieved from his position.

He was so harrowed by the experience that some described him as 'demented' and even many of his close friends didn't recognise him anymore.

After this distressing ordeal, the three-man roster was introduced, until automation began in the 1980s.

However, 177 years after the Smalls disaster, a two-man team *was* used one more time.

1979-The Isles of Scilly—off the southwestern tip of Cornwall

Billy Murphy stared longingly at the Bishop Rock lighthouse from his bedroom window. He was obsessed with it and always had been. Much of his time was passed admiring the mighty structure from afar and dreaming of one day appreciating it up close.

It stood alone in the water, completely isolated from land, teetering on the jagged rocks lurking below. The dirty, chalk-coloured cylindrical body curved 51 metres into the air, set against a black stormy canvas.

It was all alone out there on a treacherous stormy sea, its sturdy granite platform standing firm against the constant commanding barrage. He related to his beloved Bishop on so many levels.

The sea was particularly rough that night; the waves crashed high upon the side of the tower instead of licking the rocks below. The dark expanse of water swirled and shifted in formation, attacking Bishop Rock from all angles, but the black waves were thrown back from the brick in a mixture of white foam and bubbles.

Most children Billy's age were terrified of lightning and thunder, but this 12-year-old sat eagerly awaiting each bolt as it illuminated his pride and joy. Each crack of eye-splitting light provided another glimpse, and each following growl of thunder, Billy imagined was Bishop defiantly retaliating to the elements.

The deep blue curtains surrounding Billy's window billowed in the wind, fluttering back into his room like extensions of the sea's waves.

Billy opened his window out further and shuffled onto the window ledge, his legs dangling into the night. He moved further and further out until he was on the very edge of the windowsill, millimetres from falling, teetering just like his beloved Bishop. The icy winter breeze slapped his face and burned his nostrils as he took a deep, long breath. How he wished he could be out there, just him and Bishop, away from everything else.

The rickety bedroom door creaked open behind him.

"Bill, are you feeling bet—"

His words froze in the cold breeze as he spotted his son halfway out the window. "Jesus Christ, Billy! Get down from there! You're already ill! Oh, God, look at you—you're as white as a sheet, you fool!"

His pyjama top pulled tight against his chest as his father yanked him back from the open window. Warmth seeped into his cool skin as strong arms held him close. A moment later, he was weightless with his feet dangling above the floor while his father carried him to bed and tucked him into the soft sheets.

"You need to stop doing this, Billy; you're not a healthy boy at the moment," his father pleaded with him as he shut the windows and drew the curtains.

"But, Dad! What about Bish—"

His portal to Bishop was closed.

"Oh, shut up about that bloody lighthouse!" his dad snapped back before calming himself down. "Billy, you know I love you. You *have* to listen to me. The only way you're going to get better is if you stay tucked up, nice and warm in bed. Okay?"

"Okay, Dad," Billy said begrudgingly.

He was sick of this constant concern and attention. His parents had been fussing over him for some time now. Just because he would never leave the house to play with the other boys on the island and barely had anyone he could call a friend.

All he wanted to do was talk about Bishop Rock, and as if his parents worrying wasn't bad enough, he had been seriously ill for the past two months now.

The local doctors had no idea what was wrong with him, and even those on the mainland could offer no help. Billy constantly seemed to look a worryingly pale shade of white and was freezing cold to touch. His eyes were often swollen and bloodshot, red lines dancing through the whites like branches on a dying tree.

His mother and father simply didn't know what to do anymore, except wait.

"Are you going to visit him though?" Billy asked, eyes wide with wonder.

"The lighthouse? No, son. Your mother's away, and I can't leave you here on your own like this. The boys will understand if I take a night or two off work, I'm sure."

"But what if Bishop gets lonely?" Billy questioned with a worried tone.

"Get some sleep," his father sighed, stroking his head softly.

1979-Meanwhile at Bishop Rock

Thompson shielded his face from the rain as he jogged across the helipad atop Bishop Rock lighthouse, introduced three years before, to ensure that the keepers could access the lighthouse on nights like these. The sea was far too violent and treacherous to reach the rocks safely by boat, forcing Thompson and his new partner, David Wells, to be airlifted in.

Thompson gave the pilot the thumbs up before clambering down the ladder as fast as he could. The rungs were slippery and frighteningly cold, but he'd done this a thousand times.

"Watch ya step!" he screamed up to Wells, battling to be heard over the hammering and clattering of the helicopter taking off.

Thompson hopped confidently from the ladder once he was a yard or so from the platform, landing with a soft splatter of his boots against metal. He ducked inside into the top floor of the lighthouse to get some respite from the unrelenting weather. Wells followed close behind.

Thompson was in his late fifties but could easily be mistaken for a lot older. His thick, grey beard was unkempt, and his shaggy hair wasn't much better. He wore his age on his face, with wrinkles and folds from top to bottom like an un-ironed sheet. He was a bulky man, standing well over six feet, with a naturally broad and muscular body. He towered over his latest partner.

Wells was 24 and new to the island. This had been the only job he could get his hands on after looking just about everywhere else. He was good looking, with a chiselled face, flowing blonde locks and bright blue eyes. Compared to Thompson, he was a very slight, short man, and his nerves made him sink even lower still.

They had barely had time to introduce themselves back on dry land and shared a somewhat awkward and silent ride over, but Thompson now reluctantly instigated pleasantries.

"I guess we better get to know each other if we're going to be stuck out here for God-knows how long," Thompson grumbled, unable to force a sense of pleasure into his sullen tones. "It was Wells, wasn't it?"

His brown eyes were unwelcoming and, teamed up with his harsh eyebrows, always seemed so full of anger.

"David Wells, yes. Looking forward to working with you! Hell of a lighthouse this, isn't it?" Wells replied, extending his hand to shake.

"They don't call her the 'King of the Lighthouses' for nothing, kid," Thompson said, shaking his new colleague's hand eventually.

He wasn't a fan of new people; hell, he wasn't a fan of people in general, but he prided himself on being professional and getting the job done.

"Sorry, I didn't catch your first name." Wells smiled.

"Thompson'll do just fine," the older man mumbled in reply. "I s'pose I should give you a tour of the place then. Keep up, please."

The smile drifted from Wells' face, but he shrugged his shoulders and followed Thompson down a set of stairs to their right.

"The last crew would have been flown out about half an hour before we got here, so all the systems should be working fine, but it's best to check. Our job is basically to keep the bastard place running and report any wrecks or activity out there," Thompson explained, casually throwing a thumb out in the vague direction of the sea.

"Are there not meant to be three of us?" Wells enquired.

"Aye, Murphy should have been here, but I guess he's been caught up in some drama at home. His little son is very ill, you see. Poor kid," Thompson explained. "So, it should be just you and me for the time being."

"Sounds great!" Wells exclaimed, immediately regretting the level of enthusiasm. He was trying to make a good impression, but he could already tell that Thompson was a man of few words and even fewer emotions.

"We have ten floors here. These stairs take you from the lamp all the way down to floor two, then it's ladders down to the rocks from there," Thompson continued to clarify as they trudged down the steps.

The staircase was a perfect spiral, running down almost the entire body of the tower. The narrow cylinder meant that the spiral was incredibly tight, and it was almost dizzying to walk down.

"This is floor nine. The service room. This is where we do maintenance and the such; just keep the light and the horn going basically." Thompson pointed out with the passion of a brick.

Wells peered inside. The room was full of electronics, levers, and buttons, with a dull whirring, mechanical noise. In the centre stood the main control panel, painted a dark green colour which had flaked off over the years.

"Could you just run the controls by me?" Wells asked, but Thompson was already stomping his way down to the next floor. "Maybe later then."

"This here is your storeroom: food, pots and pans and such. Not a lot to see really," Thompson pointed out without stopping his decline down the stairs.

Wells didn't bother to ask any questions, he knew better than to irritate the man further. He already got the distinct impression that Thompson resented having him here, so he just followed him down further and kept his mouth shut.

"Here we have the bedroom; I'm sure you'll find it most comfortable. As you can see, it's fitted out with the latest modern trends and entertainment to pass the time."

The bedroom was a sad sight. Wells hadn't expected much, but this was even dingier than he had imagined. Three old, rickety single beds lined up, one against each wall, with a chest of drawers squeezed in next to each. The closest thing that came to home comfort or decoration was the thick layer of dust coating just about every surface. A single lightbulb hung from the ceiling, flickering every few seconds, but barely doing anything to brighten the dull space.

"It's lovely," Wells muttered, tongue-in-cheek.

Thompson ignored him. The last thing he wanted to do was start exchanging banter. He couldn't think of anything worse.

"Next floor down, we have the living room. Just a couple of armchairs and a few books and that really, but it's better than nothing."

"Sounds good. What about the rest of the place?" Wells asked.

"Oh, it's just storerooms and old oil tanks, nothing to worry yourself with. Everything we need is be'en here and the top really," Thompson assured.

"Okay, well get me up to speed with the controls, and I'll be good to go!" Wells said, hoping his teacher wouldn't just ignore him this time.

Thompson spent the next hour or so teaching his young protégé the inner workings of the lighthouse before retiring to the sleeping chambers for a rest. He found that sleep was the best way to pass the time in this line of work; plus, he wasn't as young as he used to be: the kip would do him good.

***

Thompson awoke from his sleep a couple of hours later, feeling slightly groggy and worse for wear. He headed up to the top platform for some fresh air, hoping it would clear his headache.

As he wearily climbed the spiral staircase—the circles only making his head feel worse—he could hear the muffled tones of singing. The sounds grew louder as he neared the summit:

"Come all ye young fellows that follows the sea
To me, way hey, blow the man down
Now please pay attention and listen to me
Give me some time to blow the man down..."

"Blow the man down, ay?" Thompson grinned.

Wells jumped out his skin, almost dropping the burning cigarette nestled between his fingers. It was the first time Wells had seen the faintest sign of a smile from his new housemate, so he was quite taken aback.

"Yes, sir, my dad used to sing it to me as a boy. Bad habit, I s'pose." Wells laughed uneasily.

"Not at all; nothing wrong with a good old sea shanty in this line of work, boy," Thompson chirped, slapping Wells on the back as he shuffled up next to him.

"Got another one of those?" he asked, gesturing towards the flumes of smoke escaping Wells' mouth.

"Sure do," Wells replied, thrilled that Thompson was finally trying to bond.

"Oh, actually, hold that, kid. I'm just going to go grab my book from downstairs. Won't be a tick."

Wells nodded, not wanting to seem like he was trying too hard to befriend the stubborn old man.

A couple of minutes later, Thompson's grumpy voice bellowed up the staircase.

"Wells, have you moved my book?" echoed through the night.

"Err, not that I know of!" Wells shouted back down, desperately racking his brain as to whether he'd accidentally taken it.

He could hear Thompson's grumbles and moans making their way back up the stairs, louder and louder, until his messy grey mane re-emerged.

"I could have sworn I left it next to my bed," he mumbled.

"Well, I'm sure it'll turn u—" Wells began to reassure before Thompson interjected.

"I thought you said you didn't fucking move it?"

Thompson was visibly annoyed, and as Wells followed his fiery gaze, he understood why. On the side of the balcony, next to him, stood a solitary book.

"What? I swear that wasn't there a minute ago!" Wells pleaded.

"I know some people like to joke around to pass the time in these jobs, but let me tell you right now, that shit will not fly with me!" Thompson spat, snatching his book up before barging past Wells, back down the stairway.

"Fucking prick," he kept murmuring under his breath, straining to suppress his inextinguishable anger issues.

After stamping down the stairs as loudly as possible, Thompson threw himself into the nearest armchair and settled into his book, *The Old Man and the Sea.*

The book described the journeys of fisherman Santiago who suffered a painfully unlucky streak, going 85 days without a catch. The younger fishermen mocked him and refused to work with him, out of fear of catching the curse.

A couple of chapters in, Thompson began to calm down and regretted the way he had reacted. Wells had probably forgotten he'd borrowed the book or was just playing a practical joke.

It was rare for him, but Thompson decided to go and apologise to the younger man. It was his first day after all.

It felt as if he spent his life climbing up and down these stairs, as Thompson made his way back up to the lamp.

"Come all ye young fellows that follows the sea..." he heard as he passed the 8th floor store room.

"To me, way hey, blow the man down
Now please pay attention and listen to me
Give me some time to blow the man down..."

***

At least Wells' spirits hadn't been dampened by his outburst, Thompson thought, nearing the top of his climb.

"Come all ye young fellows that follows the sea
To me, way hey, blow the man down..."

All he had to do was say sorry and share a smoke with the kid; everyone loses their temper sometimes.

"Now wait for Thompson and listen to me
Look at the rocks and throw the man down..."

Thompson bounded up the last few stairs, his rage instantly switched back on.

"What the fuck did you just say?"

Wells looked up from his perch on the side of the balcony. "What did I say when?" he asked defensively.

"Don't play fucking games with me, boy!" Thompson roared, taking a step closer to Wells to show him that he wasn't messing about.

"I literally do not know what the fuck you're on about," Wells claimed, hopping down from the railings.

"You want to throw me onto the rocks, ay?" Thompson screamed, grabbing his partner's collar and pushing his head over the side of the balcony. "You want to throw me down there?"

Wells planted two hands on Thompson's chest and pushed him away.

"What the fuck are you talking about, you crazy old bastard? You've been a prick ever since I arrived here! I didn't take your shitty book, and I sure as hell didn't say anything about throwing you onto any fucking rocks!" Wells yelled in retaliation.

"I know what I heard, you disrespectful piece of shit!" Thompson spat.

"You know what, Thompson? Maybe you're just going a little bit crazy. Losing your mind in your old age," Well's hissed mockingly as he made circle motions by his temple.

Thompson wound his arm up, preparing to smack Wells as hard as he could in the face. Something in the back of his head told him to stop. This wasn't worth losing his job over.

"You just stay out of my way!" he cried, retreating down to his bed.

"Crazy? Me? How the fuck can he call me crazy? I know what I heard! And I know that he took my book!" he whispered to himself.

Thompson's mind was full of questions, rushing around one after another, just as fast and forceful as the waves hitting the rocks below.

Why was he doing this? Was this all one big game to him? Was he playing one big joke on Thompson? Was he trying to make him think he was crazy? Maybe he was after his job! People had tried to force Thompson out of this position many times before, claiming that he was unstable, prone to rage. Yes, that was it! He was trying to make Thompson think he was crazy! But why? So he could steal his job and take the higher wage as head keeper?

Thompson stormed into the bedroom and slumped down onto his bed, his head sinking lower than expected and rebounding hard against the mattress.

"What the fuck?" he exclaimed.

He sat back up and peered behind him. His pillow was gone.

"Oh no! Oh, this is the last straw!" he said, marching back out the door straight away.

"Where the fuck is it this time? First my book and now my pillow? Are you really that immature, you little shit!"

This time Wells came down to him, striding down the steps almost as purposefully as Thompson.

"What the fuck is it this time?" Wells asked.

"You know exactly what it is: Where is my fucking pillow?" Thompson growled back.

"Oh, Jesus Christ, are you serious? You've lost it! You have actually lost it! I'm not spending another minute around you! I'm sleeping upstairs, and first thing in the morning, when the water is calm, I'm getting the fuck out of here!" Wells laughed, before leaping back up the stairs as fast as he could.

"He laughed. He actually laughed at me," Thompson whispered to himself. "As if I'm the crazy one here!"

His face was growing redder and redder by the second, and he could feel the rage bubbling from within. All he had to do was make it until tomorrow morning, then cheer and wave as Wells left, never to return.

Thompson bent over the side of the stairs, eyes shut, breathing in deep and then out, in and then out. His heart rate slowed and his breathing became more regular as he felt himself calming. After a moment or two, he opened his eyes once more.

"Oh, you've got to be kidding me!"

Thompson squinted and strained, but he was almost positive about what he could see sitting at the very bottom of the spiral staircase. His pillow.

He kept breathing steadily as he started the decline from floor seven to floor two, all the while muttering the words *"one more day."* That's all he had to endure until this plague on his life left for good. Maybe even Murphy would be back by then.

As he reached the very bottom of the stairs, he felt the real force of the wind outside. It whistled powerfully under the door and through the slim cracks in the granite bricks. The noise was so loud it muffled the profanities that spewed from Thompson's mouth when he bent down to retrieve his pillow.

Attached to it was a little note. Simply:

Thompson surrounded by a neatly drawn heart.

He resisted the urge to batter the living daylight out of Wells and instead tucked himself into bed, comforted by the promise of isolation tomorrow morning. However, his sleep was interrupted that night by a constant whispered chorus of:

"Come all ye young fellows that follows the sea
To me, way hey, blow the man down
Now wait for Thompson and listen to me
Look at the rocks and throw the man down..."

After lying there for what seemed like hours, Thompson couldn't take it anymore. What if he was crazy? What if this was all in his head? Maybe Wells was right after all.

He slid out of bed and stumbled out the doorway towards the stairs. He needed some answers. He rubbed his eyes and planted one hand against the wall to steady himself. *Rustle.* Thompson turned his head to the source of the noise and tore a scrap piece of paper from the wall.

Sprawled across it in messy red handwriting was the word: *CRAZY.*

As Thompson inspected it closer, he spotted the world *Santiago* in print and realised what the paper was. It was his book, *The Old Man and the Sea*. He glanced up the staircase, slightly blinded by the light of the lamp bursting through every five or so seconds. Page after page was stuck to the walls, spiralling up with the stairs, each brandishing the word *CRAZY* in the same red handwriting.

Thompson was sure now. He'd never been so sure of anything in his life. He was not crazy. Wells was trying to mess with him, make him think he was losing it, but Thompson swore he would get the last laugh.

As he burst out into the fresh air, he spotted Wells, fast asleep on the floor next to the lamp. Thompson's target illuminated every five seconds, like a beacon beckoning him to go in for the kill.

He leaped on top of the smaller man, pinning him to the ground with his knees.

"What the fuck?" Wells screamed as his eyes snapped open in a startled panic. "What are you doing?"

"Crazy, am I? Thought you could make me lose it? Well, who's the crazy one now?" Thompson screeched, throwing the balled-up scrap of paper at Wells' face.

Wells desperately tried to punch and claw at Thompson's face, but even though he was far older, he was much bigger and heavier than his opponent. Thompson swatted away Wells' flailing arms with one hand whilst clamping the other around his throat.

"Stop! I haven't done any—" Wells whimpered, but Thompson gripped tighter.

He now had two hands wrapped around Wells' throat, choking every last bit of air from his lungs.

All Wells could do was muster a weak whisper: "Please."

It reminded Thompson of the whispered voices he had been hearing all day.

"Stop whispering! Stop whispering! STOP WHISPERING!" he squealed. He didn't sound human anymore.

Wells' grew weaker and weaker as the oxygen left his body until, eventually, he jerked violently before coming to an eerily still rest.

Thompson clambered to his feet, manically laughing.

"I won! I won, you bastard! You tried to make me lose my mind, and I won!"

Thompson stared down at the lifeless body before him and continued to cackle. Then he stopped.

"Come all ye young fellows that follows the sea
To me, way hey, blow the man down

Now wait for Thompson and listen to me
Look at the rocks and throw the man down..."

"What? No! NO! NO! NO!" Thompson screamed. "I killed him! I won! WHY ARE YOU STILL DOING THIS!"

He kicked out at Wells' dead body, again and again, as hard as he possibly could, but the song still rang through his ears.

"Come all ye young fellows that follows the sea
To me, way hey, blow the man down
Now wait for Thompson and listen to me
Look at the rocks and throw the man down..."

He slapped the side of his head with one hand, then the other, and before long he was punching his temples with all his strength.

"Get out of there! GET OUT!"

He sank to his knees and sobbed. After everything, he had been hearing the voices all along. Wells hadn't been singing it, and he probably hadn't been moving anything either. It was all in Thompson's head. He couldn't take this anymore. Now he was crazy and a murderer.

He clambered to his feet, fighting the urge to throw up. Stumbling like a drunk, he lifted one leg over the nearest railing, followed by the other. He took one deep breath in, then leant out over the side, gripping onto the rails behind him. He took one deep breath out, then closed his eyes. Another deep breath in and loosened his grip. One last breath out, and he let go.

His body plummeted through the air, falling 51 metres and ten floors down before finally crashing down onto the rocks below. Thompson had always been surprised by how loud the waves were when they collided with the rocks at Bishop lighthouse. It was nothing compared to the crack of bones.

The top of Bishop Rock lighthouse continued to flash for 15 more seconds.

Flash...
Flash...
Flash...
Darkness...

"Come all ye young fellows that follows the sea
To me, way hey, blow the man down
Now wait for Thompson and listen to me
Look at the rocks and throw the man down..."

***

A dark figure stepped out from the doorway at the top of the lighthouse, illuminated only by his own shining, demonic, red eyes.

Billy Murphy ran his hands along the railings of his beloved Bishop.

"Now it's finally just us."

The End

Connect with Seb at the following links:

Website: www.sebjenkins.co.uk

Wattpad: https://www.wattpad.com/user/SebJenkins

Facebook: https://www.facebook.com/sebjenkins96
Amazon:
https://www.amazon.co.uk/s/ref=dp_byline_sr_book_1?ie=UTF8&text=Seb+Jenkins&search-alias=books-uk&field-author=Seb+Jenkins&sort=relevancerank

Goodreads: https://goodreads.com/author/show/16585589.Seb Jenkins

Cover by Phoebe Liang (on Wattpad as @sugarcrystals).

The Detour

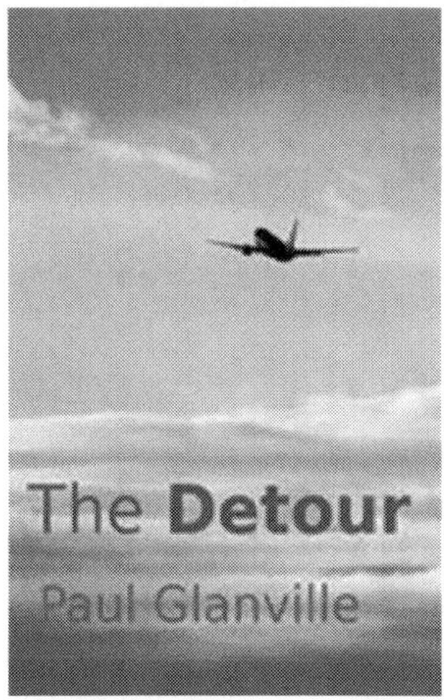

Paul Glanville

A routine day takes a detour when an airliner is hijacked.

Paul is an Embedded Systems Engineer by day and has been writing for himself since WordStar was popular. He has only recently begun to share.

***

I am a glorified bus driver.

I start every day in Jakarta. My passengers get on, and I take them to Banda Aceh, with a stop halfway at Pekanbaru. There's about an hour traveling between stops. We pull up to the terminal; a few passengers get off and some cargo from under the floor is unloaded. Then new cargo is loaded, some passengers get on, and after about a half-hour, we're on to our next stop. When we get to Banda Aceh, we turn around and do it in the opposite order on the way home.

Banda Aceh is a resort town. You may recall hearing the name; it was hit by a tsunami in 2004. That was a terrible disaster, but it's all cleaned up now, and we're the cheapest way to get there from Jakarta. We take longer than the others, who go there directly without stopping three times, but if you're one of my passengers, we'll get you to within a short taxi ride of the resorts before noon.

I've been flying for decades: first for the Indonesian Air Force, ferrying men and supplies all over the country. Now I'm the captain in a small regional carrier, doing almost the same thing as before.

The job is not nearly as glamorous as people think. It's mostly preparation for an awesome responsibility, every day.

My favorite part is taking off. You push those throttles forward, and the engines gradually spin up to full power. The A319 strains, but you have the brakes on. Finally, you release the brakes, and you're pushed into your seat as she leaps forward. About halfway down the runway, you pull on the yoke slightly, the nose gently rises, and the world disappears from view in the main windscreen. The feeling...the rumbling sound of the wheels on the tarmac goes away; it's suddenly quiet as you lift up. "Wheels up!" you command, and your copilot flips the lever. Three green lights turn red then extinguish altogether. "Wheels up!" your copilot responds. Above the clouds, the sun shines brilliantly. She wants to fly. There's no feeling like it, and I get to do it several times a day. You look over to the man in the right seat. "She's yours." You feel him take the controls and you let go. Now you can relax a bit and enjoy the ride from the best seat on the plane.

Landing is the tricky part. If you just aim the plane down, it'll accelerate like a roller coaster, and you can't land if you're going too fast. Getting up is easy, but it's a delicate balance, getting back down.

I've got thousands of hours more experience than my copilot, and he's not going to get any more if I fly the plane all day every day, so I hand it off. I usually let copilots land, too. Again, they need the experience more than me. After a while, the company changes my crew: new copilot, new cabin attendants. I've had the same flight crew for months, and we talk about each other. We know each others' personal lives: who's married, who's dating, what's happening in their families. It's less of a boring grind than it otherwise would be.

***

We just took off from Sultan Syarif Kasim II International at Pekanbaru—next stop: Banda Aceh—and we're climbing through broken cloud past 5,000 meters, up to our cruise altitude of 8,000. Ninety-seven passengers, mostly tourists. I'd just handed off the controls to my copilot, Martin Ramirez, when I got a call from the forward flight attendant's station.

"Captain, there's a disturbance..."

Then, I heard a lot of noise. "What's happening?" I asked.

The cockpit door suddenly burst open. It's not supposed to do that after I lock it.

A lot of screaming and yelling. A stewardess fell backward, landing hard on the cockpit floor, and three men followed, stepping over her as they barged in.

"We're taking control!" one of them said. He held up a hand grenade. That got our attention like nothing had ever before. I looked over to Martin. He was looking at the grenade as if he was watching his life count down.

"Martin!"

My copilot ignored me, still focused on the intruders and the weapon.

"Martin!" I yelled.

He jumped and looked back at me, his eyes wide-open like saucers.

"Martin, I'll handle this. You fly the plane!"

He blinked then nodded. "Yes, sir!" He gulped and turned to face the controls. He was scared but doing his job.

"I give the orders here!" the leader said.

I turned to him. "Sir, I'm the captain, and I can order everyone to cooperate with you."

"Fuck you! I give the orders! Do you hear me, asshole?" He was still excited.

I had to calm him down. "Loud and clear. You give the orders. I have the authority to do whatever you want, okay? Just tell me what you want, and I'll make it happen."

The leader's demeanor seemed to relax a bit, although the other two still looked pumped to their eyeballs with adrenaline.

In the calmest voice I could, I asked, "Tell me. What do you want?"

"Take us to Mecca!"

A hijacking. I was almost relieved.

"Martin, we're going to Mecca."

We've had more than our share of radical Islamic-inspired violence and terrorism, but we've been in relative peace for most of the last decade. I looked at the three again. They were certainly "True Believers," but were they part of some radical group? They got a grenade aboard somehow and the door might have been weakened—was someone in the ground crew involved?

"Uhhh." The stewardess began to stir. "Sorry, sir." She got up to her hands and knees. "I couldn't stop them."

"That's okay."

"Get her out of here," ordered the leader.

The two other men grabbed her, roughly lifted her up, and shoved her out of the cockpit. She fell on her belly and slid down the aisle. I wanted to get up and stop this—a hijacking is one thing, but nobody abuses my crew! What could I do without getting everyone killed?

The leader spotted the jump seat and sat where he could keep an eye on us. "I've got everything under control here. You two, guard the door."

"Okay." They left.

By now, even the passengers in the tail knew something was wrong.

"Good morning. This is your captain speaking. We've had a disturbance in the cockpit, and we're working on it, so there's no cause for alarm. In the meantime, please remain seated. Thank you."

We settled in for an uneasy ride.

***

Fifteen minutes later, we started our descent into Banda Aceh. The way it's done is by reducing the engine power, usually all the way to idle; when you reduce power, the plane slows and you maintain the proper airspeed by gently descending. You can hear the sound of the engines drop, and this alarmed the leader.

"What's happening? What are you doing?"

I turned. "Don't worry, we're just starting our descent into Banda Aceh."

"No! We're going to Mecca!" He waved his hand grenade around.

"We can't make it all the way to Mecca. We have to land and refuel."

"Don't fuck with me. I saw the fuel trucks at the airport. You already refueled!"

I looked at the papers from Pekanbaru.

Four hours ago, when we did our preflight preparations at Jakarta, Martin noticed that the price of jet fuel was lower at Pekanbaru, so we made sure to have enough to get there, plus the mandated reserves, of course. You have to understand that planes fly more economically when they're carrying less weight, and fuel is heavy, so you try to take off with only as much as you'll need, plus a little extra for emergencies. So, when we stopped there, we partially fueled while we unloaded and loaded passengers and cargo. We knew we'd be back in a few hours on our return trip. The plan was to completely fill our tanks on the return leg and ferry the cheaper fuel back to Jakarta for the airline. The economics of running an airline is a boring part of the job. But today, it became a real problem.

I did the math. The gauges were showing about a quarter full. Forty-eight hundred kilograms. I guessed about 1500 km, give or take. I saw Martin glancing at the gauges. He glanced over to me and shook his head. We didn't need to say a word. We'd done the same arithmetic and came to the same conclusion.

"We can only go about 1500 kilometers before we have to refuel."

"I saw the plane getting refueled." He waved his weapon. "We go to Mecca or else everyone dies!"

I turned and sat back. "Martin, set cruise at 10,000 meters. Point seventy-eight Mach."

"Captain?"

"I know," I sighed. "Just do it."

"Yes, sir."

I told the flight controller about our situation. Minutes later, we were passing Banda Aceh. I started praying for a friendly runway beyond the horizon.

Every airport in the world has a four-letter code name that our flight management autopilot understands. I asked traffic control for the airport code for Mecca. A few minutes later, I was told that Mecca has no airport, none at all, which surprised the hell out of me. Actually, I was so far beyond surprised that I can't think of a word for it. Imagine, more than a million pilgrims come to Mecca for the Hadj every year, and there's no airport in town.

The controller added that the closest airports are Jeddah and Medina; Jeddah is closer; only about eighty kilometers from Mecca.

"You heard the guy," I said. "We can't take you to Mecca, but we can get you close, so where do you want to go?"

"Medina!" he answered.

I relayed that to the ground and was given a code to enter: OEMA. I punched it into the Flight Management Console. It's more than 6300 km away.

No way we would have made it, even if we had been fully fueled, especially not with the plane loaded with ninety-seven passengers and four cargo containers.

"What makes you think we can go all the way to Mecca with this plane?"

"We looked it up on the Airbus website—an A319 can go 6750 kilometers. Banda Aceh to Mecca is less—we looked that up too—so we go to Mecca!"

Martin and I exchanged bewildered glances. This plane can do about 6000 kilometers, if she was topped off. Maybe 6300 if we exhaust the reserves—in light air, or with a slight tail wind, maybe—but a headwind would force us down early. 6700 kilometers? No way!

Martin spoke up, "Hey, boss, that plane you saw in the Airbus site, was that the A319 Neo?"

"I dunno. Who cares?"

Almost whispering, Martin addressed me, "I think Airbus is promoting their newest model on their site. The Neo's got sharklets."

Of course! You might have noticed how, on many new planes, the last couple of meters of the wings are bent to go straight up. They're called "winglets" or "sharklets" because of their shape. They dramatically improve a plane's performance by roughly ten percent.

Ours is not a brand-new plane. We don't have that feature, and even if we were full of fuel, we wouldn't make it to Mecca. As it was, we couldn't even make it a quarter of the way there. The next land, beyond the horizon, was India, and I was worried that it was too far away. I silently prayed for a stiff tailwind...

We don't carry international charts that include the Indian Ocean. Why would we? We're regional. So we really didn't know where we're going. We didn't know which waypoints to program into our Flight Management System (a super-fancy controller for the whole plane, including an autopilot), the frequencies of the navigational beacons along the way...nothing.

We were lost in a big sky.

***

"Regional two-niner two-seven." It was the flight controller.

"Regional two-niner two-seven. Roger."

"Hi. We understand you're en route to Mecca."

"Roger, Mecca."

"Vector directly to AKINO."

A waypoint! Thank goodness! We had someplace to fly to! I entered AKINO into the Flight Management Console. Course 274. Almost due west. Sounded about right. I hit the program command button. I felt the plane respond to the autopilot, banking slightly to the right from 270. "AKINO, copy."

"At AKINO, contact Colombo Control for further instruction."

"Thanks, Jakarta!" Sri Lanka! I'd forgotten, and it's closer than India! Maybe, just maybe...

"You're welcome. Good luck!"

Years ago, we only had radio beacons for navigation. After a while, they started naming the intersections of the beacons; if one beacon was at a particular angle with respect to another, you could tell the controller that you were at a particular waypoint. They're on the charts. Today, with GPS, we can program our autopilot to go anywhere, and we have a new set of waypoints that are simply latitude and longitude coordinates. Nearly all of them are five-letters long, just as most of the beacons are three and airports are four. AKINO is a GPS waypoint.

It took thirty minutes to get to AKINO. We said goodbye to Jakarta Air Traffic Control, they wished us luck, and we contacted Colombo Control. They were expecting our call and gave us more navigational waypoints in order: TEBIT, HC, MTL, VCRI. That last one grabbed my attention—four letter codes are airports! I glanced over to Martin. He looked as surprised as I felt. Dare we hope? I steadied myself and looked over my shoulder at my "guest" in the cockpit, Mr. Hand Grenade. I entered the codes into the Flight Management Console. The airport was about 80 km further than our fuel estimate.

The controller continued to give us letters and numbers. Mr. Hand Grenade didn't seem interested.

Have you ever driven your car on "E," certain that you've got another two or three liters before your engine starts sucking air and dies, certain that the gas station a dozen kilometers away is close enough? There is a big difference between certainty and knowledge, isn't there? No matter how certain you are, you still sweat up until the moment you roll into the station and stop in front of the gas pump, don't you?

Cruising at ten thousand meters and point seventy-eight Mach, it took about an hour to get to TEBIT. An hour of watching the needles slowly drop, little by little, lower and lower. Ahead, open sea, open sea, and more open sea. The closer we get to TEBIT, the more nervous I got. I watched the gauges and waited, listening for a sputter, a hiccup, anything to hint that an engine is about to cut out, and then the other. I waited for a hint that our quiet glide down to the water was about to start.

TEBIT disappeared from the console screen. I felt the plane gently change course towards HC, another waypoint...

***

"Take the controls, Cap," Martin said. "I've got to use the restroom."

"Bird's mine," I replied as I took the controls. Before our guard realized what was happening, Martin had released his seat belt and was out of his seat.

"Get back! Get back in your seat!"

"C'mon, man. I've really gotta go."

She yawed slightly then straightened out. An alarm went off. An alarm I'd been dreading.

"What's that?"

"Shit! One of the engines stopped," I said, clearing the alarm.

"What did you do? Start it back up!"

"I didn't do anything. We're running—"

Another alarm sounded as the screens went black.

"Fuck!"

***

Clearing the annunciator, the cockpit was eerily quiet. No whine of the twin turbines; only the whoosh of air.

I was piloting a 55-ton glider.

I heard something slam against something else. The cockpit door slammed. There were sounds of a struggle. I glanced quickly over my shoulder—they were on the floor—and I got back to work. More struggling and then pounding on the door. This time, it didn't open.

Martin got back in his seat. His clothes were in disarray, his tie and belt missing altogether. He smiled. "Look at this," he said. I glanced over. He had the grenade! "Notice anything?" He handed it to me. She was flying smoothly, and I didn't need my right hand for the throttles, so I reached over.

There was something, well, odd. Something caught my eye, and I turned it over—there was a hole in the bottom. "Martin, are you telling me we're going to ditch in the ocean and my passengers are in mortal danger because of a fucking practice grenade?"

Martin nodded, laughing. "Hard to tell them apart, especially when the bad guy doesn't give you a chance to examine it."

There was thumping on the other side of the cockpit door. It stopped, and I got a call on the intercom. It was Sally, one of the cabin crew.

"Some passengers took out the bad guys. We're good in here," she said.

"All clear in here too," I said, looking at our hijacker, lying on the floor, hog-tied with a tie and a belt.

"Cap," Martin said, "with all the excitement, I forgot why I got up in the first place."

I laughed. "I've got her. Go do what you have to do."

"Thanks."

"Oh, and get our 'friend' out of my cockpit!"

"Aye, Cap'n."

He opened the door and cheers erupted from the passenger compartment.

I heard something being dragged on the floor, and the door closed.

***

When the engines died, hydraulic pumps and the generators died with them, taking out the flight controls and the computers. Fortunately, planes like ours are fitted with some very basic emergency backups. When the engines' hydraulic pumps fail, there's a little windmill that pops out of the fuselage called a Ram Air Turbine, and it works a small hydraulic pump. It's just powerful enough to control the plane. There's also a set of six old-fashioned instruments so we can know how high we are, what direction we're going, and so on. So, we were flying old school.

One of those instruments, the VOR receiver, came to life. It had picked up the MTL beacon. The receiver showed the direction and the distance to the transmitter; we were 200 km away. At our altitude, that was too far to glide, but if we headed straight for it, we'd be closer to land and maybe some shipping...

It was a long fifteen minutes. Altimeters look like clocks, and I spent the whole time watching ours spin backward.

We'd been in radio contact with the Sri Lankan Air Traffic Controller, and they had us on RADAR the whole time. And, of course, the flight attendants had prepared everyone in the cabin—we didn't want a repeat of what happened to Ethiopian Airlines 961, another hijacking where half of the initial survivors didn't even make it out of the plane before it sank.

We were down to our last one thousand meters when Martin spotted a plane coming towards us. I just got a glimpse of it in the right-hand side before it disappeared up and to our rear.

Before I knew it, a big C130 was flying on my side. "Sri Lanka Air Force."

"Good afternoon," came over my headset. "We're here to help. We've got divers, medics, and a few power boats from the Special Boat Squadron ready to drop and help your people until more substantial help arrives. A navy cutter should arrive in about half an hour."

"Roger, and thanks!"

***

Our angel, in the form of a military transport, flew alongside us, talking us down. I can't begin to say what a help that was. They told us how close we were getting to the water.

I pitched the nose up and slowed the plane. The other plane gently floated away, apparently unwilling to follow us into a stall and a ditching. Then I felt the tail skimming on the water. This is what we're paid for. You've got to keep the wings absolutely level. You can't let one engine hit the water too soon before the other. If it does, it'll stop while the other is still going 200 kph, and the plane will break up.

Water washed over the windscreen. When both engines hit the water at the same time, the plane stopped, quite suddenly, from 200 to zero instantly. The nose bobbed up. I could see the sky! I looked around. We were okay. Martin and I went through the shutdown sequence and were out of the cockpit in a minute.

The cabin crew didn't need any prompting. All the doors, including the two, one over each wing, were open, and the passengers were filing out onto the inflatable ramps that double as rafts. Nobody seemed to be seriously hurt. A few scrapes here and there, but everyone was moving on their own. All in all, pretty good. I think my cabin crew is the best.

So, no casualties—except for the hijackers, that is. Nobody had thought to untie them, put them in their seats, and clip their seat belts. When the plane stopped, they didn't and they met bulkheads.

The Sri Lankans even managed to save the plane—this plane! The divers attached floats to her, preventing her from sinking before a crane and a barge could be brought to the scene. They didn't have to do that. I think they're geeks and just wanted to show off that they could.

It took a few months, but she was declared air-worthy again.

Well, I hope you liked my story. We're approaching Jakarta, and it's about time to start the descent checklist, so you'll have to leave the cockpit. Nice meeting you. Goodbye.

The End

Connect with Paul on Wattpad:

https://www.wattpad.com/user/gkp00co

Cover by Author.

Live From Garissa

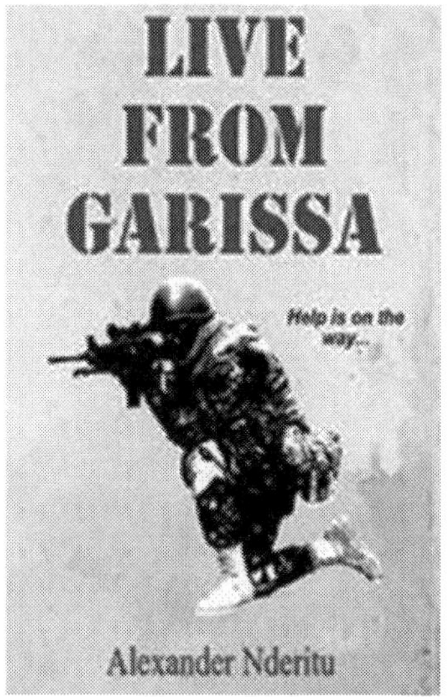

Alexander Nderitu

"Live From Garissa" was inspired by actual events that took place in my country, Kenya, in 2015. It's a work of fiction, and I enjoyed creating the female lead character and showing readers the world through her eyes. I have been a writer for just over 15 years now and written quite a number of stories, some of them based on actual events. My first novel, *When the Whirlwind Passes* (2001), was inspired by the sensational gangland-style murder of an Italian fashion baron in the 1990s.

But I have no special attraction to dark/horrific events. I am also a poet and playwright. Most of my plays are comedies, and my best poems (like "Someone in Africa Loves You") are about love or the beauty of nature. However, I am not one to shy away from reality, and that's why the Crime Fiction genre is so important to me. So, yes, the statistics and places mentioned in this story are true. The struggle against terrorists in East Africa is real. And my ambition to make the world a better place through my writing is as real as the scorching sun that rises over Garissa every morning.

***

You can always tell when there's breaking news. Groups form under the flat-screen TV monitors mounted on the walls of the newsroom at strategic points. IT-savvy journos leap into cyberspace, scanning social media sites for the latest updates. Landlines and mobile phones won't stop ringing.

This is the kind of scene I walk into when I enter my workplace at a little past 7:00 AM on a Thursday in April.

"What's going on?" I ask three male colleagues staring at a large TV screen like generals in a war room.

"Siege in Garissa," one of them answers without looking at me.

"Could be Al-Shabaab," another one adds. "They stormed a school early in the morning and are holding the students hostage."

"Oh my gosh," I say. I am not really surprised, though. Over the past three or so years, Kenya has been on the receiving end of several terrorist attacks, the worst so far being a four-day siege at the upmarket Westgate Shopping Mall that cost 67 lives. Kenya Defence Forces (KDF) have been in Somalia for a couple of years now, hunting down the Al-Qaeda-linked Al-Shabaab militants, but the battle appears to be far from won.

I proceed to my work station, leaving the three guys with the scent of my perfume.

"Morning, Jackie!" Wanjala greets me as I unsling my handbag and boot up my desktop computer.

"Morning," I say, sliding into my swivel chair.

Wanjala is our media house's oldest employee. He's a scriptwriter. Sixty-plus years of age. He's also the dirty old man of the office. He often insists on hugging female colleagues, especially interns, although he does so with considerable charm. Sometimes he sneaks in a kiss, which he refers to as 'a Christian greeting.'

"Have those hostage-takers made any demands?" I ask.

"No," Wanjala says. "But you know what they always ask for—KDF to pull out of Somalia."

My computer is up and running. I go to Twitter to see what people are saying.

My name is Jacqueline Mwende, and I am a TV reporter. I am originally from Kitui—Kambaland—but I did my Mass Communication degree in Nairobi where I now live and work. I am twenty-four years old, single and (discreetly) searching, a blogger, Daddy's girl, weight-watcher, and supporter of the Oxford comma. Basically, I am a journalist in search of her Watergate.

Twitter is not much help. No concrete news, official statements, eyewitness accounts or corroborated evidence. All I can make out is that heavily armed men stormed Garissa University College at daybreak and are terrorizing the students.

I need a cup of coffee. Looks like it's going to be a long news day. I go to a percolator at the far end of the extensive, open-plan office and fix myself a cuppa. As I return to my desk, enjoying the awesome aroma of the Arabica coffee, I notice Stanley Mbugua, the TV News Director, talking to Wanjala who in turn points at me.

"You heard about Garissa?" Mbugua asks me without greeting.

He's forty-five. Loves suspenders and loud ties. No-nonsense-type guy. He doesn't talk; he barks. But he's good at what he does: Our ratings have steadily risen since he took over the news department.

"Er…yeah," I reply. "I am looking it up online right now."

"We have chartered a plane for ten reporters from different divisions. You need to leave *now*. Kioko has been trying to reach you since dawn."

"I was driving."

"Well, he's waiting for you in the basement parking. Keep your cell phone on throughout. Carry power banks. *Chap chap!* I don't want those print guys beating us to the punch. Daniella is already at Wilson."

I can't help but smile as Mbugua retreats. Daniella Muthoni is a writer from our print division—occupying the floor below us—and she and Mbugua are reportedly dating. Although much of the information we gather is shared throughout the print and electronic divisions, there has always been a rivalry between the TV channel and the English newspaper (which often beats us in attracting advertising revenue). Which makes the Daniella-Mbugua affair all the more sensational. She often comes up to our floor and can spend hours in his office. We jokingly refer to her as an 'embedded reporter.' She's thirty-three, light-skinned, unmarried, hot-tempered, and I'll concede that she's pretty. She doesn't like us 'TV people.' One time, two male Swahili anchors complimented her admirable derriere as she sashayed past them, and she carpet-bombed them with feministic insults in English (unlike most Kenyans, she's monolingual). Catch me dead having an office affair. I like my space. I can't imagine working all day with the same person I'll spend the night with.

"Would you like a cup of coffee?" I ask Wanjala. I have no time to enjoy it now.

"Oh, yes," he replies. "I don't know whether to marry or adopt you!"

I place my steaming cup on his desk, flashing my pearly whites, and grab my handbag. I speed through the length of the newsroom like a comet, leaving a trail of Joop perfume hanging in the air. I have no time to wait for the lift, and we're on second-floor anyway, so I just dash clumsily down the winding staircase to the basement, high heels clanging. Kioko and a technician are waiting in an idling grey Mazda. Kioko opens the door as I approach. The back seat of the vehicle is stacked with broadcast equipment. As soon as I slide in, the driver throws the car into gear. Kioko is a cameraman. He also comes from Kambaland—the Masaku side—and we get on like a house on fire. He's thirty-three, married with one child.

We find Daniella and a few other colleagues at Wilson Airport, on the lip of Nairobi City. Daniella is standing on the apron, talking on her cell phone, fake reddish hair blowing in the wind. She looks pissed, and I soon find out why: the plane that has been hired for us belongs to an airline with such a bad track record that its nickname is 'East Africa Scareways.' Why do people treat journos as if they're commandos?

In the ten or so minutes we spend together waiting for some colleagues from our radio division, Daniella doesn't acknowledge our presence.

***

The most thrilling part of a flight for me is as it gathers speed just before take-off. Today, however, I am scared stiff by the groaning of the engines and the shaking of the fuselage. I close my eyes. The plane argues with some invisible demons as it climbs into the milk-white clouds, but beyond that, there's no turbulence.

Garissa is located in the northeastern flank of Kenya, bordering Somalia. Garissa University is the only public university in the area. The northeastern region is not known for educational or economic progress. It's a semi-arid area that reminds me of my hometown of Kitui. At a little past 9:00 AM, we begin our descent. I suddenly get the urge to pee. I have a feeling we're flying into a war zone.

Having landed in one piece and gone through airport controls, we scramble for taxis. I can't see Daniella, but I can hear her voice: "What a shaky plane—I thought we were flying over the Bermuda Triangle!" Kioko negotiates with a bearded driver in a battered, white Toyota Corolla. In the distance, there are two camels lounging under an acacia tree.

"Tell him if he doesn't give us a good rate, we'll go by camel," I whisper to Kioko.

Negotiations over, we haul our equipment into the cab and climb in. It's as hot as an oven inside. The driver is a wiry, elderly man with henna on his beard.

"It's a shame," he informs us in Somali-kissed Swahili. "There's a military barracks right next to the school, and the *magaidi* still attacked and took control of it."

"Would you know how many students are trapped in the campus?" I inquire.

"About eight hundred," the cabbie says. "There are no outside hostels. Everyone lives inside the compound."

We pass other people walking towards the scene of the crime. The women are conservatively dressed, some wearing the *hijab* (a scarf over the hair and chest) or even *bui bui* (totally covered up, eyes peering out like a ninja's).

Neighbours, concerned relatives, idlers, security personnel and media teams have gathered outside the college. KDF has thrown a cordon around the school. More military vehicles are issuing from a garrison about 200 metres from the college. We quickly unload our equipment. As we do so, I make the mistake of placing my hand on the roof of the taxi—it's as hot as a spaceship! We set up as close to the action as possible, but apart from some sparse gunshot sounds, there's not much to report. I fetch my smartphone and scan social media. The hashtag '#Garissa' is already trending. Around thirty students are estimated dead.

I use my jacket for shade as I browse the web. It's forty bone-dry degrees out here, and it's not even noon yet! My battery starts to wane. I attach the phone to one of Kioko's power banks and scan the crowd as I wait. Wind and sand lash at my face like a featherweight boxer in the opening rounds. I need interviewees. There's a KDF soldier engaged in crowd control near me. He's in full-camouflage uniform, lugging a huge belt-fed, shell-catching machine gun. Catch me dead interviewing an armed man under stressful conditions! I notice a large woman wearing a *hijab* talking urgently on her cell phone under a thorn tree. She seems distressed. She can't keep still. She must be connected with the hostage situation. As soon as she finishes talking, I approach her.

"I am a reporter," I say in Swahili. "You look disturbed. Do you know anybody in there?"

"My daughter is a student there," she says. "Halima Abdul-Aziz. She called me early in the morning and said, 'Mama, pray for me.' I asked what was going on, and she said that masked men had entered the school and were shooting everyone. She didn't say anything else. Her phone is still ringing but no one answers. Her father reported the matter at the police station, but they seem overwhelmed."

"Can I interview you on camera?" I ask. "You can appeal for help if you wish."

She nods her acceptance, and I return to my station.

"I've found an eyewitness," Kioko tells me, indicating a slim man with curly hair and a pronounced Adam's Apple. "And he's willing to talk."

My smartphone is ringing. Mbugua.

"We go live at eleven," he barks.

I line up my interviewees and straighten my clothes. Kioko counts down the seconds using his fingers: three, two, one...

"Garissa town woke up to shock and horror this morning when it emerged that suspected Al-Shabaab militants had stormed Garissa University College and taken the students hostage. With me here is Rashid, an area resident who witnessed the arrival of the attackers. Rashid?"

I put the microphone to his face.

"I was walking to the mosque in the school for morning prayers," he says. "This was around 5:30. As I approached the main gate, I saw four men coming out of a Toyota Probox. I thought they were cops. They had a brief argument with the two guards at the gate, and then they suddenly shot them! I turned around and ran away. I heard more shots, so I just kept running. I think they were shooting at me."

"Thank you, Rashid," I say, maneuvering to the *hijab*'d lady. "And tell us your story, madam."

I hold the microphone to her face. Her voice is coated with emotion. A lump forms in my throat. I can barely hold the mic steady. Sporadic gunshots can be heard as she talks about her daughter. *Mbugua must be loving this,* I think to myself as I nod politely to encourage the interviewee. He has a flair for the dramatic. During the tense 2013 presidential elections, someone in the newsroom joked that if there was no post-election violence, Mbugua would go out and burn tires in protest!

The interviewee is battling tears. I draw the microphone to myself and face the camera.

"Stay tuned," I say. "We'll keep you updated on the latest developments. This is Jacqueline Mwende, reporting live from Garissa."

***

At 1:00 PM. Kioko and I saunter to a nearby eatery for lunch.

"They're waiting for Recce Squad," Kioko informs me as he pushes his meaty food around a metal plate like a city council *askari* harassing a hawker. The Recce Squad is an elite squad of police commandos best known for liquidating the Westgate Mall attackers.

I ask the waiter for coffee, but they have none. He offers me tea made with camel milk. I accept. Tastes oddly nice.

***

By 2:00 PM, the crowd has swelled and gunshots can still be heard. I have to go live again, so I try to furnish enough details to keep an avid watcher interested: "...There are two hostels, three stories high, housing about four hundred students each. About two hundred metres away from them are staff quarters harbouring about 50 people..."

It's now 3:00 PM. Security personnel tell us to push back to at least two hundred metres away from the compound. A battle tank rolls into the campus, caterpillar tracks and all. Kioko and the other cameraman angle for good shots.

Shortly after 4:00 PM, a series of paramilitary vehicles zoom into the compound as if they're racing. The Recce Squad is here! The *rat-a-tat* of machine-gun fire picks up. And then silence.

At 5:00 PM, KDF soldiers begin to exit the premises. The area remains sealed, but we know the siege is over. The crowd starts to thin out. Everyone wants to catch the evening news.

***

The bearded cabbie from earlier drives us to a hotel in the town centre. Virtually all the media people are there. It's as if we have staged a siege of our own. At 7:00 PM sharp, we are all glued to a single TV set where the Interior Minister is expected to make a statement. All the attackers have been killed, he says, but a mop-up operation is currently being carried out by security forces. One killer with a suicide vest blew himself up, taking a cop with him. The death toll stands at 70, but the final count could be higher.

Supper consists of potatoes, diced carrots, boiled goat meat, uncooked ripe bananas and rice seeded with small dates. If there's one thing I'll miss about Garissa, it's the food. Everything tastes nice. "Grass-fed goats," Kioko says, watching me savour a bone. "That's why they taste so good."

***

I see my smartphone screen glow and answer it even before it rings. It's Kioko calling me to go down to breakfast. *Everyone* is at the restaurant, he says. It's 6:45 on Friday. I barely slept a wink. Yesterday's horror and the unfamiliarity of my surroundings kept my mind alert. I could hear the gunshots echoing in my head. I go downstairs.

Everyone seems to be having fruit and juice so I do the same. I order a salad containing watermelon, pineapple, avocado, beetroot, paw paw, and peaches and a tall glass of fresh mango juice. Scenes from yesterday's media conference and interviews dominate the morning news.

"Some survivors have been rushed to Garissa General Hospital," Kioko informs me. "We need to get there, *pronto*. The campus is still on lockdown."

We get into the Toyota cab from yesterday. Luckily, the bearded driver has purchased our newspaper, *The Kenyan Spectator*. "KENYA UNDER ATTACK!" roars the banner headline and below that is a picture of the battle tank rolling into the college. The cover story is by Daniella Muthoni. She and Mbugua are two sides of the same coin. They deserve each other.

"What was the tank for?" Kioko says. "There were, like, six attackers!"

"Are you serious?" I say, unbelieving.

"The witnesses say there were between four and six attackers, some of them hooded."

Mbugua calls.

"You go live at eleven," he says. "We'll be having a studio discussion and intercutting with you guys in the field."

"OK," I say. "I am on the way to the hospital to interview survivors."

"Get details: names, courses they were studying, age, what happened at what time, who shot whom."

After a short ride along bone-juggling roads, we arrive at Garissa Hospital. Everybody and his uncle is here. Security is tight. Ambulances and police cars are the only vehicles being allowed in and out. Daniella is here already. She's animatedly trying to get an AK-47-wielding cop to let her through. He seems adamant, but I wouldn't be surprised if she succeeds. She's a go-getter. She would sleep with a terrorist for a scoop.

"Come on, Jackie," Kioko says, off a phone call. "Unhurt survivors are being screened and released. Let's go talk to them."

We hop back into the taxi and peel out.

I use my phone to scan social media. "Outrage" is the word I would use to describe the general sentiment of the nation. Kenyan netizens feel that the security forces' slow response cost many lives. The attackers made their way in at around 5:30 AM after shooting the guards at the main gate. They switched off some of the power at the mains and proceeded to go on a killing spree, shooting students holding morning prayers in a mosque and a classroom. One campus cop engaged them for ten minutes but ran out of bullets and was swiftly obliterated. At 6:00 AM, an alarm was raised at the headquarters of the Recce Squad in Nairobi. By 7:00 AM, the commandos were ready to leave, but there was no air transport available. Police and KDF in Garissa began to respond. At 9:00 AM, the Recce Squad were driven towards Wilson Airport. This means that Kioko and I actually got here hours before the rescuers! At 12:30 PM, two planes were finally availed to the commandos. The Squad arrived in Garissa at around 1:55 PM and were briefed. By this time, KDF had confined the attackers to one building, where the latter had adopted sniper tactics. At around 5:00 PM, the Recce Squad moved in and zapped the remaining terrorists within minutes.

Kenyans are incandescent with rage. Heads must roll, they say. Security chiefs must resign or be fired over the delayed deployment of the Recce Squad. The death toll is now over one hundred.

We arrive at a residential area adjacent to the college. Most adult men are wearing *kanzus* (ankle-length tunics), some headed for nearby mosques. Friday is a holy day in Islam.

There are plenty of survivors now that the siege is over. I line up two of them for my eleven o'clock broadcast.

"As of now, about 615 students and 50 staff members have been rescued. Those injured have been rushed to Garissa Hospital. With me here are two students who survived the attack. We will begin with Ibrahim Hassan, a twenty-four-year-old Bachelor of Education student from Garissa. Tell us what happened, Ibrahim."

I put the microphone to him.

"I was woken up by gunshots at around five-twenty, but I thought they were coming from the barracks near the college. After a few minutes, I heard screaming and more gunshots. My room is on the third floor. I went to the window and looked down. I saw four armed men with covered faces walking towards a room where Christian Union students hold morning prayers. I panicked and ran out of my room. Other students were also running in the corridors, towards the stairs. We escaped from the hostel through a back door and then jumped over the campus fence. I later heard that all the CU students were killed."

I take away the mic.

"And this is Wairimu Kago, twenty-six years old, a fourth-year English Literature student from Nyeri. Wairimu?"

I put the mic to her.

"What I can say," she whispers, "is that God saved my life. We had just began our morning prayers when four men burst in and started shooting. At first they all stood side-by-side at the front of the classroom, heavily armed, as if they were acting in a play, and then one of them shouted 'Today you will swim in your own blood!' and the gunshots started. I think I fainted immediately because the next thing I remember was lying on the floor with two bleeding people on top of me. I could hear the killers talking. I touched some blood on the floor and slowly smeared it on my face so that they would think that I was dead. What I can say is that I stayed like that until KDF soldiers came and rescued me, hours later. I had lost track of time."

"Thank you for your testimonies," I say. I neglect to mention that Wairimu is pregnant in case her folks at home are not aware. "This is Jacqueline Mwende in Garissa. Back to you in the studio."

***

It's sauna-hot inside the car as we head back to the hotel for lunch. I doze all the way there. By evening, we are all gathered in front of the hotel TV to watch an update from the national security brass. They know that Kenyans are angry about the lapses. There have been calls for a complete overhaul of the internal security machinery. The Interior Minister looks like a general who has just lost a war. The police spokesman's face is so staid, it wouldn't be out of place on Mount Rushmore. And then comes the zinger: the final death toll is 147. Kioko whistles in shock.

***

Saturday dawns bright. Once again, I had a fitful sleep. The president announces three days of mourning. The university has been closed indefinitely. The security chiefs are as unpopular as second-hand underwear. Air force planes will be used to ferry the corpses to Nairobi for identification, says the government spokesman. If only those same planes had been availed to the Recce Squad!

When I'm stressed, I seek refuge in the ark of solitude. So after breakfast, I sneak off for a long walk. A fierce sun has a monopoly of the ultramarine sky, and the wind is a tyrant. I think of the massacred students. What a grim harvest of innocent lives! Just two days ago, each of those one-hundred-plus people had an identity card, school ID, a mobile phone, a dream, friends, family, religion. Now they're past tense; statistics in the "war on terror." In my mind's eye, I can envision international TV anchors covering the tragedy: a gorgeous, thirty-something blonde sitting behind a shiny desk with a backdrop of a busy newsroom going, "...and the latest news from Kenya is that 147 people have been confirmed dead following last Thursday's terrorist attack by Al-Shabaab militants. Kenya has of late been a hotbed of terrorist activity..."

***

The reflection of the full moon floats and wobbles on the dark water of the Uhuru Park lake. It is now just over a week since the end of the siege. The time is 8:01 PM and more and more people are streaming into the public park for an all-night vigil organized by a consortium of "civil society group." As you might expect, the majority of attendees are college-age youths from the nearby universities, here to mourn their "fallen comrades." A stage has been erected in one corner of the park, complete with sound equipment and flashing lights. Beside the stage, is a shrine to the victims. 147 plastic face masks with the black-white-green stripes of the flag painted on them lie on the grass surrounded by burning candles, flowers, photographs and farewell cards. The masks have hollowed-out eyes and mouths and look rather spooky, partly because there are so many of them gazing quietly at the starless night and partly because of the candles burning around them. From a distance, the people standing around them must look like witches and wizards conducting a ritual. Along the live fences of the park, silhouettes of armed cops patrol silently. As often happens, it's hard to tell whose side they're on: Are they there to protect our vigil or to prevent a spontaneous riot caused by charged emotions? One issue with events in this venue is that it is uncomfortably close to parliament buildings, the senate and the president's official residence. Crowd control is always a factor.

One of the event organizers, a twenty-something young lady in a white t-shirt and blue jeans, climbs onto the stage, grabs the microphone and begins to address the dark, viscous crowd.

"Tonight," her electronically distorted voice booms out of the stadium-standard speakers, "we are here to ensure that what happened in Garissa is not forgotten and to show the terrorists that Kenya remains unbowed." (Cheers) "You will not divide us!" (Louder cheers) "There are Muslims even here. You will not make us hate our brothers and sisters! You will not divide us along religious lines!" (Cheers, whistles) "You will not divide us along tribal lines!" (More cheers and whistles). "We remain one country, one people, one nation!"

Why am I cheering? Why am I standing up? Why am I punching the air with my fist? And why are tears streaming down my cheeks? I sit back down on the cold grass and clumsily wipe the tears away from my eyes, but the warm, salty streams continue to flow. Something that feels like a potato in my throat starts to grow. Images from the corpse-strewn classrooms flash through my mind. The metallic smell of blood returns to my nostrils, and the sound of sporadic machine-gun fire echoes in my ears. As a journalist, you see or hear a lot of gut-wrenching stuff over the months and years, but no assignment has ever affected me as much as the Garissa siege. The violence was so sudden, unnecessary and horrific that I sometimes wake up thinking it was a nightmare, just moments before I become *compos mentis*. Every day since we returned from Garissa, I remember the traumatized survivor who told me *"One of them shouted, 'Today you will swim in your own blood!' and the gunshots started."*

The lady host is welcoming someone to the stage, a tall, dreadlocked young man wearing a Bob Marley t-shirt and combat boots. Judging from the roar of the crowd, he's quite popular.

"We will be having poetry and music performances as well as tributes and speeches throughout the night," the host says. "And to start us off is Dawa Kali with a spoken word piece. Welcome."

She hands him the microphone. The crowd cheers. I finally manage to swallow the potato in my throat. The poet speaks:

"147 is not just a number!
We will not forgive or forget what happened in Garissa
We not forget to remember what they did to our brothers and sisters
In the dark of night, on a mission of terror
A mission carried out by cowardly murderers
Who attacked defenseless students in their slumber
Extinguishing whatever potential was in their future
Unbothered by the sight of crying mothers
And the innocent blood scattered all over
We shall not rest until they also suffer
The same fate that they delivered to others
And their own mothers will remember to remember
That 147 is not just a number!"

As the crowd goes wild, a thought strikes me: My blog has been dormant for several weeks now. When I opened it, I was excited about having a little corner of the Internet all to myself. A place where I could just share my thoughts and opinions outside the editorial limits of my journalistic work. But I only blog when I am inspired, and I haven't been inspired for a long time. Like Dawa Kali and the other people gathered before me in the gloom tonight, I want to *feel* that I am doing something about the tragedy. I am going to document the lives of as many of the victims as possible. I am going to make sure that 147 won't just be a number, a statistic. I will bring out the lives, images, hopes and dreams of the victims—an online memoriam of sorts. I already have quite a bit of information from my interviews, but I need more. And in order to get it, I will have to go back to Garissa.

The End

Connect with Alexander at the following sites:

Website: www.AlexanderNderitu.com

Facebook: https://www.facebook.com/alexandernderitu

Instagram: @alexander_nderitu

Twitter: @nderitubooks

Lulu spotlight (for paperbacks and e-books):
www.lulu.com/spotlight/NewShalespeare

Cover by Author.

Redshirted

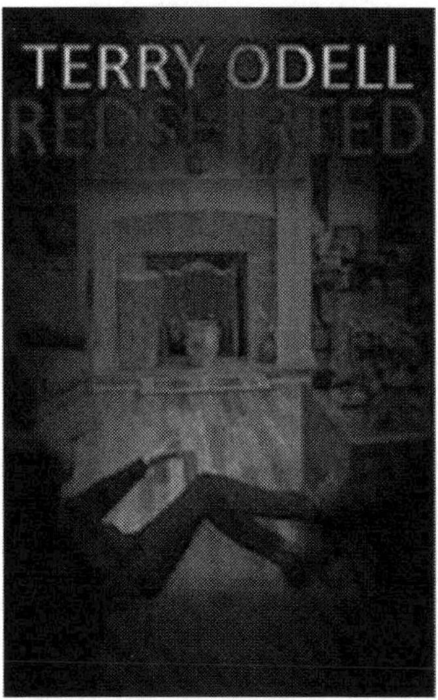

Terry Odell

Terry Odell was born in Los Angeles, moved to Florida, and now makes her home in Divide, Colorado. An avid reader (her parents tell everyone they had to move from their first home because she finished the local library), she always wanted to "fix" stories so the characters did what she wanted. Once she began writing, she found this wasn't always possible, as evinced when the mystery she intended to write rapidly became a romance. Her writing credits include the *Triple-D Ranch* series, the *Pine Hills Police* series, the *Blackthorne, Inc.* series, and the *Mapleton Mystery* series. Her awards include the HOLT Medallion and the Colorado Romance Writers Award of Excellence.

I'd always wanted to use the line "He's dead, Jim" in a story, and this is what resulted. It's also the first time a character demanded the story be told in first person, and I decided not to argue. "Redshirted" is part of the 2015 Silver Falchion Award-Winning Short Story Collection *Seeing Red*. "He's dead, Jim." Homicide

Detective James T. Kirkland dreads the *Star Trek*-loving medical examiner's joy in stating the obvious. This time, the victim was wearing a red shirt, and when what looked like a death from natural causes turns into a homicide, Kirkland is called upon to solve the crime, red shirt and all.

***

The cloying odor of death wasn't what bothered me as I signed the patrol officer's clipboard and ducked under the yellow tape fastened across the door. It was seeing the name Frank McCoy printed on the sheet. I'd been chasing down dead-end leads on an ugly double-homicide for the last thirty-six hours, and I was *not* in the mood for his damn humor. Still, if I didn't play the medical examiner's game, I might never get out of here. I added my name under his, braced myself, and stepped into the apartment.

"What do we have?" I asked, knowing exactly what I'd hear.

McCoy raised his gaze from the corpse, which lay face up on the carpet. He grinned, saying the same thing he said every time he showed up at one of my homicides. "He's dead, Jim."

It's not my fault my mother named me James. Middle name Thackery after her late father. Last name Kirkland, which made me James T. Kirkland. Not precisely James Tiberius Kirk, but close enough for Frank, a *Star Trek* aficionado, to deliver that damn clichéd line every chance he got.

"Any speculation as to cause of death—" I scrubbed my hands across my eyes, trying to erase the fatigue and bring the room into sharper focus—"*Bones*?" Might as well go along with the *Star Trek* game, if I wanted to move things along.

"This one's easy. Should be obvious even to a mere cop such as yourself. What do you see?"

"I see a dead man on the living room floor. A peaceful looking corpse, as corpses go. Please tell me this is going to be a slam-dunk."

Bones gave a snorting chuckle. "Cause of death is obvious. He's wearing a red shirt."

My pulse tripped. Had I missed a new serial killer? "What the hell are you talking about?"

Bones made a *tsking* sound and gave an indulgent headshake. "Jim, Jim, Jim. Have you no respect for television history? Everyone knows if *Star Trek* put an away team extra in a red shirt, he'd be dead before act two."

Relief that I wouldn't have a serial killer added to my currently overflowing caseload outweighed my exasperation with McCoy's obsession. "I don't think you can put that in your report."

"Probably not." Bones tossed banter aside and assumed his professional demeanor. "I'll know more when I get him on the table."

Normally, the ME was last on scene, but I'd been running all over town and was at the opposite end of the county when I got the call. I trusted Bones not to have messed with any evidence. From the looks of things, there wasn't much to mess. Place was immaculate. If you didn't count the body, of course.

"Sorry I'm late." I tried to keep the resentment out of my tone. But what looked like a simple heart attack had pulled me off a high-profile murder investigation, and I wanted out of here.

He looked over my shoulder. "Where's your stalwart partner?"

"Home getting some required shut-eye, as ordered." When the call came in for this one, I didn't see any reason to wake Rocky until I checked it out. The way things looked, maybe I'd be able to grab a few hours myself.

"Let's roll him," Bones said.

I snapped on my gloves and crouched beside the body. Nothing unusual on the back, either. Natural causes was looking good. "You get any skinny on him?" I asked.

"Deceased is Randall Palmer, lives alone, thirty-one. Neighbor's dog started going nuts at the door. Neighbor knocked, phoned. No answer, so she called it in. Nice young man, she said. Brought her dog leftovers when he ate out. Polite, asked about her children, grandchildren, but never shared much of his own life. I'd say he's been dead two, maybe three days, given the cold snap, the open window, and no heat."

Hardly anyone in central Florida used heat. We had maybe ten days a year where the temperatures dipped below forty. Our luck to be in the midst of three of them, complete with freeze warnings.

"As I recall, it was in the low seventies on Saturday. The front didn't blow through until about two a.m. Sunday. So he died before then, or he'd have closed the windows, right?" I looked again. Red or not, his shirt was a short-sleeved polo. "And put on a sweater, or a warmer shirt."

Bones glared at me. I shrugged. He didn't like the gray areas where forensic science overlapped the unquantifiable, gut-response observations of a detective. He'd go to his lab and analyze body temperature, livor mortis, stomach contents and God knows what else, but my money said we'd end up in the same place.

I glanced at Palmer's arms. No needle tracks. "You think it's natural causes?" I couldn't disguise the hope in my tone. Even if wearing a red shirt wasn't a legitimate cause of death, a slam-dunk would be welcome so I could get back to my other cases.

Bones peered over the top of his frameless spectacles. "You know I won't answer that here."

So much for wishful thinking. "Right. Sorry. Let me give the place the once-over."

Nothing unusual in the living room. Upholstered couch, leather reading chair, matching wooden coffee and end tables. Shades of brown and beige everywhere. Entertainment center with a moderate sized television, CD player, with the CDs arranged by music type and subdivided alphabetically by artist.

The room dog-legged to the right and what normally would have been a dining area was Palmer's den. Desk, wooden bookshelves filled with books. No photographs. No bric-a-brac.

I gave the rest of the apartment a quick walk-through, snapping pictures as I roamed. No signs of a struggle. Windows were open about six inches, and the temperature was dropping rapidly as evening approached. I shivered and hurried toward Palmer's single bedroom.

Neat, as expected. Bed made, nothing on the floor. Housekeeper? Girlfriend? Obsessive neatnik? Images of my bed, even in its rumpled state, beckoned. I moved along. Condoms in the nightstand drawer. A careful man.

The bathroom almost sparkled. Almost. Faint whiff of vomit from the toilet, consistent enough with a heart attack or drug OD. Continuing my exploration, I opened the medicine cabinet. No signs of drug paraphernalia, nothing but a bottle of generic acetaminophen. I checked the contents. Almost full. Box of Band-Aids, bottle of mouthwash, tube of toothpaste. Fluoride with breath freshener. Antiperspirant. Extra strength.

In the kitchen, the death smell was less prevalent, overlaid by garlic and seafood. A peek under the kitchen sink revealed takeout food containers in the trash, about the only indication someone truly had lived here. I sniffed. Asian. Chinese? Thai? Not my area of culinary expertise. I made a mental note to have the techs bag it.

Everything else was spotless. No dishes in the sink, clean or dirty. Dishwasher was empty. Round wooden table, two chairs, two placemats. No crumbs, no sticky smudges. By now, I felt decidedly slovenly.

I went back to Bones and reported my findings, including my thoughts about possible food poisoning, or poisoned food.

He nodded. "Thought I smelled it when I came in. Garlic, right? Some kind of shellfish?"

I hadn't noticed until I got to the kitchen. But Bones dealt with death all the time. His brain probably filtered out the decomp odor and let the others come through. "Right on."

"I'll order a full tox screen, make sure I test his stomach contents." Bones replaced his instruments in his kit. "I'm done."

As if by magic, or at least telepathy, two uniforms appeared at the exact instant Bones said, "Okay, let's bag him and take him downtown."

"What's your take? Off the record," I added.

He rubbed his chin. "If I were going to jump to conclusions, I'd say heart attack or drug overdose, but I never jump to conclusions. I'd keep the scene secure until I get some preliminary results, just to be safe. I'll let you know what I find." Bones's knees cracked as he stood. "Don't work too hard."

Right. Like being a homicide detective was a walk in the park. But it was what I did, and I couldn't imagine doing anything else.

Bones and the body left. Time to figure out more about who our victim was, see if there was a logical reason for him to have dropped dead. Much as I wanted to buy into the heart attack, the guy was young. And healthy looking.

A day planner sat by the phone on his desk. I leafed through the pages, noting an appointment with a Dr. Blair ten days ago. Lots of things listed under "returns." It took me a minute to figure out they were library books and DVDs. Oh yeah, I was definitely overdue for some rack time. I rubbed my eyes, worked some of the tension out of my neck and shoulders and went back to his entries.

Neat printing. All black ink. Every errand, every appointment duly recorded. Hell, the guy even noted his workouts—every Monday, Wednesday and Friday at seven-thirty a.m. You think he'd remember something that routine. I'd have to find out what kind of a doctor Blair was, but shrink came to mind. OCD was bouncing around my brain. Health-wise, Palmer seemed to be taking damn good care of himself. Heart attack was sliding down my list of possible causes of death.

The name Juliet appeared often. I flipped back. Started showing up six months ago, once or twice a month, then with increasing frequency. Several times a week now. Usually circled. Big letters. No time slot. Someone special for Palmer to deviate from his meticulous record keeping. Last entry was for Saturday, three days ago. I snapped pictures of the pages and wrote the name in my notebook. No addresses. I took another look. That's when the bell went off. This wasn't a planner, or an appointment book. Palmer used it as a diary. A boring diary. Nothing written down after Saturday. Today was Tuesday. Agreed with what Bones guessed was time of death.

I was searching for an address book or PDA when I heard a voice call my name. Female. I turned to see a patrol cop I didn't recognize, waiting outside the tape, holding a metal thermos.

"Coffee?" She raised the thermos and gave a hesitant smile.

"You signed the sheet?"

She nodded. "Yes, sir."

"Then come on in."

She crossed the room, and I caught the nametag on her chest. Not a bad chest, probably, once she lost the Kevlar. "Officer Stroup."

"Charlene, sir, but everyone calls me Charlie." She extended the thermos. "Black, extra sugar."

I'd probably downed two gallons of the stuff, but I wasn't going to refuse all that stood between me and collapsing on the carpet, which was still part of a possible crime scene. "Thanks." I tried for a friendly smile. "Someone's filled you in."

She actually blushed.

"You're new, right?" I said.

"First week on patrol, sir."

"Relax, Charlie. The rumors that I eat rookies for breakfast are grossly overstated."

I looked at her more closely. There was something about her eyes. More than that they were big and brown. They'd held mine when she spoke, but only for a moment before she gazed around the room, taking everything in. Eyes of a good cop. Eager. The eyes of a new cop. Eyes I'd seen in my bathroom mirror twenty years ago.

I took the thermos, unscrewed the cap and inhaled. "Where'd you get this? You can't tell me you happened to have a thermos of coffee just the way I like it on the off chance there'd be a homicide and I'd show up."

"No, sir. Henderson sent me."

So she'd drawn Henderson as her training partner. A career patrol officer with an overactive male chauvinist gene who sent her to fetch coffee instead of letting her learn how to assess a scene. He had a major suck-up gene as well. I wondered why he'd let her deliver the coffee instead of taking the credit himself.

Speak of the devil. Henderson's wheezing announced his arrival. Hell, it was only one flight of stairs. The man ought to hit the gym once in a while.

"Kirkland. How's it hanging?" Henderson said. He turned to Charlie. "Hey, rookie. I thought I told you to get coffee for the detective."

Charlie's jaw clenched. Her mouth opened and closed.

"And she did." I waved the thermos under his nose. "And damn fine coffee it is." I winked at Charlie.

Henderson grunted.

"What do you have for me?" I asked him.

"Not much." He consulted his notebook. "Mrs. Levitz in 2-B next door called it in."

"What do you know about our victim?"

He took off his hat and scratched his balding head. "Not much," he repeated. His report confirmed what Bones had given me.

"Any health problems? Family? Next of kin? Where he works?"

Henderson shook his head. "Only that he's an accountant."

Fit the image. "So what *have* you been doing? Aside from organizing coffee runs?"

Charlie had backed off, halfway to the door. I caught her eye and held up my hand, indicating she should wait. Her eyebrows lifted, but she stopped, her body tense, almost at attention.

Henderson's shoulders stiffened. "The guy dropped dead. Not much to do until the *detectives* showed up. I called the ME and the tech crew. As per regs."

I managed to keep from whacking him in the jaw with my fist. Might spill my coffee. "So you haven't talked to anyone else in the building?"

"No. I waited for you." He threw a look at Charlie. "You can wait downstairs, rookie."

"No, she can't," I said. "She's with me. You can relieve Wilkes until the techs get here. Call me when they do."

His mouth gaped, reminding me of my sister's goldfish. "But she's a—"

"A cop," I replied. "And since she's new, she'll benefit from the experience. You, on the other hand, have done this countless times, and I'm sure you'd be bored."

Henderson hesitated, but seemed to think better than to retort.

He spun on his heels and marched out of the room.

"Why?" Charlie asked. "Henderson's got at least twenty years on me."

"I trust my instincts. How about a rundown?"

Charlie pulled herself up to her full height, which I estimated to be about five-eight, allowing for the thick soles of her shoes. Only a few inches shorter than me. After a deep breath, she began.

Her report was concise. She and Henderson answered the call from Dispatch, talked to Mrs. Levitz, and rounded up the landlord, who unlocked Palmer's apartment.

She swallowed a few times, obviously reliving discovering her first corpse. After two or three days, any corpse is ugly. And smells. This, however, was a relatively easy one, and I was glad. She'd have plenty of chances to see the *really* ugly ones. Like the Grosvenor case, which insisted on weaving through my thoughts. A genuine hatchet job. If I could only find the hatchet, not to mention the killer who wielded it.

Charlie cleared her throat, which reminded me I was working the Palmer case now. I blinked her back into focus. She fished a slip of paper from her pocket. "Landlord gave us a list of tenants. Henderson sent me for coffee. Said the guy probably had a heart attack, no need to upset the neighbors. He and Wilkes set the tape."

Henderson might be a lazy SOB, but he was enough of a cop to know every unattended death was a potential crime scene and was investigated like a homicide until proven otherwise. I hoped we'd get to the otherwise fast. And I knew I wasn't going to write this off without a basic investigation, no matter how loud my bed was screaming.

"Glove up," I told her and went back to Palmer's desk. She followed, slipping her hands into blue latex gloves. "I'll take pictures, you look for whatever he used for addresses. Phone, PDA, whatever."

She put her hand on the pull of the top side drawer, then stopped. "Are we allowed to do this? Open a drawer? Without a warrant?"

"He's dead. Can't have any more expectation of privacy. And we're trying to help. Find next of kin, find someone who knows him, who might help us understand why an apparently healthy man up and died in his living room."

She tugged the drawer open. "How about this?" She pulled out one of those new electronic do-it-all gizmos. I had a relatively sophisticated cell phone, department issue, but this was state of the art. Probably made coffee, too.

"Okay, we're looking for someone named Juliet," I said. "She was probably the last person to see Palmer alive."

"Last name?" she asked.

"No clue," I said. "But this guy doesn't strike me as the sort to alphabetize by first name."

She pushed buttons and studied the display. "You're right. But I don't think you're going to like this."

I lowered the camera from my eye. "Why?"

She handed me the phone. "Last names. Period. No first names at all, unless there are duplicates, and then it's only an initial."

The rest of the contact list was the same. Great. Maybe two hundred names. It would take hours, maybe days, to track them down. "Okay, let's try something else."

"Sir?"

I rubbed my stubble-covered jaw. Thanks to my mother's Nordic genes, my blond hair meant it wasn't too conspicuous, but I felt scruffy. I'd put on a clean shirt sometime in the last twenty-four hours, but my pants were hopelessly wrinkled, and my sport coat was ready for a trip to the cleaners as well. In a futile effort to present a more professional appearance, I straightened my tie. "Let's go talk to some neighbors."

Brad Talbot and his crime scene techs appeared on the stairs before we hit the landing. Trying to shrug off the blanket of exhaustion that clung to me, I did a one-eighty and hauled myself back to Palmer's apartment.

"Sorry it took so long to get here," Brad said. "Things are busy."

And this probably didn't seem like much of a case. While I hoped Bones would find a ruptured aneurism or other natural cause of death, I'd poke and prod at the possible foul play angle a little longer.

Brad and I walked the place. "Doesn't look like a crime scene," I said. "He's got a day planner, a fancy cell phone. Take the food under the sink. Maybe someone poisoned it." My eyeballs felt three sizes too big for their sockets and I sucked down some more of Charlie's coffee. "Do a little of your fingerprint magic. You should be in and out in nothing flat."

I trusted Brad and left the techs to their work. Charlie and I went on with my original mission. First stop, the landlord's apartment, where I got a copy of Palmer's rental application. "Always glad to help the police," he said, handing me a single sheet of paper. "Hard to believe Mr. Palmer's dead. He was so young."

Palmer had given an accounting firm as his place of employment. Worked there seven years at the time he filled out the paperwork. Would make it ten now. Two other references, neither of whom was named Juliet. I copied the name and phone number of his emergency contact, thanked the landlord, and moved on.

Charlie and I worked our way down the hall. When Mrs. Grimaldi invited us in for tea, I declined. Her apartment was heated to womb-temperature and smelled like apple pie. I was afraid my sleep-deprived body would curl up on what appeared to be a very comfortable recliner in front of a gas fireplace and never return.

"I didn't see much of him," she said. "The occasional encounter at the mailboxes. How did he die?"

"We don't know yet, ma'am," I said. "Were you aware of any health conditions? Did he talk about seeing a doctor?"

She shook her head. "Seemed the picture of health to me."

"What about visitors?"

"I wouldn't know," she said. "People come and go, and I'm at the end of the hall. I wouldn't know who visits whom upstairs."

"Thanks for your time." As with the other tenants, I handed her my card telling her to call if she thought of anything else.

I hoped for better luck on the second floor. Charlie dogged my heels. She'd been a silent observer, jotting notes in her notepad. If Henderson didn't sour her on the job, she'd do well.

"You'll notice there are two kinds of people in situations like this," I said. "The ones who won't give you the time of day, and the ones you can't get to shut up. But the best way to get information is to keep quiet. People hate silence, and they'll usually fill it."

"Like with Mr. Fox in 1-C," she said.

"Right. Of course, I don't think there was anything useful in what he told us, but I did learn more about growing tomatoes than I'll ever be able to use."

"It was nice of you to listen. He seemed lonely."

"No point in antagonizing people without a reason," I muttered.

She grinned. "Don't worry. I won't tell anyone there's a human being buried under the cop façade."

I stopped midway up the staircase. "Keeping hold of a thread of humanity is the most important thing you can do. Seeing the things we do, day after day, will eat you alive if you let it." My words bounced off the narrow walls, sounding harsher than I'd meant them.

Charlie met my gaze, eyes narrowed, brow furrowed. "Yes, sir. I understand."

Two of the four occupants of the second floor were no more helpful than Mrs. Grimaldi. Mrs. Levitz didn't mind talking to us again, but she merely repeated everything we already knew. I left my card, my gut telling me she'd be calling the department often with useless tidbits she'd just remembered. Her dust mop of a dog was sniffing around my ankles and I was glad to get out of there.

"Last one for this floor," I said when we escaped Mrs. Levitz's chatter. I dragged my feet to 2-D and rapped on the door. It opened so fast I almost fell inside. Someone had been waiting. I identified myself and Charlie.

"I'm Douglas Downing," a seventy-something man said. Tall, reed-thin, a fringe of white hair surrounded his age-spotted pate. While most of the other tenants had been in comfortable garb, he wore an old but neatly pressed suit. Charcoal gray. White shirt, gold cufflinks, blue tie. "I wondered when you'd get to me. Why don't you come in?" He backed away from the door and gestured us inside.

Mr. Downing sat on an overstuffed sofa and cleaned his black-framed glasses. "Sit." He slid the spectacles on and pushed them up the bridge of his pointy nose. "Ask your questions."

"We don't have a lot of questions," I said. "We're trying to locate someone who might have been the last person to see Mr. Palmer alive, to see if we can find out how he died."

"I suppose that could have been me," he said, not looking surprised at the death notice. But, by now, the news was sure to have spread through the building. "When did he die? I saw him Saturday evening."

Several layers of tired peeled away. My heart rate kicked up half a notch. "About what time?" I felt the first glimmer of a possible lead.

"Would have been before eight. I was just getting back from my book club meeting."

The right timetable. I scooted a little closer to the edge of my chair. "What was his condition when you saw him? Was he complaining about anything?"

"Nothing at all, although he didn't look too happy."

I waited. True to form, he continued, filling the vacuum.

"He was saying goodbye to his lady friend. Juliet, he called her. He didn't appear to like that she was leaving so early."

"What can you tell me about her? Did they get along, fight? What does she look like? Anything will help."

He gave a halfhearted shrug. "Good looking woman. About Mr. Palmer's age, I'd say. Maybe five-three. Well-endowed, but skinny for my taste. Blonde hair, down to her shoulders. Never heard them fight."

I scribbled in my notebook. "Go on, please."

"She's been coming over regularly for six months now, I guess." He glanced in Charlie's direction, then leaned forward, his voice lowered, as if he didn't want her to hear. "Normally, she doesn't leave so early. Or maybe it's she usually leaves very early, if you know what I mean." He gave a conspiratorial nod.

In deference to his manner, I lowered my voice as well. "So, she usually spent the night?"

He bobbed his head, his narrow lips pressed together.

"Would you know anything more about Juliet?" I asked. "Her last name, where she works, where she lives?"

He rolled his eyes toward the ceiling. Mine automatically followed, as if the answer might be camouflaged in the bumpy popcorn coating.

"She worked at a health food store, I'm pretty sure of that," Mr. Downing said. "Sometimes she'd show up in one of those smock top things. Burgundy. I saw it up close when I held the front door open for her. She looked surprised, like nobody ever did that for her." He sighed. "Maybe nobody did. Times sure have changed. Used to be women liked it when you did the polite thing."

"That's very true," I said, interrupting his reverie. "Back to Juliet, if you don't mind. Did you notice which health food store? Something on her smock, perhaps?"

He furrowed his brow, his bushy white eyebrows almost meeting in the center. "Come to think of it, maybe there was. But I don't remember paying it much mind. I'm not into that health food stuff. Weeds and twigs, I say."

Charlie cleared her throat. I glanced in her direction. She gave me a questioning look. Might as well give her a shot. I nodded.

"Mr. Downing," she said. "Sometimes when I try to remember something I've seen, I close my eyes and picture myself exactly where I was at the time. Maybe that would help."

Even though she was in uniform and I wore street clothes, he looked at her as if he saw her as a cop for the first time. Along with opening doors for women, he was of the generation where women stayed home and raised the kids. The expression shifted almost immediately, and he closed his eyes.

"You're right, Miss. I can see it clearly now. Crenshaw Natural Foods. And she had a nametag on, too, right above it. Juliet Yates." His eyes popped open and he smiled at Charlie, revealing a row of yellowed teeth. "Clever girl."

If Charlie took exception to being called "miss" and "girl," she had the smarts not to let it show. "I'm glad you remembered, Mr. Downing. That was very helpful."

"Thank you, Mr. Downing." I handed him my card. "If you remember anything more, you can get in touch with me. Have a good evening."

"I want another look at Randall Palmer's addresses," I said to Charlie when we were in the hall. We retraced our steps to Palmer's apartment. Henderson glowered at the doorway, especially when I nodded Charlie into the apartment with me.

"Hey, Brad," I called. "I need a peek at that cell phone thing."

He tipped his head toward the evidence bags. "No prints," he said. "Help yourself."

I handed the bag to Charlie. "Too much technology for my blood."

She ran her fingers over the buttons. "There's a Yamada, a Yeager, a York, a Young and a Yurk. No Yates."

"What about the health food store? Maybe he called her at work."

Her brow furrowed as she studied the display. "Nope. Not under the Hs or the Cs."

The hair on the back of my neck prickled. I resealed the bag, signed it to preserve the chain of evidence.

"What now?" Charlie asked.

For an instant, I thought about letting her tag along, but I didn't need any grief for taking a green rookie away from her training partner, no matter what I thought of him. I gave her an apologetic smile. "I'm afraid this is where you go back to your patrol officer duties and I try to locate Miss Yates."

She accepted her fate with a resigned nod and turned away.

"Charlie," I said, before she got to the door.

She twisted around, her gaze meeting mine. "Sir?"

"You're a good cop. Listen to Henderson, but don't judge the job by the way he does it."

She grinned. "Yes, sir. Good luck with the case."

I made the trip downstairs and out of the building. Day and night had lost all meaning, so I glanced at my watch as I walked toward my unmarked unit. Nineteen-thirty. I was working on something like my sixth wind by now, but I knew I wouldn't sleep until I followed up on this lead. There were probably a dozen good reasons why Juliet's name wasn't in Palmer's phone, but I couldn't think of one that would let me go home yet. If Juliet could give me what I needed, I'd crash for at least eight hours.

Back at the station, I checked for anything new on my double homicide, almost glad when there wasn't. I could deal with Juliet Yates and get my rack time. I found Juliet's DMV record, including a better-than-average driver's license photo confirming what Mr. Downing had said about her looks. I ran her through a couple of criminal databases and came up empty. Time to pay Miss Yates a visit. I logged off the computer and headed for the elevator.

Charlie waited there, dressed in street clothes, a parka slung over her arm.

She turned at my approach. As expected, she looked fine minus the Kevlar. She smiled. "Hello, Detective. Any luck finding Juliet Yates?"

I jerked my gaze to her face. "An address. I'm on my way there now."

"Um...would it be all right if I came along? I'm off duty. I'd like to see more of the investigation." She hesitated. "I'm shooting for detective someday."

Against regulations, letting her tag along, but I didn't want to put out the light in her eyes. "Why not?" Besides, having a woman around when I broke the news to Juliet that Palmer was dead might be helpful. It would take at least an hour to get one of the department chaplains to come on a death notification call.

I tossed the coffee cups and fast food bags off the passenger seat in my unit and Charlie slid in. "Thanks. I'll stay out of your way."

"You'll be fine," I said. "You were great with the neighbors. This is just one more interview."

I plugged Juliet's address into the GPS and followed the route to an upscale condominium apartment complex, one of those gated communities that popped up like mushrooms around sinkholes and retention ponds the developers called lakes.

Four minutes later, after badging the guard at the gate and weaving through a winding maze of pink stucco two-story townhouse apartments, I parked three units down from Juliet's building. The wind chill kicked in and I crossed my arms trying to keep warm. I wore the same slacks and sport coat I'd put on this morning when it was sunny. Charlie looked like she wanted to offer her parka. She didn't. Smart move.

I knocked on Juliet Yates' door, Charlie standing to my left, behind me. Rock music blared from inside. I waited, knocked again, then pressed the doorbell.

"Through there." Charlie pointed through a picture window.

I looked over her shoulder. The living room opened onto a glass-enclosed Florida room, where a woman ran on a treadmill, staring straight ahead, apparently oblivious to everything around her. I hit the doorbell several times and pounded on the door.

The music stopped. The woman slowed her pace, then grabbed a towel and strode to the door, daubing her brow. "Who's there?" she asked.

"Police officers," I said, and the door opened.

Based on Mr. Downing's description and the driver's license photo, Juliet Yates stood in front of me, dressed in skin-tight leggings and a sports top revealing abundant cleavage and slim midriff. She patted her brow with the towel once more. "Sorry, I was working out. In the zone, you know."

I grunted in acknowledgment. "I'd like to ask you some questions," I said. "May we come in?"

"Questions? Me? About what?" However, she stepped back and motioned us inside.

I followed her tight derriere to the living room where she indicated a floral print rattan couch. Charlie took one end, I sat on the other. Juliet seated herself across from us in a matching chair.

"I understand you're acquainted with Randall Palmer," I began.

"Yes, I am." She draped the towel around her neck. "Has he done something wrong?"

I avoided the direct answer. "When's the last time you saw him?"

Without missing a beat, she answered, "Saturday night. We had dinner at his place."

"How long were you two involved?"

This time, she hesitated. Had she grasped my use of the past tense?

"We dated about six months," she said. "Saturday I told him I thought we should, you know, maybe start seeing other people. It wasn't working as a long-term relationship."

"How did he react?"

She shrugged. "I suppose my ego would prefer to say he was heartbroken, but I think he accepted it. We parted on friendly enough terms."

Maybe not so friendly. He hadn't wasted any time erasing her from his contact list.

More sweat dripped from her bangs and she patted her forehead with the towel. "You still haven't told me why you're here."

I glanced at Charlie who leaned forward a hair, as if to offer comfort if needed. Best way I'd learned was to get straight to the point. "I'm sorry, Miss Yates, but Randall Palmer is dead."

She lowered her face in the towel. When she looked up, her features were controlled. "How?"

"That's what I hoped you could help with. Were you aware of any health problems?"

She shook her head. "No, he took very good care of himself. We met in the health food store where I work. I don't think he had as much as a cold since I met him."

"Do you know his family? Anyone we should notify to make ...arrangements?"

"I'm sorry," she said. "I never met them. I think he mentioned a sister once. Samantha? Lives somewhere up north. Chicago, maybe."

That agreed with the emergency contact number from his rental agreement. "Thank you."

"If there's nothing else," she said, "I think I'd like to be alone. The news shook me, I guess."

She did look a little off-color. "Let me get you some water," I said.

"I'm all right, really," she said. "It was just, you know, a shock. That he's dead. So suddenly."

"Water will help, especially if you've been exercising," Charlie said. A bar-height counter separated the living room from the kitchen, and she headed in that direction.

"I can get it." Juliet jumped up. I followed. She pushed past Charlie and opened a cabinet, extracting an oblong-shaped bottle of designer water. "Want one? It's not cold, but given the weather..."

Charlie accepted the bottle, and Juliet pulled out another one for herself, offering me a third. She cracked off the top and swigged half the contents. "I'm fine. There's no need for you to stay."

"I'll feel better if we wait a couple of minutes." I wandered toward a collection of potted plants snuggled against the doors. "Just to make sure you're all right." Charlie hung back, staying near the counter. I took in as much as I could, treading a very fine line with the expectation of privacy rule. Juliet Yates was far from dead. "Prepared for the freeze warnings, right?"

She nodded. "My herbs. Most of them can't handle the cold. I should get outside and cover my outdoor plants, too." She pointed to a pile of sheets in the corner.

"You must have a green thumb," Charlie said. "I can barely keep a silk plant alive."

"It's a hobby," Juliet said.

"Would you like some help covering them?" Charlie asked.

"No, there's plenty of time. I want to shower and change before I go outside. If you'll excuse me?"

My sleep-deprived brain wasn't firing worth a damn. I handed her my card and gave her the usual spiel about calling me. She saw us to the door, practically shoving us outside. I turned up my collar and bee-lined down the block to my cruiser. Charlie climbed in, set her water bottle in a cup holder, and I cranked up the heat.

"Impressions?" I asked her.

"Not really, other than she's a self-centered fake."

I felt an unexpected burst of pride. "Explain," I said.

She met my eyes. "With all due respect, sir, I know how men look at women. They're hard-wired that way. But her—" she cupped her hands in front of her chest—"they're not original equipment. The hair's not her natural color, and I'll bet half my next check the nose isn't the one she was born with, either. And she probably gets Botox injections in her forehead."

I'd wondered about the boobs, caught the hair, but not the Botox. "So, she's been sucked in by all the emphasis our society puts on image. Along with half the female population."

"All the way," Charlie said. "She didn't seem too shook up by Palmer's death, or is that a common reaction?"

"In this job, you get it all. She might be one of those who refuses to show her feelings. Or it'll sink in later and she'll fall apart."

"You think she had something to do with Palmer's death?"

"What do you think? She had the opportunity, maybe put something in his food. But motive?"

She pondered that for a while. "I have no idea."

"Neither do I, and we can't do anything else tonight. I'll drop you back at the station."

When I let her off by her car, she smiled. "Thanks again."

"Hang in there." I watched her drive away, remembering when I'd been that eager. I parked and went to my desk, figuring I could finish my reports and put the case behind me until Bones and the techs filed theirs. Notifying his sister could wait, too. I'd see if I could get someone in Chicago to handle that end.

I wondered if I could get Charlie a new training partner. Someone who'd give her room to grow. I knew if I was still around when she put in for detective, I'd volunteer.

My cell went off. "Kirkland."

"Hey, Jim, it's Brad Talbot. We lifted a couple of good latents from the Palmer place and got a hit from IAFIS. Jane Keats. Arrested in a kegger party roundup in Boston thirteen years ago. Alcohol and drugs. Suspended sentence. Not the greatest way to spend her eighteenth birthday."

Interesting. What would she have been doing at Palmer's place? Didn't fit his image. Worth another trip through the search engines.

I clicked a few times and found a Boston newspaper article with a photo of four kids hoisting a trophy. National Quiz Bowl winners. I squinted at the caption under the picture. Isaac (Izzy) Horowitz, Jane Keats, Gordon (Gonzo) Stevens and Randall (Rowdy) Palmer.

I studied Jane more carefully. Short, round, with the requisite bottle-thick glasses and an overbite. Whatever her nickname was, it wasn't the sort to be printed in the paper. Remembering the cruelty of kids, I couldn't help thinking Plain Jane or Blubber.

I read the article. An obituary for Gordon Stevens, dead of a heart attack five years ago. Curious, I continued surfing. Isaac Horowitz died three years ago, cause of death: heart attack.

Three young men, all connected, all dying of heart attacks? That was too much coincidence for me. I'd have to call Bones and make sure he ran more than the basic tox screen.

A stab of worry pierced my gut. What if Jane was going to be victim number four? Someone should find her. Warn her. Maybe give some poor homicide dick one less case to solve. One less face to see when he closed his eyes at night.

I told myself sleep was a highly overrated commodity and clicked some more, looking for Jane Keats. If she'd married, she might have changed her name. She could have moved anywhere.

I swore out loud. Jane's prints had been in Palmer's apartment. But Juliet had been there. Her prints should have been, too. Hell, they probably were, but we didn't have hers as exemplars.

I stared at the picture of Jane. Pulled up the picture of Juliet. Stared some more.

I sprinted downstairs to my car, pulling on gloves as I ran. I clicked the remote, yanked the door open and lifted out the water bottle Charlie had left behind.

I found Brad in the lab. "Print this." At his cocked eyebrows, I added a please.

He shrugged, but reached for his print kit. "Okay, what am I looking for?"

"Just tell me if any of the prints match the ones for Jane Keats."

I paced while he worked, not sure what I wanted him to find. When he gave me his answer, I exhaled the breath I'd been holding. "Thanks. Next round's on me."

I high-tailed it back to Juliet's apartment. The lights were off in the living room. When there was no answer, I walked around back. Her garden was well-illuminated, and I had no trouble finding her covering her shrubs with the sheets I'd seen in her kitchen.

"Hello, Jane," I said.

She tensed. Slowly, she rose and faced me. "My name is Juliet, not Jane."

"But you used to be Jane."

"I don't know what you're talking about, but you clearly have me confused with someone else." Her back to me, she flapped a sheet in the air and let it drift over a bush.

"Your fingerprints say otherwise. The ones on the bottle of water match the prints of Jane Keats we found in Randall Palmer's apartment."

She turned, wiped her hands on her jeans, and folded her arms across her chest. "Are you going to arrest me?"

"I'd rather talk first. Tell me about it." I waited. I pegged her as a babbler.

"They deserved to die," she said. She leaned over and adjusted a sheet. "I wasn't good enough for them. Sure, when they needed someone to help them with math, or physics, or write their English papers, I was who they called. Without me, we'd never have won Quiz Bowl."

Sad that a high school triumph thirteen years past was the defining event in her life.

She brushed her hands together and strolled through the yard, which now appeared to be covered with pastel snow drifts. She wandered onto her screened patio, fingered some plants, then stopped in front of the potted herbs along the glass door into the house. "You think they'll be all right out here? They're sheltered from the wind, and if I run the heat in the house, they'll stay warm enough."

Apparently satisfied she'd answered her own question, she slid the door open and sidled past the pots. She filled a teakettle, put it on the burner. "I'm going to make some herbal tea," she said. "Would you like some?"

"I think I'll pass."

She looked at me, a profound sadness in her eyes. "It wasn't supposed to be like this. I thought once they paid for what they did, I'd be happy."

"What did they do?"

"Ruined my life."

I waited.

"They invited me to a frat party. Gordon's older brother's house. It was my birthday. Everyone treated me like I was popular. I thought they'd finally accepted me." She took two mugs from the cabinet. "You sure you don't want some?"

"I'm fine. Go on, please."

She put the second mug back. "I'd never had a drink before that night. Or smelled marijuana. I didn't like beer, so I drank the punch, no clue it was spiked. I was totally out of it. Later, I found out I was on the agenda for a group encounter of the intimate kind upstairs." She snorted. "At least there was no YouTube in those days. No Facebook. No Twitter. Just Polaroids. Lucky for me, the cops showed up before it went that far. I don't remember anything until my parents bailed me out of jail."

She spun around, venom in her eyes. "You know what that did to them? My dad was a minister. Bailing his underage daughter out of jail devastated him and my mom. Being arrested meant I lost my scholarship. We had no money. That was the only way I could afford college. So now I work in a damn health food store."

I refrained from pointing out there were lots of people who overcame far greater obstacles. She'd spent years blaming others for her misfortune, and nothing I could say would change that. Instead, I Mirandized her.

Defeat replaced the venom in her eyes. She said she understood her rights. "I can forgive them for not recognizing me. All the dieting, the exercise, the cosmetic surgery. Gordon enjoyed my company until I told him my name, and then he did a complete one-eighty. All he saw was the Jane I'd been."

She shrugged and sat down. "After Gordon...died...and the cops started asking questions, I decided Jane needed to disappear, so I moved away, changed my name to Juliet."

"And you went after the others."

"They liked Juliet. After we dated awhile, I told them who I'd been. Gave them a chance to make amends. All they had to do was apologize, and nothing would have happened."

"But they didn't."

Her hands, resting on the table, clenched into tight fists. "Juliet's all on the outside. Inside, I'm still Jane. But they would have liked Jane if they'd given her half a chance. They never knew how much it hurt."

The kettle whistled. She rose and pulled a jar of dried leaves from a cabinet. I jumped to my feet and stayed her hand.

"Relax." She waved the jar under my nose. "It's only dried mint. Perfectly harmless. Soothing, actually." She tipped some leaves into a ceramic teapot, then filled it with boiling water. A minty aroma filled the kitchen.

"What did you give them?" I asked.

She pointed to a potted plant in the corner of the patio. I followed the direction her finger indicated. Nothing spectacular. The innocuous plant with its dull green leaves and dark berries looked more like an overgrown weed to me.

"*Atropa belladonna,*" she said. "It's actually related to tomatoes and eggplant. But far more deadly."

Apparently so. "What did you do?" I asked. "Grind the berries? Make tea out of the leaves?"

"Nothing so commonplace." She leaned forward and explained how she got the poison into their systems.

"Damn," I said, taking in her dilated pupils. Juliet. Romeo. Both dead at the end of the play. "There's more than mint in your tea, isn't there?"

She smiled and closed her eyes. I called the medics and waited in the empty silence.

Once the medics had her in the ambulance, I sat at the table, bracing myself for the call I had to make. Damn, it was going to be tough, but I pulled out my cell and punched in Bones's number.

"Hey, Bones," I said. "I've got the cause of death on Palmer. The killer confessed. Belladonna poisoning. I'm sure your fancy lab tests will find it in his system."

"Atropine." I visualized Bones rubbing his chin. "I'll be sure to have them run the test for it. In the food?"

"Nope. The girlfriend made some concoction of nightshade, mixed it with DMSO and delivered it topically."

Another pause, another image of chin-rubbing. "DMSO explains the garlic odor," Bones said. "Fascinating, to quote the intrepid Vulcan. Topically, you say. Contact with the skin, then the DMSO conducts it right into the bloodstream. So—"

I took a deep breath. This was the hard part. "Yep. The red shirt he was wearing? Her gift to him. She'd soaked it in atropine and DMSO. You were right all along. His shirt killed him."

The End

You can find Terry at:

www.terryodell.com

Facebook: https://www.facebook.com/AuthorTerryOdell

Twitter: https://twitter.com/authorterryo

Blog: https://terryodell.com/terrysplace/

Cover by Zach Saltos.

Crossing the Line

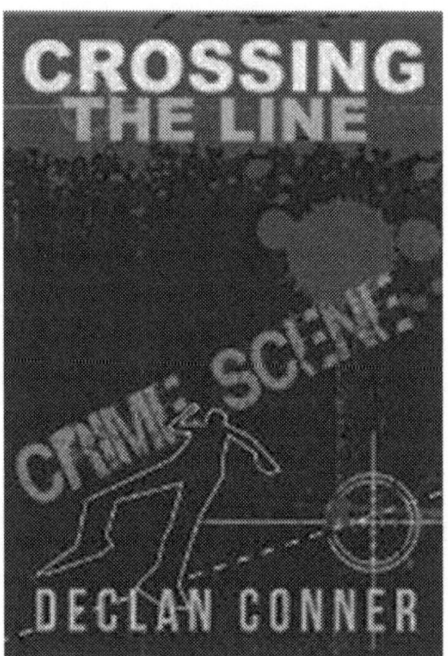

Declan Conner

Detective Grace Rutherford is called to the scene of a young woman's murder. She knows all the clues are at the scene for all to see, but sometimes it's hard to see what's in front of your face when your mind is beset with personal problems. It should be an open and shut case once the DNA results are back. At least that's what the murderer hopes for.

Declan Conner lives in Brazil, where he writes crime thrillers full time. For the better part of 2011, his collection of shorts, *Lunch Break Thrillers*, rose to the top ten for anthologies on Amazon UK, rubbing shoulders and changing chart position with the likes of Agatha Christie, Lee Child, Stephen King, and Edgar Allan Poe. Currently he has six full-length works published via Amazon, with more to come.

***

Grace Rutherford rolled over on her mattress. She grabbed at the source of the annoying ringing coming from her nightstand and cracked open one eye, then the other. The number on the screen of her cell phone blurred.

"Who is it?" she croaked out, then cleared her throat.

"Dispatch. We have a code two-zero-seven over on the sixty-five highway in a rest area two miles out of town. The victim is Jane Rhodes, a known prostitute. We have a highway patrol officer at the scene. Forensics and the coroner's office have been informed."

She wanted to protest, but then she knew it wasn't the dispatcher's fault they were calling her on her scheduled day off. Not with half of her colleagues down with flu.

"I'm on it," she said, then closed the call. Reaching out, the phone slipped from her fingers back onto the nightstand.

Her shoulders hit south. She groaned. There wasn't a note left on the nightstand with a single rose. No aroma of coffee awaiting her. All there was to say that her visitor had been there was a dent in the pillow next to her and the duvet turned back at his side of the bed. Dick, she recalled he'd said his name was, short for Richard. *Some dick*, she thought. Rutherford smiled at the recollection of exchanging body fluids; an itch scratched. It was a failed visit to see her daughter that had sent her on a bar crawl and into revenge-screwing mode.

"You're an hour and a half late," her ex had said. "You can't see her; she has homework."

It wasn't just the pain of her foot trapped in the door that had annoyed her. She grasped at an image of his secretary, and now his wife, dancing up and down on her toes behind him, working him like a ventriloquist's dummy. A bullet to Bimbo's forehead would have solved the problem but created another. Rutherford didn't think Bimbo was worth the effort of her drawing her pistol, only to be banged up for life with no visitation rights at all to her daughter. What really pained her was walking down the drive and glancing back to see her daughter Jess, crying at her upstairs bedroom window. She cursed under her breath that the hours she worked had cost her custody.

Rutherford threw her legs over the side of the bed. She rose to her feet then slipped her silk wrap around her and stumbled into the living room, picking up her discarded clothes trail from the night before all the way to her front door.

Her head pounded on the way back to her bedroom and on into

her bathroom. She glanced in the mirror and shrugged. The sculptured face that she'd laboriously put on the night before was now streaked with mascara and smudged lipstick. She took a quick shower and dressed.

Detective mode took over as she slipped her pistol into her shoulder holster and then locked the apartment door behind her. Somehow, wearing her black trouser suit and carrying her pistol gave her a sense of purpose and a surge of power. Restored to a semblance of normality, the feelings of worthlessness that had engulfed her were swiped away in that moment. Her mind darted in a multitude of directions as she climbed into her car and pulled out of the parking lot. It was always the same on a new case. The anticipation of what she'd find at the scene started her adrenaline flowing.

As she approached the rest area, there was just the one highway patrol car. The officer was sitting with his backside on the hood of his car and smoking a cigarette. She pulled up behind him and parked.

"What have we got?" she asked.

"See for yourself," he said, then stubbed out his cigarette, adding to a pile of other stubs.

The forensic crime investigator's vehicle pulled up behind her as she hauled herself out of her seat.

"Have you run a license plate check?" Rutherford asked the officer.

"Yeah, it belongs to the victim. Her rap sheet shows the same tattoo on her arm."

Rutherford noticed the passenger door was wide open to the victim's car.

"Was it like that when you arrived?"

"No, I thought she was asleep, but she didn't respond. It was partly open off the catch when I arrived around an hour ago. Checked her pulse to confirm she was dead rather than drugged up on heroin, then phoned it in."

"Leave me to it," said James, the forensic guy.

"Where does her rap sheet say she works her tricks?" she asked.

"Main Street."

Rutherford glanced around. There wasn't a house in sight to start pounding doors for any witnesses. The rest area where she'd parked was masked by thick foliage on what was a country road. It was a good spot for a prostitute to bring her tricks, with no prying cameras, except it was miles out of town, and time was money in their game. Not only that, it was her vehicle. If she worked Main Street, she'd solicit on foot, climb into her trick's vehicle and likely have a spot nearby to take them.

"No blood. It looks as though she's been strangled," James called out. "We've had a break, though," he said, and held up a condom with his tweezers, then dropped it into an evidence bag. "You can come and see now. I found the condom in her clenched hand."

Stepping over to the victim's vehicle, she thought that finding the condom in her hand didn't make sense. Not for a murderer to have missed looking for it as a priority before leaving. Her eyes coursed over the ground, but there wasn't the usual telltale sign of discarded condoms for it to be a regular spot to take clients.

"I've arranged for the vehicle to be collected and taken to our garage for further forensic tests," James said. "Once we have the DNA from the sperm, you'll likely have your murderer. She had false nails, but there isn't any blood on them and none of them are broken. But just in case she fought back and scratched him, the medical examiner will take scrapings at the autopsy."

"What's in her purse?"

"Driver's license, unused condoms, four hundred dollars in crumpled notes, and the usual makeup. Oh yeah, and she had a cell phone with the battery dead."

"Pass her license here."

She made a note of the address. Rutherford wasn't looking forward to her next port of call, however many times she had trodden the path. As a young woman, she dreaded there would be children at the victim's home. Fishing her cell phone from her pocket, she dialed dispatch.

"Detective Rutherford here. Can you run a check to see if anyone reported a missing person overnight?" She reeled off the victim's name and address.

"One moment."

Rutherford had avoided looking at the corpse. Not having had any breakfast, she hadn't thought her stomach would have taken it. A quick glance and she averted her gaze, relieved that it wasn't a bloody scene. It was like the officer had said. Jane's seat was wound down, and she looked as though she was asleep. The odd things were her skirt was in place and her pants weren't around one of her ankles. The murderer must have strangled her after they'd done the deed.

"Sorry it took some time. I have it. It was typed in misspelt. Her partner phoned it in at two in the morning. It's down for an officer to call later this morning."

"Scrub it. I'm on my way there now. Give me the name of her partner."

"Harvey Logan."

The coroner's body snatcher van and the tow truck arrived at the same time. She turned to the officer.

"As soon as they're done here, you can go. Send your report over to robbery and homicide, and mark it for my attention."

He tipped her a salute and climbed into his car.

Rutherford shuffled onto her seat and set off for town. She knew the area, but she hadn't been there for many years. The journey was something of a haze until she arrived. It wasn't like the last time she visited as she pulled over at the victim's apartment block. What had been a pristine new build was now blighted with graffiti. The entrance door was hanging to one side with a broken hinge and a spider's web of glass where someone had kicked in the bottom panel. A smell of urine hit her nose, and she walked inside and up to the apartment door. The overbearing odor had her retching. She gave the door her best detective knock. Thankfully the door opened right away. She stepped back. Rutherford hadn't been expecting to see a well-dressed woman answer.

"Detective Rutherford. Jane's partner Harvey reported her missing last night. I have bad news I'm afraid."

"You'd better come in. I'm Alice Gibson from child protection services."

"Is Harvey here?" she asked, as she followed her down the hallway.

"No, that's why I'm here. He phoned to say the kids weren't his problem and he had to go."

"What time will he be back?" Rutherford asked.

"We'd better talk in the kitchen," she said, and then beckoned her through an open door. "He won't be back. Her children are in the living room. I'm trying to get a hold of relatives but not having any luck. The office is arranging for them to go into care unless you've found her. Has she been in an accident?"

"No, not that. We've found her, but unfortunately, she's dead."

The social worker tished, then sighed, like it was an inconvenience.

In a way, she was pleased there were no relatives to break the news to, followed by floods of tears. It was matter of fact giving the news to the social worker, free of emotion.

"That's all I need. That means I'll have to take them."

"Did he say where he was going?"

"No, he had his bags packed at the door waiting. He's not on our records, so he must have been a new boyfriend."

Rutherford sighed. "I'll need to talk to the children. How old are they?"

"I'm not sure I can allow that. We'll have to break the news to them after consulting with our resident psychiatrist. Any contact with them will have to be arranged through our attorney."

Rutherford rolled her eyes and thought that was all she needed: a do-gooder social worker going by the book.

"Listen, this is a murder enquiry. I need to know what they knew about her partner. He could be a person of interest."

"No, it's out of the question. Maybe the neighbors will know. Ask them. Her two youngest are only three and four. And her eldest has learning difficulties, but regardless, I can't allow it." She handed the apartment keys to Rutherford. "I'd better take them to the office under the circumstances. I'll let you lock up. I've already packed some of their clothes."

A young girl around her daughter's age ran into the kitchen.

"Where's Mom? I want my mom," she said, clearly distressed, tears running down her cheeks. A vision of Jess, her own daughter, crying at her bedroom window flashed in her mind.

"I'll leave you to it. You can pull the door to on the Yale catch," said Rutherford, trying to hold herself together. She could barely contain herself until she arrived at her car, and yanking her door open, she slid onto the seat. Rutherford repeatedly head butted the center of the steering wheel, but it didn't stop the tears. Guilt had struck her for the many times she'd been late for her visits to see Jess and for the times she couldn't make it when she'd put work first. It hadn't mattered when her husband was at home to see to her, but she knew that she hadn't adjusted since the divorce. She pushed back into her seat and wondered how Jess would cope if that last vision of her was when she'd walked down the drive.

Rutherford slapped the steering wheel. A sense of determination rolled through her. The failed access visit would be the last time she would ever let Jess down.

The social worker ushered the children out to her car. The eldest child sent a soulful stare at Rutherford, tears still streaking down both her cheeks. "Don't worry, I'll find your mom's killer," she mouthed under her breath. "That's a promise."

***

Rutherford drove slowly along Main Street. The bars were due for closing, so she knew she would have to work fast before the girls started to thin out. The rain didn't stop some of the younger ones propping up the lampposts with their umbrellas protecting them, if not their scanty clothing. They weren't the ones she was looking for. Pimps would have the street marked out, and they'd be watching their investments. She was looking for Candice, when she spotted her in an alcove of a storefront. She pulled over, stopped, then powered down her passenger window. Candice stepped over and leaned inside.

"Oh, it's you!"

"Yeah, it's me. Get in," she said, and reaching over, she pulled on the door release.

Candice retracted her umbrella and sidled onto the seat.

"Is this business, or police business?"

"You'll get paid for the usual, don't worry."

As soon as they cleared Main Street, she checked her rearview to make sure no one was following. Rutherford turned left into an industrial complex and parked at a loading bay then pulled down the hood to her sweatshirt. She opened her purse, took out a twenty and handed it over.

"Better make it quick for twenty," Candice said.

Rutherford reached over and opened her glove compartment then switched on the vanity light. Candice was well past her sell by date for her line of work, but at least she knew that with her earning power diminished, she didn't have to worry about her having a pimp. Not only that, she knew that the working girls looked to her for advice as a mother figure.

"Do you know her?" she asked, and held up the mug shot of Jane Rhodes.

"Yeah. I heard she'd been murdered. How can I help?"

"I need you to talk to the girls on the street. I can't go questioning them all when their pimps are watching, or we could end up with more corpses. She had a boyfriend called Harvey. I need to find him."

"Never heard of him. What does he look like?"

"White. In his forties, bald head, scar on his cheek. Powerful build."

"Shit, that sounds like her pimp, but he's called Hulk Logan. Least that's what we call him on the street. Don't wanna go messin' with him. He's one bad dude."

"Where can I find him?"

"The Rubber Duck Bar on the edge of town. D'ya think he killed her?"

"We don't know anything yet, but I want to give him a tongue lashing for abandoning her kids."

"Well, good luck with that." She looked at her watch. "Better get back. The bars'll be closing soon. Drop me at the end of the street in case anyone recognizes your car."

On the drive back, the scene of the murder flashed through her mind.

"Did you see her on the night of the murder?"

"Yeah, she was working the street."

"So, seeing as she was found in her own vehicle, would you say she'd finished and she was on her way home?"

"From what I saw on the news report, they found her in the opposite direction to where she lived. Maybe she had a regular phone her and met up with him."

"Maybe. Did you speak to her at all on the night?"

"Yeah, she was on edge. Said a cop followed her on her last trick, and he was drunk, but he didn't stop them."

"What time?"

"Midnight. That's when we all finish."

Rutherford dropped her off. There wouldn't be time to get to the Rubber Duck Bar before it closed, but she headed in that direction anyway. The bar was in darkness when she arrived, but not so dark that she couldn't see that someone had painted over the "D" on the name on the sign and replaced it with an "F." She tapped in the street name for Jane's boyfriend on her keyboard. The result appeared on her inboard computer screen. It came back with a rap sheet as long as her arm and a stack of outstanding warrants. With a history of violence, she was relieved the bar was closed. She called dispatch on her radio, only to find the Marshals were already looking for him. She left a message with details of the bar where he hung out and for them to call her if they got a result. Calling it a day, she drove home.

Climbing the stairway, she was worn out. She opened the door and trudged through to her bedroom, then dove on the bed, exhausted. Her boss had said to put the case to one side until the DNA came back, but she'd spent most of her spare time trying to track down her boyfriend. Rutherford was sure he would be involved for him to skip out on the kids.

She reached out and turned on the bedside lamp then picked up the file with her case notes from the nightstand and rolled over. She read through Officer Clive Woodward's report and chewed on her lip. Jane's cell phone records confirmed what Candice had said. The cell tower had her in the vicinity of Main Street all night, then one picked her up when she was almost home. For some reason, she changed direction, and two more cell towers picked her up on the way to where she was found until the battery died. There were no calls from anyone, so Candice had gotten that part wrong about a customer phoning her. She wondered if perhaps her partner had arranged to meet her at the rest area after work. But then no self-respecting pimp would have left four hundred dollars in her purse, never mind leaving a condom behind.

The lubricants from the condom and other particles confirmed it was from the same manufacturer as the ones in her purse and they weren't the sort that used added spermicide. All her leads for the past week had run her up a blind alley. She wondered if her boss had been right and she should have waited for the DNA results.

***

It was daylight when she awoke to her phone ringing, still fully dressed and pistol in holster.

"Who is it?"

"James from forensics. I have one of the DNA results back, and the autopsy has determined the cause and time of death."

"Well, don't keep me in suspense."

"We have a match on the DNA. One Harvey Logan, alias Hulk Logan."

"Bingo, I knew it. That's her boyfriend."

"Not so fast. That sperm sample taken from the cervix had a good percentage of live sperms. It can live for up to five days there before they all die off, and there was no rupture in the condom. If the DNA is from her boyfriend, there's every reason for it to be there, alive and kicking. She did die from strangulation though. The time of death was around midnight to one o'clock."

"That's not much help just now. She was seen on Main Street at midnight. From the route she took, I think it would be nearer one when she died."

"You're right there. I saw the cell phone records, but see, there lies a problem."

"What problem?"

"Sperm in a condom doesn't survive as long as it would in the cervix, but it doesn't die right away. The sperm in the condom was mostly dead with only a few on their last legs, and I was back at the lab to run the test at seven forty-five."

"So, what does that mean?"

"It means that the sperm must have ejaculated a while before the time of death. Say around ten to midnight. One other thing. There wasn't an open condom wrapper inside or outside the vehicle. Look, I have to go. I'm expecting the other DNA result on the content of the condom this afternoon, and I have a ton of work."

"Speak to you as soon as you know something," she said, then hung up.

Rutherford stripped and walked into the bathroom to take a shower. As the water cascaded over her, she had a light bulb moment and closed the faucet. It was a long shot, but Candice mentioning that a cop car followed the victim with her last trick of the night got her to thinking. There was a chance that her last customer, or a different one, could have followed her, pulled her over, then asked for second helpings and suggested the rest area. She quickly dried herself then dressed.

Rutherford dropped her backside on the mattress, picked up her phone and phoned the sheriff's office.

"Detective Rutherford here. I hope you can help me. I could do with the roster for highway patrol vehicles that cover central. Main Street in particular. I'm hoping that one of your officers either had their dash cam on, or, if maybe they can recall a vehicle in front of them as they drove along Main Street. It's relating to a murder case I'm investigating."

"What date and time?"

She rhymed off the date and the approximate time.

"That would be the night shift. I'll get back to you."

Rutherford closed the call and picked up a photograph of her daughter from the nightstand. She wondered if, when Jess grew up, she'd understand that if it wasn't for her doing her job, there would be anarchy on the streets, and it was her way of protecting her future. She doubted it. Likely all she'd recall would be the hurt of her not being there for her. She sighed, kissed the photo, then placed it back under the lamp.

Her phone rang. She crossed her fingers it would be the results of the DNA test.

"Hello."

"Jack from the sheriff's office. I have the officer's name. Highway Patrol Officer Clive Woodward."

"Really!"

"Don't know how he does it."

"Does what?"

"Work after his wife was mown down by a hit-and-run drunk driver. She died a few days later."

"When was that?"

"Around six weeks ago. Bastard's out on bail. Knowing the justices around here, he'll probably get a slap on the wrist."

"Yeah, I give you that. Who was the driver?"

"Gordon Hughes. We're all hoping he'll step out of line while he's out on bail."

"I wouldn't hold my breath," she said, and thanked him, then hung up.

Revenge would be sweet, she thought, if he did step out of line, recalling wanting to put a bullet in Bimbo's forehead. But then all she had lost was one visitation. She had the rest of her life to make amends. Poor Officer Clive Woodward had lost his wife for good.

The scene of Jane's murder had been bugging her all along. Now she knew the condom wrapper wasn't found at the scene; it was likely opened somewhere else. She was betting that the condom was used somewhere else, too, and then discarded from what James had said about the lifespan of the sperm. With Jane laid down on the retracted seat, the officer wouldn't have seen her. All the same, he would have approached the driver's side and opened that door to check her pulse. Why open the passenger side door unless he climbed over her? The phone rang and she answered.

"Hi, it's James again. I have that other DNA result."

"Don't tell me, you have a match to a hit and run DUI driver, Gordon Hughes, and I'm guessing he has a prior for soliciting prostitutes."

"How the hell did you know?"

"I'd like to say I could read your mind, but I'd be lying. Let's just say an open car door told me, together with a pile of discarded cigarette butts, and another door that closed on my foot."

"I'm not even going to ask what that means. What are you going to do, arrest Hughes?"

"Under normal circumstances, I would and leave it at that for a jury to decide with my conscience clear, but I made a young girl a promise. If you want to know what I'm doing, I'm not doing anything today, only phoning the office to give them the name of the murderer and the motive, and it isn't Gordon Hughes. Though I'm betting Hughes was her last trick on Main Street. They can deal with it. It's Saturday and I have a whole day with my daughter."

The End

Connect with Declan at:

Blog: declanconner.com

Amazon: All his books are available on all sites and are enrolled in Kindle Unlimited and Prime. Publisher Scorpion Books: Simply search Declan Conner.

Cover by Author.

Luck of the Draw

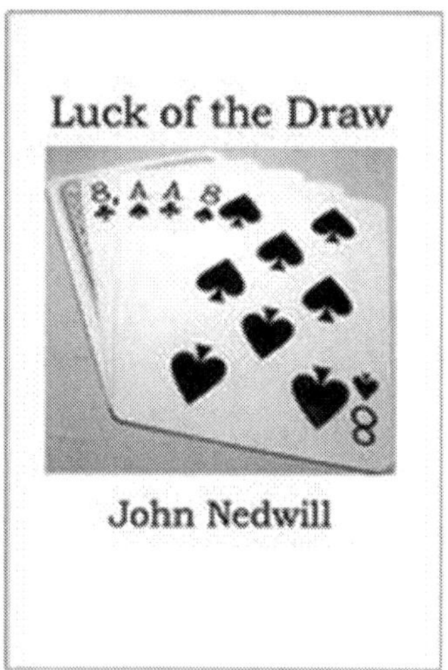

John Nedwill

In "Luck of the Draw," two Belfast detectives set out to find their way to the heart of a murder. Unfortunately nothing is ever simple, but Detective Inspector Corrigan and Detective Sergeant Beaulieu of the PSNI are determined to find out the truth behind the death of a gambler.

John Nedwill wishes he was a published author. It would get him away from the day job of being a nuclear engineer and editor of soul-destroyingly bad technical reports. In order to maintain his secret identity and avoid attention from his work colleagues, he has taken up his *nom de plume*. His ambitions are to obtain a sample of trinitite and to verify the truth behind the apocryphal *Fat Man Hypothesis.*

***

It was a cold spring morning in Belfast. The rush hour traffic was standing nose to tail on the University Road, the fumes from their exhausts adding to the grey clouds that hung over the city's Botanic Gardens. Despite the early hour, the groundskeepers were already busy amongst the borders and lawns of the park, preparing it for the warmer weather to come.

Jack Finch had been a gardener with the city's Parks Department for over twenty years. This morning he had parked his pickup in the lee of the Ulster Museum and was now making his way to the flowerbeds in front of the garden's Victorian greenhouse. As he strode across the damp grass, he noticed that the part of the bed had already been cleared of the old growth and something had been planted in it.

"That's my job," Jack announced to no one in particular. He bent down to look at the strange thing growing out of the middle of the flowerbed. It was like no plant that he was familiar with. This looked like a gnarled stump with five leathery twigs growing from it. A deck of cards had been scattered beneath it, and some of them had been blown against the greenhouse's panes.

"Bloody vandals," Jack cursed. Then he paused. In his experience, vandals were only interested in destruction, not gardening. He knelt down to start digging up the strange plant. Just because it wasn't meant to be here didn't mean that it shouldn't be treated with respect. As he cleared the freshly turned earth away, Jack started to worry. The strange plant didn't have roots—just a hairy stem that seemed to grow thicker the further down he dug—and it had fingernails on the ends of the twigs. Jack Finch stood up and reached for the radio on his belt.

"This is Jack, down by the palm house. I think I need the peelers here," he said quietly.

***

A few hours later, the entrance to the park had been closed. Uniformed policemen were stationed at the gates to keep the curious back, while inside the park a number of white-painted police cars were parked on the road at the edge of the grass. A plastic tent had been placed over the flowerbed to protect the corpse and the shallow grave it lay in. Outside the tent, a small group of people had gathered. Most of them were dressed in white, hooded oversuits, with the rest dressed in the green uniforms of the Police Service of Northern Ireland.

Two men in creased suits pushed their way through the

onlookers and showed passes to the officer on guard at the gates. He stood aside to let the men in and pointed towards the tent. The shorter of the two men nodded, then they made their way across the still damp grass.

"Hey!" called the shorter one. "Is that you, Máire?"

One of the suited figures waved in reply. "Inspector! Come on over!"

Detective Inspector Corrigan shook the gloved hand of Máire Brennan, one of Belfast's foremost forensic technicians. "So, what do we have here?"

Máire pointed into the tent. "D'ye want to see? You'll need to put these on." She dangled two pairs of paper overshoes in front of Corrigan and his colleague, Detective Sergeant Beaulieu.

Corrigan shook his head. "I think I'll pass. What have you got?"

Máire passed him a clipboard with a sheaf of papers attached to it. "Murder victim. Male. Forty-eight years old. His name is Peter Milton and he lives in the Strandtown area."

Beaulieu grimaced. "Let me guess—you found his wallet?"

"Complete with driving license." Máire handed the sergeant a plastic card with a black and white photograph on it. Beaulieu looked at it then handed the license to Corrigan.

"If only they were always so obliging," Corrigan said. "I suppose we'll have to tell his family."

***

The unmarked police car cruised slowly through the streets of Strandtown. One of the suburbs on the eastern side of Belfast, Strandtown was a mixture of Victorian terraces and dilapidated 1960s maisonettes. Many of the older buildings had paintings on their gable ends: murals depicting Protestant folk heroes and significant events in the history of Northern Ireland. Stern visages of old men glared down from their exalted positions onto gangs of shaven-headed boys playing football. As the car came towards them, the children scattered to the pavements and stared. A few of them displayed their contempt for the strangers by pulling faces and raising two fingers at them.

"Charming," Corrigan muttered.

"Sure, they're just a bunch of wee shites," Beaulieu remarked. "If my da had caught me doin' that, he'd have given me a right hiding."

Corrigan shook his head. "Try that and they'll have you up in front of the disciplinary committee." He looked up at sign on a wall. "Turn left here."

Beaulieu followed the inspector's directions and stopped outside a maisonette—one of over fifty superficially identical buildings. The kerbstones in front of the house, like all those in the rest of the street, were painted red, white and blue. The two policemen got out of their car and walked up the short path to the front door of the dwelling. Corrigan shuffled his feet and composed himself before knocking on the door.

A cry of "Hold on!" came from inside the house, and a blurred shadow could be seen through the door's frosted glass. There was a clattering as somebody fumbled with the bolts, and then the door was opened. A young woman in velour leggings and a loose sweatshirt stared at Corrigan. "What does yez want?" she asked.

"Mrs. Milton?" Corrigan asked, trying to look past the young woman's bulky frame.

"That's me ma," the young woman replied. "What does yez want?"

Corrigan held out his warrant card. "I'm Detective Inspector Corrigan. This is Detective Sergeant Beaulieu. May we come in?"

The young woman moved to one side. "I suppose so." She called over her shoulder, "Ma! It's the peelers!"

"All right!" A middle-aged woman emerged from the kitchen. "I'm Agnes Milton," she announced.

Corrigan stepped forward. "You're married to Peter Milton?"

"Aye."

Corrigan lowered his eyes. "I'm sorry to say, Mrs. Milton, that your husband is dead." Mrs. Milton's florid cheeks turned pale. "We believe that he was murdered." At this Mrs. Milton seemed to sag, her legs starting to buckle under her.

Beaulieu, well-practiced in situations like this, moved quickly to ease the older woman into a nearby armchair. The sergeant turned to the younger woman. "I think she might need a cup of tea. Would you go and make a pot, please?" The young woman nodded and hurried into the kitchen.

Corrigan lowered himself until he was on a level with Mrs. Milton. He could see tears beginning to form in her eyes. "We may need to ask you some questions. But I don't think now is the time. If you want, I can get a female officer to sit with you." Mrs. Milton started to shake. Corrigan glanced up at his sergeant. "Where's that tea?"

"Just coming, sir." Beaulieu went into the kitchen and came back bearing a steaming cup. He put this into Mrs. Milton's hands and watched as she drank mechanically from it, making sure she didn't spill any of the hot liquid. Corrigan nodded, then went into the kitchen himself.

The young woman who had answered the door was there, staring at three mugs set by the kettle. Corrigan gently touched her shoulder. "Are you all right?"

"No." The young woman took a deep breath. "No. I'm not. Look, I think Ma is going to need some time."

Corrigan nodded. "Of course. I understand. But, when you're ready, I've got some questions that I'll have to ask. They may sound callous, but..."

"I know. You have to ask them. Sure, I've seen enough of them crime shows on the television to know that. D'ye have a card?"

Corrigan pulled his wallet out of his pocket, took a card from it, and passed the card to the woman. "Detective Inspector Corrigan. That's my number there. When you're ready, give me a call. Now, do you want anyone to sit with you or your mother?"

The young woman shook her head. "No. I don't think so. I'll call me aunties, and they'll be over." She reached for the kettle and started to pour hot water from it into the mugs. "Will ye stay for the cup in your hand?"

"No. I don't think we will. Remember to give us a call—when you're ready."

"I will."

***

A half-hour later, Corrigan and Beaulieu had returned to police headquarters on the Knock Road. Although the sangars and the anti-mortar fence had vanished many years ago, the building still carried many holdovers from the dark days of the 'Troubles.' A wide no-man's-land still surrounded the main office block, and the roads inside the compound still were littered with concrete barriers designed to prevent a car bomber from approaching the building directly. Although the homegrown threat had receded significantly, the old methods of protecting against them were just as useful against the new breed of religious fanatics. Fortunately, Belfast had been spared their attentions—so far! But the older officers still took comfort in the remaining fortifications.

Máire was waiting by Corrigan's desk. She handed him a slim manilla folder. "There you go. I've done the preliminary autopsy."

Corrigan opened the folder and read the summary notes. While his job brought him into contact with the dead all too frequently, he did not like to delve into the details of their demise. He sometimes wondered how the forensic officers could treat the subject of death with so much detachment, but he had never asked them, afraid that the answer would prove too alienating.

"Blunt force trauma to the skull," Corrigan remarked. "Any idea what did it?"

Máire shrugged. "Nothing too big. Looking at the wounds, I'd say it was something like a scaffolding pole or a pipe. And it wasn't a clean blow. There are signs of bruising along the spine and shoulders. Our assailant must have hit the victim at least five or six times, probably after knocking him to the ground, if the broken jaw is anything to go by."

Corrigan winced at the images that Máire's description brought to mind. "So, somebody was in a bad mood."

Beaulieu took the folder from the inspector and started to read the report. "I can't say that I disagree with that." He turned his attention to Máire. "Did you take a look at the cards?"

"We did. They're 555s. You can buy them in any shop. We're going to try and lift some prints from them, but they're laminated. We might be lucky, but it would help if you could find the murder weapon."

Beaulieu clicked his fingers. "James Bond. *Diamonds are Forever.*" Both Máire and Corrigan looked blankly at him. Beaulieu shook his head. "You're a right pair of culchies, aren't you?"

"I've seen it on the telly, but I don't remember anything like that. Just a load of diamonds and a laser beam."

"God preserve me," Beaulieu muttered. "It's in the book. The one that Ian Fleming wrote. Bond is talking to Felix Leiter, who tells him about some poor sod who the Las Vegas mob caught cheating in one of their casinos. He was buried in the desert with only his arm showing and a deck of cards in his hand."

"So," Máire said carefully, "you reckon that Milton was killed by one of the local gangs because they caught him cheating at cards?"

Corrigan spoke up. "Either that or it was someone who reads too much trash."

"Bond is not trash!" Beaulieu said defensively. "All right, my ma was always ashamed to be seen reading him on the bus, but that was fifty years ago."

"Still, that gives us a possible place to start." Corrigan took the folder from his sergeant and handed it back to Máire. "If you get any dabs off them cards, let us know. In the meantime, we need to find out who's running the rackets down in Strandtown."

"I hate talking to the UDA," Beaulieu muttered. "They're a load of heid-the-ba's."

"Same here. Let's just hope that Mrs. Milton or her daughter decides to talk to us. It'll save us some bother."

***

Corrigan and Beaulieu began their investigations in Strandtown. The suburb had been built in the shadow of the shipyard, back when a job at Harland and Wolff had been a job for life. Back then, Strandtown had been intended to replace the rows of Victorian terraced housing that had spread out from the Lagan like a tide of red. The new buildings were meant to be homes for the shipyard workers, meant to reflect their increasing wealth. Then, in the 1970s, the Troubles had hit Belfast. The city, always divided along sectarian lines, had become a hotbed of violence. Families had fled the choked city centre, seeking security amongst those who had the same religious and political affiliations. Strandtown had survived the arrival of the newcomers; indeed, they had been welcomed.

It wasn't until the 1980s, when the shipyard started to lose business, that the area had turned bad. When the workers had been laid off, they had sought someone to blame it on. Strandtown became an area that was fanatically Loyalist. The young men, seeing no future, had become easy targets for the propaganda of the paramilitary groups. The so-called 'hard men' had moved in, bringing with them the trappings of organized crime. Flags—the Union Flag and the Red Hand—were flown from lampposts and buildings, and the kerbstones were painted. It was a warning to everyone: 'Here be Dragons!'

Both Beaulieu and Corrigan had served their time in Strandtown. As uniformed police officers, they had patrolled the area in armoured Land Rovers, staring at the streets through inch-thick plexiglass and narrow vision slits. Then, when they had entered the plain clothes branch, they had got to know the inhabitants of Strandtown and their businesses, both legal and illegal. They had made contacts in the area—'touts' in the local parlance— and become grudgingly trusted as men of their word. Now they were going to draw on the credit they had built up.

They spent most of the day tracking down Mahoney. Mahoney was one of the 'soft men': people who associated with Loyalist paramilitaries but were not active members. Beaulieu had done him favours in the past, such as overlooking minor offenses and fixing administrative problems. Eventually, they ran him to earth in a bedsit above a chip shop.

"Neville Beaulieu—as I live and breathe!" Mahoney greeted the sergeant with a pat on the back. "Will ye no' come in and have a glass of whiskey?"

Beaulieu glanced back at Corrigan. "I would, but I'm on duty. We need some help."

Mahoney shook his head in mock despair. "Ach, sure no one will mind. It's even legal." He held up a bottle of Bushmills, showing off the tax stamp on the label.

"Aye. Right. Poítin and tea leaves, if I remember your recipe."

Corrigan interrupted the conversation. "We need some information. We need to know who's running the loan sharking and gambling rackets."

Mahoney shook his head. "Sure, why would I know such a thing? I'm just a poor old man, eking out his pension as best he can." He gestured around the room with the whiskey bottle. "If I was in with those lot, d'ye think I'd be livin' here?"

"Ach, sure you've never been short of the money," Beaulieu remarked. "You've always managed to find it. Besides, if you can afford a drop of the good stuff, you're doing fine."

"A present from a friend."

"And didn't I give you enough presents?"

"That you did. And I'm grateful." Mahoney drank a slug of whiskey from a cut-glass tumbler. "But you know whose side I'm on."

"This isn't to do with the chuckies," Beaulieu said. "It's one of the Strandtown residents as has been murdered. We're trying to find any possible leads."

Corrigan fixed Mahoney with a stare. "His name was Milton. Peter Milton. He was beaten to death with some kind of pipe. We believe that he was gambling and got in debt to someone."

Mahoney finished his whiskey then poured himself another measure from the bottle beside him. "Peter Milton? Husband of Aggie? I'd heard that he had died. I didn't know that it was one of the boys what did it. But I'm not one to tell tales."

"You don't have to," Beaulieu said. "Just give us some names.

We'll do the rest. That's all. Like you said, present from a friend."

Mahoney got up from his faded armchair and crossed the room to an old bureau. There, he took out a notepad and scribbled something on one of its pages. He ripped the page out, folded it, and passed the paper to Beaulieu. "There you are. But you didn't get them from me, mind?"

"Course not," said Beaulieu. "We know whose side you're on."

In their car, Beaulieu and Corrigan pored over the names on Mahoney's note. "How are we going to tell which one is our man?" Beaulieu asked. "We can't go around asking everyone if they know who murdered Peter Milton. After the first two, word'll get out that we're looking for someone."

"There's only one person we need to talk to," Corrigan replied. "Agnes Milton."

***

Mrs. Milton was holding an open house. The front door of the Milton home was on the latch, and a picture of Peter Milton draped with a black ribbon had been placed in the window. A small knot of respectably dressed women were gathered in the lounge, clutching cups of tea and slices of cake. Corrigan and Beaulieu waited, silent and respectful, until the last of the visitors had said their goodbyes.

"Mrs. Milton," Detective Inspector Corrigan began, "we've come to pay our respects. We've also come to ask you a few questions."

Mrs. Milton's daughter intervened. "Can't it wait? You can see that Ma's still in a state."

"With respect, we really do need to ask some questions. There have been some leads in our inquiry, and we need the answers quickly if we're to continue."

Mrs. Milton eased her daughter aside. "I'll talk to them, May. Then we can put this all behind us."

Corrigan cleared his throat. "Mrs. Milton, we believe that your husband might have been in debt to someone. Probably as a result of illegal gambling. We have obtained some names, and we were hoping that you might recognize one of them."

Mrs. Milton blinked in surprise. "Gambling debts?"

"Yes. Now if you could..."

"My husband wasn't in debt. He said he'd had a big win. He was going to use it to take us on holiday for our anniversary. He said he was going to take us to America." It looked like Mrs. Milton was about to burst into tears.

"Did he mention any of these names?" Corrigan read from the list.

Mrs. Milton stopped him. "He couldn't help but talk about it! He said he'd won the money from Mitchell O'Connell."

Beaulieu looked at the list. "Third one down, sir."

"Thank you, Mrs. Milton," Corrigan said. "And we're sorry for your trouble."

The two detectives made their excuses and headed back to their car. "O'Connell," Beaulieu remarked. "I know him. He's got a right temper."

"Just the sort of man who would bludgeon someone because he lost at cards?" Corrigan asked.

"I wouldn't swear to it in court, sir. But let's see if it's good enough for a warrant."

***

Corrigan, Beaulieu and a platoon of uniformed officers arrived outside the builder's yard that belonged to Mitchell O'Connell. Corrigan was chafing under the unfamiliar weight of his flak jacket. He addressed the policemen. "We are searching for a weapon—likely a pipe of some kind or an iron bar small enough to be used as a weapon. If you find something, don't touch it! Wait for the forensics officers to turn up and collect it. Also, remember our suspect is in with the local paramilitaries and he has convictions for affray. If he shows the slightest trouble, we arrest him. Everyone clear?" The officers murmured their understanding. "Right. Let's go."

The uniformed officers fanned out, covering the main gate of the yard and its surrounding wall. Two of them accompanied Beaulieu and Corrigan to the front door of the O'Connell house. "Be my guest," Corrigan said to Beaulieu.

Beaulieu hammered on the door. "Mitchell O'Connell! Open up!"

The door opened enough for a bloodshot eye to peer through the gap. "What do you—Shite!" Whoever was behind the door tried to slam it shut, but Beaulieu was too quick. The sergeant aimed a vicious kick at the door, forcing it open, then followed through. Corrigan and the remaining police officers came in behind him.

"Ye can't come in here!" O'Connell yelled. "I've got rights!"

"And we've got a warrant!" Beaulieu shouted back. "Now sit down and shut up!" He pushed at O'Connell, knocking him against the staircase banister.

O'Connell's face reddened. "Lay a bloody han' on me, will ye?" He threw himself towards Beaulieu, his fists ready.

"Ye're just givin' me an excuse!" Beaulieu grinned as he sidestepped the attack then grabbed O'Connell, twisting his arm behind his back. "You're under arrest, son." He pushed O'Connell into the arms of the waiting policemen.

"I'll bloody have yez!" O'Connell screamed as he was shoved towards the waiting Land Rover.

"A bit unnecessary, that." Corrigan glanced at his colleague.

"I won't let it happen again, sir." Beaulieu straightened his jacket. "Now, shall we get looking for that weapon?"

***

Máire placed a manilla folder on Corrigan's desk. "Bad news, sir. O'Connell might be an arrogant eejit, but there's no proof that he was the one who did for Milton."

"You mean there was no evidence on any of that stuff we brought back?" Corrigan sighed and leaned back in his chair. "I suppose we'll have to let him go then. Beaulieu?"

"Sir?" Detective Sergeant Beaulieu moved to Corrigan's side.

"Not so fast." Máire grinned. "I said there's no proof he killed Milton. That doesn't mean we can't link him to the crime. I managed to get some prints off those cards. Not good ones, mind you, but they should stand as evidence."

Corrigan shifted so he was leaning across the desk, the very picture of attention. "Was O'Connell's on them?"

"They were. And so were Milton's, as well as a couple of others who are in our files. I think those cards were the ones that were used in Milton's last game."

Corrigan stood up. "One of them has to know something."

"At the very least," Beaulieu added. "I'm sure we can persuade one of them to tell us what went on."

"Let's see what we can salvage from this mess."

The End

Find John Nedwill at the following link:

Wattpad: https://www.wattpad.com/user/johnnewill

Cover by Author.

Grudge

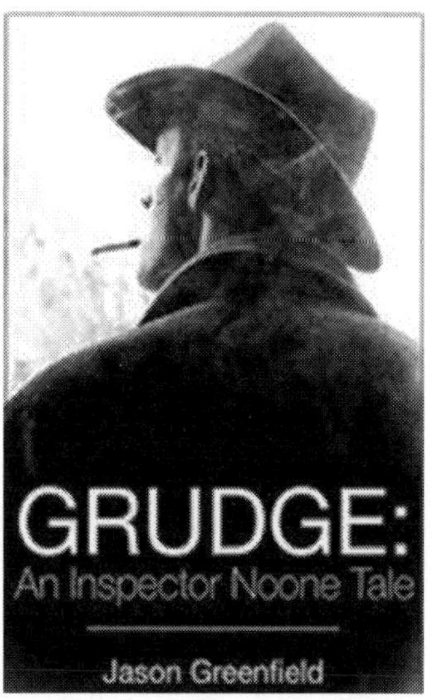

Jason Greenfield

A Little about me and the story.

Inspector Noone came about sort of by accident. Way back in the dawn of time, primary school-aged me discovered a love of writing, and that has never left me. Fast-forward decades later and after all this time, I really know what I want and don't want to do with my writing—I want variety (experimenting with all different types of genres and writing styles/formats—some are pretty wild and crazy), and also I'm not one for planning out and re-writing/ redrafting/overthinking every little word. I just tend to write.

And I'm not a fan of crime fiction/police detective (with the exception of Victorian—big Sherlock Holmes fan!)—much too formulaic for me. But one day, I discovered a writing site and started doing writing challenges—being limited by word count and a prompt was an exciting way to push myself to try new things. And so I did this one-off flash fiction called 'AND IN WALKS JEFF BECK,' where an unnamed policeman arrests a rock star for murder. The next week, I did another story, and this time I named the copper, and Inspector Noone was born. And I kept on returning to him, but rather than follow the tired old formula, I decided (unconsciously—it just happened!) to do a series of vignettes about his life, and hopefully in the process, I produced some interesting bits.

There are Noone stories dealing with workplace bullying, a flashback to young Noone in the army, one focused on his dad, another couple dealing with his Victorian ancestor, interacting with villains and informants, etc.—'Grudge' is one of the longest and maybe one of the more 'traditional cop-like' as it deals with getting information and an actual police operation. I also do a fair bit of phonetic slang in some of my stories—Western/cowboy, cockney/chav, Scots, etc.—this one has an Irish/Northern Irish element, but it's set in London. One or two short Noone bonus stories follow 'Grudge' to give you more of a flavour…and to increase my word count!

Sack of Gobshite

'Well, now. So here we are.'

'We are indeed.'

'Will ye be takin' a wee drop, Mr Noone?'

'Depends what's on offer.'

The old boxer smiled and opened his desk drawer. 'Only the good stuff, to be sure. None o' yer shite brands.'

'I don't doubt it, Pat. Thank you again for setting this up.'

'Yer man there looks fidgety.'

'DS Lyndsay's a bit new to the art of the tête-à-tête. Besides he's been playin' silly beggars recently and, as a consequence, is on his best behaviour. Ain't that right, Steve?'

The Detective Sergeant nodded briefly and looked down.

Trimble gave them both a brief look and reached into his drawer for a third glass.

'Your boy don't drink?'

'He drinks, all right. A bit too much, if you know what Oi mean. Best not to fuel any fires.'

'Where is he?'

'He'll be here soon enough.'

'Good. As for fueling fires, Pat, I'm very much afraid that it don't matter what gets young Mr Brennan's boilers going. In fact, that'll be a definite advantage to him.'

Pat Trimble looked closely at Noone. 'So it's not a talk you're after then, Inspector?'

'From what I've heard, your boy doesn't do much talking to anyone, let alone Old Bill.'

'Well, ye have half o' the right o' it. He don't talk to the guards, but the rest o' the toime, ye can't keep the gobshite from spilling from his mouth.'

'So I hear. I also hear that if we were to pull him in, he'd clam right up, hence my visit today.'

'An' you're resolved to settle it accordin' to the house rules.'

'Yeah.'

'You're doubly sure now, Inspector. Ye've only witnessed the goings on here after hours, but are ye sure you're up for a spot a participation?'

'I am if I know the rules will be abided by.'

'Aye, ye've no fear on that score. If young Sean reneges, he knows what'll happen an' Oi will personally enforce that.'

'Good.'

'Well then, I'll call an' tell the lads ta send that sack o' gobshite in. Though, per'haps, ye'll be doin' me curiosity the favour o' telling me, what's stoking your fires, Inspector?'

Noone said nothing for a moment.

'Just the usual, Pat. A whole heap of steaming shite, an' that's par for the course. I can deal with it, but then comes a day when the pile gets topped off. Just a small additional dollop of shit, but it turns out to be the turd that sets off an avalanche.'

'A shit storm,' added Lyndsay.

'Right you are, Steve. A shit storm precipitated by a particular steaming turd.'

'Would the turd have a name, Inspector?'

'Yeah. You might recall an old colleague of mine. Clive Slinkard by name.'

'Aye. Oily, weaselly fella, if Oi am not very much mistaken.'

'That's the one. Turns out his dismissal from the force was not quite as set in stone as I once suspected. More of a quiet transfer, following extended leave. Steve, who are the biggest bunch of wankers, outside this fair Metropolis, who we have occasional and never very pleasant dealings with?'

'Regional Crime Squad, boss.'

'Yeah. Regional Crime Squad, and who is currently liaising with our nick as their head?'

'DI Clive Slinkard, boss. The tosser.'

'Now, now, Steve, you know that's not the proper term of address for the gent.'

'Sorry, boss. DI Clive "Fucking" Slinkard.'

'That's the one. Now, Pat, I'd like to give your boy Brennan the opportunity to talk before we move to the alternate option.'

Trimble nodded and reached for his phone.

'U'v' a Head on Yee Lyk a Box of Harp

'Youse fuckin' guards. Away and wash the back of yer bollox.'

'Now, now, Sean. You'll have to speak clearly as my colleague, DS Lyndsay here, don't speak the vernacular.'

'Oi'll make me'sel' clearer then, loike yer da did ya ma before the rape.'

'Original.'

'Eighty-four three hundred, big-face.'

'Well now, you're just repeating yourself in different ways.'

'Boss?'

'He's tellin' us to fuck off, Sergeant.'

'De ye know who ah am? DO YE KNOW WHO AH AM?'

'You're a mouthy, little toerag that has information I am currently in need of. You'll oblige me by disgorging said information, or I will be forced to remove it from you in less pleasant ways.'

'Is that right, peeler?'

'SIT DOWN, ya eejit. Yer runnin' around like a blue-arsed fly.'

'But, Pat.'

'Sit. Now it's obvious yer man here is not one for talking, so we'll do it the other way.'

Sean Brennan goggled at him. 'You're not...but he's a fockin' guard.'

'Mr Noone here is respected in these parts, Sean. He's always been as good as his word. Question is, will you be?'

'I ...'

'Jaysus, the wheel's turning but the hamster's dead!'

Noone stood. 'Right. If that's settled, let's discuss the terms.'

***

She Could Eat Apples Through a Letter Box

They stood facing each other...the dark-haired Irishman in his early twenties and the fair-haired Englishman who was a decade older.

Sean Brennan grinned.

'See yuir ma, Inspector? Oi hear she's no show pony, but she'd do for a ride around the house!'

Noone said nothing.

'In case yuir not understandin' the Ulster, Oi'm callin' ya ma a hoor an' that's bit horsey, so she is.'

Noone's eyes stared unblinkingly.

'Oi mean, Jaysus, she's teeth on her like a Donegal graveyard. She could eat apples through a letter box.'

Noone continued to look right into the Irishman's eyes.

'Now me, Oi wouldn't ride her if she came wi' pedals. Yore da though, he'd empty the bag even though she's a head like a burst trout.'

Still nothing.

'Or do you not know? Ask yuir ma who yuir da is. Bet he was clean ratten!'

The bell rang.

The crowd roared as Noone delivered the first punch.

Brennan stumbled backwards, his cockiness evaporating like an early morning mist.

'Smash his cranium!' shouted a voice from outside the boxing ring.

The crowd at Trimble's Gym were roaring now...Some chanting for Brennan, and others supporting his opponent.

'Keep yer guard up, ye gobdaw!!' screamed the voice of someone who obviously didn't like Brennan but was loathe to see a policeman take out one of their own.

'Give 'im one, boss!' Lyndsay was perched by the side, as carried away as the rest.

Noone didn't hear him. He didn't hear any of them. It had all faded to white noise. For him it was just a flurry of movements—punch and be punched. Attack and defend then counter attack.

Brennan had got in a few good blows and drawn blood. Noone's nose felt like it may have been broken, and he had a sharp pain in his left eye. Had he been able to take even a split second to think, he would have contemplated the certainty of half his face looking black and purple on the morrow, and that was just in the right now, without further damage potentially to come.

But Noone wasn't thinking anything...It was all instinct. Instinct that made him hold his gloves to ward off repeated blows to his face. The Irishman was screaming insults and dancing around him, jabbing and darting in a miasma of violent action.

Screaming. Shouting. Moving. Expelling air. Using up energy.

Noone's feet were firmly planted on the ground, his arms protecting his face at the expense of blows to his body.

The world slowed down. Figures flashed before him...Detective Inspector Clive Slinkard...a man who seemed unconsciously determined to play up his resemblance to Boycie from *Only Fools and Horses*, not only in coiffure and mustache but in a penchant for tacky but expensive suits and camel hair overcoats. Maybe it was deliberate, and out of this moment, out of the ring, Noone would have thought—down to the cigars and brandy. Though, to be fair, who didn't like a Cuban and a nice snifter.

Without attempting to conjure them, he saw a blur of images come to him as the white noise grew to block out everything but himself and the man before him, who was starting to slow and breathe in a more laboured fashion.

More Slinkard...his triumphant return with the RCS, the platitudes and veiled threats. Mention of his ex-wife. The cases of the past number of months...dead informer, murdered spouses, bodies alive and in pain and ones that were snuffed out forever. Traumatised witnesses, grieving relatives, shocked business owners contemplating the destruction of their livelihood. Gloating criminals leaving court, slipping the net...those who avoided charges, intimidated witnesses recanting their testimony, the long, long hours all piling together. Sally's face, understanding, but her eyes sad as he cancelled arrangement after arrangement or left in the middle. All of it mounting up...the never-ending mountain of shit.

Slinkard's return. That sneer on his face.

Brennan had slowed to a crawl. Noone's arms lowered, and it all sharpened into a single point. Suddenly sound came rushing back, and he was aware of a piercing, feral scream of rage—his right fist thundered forward and connected hard. A spray of blood seemed to hang in the air like a slow-motion capture on an episode of *Spartacus*. Then time sped up, and he connected again and again, sending more blood and teeth flying.

Then a second roar erupted. The crowd was going wild, screaming in celebration or anger. It was only later that Steve told him that it was he who uttered the first roar… as understated a description as 'uttered' was.

He stood, bending over his fallen opponent, panting heavily, and the world began to swim before him.

Hands grabbed him and gently led him to sit in the corner of the ring. Pat Trimble wiped his head with a damp towel, while his DS helped him sip at some water.

He was nearly about to pass out but managed to grab Lyndsay's collar first.

'When he wakes up, you get everything from him, right? Steve.'

'Yeah, boss. Don't worry. Take it easy.'

Noone nodded, and then he lost consciousness.

Wrong Bus

He couldn't drive. He could barely see. He ought to be in hospital. Concussion at the very least, they said.

He told them he'd get himself checked out later. He could see well enough through his one unswollen eye.

He conceded the need for a driver.

'Where to?' WPC Rhonda MacIntrye had asked him.

'Follow the number 25 route.'

They had started, parked across the road from Aldgate East Station. DS Lyndsay and DC Hussein occupied the back seats.

The 13:10 was a minute late, probably due to the roadworks in St Boltoph Street.

Eight minutes later, when they were passing the Royal London in Whitechapel, Farouk Hussein broke the silence. 'Are we sure he'll be there?'

Noone glanced back at the detective constable. 'He'll be there.'

Lyndsay nodded. 'Sean Brennan's a mouthy little c&*t, but he wouldn't lie after the Inspector beat him fair 'n' square in the ring. Be more than his life was worth, Trimble'd see to that.'

They were coming up on Stepney Green station.

'All right, gents…lady…stay alert. Our boy'll be wearing a green parker and gettin' on down Bancroft Road.'

'Sir, I think I see him.'

'Whereabouts, Rhonda?'

'He's running…gonna miss it.'

'Jesus!' swore Lyndsay. 'Fuckin' amateur.'

'Do we pick him up, Sir?'

'Nah, there'll be another 25 along in 6 to 10 minutes. Pull in opposite, Rhonda.'

***

'Suspect, IC one Caucasian male, seen boarding a number 25 bus near the Ocean Estate.'

'Knock off that Bill crap, Farouk. Rhonda?'

'Already on it, Inspector.' Their car pulled out.

'Right, two possibilities according to Brennan. Either he's doing a drop off near Stratford High Street, in which case we split and maintain surveillance, or...he'll stay on until past the North Circular and get off near Ilford Hill. That's where it gets sketchy. Brennan doesn't know where he goes next, but he does know it'll be a meet with the man in charge. We get him, and not only do we close the books on the store robberies, but we shut down the scumbags who have been dealing to schools on our patch.'

***

'He's not got off.'

'Keep driving. Twenty-five more minutes 'til the North Circular. If he alights at the aforementioned spot, we'll know our boy wasn't telling porkies.'

***

'It's him...green parker, exact same spot we were told.' DS Lyndsay couldn't keep the excitement from his voice.

'Keep 'em sharp, Steve. Rhonda, go slow. He might turn off down by the towpath.'

'Looks like he's heading towards that diner.'

'Right...pull up next road up. Farouk, you're round the back. Rhonda, stay with the motor. Steve, we'll have a butchers from that alleyway opposite. Get the binoculars.'

'Roger that.'

***

'What do you see, Steve?'

'Bloody hell, it's like somethin' out of *Breaking Bad*...Have a look yourself, Sir...uh, sorry.'

'Never mind that; what's going on?'

'Small geezer came in with two heavies; our boy was sat at the table, drinking tea. Then the geezer goes in back, and the heavies sat 'emself opposite and then...you ain't gonna believe this, Sir!'

'What?'

'The geezer's come out dressed as the fuckin' busboy, an' he's taken an order from green parker.'

'Keep watching. You're sure this is our man. The heavies might just be an escort.'

'Well, unless busboys come to work wearing expensive Rolexes, you tell me, Sir.'

'All right, keep watching. The moment you see anything exchange hands, I want this scumbag caught in the act.'

'I seen it...He handed over an envelope. Instructions?'

'Let's go have a chat with our busboy and find out. Radio DC Hussein...We're going in.'

BONUS STORIES

A THRILLING ADVENTURE OF INSPECTOR ALBERT NOONE:

The Deadly Trap

Fiends of East London

The East End of London Town, the year of our Lord 1893.

In the last thrilling installment, our heroic boys in blue, led by the intrepid and most nobly heroic Inspector Albert Noone, had pursued the Doggert Gang with verve and vigour, relentlessly running those most despicable of fiends to ground within the fetid alleyways and slum tenement courts of that hive of wretched humanity that is known to the residents as Spitalfields.

By a series of clever and intuitive deductions, the good Inspector had determined that the missing girl, one Beth Arborwright, recently come to London from the wilds of Yorkshire to take on good, honest work as a governess to the toff banker Mr Gemston, and lately missing, suspected abducted by the hands of the lascivious Tam Doggert and his gang of cutthroat reprobates, was being held within the slums, subject to who knows what indignities!

Yes, dear friends and readers—Albert Noone, whose courage was known the length and breadth of the Empire, had by diligent application of policing and the latest in forensic techniques, proven his Holmesian skill once more by careful examination of a trail of clues that led him from the chambermaid, Lally (who had broken down under the rigorous questioning of our old chum Sgt Alf Smithie), to the very doors of the Eastend's most pernicious lawbreakers. Furthermore, the Inspector had reasoned out that 19-year-old Beth had been taken as part of a scheme to extort plans to her Majesty's treasuries from the aforementioned gent by the name of Gemston, who it was secretly revealed was none other than the uncle of the young lady, by way of a youthful indiscretion by his deceased brother, Mr Phillip Gemston!

Read on dear friend, as the finest coppers in all of London Town brave the deadly trap set for them by the fiendish Doggerts!

'Blimey, guv'nor!' declared the ever-loyal Sgt Smithie. 'Them downy coves is lain in wait an' no mistake! Per'haps we'd best call on more rozzers before we give 'em a jolly!'

'No,' said Noone firmly. 'A young lady's life is at stake, Sergeant. We'll not dally like lowly blowers but do this on the fly. I want every crusher present to give a good account, by gadfy or I'll know why! That girl will be rescued and brought to safety, and the Doggerts up before the beak by evensong!'

The loyal cockney gave him an admiring smile. 'Right you are, Sir!' Smithie blew on his whistle, and in they rushed, out for a violent jolly, come what may!

***

Noone snatched the book.

'Oi, have a heart, guv, I was reading that!'

'A Thrilling Adventure of Inspector Albert Noone: The Deadly Trap? More like claptrap, Steve.'

DS Lyndsay was affronted. 'Nah, this actually happened. The author says so in the introduction, and he'd know, being old Albert's grandson.' He paused. 'Your granddad?'

'My great uncle. Yeah, these cases happened, but Nathanial Noone was a hack writer. He banged out at least forty of these back in the 1930s. Lurid pulp crap. He was paid by the word, and it shows. Exaggerations and distortions. Albert didn't walk knowingly into a trap—he was taken completely by surprise.'

'Did he rescue the girl?'

'Yeah, though she weren't no secret love child relation, whatever.'

'Still, it's a good story.'

Noone sniffed. 'If you like that kinda thing.'

Filth

Lesser of …

'Cigarette?'

His hand tapped nervously, but I could see he was dying for one. Nerves can do that to a man.

I tipped the pack forward and let a fag drop free, leaving two more in the packet. 'Don't mind if I have one me'self, do you?'

He nodded and eyed the remainder.

I lit up and inhaled deeply. 'Course, I'm trying to give em up. The girlfriend don't like me smoking around the house, but…'

My hand reached out and nudged the pack forward. '…It's been one of those days,' I concluded and flashed a comradely smile at the bloke, signalling with my eyes that it was all right to take a cig.

With great timidity, he moved his hand forward from where it was resting on the edge of the desk. I smiled again, all friendly like, and nodded to encourage the action. He looked like he needed one, and of course, I'd noted the yellow staining on his fingertips—nails were dirty and the pale, white bony hand had a tell. Slight tremor.

He almost fumbled—cigarette coming close to dropping between two long, tapering fingers—but he managed it and got the cancer stick up to his thin-lipped mouth. I half stood and leaned over, silver Bic at the ready.

'Tea should be coming soon,' I told him. 'How d'ya take yours, Simon?'

He looked up startled—it was the first time I'd called him by his first name.

Before he could answer, the door opened and my missus came in, holding a tray with two cups, a small teapot and…

'Are those custard creams?' I asked. Smiling at us both, she nodded, but then her eyes took in the cig in my hand. Hastily, I extinguished it and grinned sheepishly at Simon.

'Caught red-handed, Simon. Oh yeah, you ain't met my girlfriend, have you...forgot to say we work together.'

She rolled her eyes and sighed. 'I'll let you off this one time, but **do not** bring those home.'

'Sorry, love.' I lowered my head, slightly abashed, and caught Simon's gaze, flicking my eyes slightly.

He nodded in return.

The girlfriend was giving me evils—a stern rebuke with her peepers, but she was all smiles when she turned to our guest. 'Would you like a biscuit, Simon?'

Simon was obviously shy around women, and he blushed a bit but accepted.

'Go on, take two,' she told him and flashed him a beaming smile.

After she'd gone, Simon sipped his tea, and we both smoked awhile in silence. I took a bite of the custard cream and nodded that he should feel free to do the same. He looked more relaxed now.

'A'right mate...I want to be straight up with you here,' I started.

He sat up, nodding, alert.

'I know you're not a bad bloke, Simon'—pause—'but you're easily led. Everyone says so. Your mum, the landlady, nobody had a bad word to say about you, but...' I stressed the word and gave him the sympathetic eyes. 'They also all agreed that Gwyn'—I looked at my notes—'Mr Gwyn Phillips, that is...a bad lot they say an' yeah, I can believe it. Your mum said, "has an unholy influence on Simon." Is that true?'

Simon's eyes watered up.

I leaned closer. 'He's the one we want. Production and distribution of obscene materials featuring children...We found the vids, and we have an email chain, but he's a clever bastard, Si. Used fake IPs and never put his name to anything.'

'Mhh mhhh,'

'Take it easy, mate. We know you have...pics. We seen your hard drive, son, but there's a hell of a difference between downloading images and being responsible for them.'

'I-I didn't know about the...that he...abroad, he said...'

I nodded sympathetically. 'I believe you, Simon. Trouble is, unless we get some tangible proof that Gwyn was making the...stuff, well, chances are he's gonna walk on lack of evidence, which leaves you all on your lonesome in front of the magistrates. Now, I can put in a word, vouch for you, say you're a decent lad that got led astray, but the judge ain't going to listen—somebody has to go down for this, understand?'

Simon nodded, eyes full of terror. 'I can...tell you...what I know. You'll protect me, Inspector Noone?'

I placed a hand over his. 'I'll do my best, son.'

Then I turned on the recorder, and he began to speak.

***

The first thing I did when I left was head straight to the bathroom and wash my hands. Then I threw out the last cig...hate the damn things. I only ever smoke cigars.

DS Lyndsay fished the cig out of the waste paper bin and tucked it behind his ear. 'Good job in there, guv. You gonna speak up for the nonce then?'

I turned towards him. 'I ain't gonna say a word, Steve. They can throw the fuckin' book at that piece of filth. As far as I'm concerned, there ain't no difference between Simon and his mate.'

Sally had her coat on and was coming over. She knew how I was feeling. 'Pub?' she asked.

'Pub,' I agreed.

The End

If you'd like to see more of my work or say hi/comment, you can find me on the following links.

LINKS:

Facebook: https://www.facebook.com/TheJasonGreenfield/

Facebook:
https://www.facebook.com/ForeverTornByJasonGreenfield/

Facebook: https://www.facebook.com/TheUnseenManBook/

Twitter: https://twitter.com/JayGreenfield?lang=en – doubles as OMP Twitter.

Amazon.com books: https://www.amazon.com/Jason-Greenfield/e/B00CBFLI1W/

Amazon.co.uk books: https://www.amazon.co.uk/Jason-Greenfield/e/B00CBFLI1W/

Cover by Nicole Bea.

Only Human

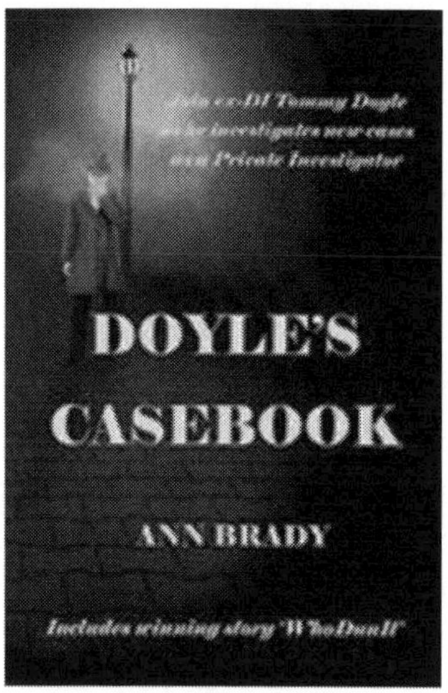

Ann Brady

The one thing ex-DI Tommy Doyle is good at is solving crime. He had left the police force three years previously, having been forced out by an over-ambitious sergeant trying to incriminate him in a crime. Being hauled before a disciplinary committee before finally being exonerated, Tommy had been left feeling disappointed and disillusioned. Four months after being cleared, he had retired—or resigned depending upon your point of view—and set himself up as a private investigator. But being a PI can sometimes be dangerous. Doyle, however, is an astute man, having learnt the hard way how to look after himself and his clients. The following stories are some of Tommy Doyle's cases. There are more to follow.

Ann Brady has been a factual writer for some 30 years, taking up fictional writing when she retired from business. During her career, she created and worked on an award-winning website and had work published in leading magazines, media, and in A-Level Educational Tutorial Booklets. Since retiring, Ann has been experimenting with historical fiction, mystery short stories and children's picture books.

Her current series of picture books, *Little Friends: Woodland Adventures,* is available in print, ebook and app formats. There are another two sets of books (6) due out shortly: *Little Friends: In the Garden* and *Little Friends: Farmyard Fun.* Ann also mentors younger writers, reviewing and editing their manuscripts through the Kids4Kids Organization.

***

The phone was ringing in the office as Doyle let himself into the building. Climbing the stairs, he was tempted to ignore it, but the persistent way in which it rang called out to him. "Answer me now!" it seemed to say. Opening the office door, he crossed to the desk and picked the receiver up.

"Doyle Investigations."

There was no reply, just silence.

About to put the receiver down, he stopped as a timid voice said, "Mr. Doyle, I need your help." It was an older man; at least he sounded older.

"And how can I help you Mr.—err?" Doyle asked.

There was hesitation before the man said, "I'm being blackmailed, and I don't know what to do. Can you help me?"

Doyle thought for a moment, replying, "Can't you go to the police?"

There was a short pause. "I cannot do that. The matter is very delicate, and the outcome would hurt someone else. Do you think you can help? I can pay you for your time," the gentleman explained.

Doyle sighed. "Can you come to my office in the morning? I'll need to meet you and get more information. Say about ten o'clock?"

There was silence as the man thought about it. Finally, he responded, "Okay, I'll be there at ten. Thank you, Mr. Doyle." And the caller hung up, leaving Doyle listening to the dial tone.

Putting the receiver down, he left the office and went upstairs to his apartment. He wasn't sure what to make of the phone call. Mind you, it wasn't the first time he'd helped someone being blackmailed. To be honest, this was the one part of his business he disliked the most. Basically because he hated with a passion the perpetrators of such actions. There was little he could but leave it until tomorrow.

***

The following morning about ten o'clock, Doyle heard a gentle knock. Opening the door, he found a man dressed in a smart suit and overcoat, holding a hat in his hand. He stood silently waiting to enter. Doyle put his age at about sixty. He also seemed very nervous.

Moving to one side, he said, "Come in. Take a seat. I'm Tommy Doyle. You rang me last night about blackmail, yes?"

Passing into the room, the man sat, finally managing to say, "Yes. I did, Mr. Doyle. Can you help me?" He appeared to be extremely nervous, so Doyle realised he would have to tread carefully.

Offering the man some coffee, which he refused, Doyle sat in his chair on the other side of the desk, asking, "So, tell me, what do I call you?"

Swallowing hard, the gentleman looked around the office then said, "Merton. My name is Phillip Merton."

"Okay, Mr. Merton," replied Doyle. "So, tell me, why you are being blackmailed and by whom?"

It was obvious Mr. Merton didn't know where to start, probably due to being embarrassed by whatever it was that had left him vulnerable.

Doyle gave him a moment or two to gather his thoughts before saying, "I know you are probably feeling awkward about telling me your personal problems, but, if I am to help you, I need you to be honest and truthful with me. You must tell me everything, okay?"

Looking at Doyle, Merton must have seen the sincerity in his face and eyes. Taking a deep breath, he began explaining what had happened that had led to his current predicament. He had lived in town most of his life. Whilst still married, he and his wife had drifted apart so led separate lives. Life had not been that good for him until about nine months ago when he had met a delightful young woman called Annabel. "Oh! I know I was probably stupid, Mr. Doyle. After all she is some fifteen years younger than me, but she is a lovely girl." He paused before saying, "I am afraid I fell for her." And he smiled sheepishly at the confession.

Doyle smiled back, saying, "You are not the first gentleman to be taken in by a pretty face, and I'm sure you won't be the last. Tell me, what went wrong?"

"That obvious?" replied Mr. Merton. Doyle nodded, waiting for him to continue. "I thoroughly enjoyed the experience. Annabel makes me laugh and feel good about myself. In fact, I was ready to leave my wife for good and ask for a divorce. Everything was going fine until recently when my wife announced that she has terminal cancer. What was I to do? I felt unable to leave her at this time, so I told Annabel I had to break off our relationship."

"And how did the young lady take the news?" asked Doyle.

"She was not pleased. Actually, she was quite distressed but then appeared to understand my reasons and accept my decision. I thought everything was okay until about a month ago when I got some rather compromising photographs through the post." He blushed. "I don't know how or when they were taken. I really thought she loved me, daft as it sounds. That she really cared for me, and we would eventually be together. Now I feel so foolish." His voice trailed off as once more he filled with embarrassment.

"Right, Mr. Merton," said Doyle. "Firstly, I need you to tell me, is it Annabel who is blackmailing you?"

Looking up in surprise, Merton replied, "Oh no, it's not Annabel. At least, I don't think it is. I can't tell. All I know is I have been asked for twenty-thousand dollars. I haven't got that sort of money to spare, especially with my wife needing treatment. Do you think you can assist me, Mr. Doyle?"

Doyle sighed; he saw no reason why not, saying, "I'm sure I can. Err, have you brought the photographs with you? Was there a note included?"

"Yes," responded Mr. Merton, "there is one inside." With some slight reluctance, he passed over a large manila envelope.

Sliding the photographs from the envelope and putting the note to one side, Doyle studied the images. Having looked at them, he picked up the note by the corner and read the contents. It was an A4-size piece of paper. The message had been made up from letters cut from old newspapers and magazines.

It read: These are copies. We want $20 thousand dollars. Will contact you with the details. Pay up or the wife gets the pics.

Doyle was annoyed by the note. He didn't like blackmailers. Carefully, he placed the note inside a plastic folder. He would ask Mac to check for fingerprints. Criminals didn't realise these days, it was often quite easy to get fingerprints from paper. Having placed it in the plastic folder, he took it to the photocopier, copying the sheet for his files.

Returning to his desk, Doyle asked, "Mr. Merton, when do they want you to hand the money over?"

Looking at him, Mr. Merton said, "I don't know. I haven't heard anything more since. What shall I do, Mr. Doyle?"

Thinking about it for a moment, Doyle said, "Okay, the first thing we do is get as much detail down as possible. I will need Annabel's full name, address and where you met her. We also need to get you fingerprinted."

"What for?" asked Merton, shocked by the suggestion.

"To eliminate yours from any we find on the paper. If we can find out who has been doing this, we will need the evidence to prosecute them," responded Doyle.

"What? I don't want to prosecute Annabel. She can't be involved in this. Besides, I, err, I don't know her full name and address. I never thought to ask her," he responded, aghast at the very idea of her being involved. And yet, suddenly, he began to realise it might just be possible. After all, he didn't know very much about her. What a fool he had been!

It also dawned on Doyle he might have problems with the man, unless he could make him understand exactly what he had got himself involved in. Taking a deep breath, he decided to speak firmly, "Now look here, Mr. Merton. I don't think you fully understand what a mess you are in. Whether you want to admit it or not, this Annabel is certainly involved in the affair, somehow. How do you think they got these photographs? Probably through her. I'll bet money this isn't the first time she's done something like this. If past experience is anything to go by, you won't have been the first to fall under her spell."

Doyle stopped, allowing what he had just said to sink in. Watching Merton, he saw how deflated the man now felt as he tried to accept what he had just been told could well be true. It was driving him crazy.

Waiting a moment, Doyle continued, "Unless we get to the bottom of this, Mr. Merton, they will not leave you alone. And, if you pay up once, they'll keep coming back again and again until they have bled you dry. Do you want that?"

Merton shook his head, saddened by the turn of events and surprised Doyle had sussed out what was already in his mind. He admitted to himself if he paid up, then they would come back for more. He felt an absolute idiot.

Finally, he said, "Okay, Mr. Doyle. I am in your hands. What do you suggest we do next?"

Doyle, satisfied that Merton had seen sense and agreed to cooperate, replied, "First thing we do is go and see my friend Inspector Mackintosh. He will do his level best to keep the matter as quiet as possible."

"What about my wife?"

"What about her?" Doyle asked.

"Does she have to be involved?" questioned Merton.

Shaking his head, Doyle said, "No. I'm sure we can keep her out of this."

Satisfied Doyle would do his best for him, Phillip Merton resigned himself to what was to happen next. Shortly afterwards, they left the office, making their way to see Mac.

***

Arriving at Mac's office, Merton's fingerprints were quickly taken. Mac kept the note, sending it for forensic testing. He also kept the pictures, locking them away securely in his special safe, promising to return them to Mr. Merton to be destroyed once the matter was complete.

In the meantime, Doyle instructed Merton not to communicate with Annabel. If she did contact him, he was to arrange to meet, but Doyle would go in his place as he wanted to see what she looked like. Afterwards, when she contacted Merton to complain about him not turning up, he was to say his wife was bad and couldn't be left. After that, he was to make any excuse he could not to meet her at all. Merton was also to contact him the moment he received any envelope that looked suspicious, which the man promised to do.

Later, when Mac met up with Doyle, he had some interesting information to divulge. It appeared Mr. Merton was not the first person to be caught in the blackmail trap. A young woman called Sonia had been reported as trying to do something similar last year. Unfortunately, the person concerned wouldn't cooperate with the police and had later confessed everything to his wife. They had moved out of town shortly afterwards. The cases seemed the same in both format and by the fact Sonia and Annabel were described as looking the same.

Not hearing anything from Merton for over three days, Doyle wondered if the man had succumbed and paid the blackmail money. He was therefore surprised, when the following morning, a knock at his office door announced his arrival. Entering the room, Merton said, "I don't think you expected me to return, did you, Mr. Doyle?"

Grinning, Doyle said, "If I am truthful, Mr. Merton, then the answer has to be no. I didn't. I presume you've received another envelope."

Nodding, Merton quickly handed a large manila envelope over to Doyle, who made sure he handled it by the corner only. Laying it down on the desk, he opened a drawer, taking out a pair of forensic gloves, some tweezers and a new plastic folder. Carefully slitting the envelope open, he used the tweezers to gently remove the note inside. The message was like the first one, made up by using cuttings from newspapers and magazines. It read: Put $20K in a plain bag. Leave in locker at LA railway station.

Tipping the envelope upside down, a locker key fell onto the desk. Merton reached out to pick it up, but Doyle stopped him. Using the point of the paper knife, he picked the key up to examine it. It had the number "321" and the words "LA Station" embossed on the sides.

Picking up the phone, Doyle rang Mac. "Hi, Mac. I have Mr. Merton here. He's received an envelope containing a note like last time and a key for a locker at LA Station. Do you want me to bring them in?"

Doyle listened, acknowledged they would be at the precinct within the next half hour, then hung up the phone. Carefully, he gathered the items together, placing them in a clean plastic bag. Shortly afterwards, they left the office.

***

Sitting in the precinct, the pair waited for Mac to return from forensics. Merton was lost in his own thoughts. He felt a real idiot for getting himself into this mess in the first place. The only consolation was that Doyle was being considerate in the way he was handling the matter. He hadn't shown any disgust at his indiscretion; he presumed Doyle was used to such things happening.

"Okay, guys," Mac announced, entering his office. "Preliminary tests seem to show it's the same person sending the notes. Whoever it is, he's an idiot. He's so cocky about what he's doing, he hasn't even bothered to use gloves when making the note up."

Both Doyle and Merton looked up in surprise. "So, what do we do next, Inspector," asked Merton.

"Well, I presume, Mr. Merton, you don't have the money to pay these guys, so we need to set up a sting. Are you able to cooperate with us on this?" asked Mac.

"If I don't have the money, I don't see how I can."

"Oh, don't worry about the money. We can sort that out," responded Mac.

"Well, in that case, I am in your hands, Inspector. Just tell me what I have to do," Merton replied.

Over the next hour, plans were put in place for a sting. The drop was to take place in three days. Mac would use Doyle as the go-between as well as have him keep an eye on Mr. Merton, who had returned home to look after his sick wife.

Doyle returned to his office but not before going to the railway station to suss out the layout of the place, ready for the day of the drop. That evening, when Mac called to see him, they went over the plans made earlier in the day, along with a few extras they hadn't told Merton about.

***

Three days later, Merton arrived at Doyle's office. He was nervous about the forthcoming event as well as being worried about his wife. She had been admitted into hospital during the night; he had very little sleep and looked tired.

Mac arrived half an hour later with the money or, more appropriately, "funny money." It was part of a batch of counterfeit dollars they had recovered from another sting the previous year. The outer dollars were genuine, but the rest were false. A quick glance would fool anyone who wasn't an expert.

At the given time, the three men left Doyle's office. Merton and Doyle went directly to the station, whilst Mac made his own way there via a different route. He needed to check in with his men to ensure they were all in place and ready.

Approaching the station, Doyle instructed Merton on what he was to do. "Okay, Mr. Merton," he said, "you go in, find the locker, open the door and drop the money in. Lock the door and leave. Go straight home; don't hesitate and don't look back."

Merton nodded his agreement. As they neared the station, Doyle whispered, "Right. Off you go. Remember, do as I told you and don't look at me. Walk away. Ignore me. Do not, under any circumstances, acknowledge me." And on that note, Doyle turned away, entering the station by a different door.

Despite taking a sneaky look around, Merton couldn't see Mac anywhere. Following the instructions, he found the lockers. Opening the door to Locker 321, he quickly pushed the bag inside, locked the door, had another sneaky look around, then turned, leaving the station. As he left, he caught sight of Doyle standing and reading a paper, but he ignored him. Doyle, seeing Merton, acted as if he didn't exist: the sign of a good undercover cop.

The wait for someone to visit the locker would last at least three hours. Whoever the blackmailer was, he or she was being very careful, waiting until they were sure the coast was clear. Doyle acted the impatient husband, choosing a train that was delayed as cover for him being in the station so long. Every so often, he would look at the notice board or go to the information desk as if chasing information.

Mac sat in the coffee bar within sight of the lockers, hiding behind a newspaper. One of the police officers was acting as a cleaner, sweeping the floor and tidying up the seats close to the lockers. A couple of other officers were moving in and out of the station, often disappearing into the toilets so they could change coats and hats.

After a long wait, a young woman finally approached the lockers, carefully looking around for anything suspicious. Once she was sure the coast was clear, she put the key in Locker 321 and grabbed the bag. The officer acting as the cleaner and Doyle moved in fast with Mac and the other guys following.

"Annabel, I presume?" stated Doyle, smiling. He blocked the young woman's path.

Hesitating, she tried to go around him, but the other officers had her surrounded. She had nowhere to run.

"I don't believe this belongs to you, does it?" said Doyle placing his hand on the bag and gripping it fast.

Trying to pull the bag away, Annabel looked around for a means of escape before saying, "I think you are mistaken. My name is not Annabel and this bag is mine. I do have the locker key." And she flashed the key at Doyle.

Mac stepped forward, showing his ID card, and asked, "Well then, you won't mind telling us what's inside the bag, will you?"

It was obvious the young woman was going to try and bluff it out, responding, "It's just some old papers, that's all." She tried to wrap her arms around the bag.

Doyle waited a moment then with a quick tug, he pulled the bag from her arms, surprising her. Realising the game might be up, Annabel slipped round the officers and made a dash for the exit. She didn't get far, coming up short against a group of people who were blocking her way.

Catching up with her, Mac quickly slipped the handcuffs around her wrists and proceeded to tell her she was under arrest. Reading her Miranda Rights, he allowed the other two officers to escort her outside to a waiting police car.

"Slippy little thing," announced Doyle as he approached Mac, handing him the bag of money.

"Sure is," replied Mac. "Are you coming down to the station?"

Saying yes, Doyle got in Mac's car, and they made their way to the precinct.

***

After the young woman had been fingerprinted, Mac interviewed her, Doyle watching and listening from the next room through a two-way mirror. It took Mac some time to break through the young woman's defences. It was obvious, even at so young an age, she was an old hand at being interviewed, quickly demanding a lawyer.

Whilst they waited, Doyle rang Mr. Merton, telling him what had happened and asking him to come to the precinct to identify the young woman. He arrived an hour later, looking extremely depressed.

Doyle asked, "Are you okay, Mr. Merton?"

Merton swallowed hard before looking at Doyle, who noted a small tear in the corner of his eye. Taking a deep breath, he swallowed before replying, "My wife passed away two hours ago. That's why it took me so long to get here. She never came out of the coma from last night. But I'll be okay."

Having heard similar words many times in the past, Doyle was adept at saying the right thing. "I'm very sorry, Phillip. Would you prefer to leave it for today and come back tomorrow? It's just that we've arrested a young woman and wondered if she was Annabel."

Merton's head went up at the sound of Annabel's name. Doyle wondered if he was going to have second thoughts about her, so he decided to let Merton see and listen to what she was saying. Taking Mr. Merton through to the room next to the interview room, he turned the speaker up so he could hear what was being said.

Mac was speaking. "Is Annabel your real name or is it Sonia Dobson as it shows here in your record?"

The young woman listened to what the lawyer had to say before replying, "No comment."

Mac sighed, continuing. "To be honest, Sonia, I don't need you to confirm your name as your fingerprints match those of Sonia Dobson. It's not worth your effort wasting my time with all this no comment crap."

"Well, if you have the information, why are you asking me?" sniggered Sonia.

"Tell me about your relationship with Phillip Merton and about the blackmail."

After listening to her lawyer, Sonia argued the point with him, finally responding, "What do you want to know?"

"What made you take up with Mr. Merton?" asked Mac.

"He was okay. He was lonely and had money. And he showed me a good time," she responded.

"Was it your idea to blackmail him or someone else's?" asked Mac.

"I don't know what you mean. Okay, so I went out with the old guy, and maybe I used him. God knows he was desperate, what with that wife of his, but that's all it was, just a bit of fun, whilst it lasted. Besides he spent money showing me a good time." She laughed.

In the other room, Doyle watched Merton's face. It had finally begun to dawn on him what a user Annabel had been. Doyle hoped anger would take over, and he would admit who she was.

Realising he was being watched, Merton turned towards Doyle, saying, "I've been a fool, haven't I? A stupid, dull old fool. Here was I thinking she cared about me, and all the while she was using me, taking what she could. That's Annabel, or Sonia, or whatever her name is, but yes that is her." He paused, sighing sadly. "Can I go home now, Mr. Doyle?"

Nodding his head in agreement, Doyle had a young officer show him out, telling him he would be in touch shortly. He felt sorry for the man; he'd just lost his wife, and now he had lost something he thought was real.

After Merton had left, Doyle went back to listening as Mac continued interviewing the young woman. When he read out the names of a number of other people who had been blackmailed, telling her they were prepared to bring charges against her for these as well, she finally cracked, confessing that it hadn't been her idea to blackmail anybody.

What she said next, almost, but not quite, shocked Mac and Doyle. "It was my husband, Caleb. He planned it all." She proceeded to tell the whole story. Two hours later, Caleb Dobson was found, arrested and charged with as much as Mac could throw at him. Doyle returned to his office, pleased at the final outcome.

***

The following day Mr. Merton arrived at Doyle's office. He seemed more in control of his emotions as he sat and listened to the whole sorry affair of Annabel. Once Doyle had finished telling him the details, Merton handed over a cheque to cover what he owed. As he left, he said, "I want to thank you, Mr. Doyle. At least my wife died without knowing anything of my disgraceful behaviour. I have learnt a valuable lesson in life. Thank you."

Doyle shook his hand, responded, "No problem, Mr. Merton. I am just glad it was all sorted for you. Remember, we men can sometimes be victims of our own egos. Who wouldn't have their head turned when a pretty girl shows interest in them, especially at a time when we are vulnerable. You take care, Mr. Merton."

After he had gone, Doyle thought about the case. How would he react if a pretty, young woman showed interest in him? Would he fall under her spell? No, he wouldn't.

But then again, maybe he would. After all, he was only human.

The End

Connect with Ann at the following sites:

www.ann-brady.co.uk

www.little friendsbooks.co.uk

www.kids4kids.org.uk

www.facebook.com/AnnBradyBooks

Cover by Author.

Miranda's Vacation

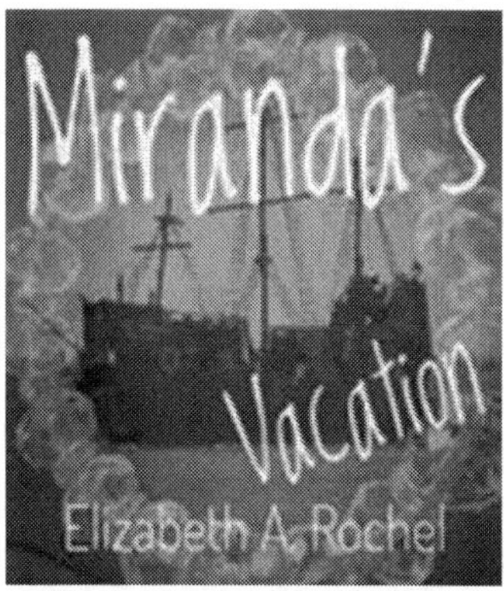

Elizabeth A. Rochel

In this short story, we find Miranda, the absent-minded sleuth, taking a cruise to avoid anything related to solving mysteries of any kind. But certain angelic forces just won't let her rest. Will they encourage her to help a couple of treasure hunters or will she end up a casualty?

Hi, y'all, EAR here. When I'm not drinking a special brew of bulletproof coffee with dignitaries from other worlds or chasing someone's grandkids or the boogie man, I'm a digital nutcase, a writer in disguise. I've written quite a few short stories and three novels thus far. Even had one published, a short one that is. It's titled "Jump," and it's in Jason Greenfield's Bite Size Stories Vol 4. I joined The One Million Project, a very worthy cause, in memory of three of my special loved ones who lost their battles with cancer. And also for the soldiers who've taken care of our freedom. I think it's only fair that we in return take care of their freedom to have a safe, clean place to live.

So, I invite you to sit back and enjoy the ride with me, along with some very talented artists into a world, a galaxy, or even a thought like you've never been before.

***

Chapter 1

It was another hot and sunny day at the Cozumel port as the passengers of the latest cruise ship disembarked. A multitude of store owners and workers got ready to attract new tourists to their stores to spend their American money.

Miranda decided not to take an excursion but to just stay at the port mall to shop and walk the beach at her leisure. Throngs of people passed her as they headed to their particular excursion signs and tour guides. Some were lined up for snorkeling, some fishing, and others were taking shopping tours and sightseeing. Still others, like her, walked along the route and browsed through the shops.

She walked past a few stores with various forms of alcohol and tobaccos as their wares. Then she was drawn to the front of a small trinket store that boasted of having a twenty-dollar sale on real silver. Miranda couldn't resist shiny trinkets and jewelry, especially the fake stuff, since it fit best with her pocketbook.

After gazing through the window for a few minutes, she went in to browse. She noticed the store clerk sitting behind the register with his cell phone pointed at a magazine he was holding. *That's goofy*, she thought. *Why doesn't he just set the magazine down then take the picture?* She turned and walked further into the store and away from the clerk, who made her feel like she was being watched.

From behind her, Miranda heard him say, "This is going to be awesome!" as he snapped more pictures.

I hate it when store clerks watch you like a hawk and think everyone is out to steal from them. I'm not a thief, so stop watching me. Grr, she thought until she spotted a shelf with books by her favorite author, which instantly distracted her. She walked over to the case, unconsciously fiddling with the crystal bracelet attached to her bag, and continued to browse the titles.

Chapter 2

Joe's eye was first caught by her extremely long, straight hair, then by the glint of the crystal keychain attached to her purse as she stood outside his store. Before his thought could be lost to his ever-wandering mind, he pulled out his phone to take a picture of the keychain. Then, he realized that she was looking right at him. He smiled, picked up a magazine, and acted like he was taking a picture of an article. But in fact, just past the magazine, his camera's focus was on her and her crystals.

Why had I not thought of this before?! he thought, then he hit his forehead with the heel of his hand. He grabbed the store phone and dialed Pops' number. "I can have my contact in town rig up a duplicate!" he said before Pop answered.

"Pops! I got a plan!" he said as a couple of new customers turned and looked at him. He smiled at them, turned his back, and spoke quieter. "Pops, we're saved! I got the answer to our problem."

On the other end of the line: "Son, you have to quit with the drama and the daydreams and face facts. We are all doomed, and nothing is going to help us. There is just no way!"

"But, Pops, listen. I got the answer," he pleaded. "I'm going to sort this out, and then I'll get back with you. But this will work. We can get the...huh...We can do this, Pops!" He nervously ran his hands through his hair. "This will work, I know it." With no response from Pops, he hung up and started searching for Jethro's number, his designer jewelry friend.

Chapter 3

Miranda purchased a couple of books she couldn't live without and started out of the store.

"Come again," Joe said with a toothy smile. "Have a good day." He nodded. He picked up his cell phone and once again held it up like he was taking a picture.

Good grief, he is not taking your picture! No one in their right mind would do that: You're as homely as a pigeon, she chided herself, echoes of voices from days gone by running through her head. She turned and headed back out to the river of tourists flowing through the mall.

With no more strange encounters, Miranda decided to shop a few more stores then head for the beach. She found an unoccupied lounge chair with an umbrella and watched the surf roll in. After a while, she started on one of her new books and leisurely led the life of a tourist.

When her phone's alarm clock went off, she gathered her things in one hand, picked up her cheesy souvenir Nahdah Colada drink with the little umbrellas and Cozumel splashed across it for good measure in the other, and headed for the ship.

Feeling quite the tourist, she stopped in one last store on the way back for a couple of souvenir t-shirts for her niece and nephew. She noticed when she walked past the trinket store that the clerk from earlier was gone.

Chapter 4

While at dinner on the third night of her five-day cruise, Miranda and the other guests in the dining hall heard gunshots from the deck outside, and they all jumped and took cover under the tables, fearing for their lives. Then, shortly after that, sounds of a shuffle were heard as the shooters were apparently apprehended.

Miranda raised her head and looked around. An alarm sounded throughout the ship with instructions from the captain for passengers to stay in the areas where they were and to stay calm. He went on to assure everyone they were safe.

The security on the ship organized the chaos professionally and instructed the people to return to their rooms, and, in the process, they had them pass through security gates so all passengers and crew were accounted for. When Miranda and her fellow neighbors finally got to their floor, they discovered their rooms had been broken into and called security.

Miranda reported she was missing nothing. She noticed her lucky charm crystal bracelets were moved but not taken. She thought that was odd and voiced her concern to the investigator. "The thief was definitely in here because everything's been pulled out, sir, but my valuables, they're still here. Nothing was stolen; granted, they are only crystals. Though, I'm stumped at why a thief looking for jewelry would pass up such a find?"

"Ma'am, there is no telling. Maybe yours was the last room they broke into, and they didn't get to snatch anything further due to time restraints," he said distractedly as he looked down the hallway. He turned back to her and shrugged his shoulders. "Ma'am, I really couldn't tell you. Maybe the thieves are keen on what's worth something and what is not."

"Well, I'm very lucky. These don't have any value except to me. I have two more in my suitcase just in case I lose these," Miranda said and chuckled to herself as she headed back into her room.

"Huh, ma'am, I need your signature here on this report. We'll get to the bottom of this, and we want to reassure you that you are safe on our ship. We've never had a pirate attack who didn't get caught," he said and stood a little taller. He took the clipboard back from her and went on to the next room.

"Sir, do you have any missing items?" the investigator asked the guest at the next cabin.

"No, sir, I don't. Nothing's been touched in our room," she heard him reply.

Miranda stood in her doorway for a few more minutes and noticed that only about six of the rooms on her end of the long hallway had been broken into. Scratching her head in thought, she went back into her room. She got a cold bottle of water and went out to sit on her private balcony. Thinking over the incidents and things she'd noted, like the officer's comment, left her wondering just how many other pirate attacks there had been.

I am not going to investigate this case. I will not. I'm on vacation, she told herself. She watched as a coast guard boat pulled up alongside the ship and several more officers embarked the ship.

Is that how the bad guys got on? It looks pretty easy. Why didn't the ship's captain know there was a boat pulled up alongside his ship?

"No, Miranda!" she said as she got up and walked into her room. "You are not investigating."

Chapter 5

"Joe, you can be such a pain. I hope this works," Pops said.

"It has to. It can't go wrong, Pops," Joe replied.

"As soon as the ship gets to America, we can mug the lady and get the stones to the Master. It'll be a piece of cake," he continued. "I'm sure this will go okay. We've already done the drop. Now we just wait for her to get to shore, and then we can rescue those kids."

"You really believe the Master won't kill the kids or hasn't already?" Pops asked.

"Yes. He said he would trade the rest of the diamonds for them," Joe pleaded. "Anytime I've dealt with him, he's been on the up and up."

"Ha, oh sure, a bad guy with morals, right?" Pops asked.

"Well, Pops, we have to trust him—it's all we got. Since those kids were abducted, I haven't slept a wink. I can only imagine what you're going through."

Pops walked over to the kitchen window and stared blankly outside, then placed his coffee cup in the sink. "This just has to work, son. I can't let those kids be harmed because of me and my mouth. No one would have known they even existed had I not put the word out for bids."

"The police can't do anything about it until so many hours have passed. I've called several times already. I keep getting the runaround from them," Joe said. "It's not like I haven't tried to do it the right way."

"I know, son. I know," Pops said.

Chapter 6

Miranda stretched as she woke at the start of a beautiful, sunny morning. She scratched her head as she tried to shake the thoughts she had all night long out of her mind.

Sitting up, she said to herself, "Why didn't they take my lucky charms? They are very flashy, and normally, a thief would be attracted to them."

Smelling a case that's as fresh as the morning dew, she shrugged her shoulders and reprimanded herself again. "Nope, not this time. I'm on vacation, I said. I'm not going to work on this case. That's for the appropriate authorities," she said as she picked up the phone to call room service for coffee and a Danish. Then she continued out to the balcony, which was calling her name.

Taking a deep breath to clear the remaining cobwebs of sleep from her mind, she sat down, finally giving in and pondering the bothersome thoughts.

She ran her hands through her hair, feeling the slight tug of tangles, and spoke to the wind: "I know you're there. I can sense it."

"Ah ha! Yes, Miranda, listen to your thoughts." Snoops' white trails of mist floated around him as he spun around and around in front of her.

Gazing out across the water, she said, "There's a case here, I know it. Because you sure are nagging me."

"Yes, there is a case, and you need to solve it. You have to save those kids!" Snoops screamed out "Yay! Oh yeah! I know she got the hint!" as he flew figure eights up and down in front of the balcony, totally unseen by her. "I've got to tell the others." Then he flew straight up and due east towards the others.

Miranda heard a knock on her door. "Wow, that was fast." She walked into her room and opened the door. "Oh, hi. Huh, I thought you were room service," she stammered as she tugged her housecoat closer around her.

"I'm sorry to disturb you, miss. I'm Sargent Merrill, and I have your report here. We are required to interview the passengers involved one more time. I know things were a little unsettling yesterday so we thought, maybe after a good night's sleep, you might remember something from the incident, something you might not have noticed at the time," he said.

Miranda invited him in with a wave of her hand. "Sure, come in. I don't have anything to add, really. I was in the dining hall when there was a commotion on the deck outside. We heard a couple of pops, and we all hit the floor. I didn't see anyone except other passengers on the floor and under tables like me."

"When you came to your room, did you see anyone around the hallway or the elevators?" he asked.

"No, sir, there wasn't anyone. I came to my door, it was locked, and I went in. That's when I discovered the room in a mess. But there is nothing missing from my room. I didn't have anything of value to steal anyway."

He looked at the clipboard in his hands, read the report she gave last night, and smiled. "Ok, miss, I guess that's it then. Sorry for the bother," he said and put his hand out to shake hers.

"Ok, Sargent Merrill, I'll let you know if I think of anything," she said as he walked to the door. "Oh, but could you tell me what actually happened? It is quite unsettling to not know what took place. It's not a problem for you to tell me, is it?"

"Well, there's not a lot to tell. Some thugs boarded the ship, like pirates. We thought they were the only ones, but apparently there were others, possibly earlier. They managed to rob some cabins on a few floors. Then, in all the commotion, they escaped. It was quite strange they took such risks with only gaining a few stolen items. And especially strange that they all got off the boat before we could apprehend any of them. We have footage from the elevators we're reviewing now."

"So you think they're all off the ship, right? We are safe, huh?" Miranda asked.

"Yes, ma'am. To the best of our knowledge, there are no stowaways. We've accounted for all the passengers and crew," he said. "If there'll be nothing else, I need to go to the next cabin."

"No, sir, that's all. I was just curious." She stepped back to shut her door. "And thank you," she interjected.

***

Chapter 7

They laid in an old mysterious combination box; there used to be hundreds of them buried in the ground, never to be found again. Until one day...

"Joey! Hey, come 'ere! I found something!" Ben hollered as he continued to remove dirt from the hole he had been working on. They had taken turns digging and gotten about five feet down when Ben's shovel sounded out with a strange twang.

"Oh, man! You told me there wouldn't be any graves here. Man! I hate this. This is going to be real bad," Ben whined.

Joey got up from under the old oak tree, walked over to Ben, and grabbed the shovel. "I told you there ain't no graves here! So shut up, and let's see what it is," he said while scraping and digging around the edges to reveal it in more detail.

"See, this thing ain't big enough for a casket. Somebody buried it, and we get to see what it is," Joey said.

After more digging, the two boys got down on their knees and dug with their hands until the top was completely uncovered.

"Are you sure it's not a casket? Could be a kid's casket, huh? What is it?" Ben said.

"I dunno." Joey wiped sweat from his brow. "It's strange. It doesn't appear to be made out of metal or wood."

Joey took the shovel and dug around all the sides until he thought he found the bottom.

"C'mon, man, help me here. Don't just stand there," Joey ordered.

"Hey, I've been diggin' the longest. I think I've done my part and then some, I'm tired," Ben shot back, but he reached for his shovel and started helping again.

After more digging, they managed to get to the bottom of the case. It was made out of some sort of pottery and had strange-looking pictures carved into the top and on the sides. They managed to get a couple of ropes under it and heaved it out of the ground.

When they looked at their prize, they were each in their own little dreamland, imagining all sorts of things they could have unearthed.

"Well, aren't we going to open it?" Ben asked out of breath from the exertion and excitement.

"Nah, not just yet. I'm savoring the moment," Joey said sarcastically as he scooted back from the case, wiping the sweat from his brow.

Ben sat on it and tapped loudly, looking at Joey with total amazement in his eyes. "I can't believe you. This is the greatest treasure we've ever found! If you don't open it right now, I'm gonna."

"Oh, really, are you now? And just how are you going to do that?" Joey asked in frustration.

Ben got up and closely inspected the case for a lock or latch. "I dunno," he said with a shrug.

Chapter 8

Despite their best efforts, Joey and Ben couldn't figure out how to open the case. During an Internet search for "antique cases," they came across Pops' Authentic Antiques Dealer in New Mexico. After speaking with the dealer at Pops', they were convinced they had to get the case open. But, he warned them, if they didn't follow the proper steps, the case would self-destruct, taking the contents with it.

They worked overtime at their jobs the next few weeks till they were able to get enough money for a trip to New Mexico. When they arrived, they located Pops' shop and showed him pictures of the case, which they had safely hidden in their hotel room.

Pops didn't know how to read the writing on the case. So, while the boys waited, he did some research and found the writings to be hieroglyphics. Once he found a local person who could read them, they emailed the pictures of the case to the man.

"Joey, we got an email from a Mr. Master, come quick," Ben said a short time later.

Mr. Master's email told them cases such as theirs usually had a story or riddle engraved on them, which was a code to opening it. He, however, had found nothing of the sort on this one. To the best of his knowledge, the only thing written on the case were words of warning and danger. It showed hundreds of people suffering and dying because of the contents.

The email went on to plead to let him see the case. Mr. Master claimed he had the resources to have a team of scientists investigate it and its contents. If they would bring it to him, he would be willing to pay a handsome price for it.

The boys looked at each other with uncertainty. "Do you suppose this is legit?" Ben said.

"Huh, I don't know," Joey replied.

Unnoticed, Pops had walked into the backroom; the boys heard someone talking loudly then a phone slamming down from the back. They looked at each other and shrugged their shoulders.

When Pops came back into the room, he pointed the boys to the door. "You have to leave now, and don't come back."

When they got to their hotel room, curiosity was killing them.

Joey said, "I got it! Let's just smash it and see what's inside. If there's nothing, we are out nothing. But if there is something, then I'm sure we're rich!"

Chapter 9

After they finally settled down in their hotel room, they discussed the way Pops just switched from being so helpful to practically kicking them out.

"Yeah, that was strange," Joey said.

"I wonder what ol' Pops knows that we don't," Ben said.

Joey shrugged and simply said, "I dunno. But let's get this thing open and just see."

He took the tools they brought with them and started beating on the box with a large hammer. After a few well-placed hits to the front of the case, it started to cave in, and soon the entire box turned into shattered pieces, dust flying out in every direction.

Under the rubble, they dug out a small leather bag. "Open it, man. What do you think it is?" Ben asked. "Do you suppose we're gonna be OK? They said it had warnings written on it. Maybe we're not supposed to open it."

Joey shrugged and pulled open the leather strings. He poured out the contents onto the bed. To their amazement, it looked like a hundred diamonds glittering in front of them.

"Oh, no! This can't be for real!" Ben shrieked with excitement.

"Yeah, man, I think it is," Joey replied, dumbfounded. "We're gonna be rich! We have to get home and figure out how to sell these babies."

"For sure we do!" Ben said.

"Tomorrow, we go home and see what we can do," Joey said and held his hand up for a high-five from Ben.

"Maybe there's even a reward for them," Ben said.

On their way home, they decided it would be best if they split the diamonds up and hid them in separate places. Ben hid his in a special hiding spot under the stairs of his house, and Joey just hid his in plain sight in his room.

The next day, they met up at Joey's and discussed selling the diamonds. Joey told Ben Mr. Master had emailed him again, offering even more money for the box.

After discussing it, they decided to let Mr. Master know they'd opened the box and wanted to sell the contents. They figured a cool million would be enough for the stones.

Joey said, "I think first, we need to see if there is a reward out there. Surely, someone's interested in them. We might be able to make even more money."

They surfed the 'Net until they came across an old article titled "Hidden Treasure of Cursed Diamonds: Fact or Fiction." As they read the article, they learned the markings were from the Mayans in Cozumel. And it appeared the curse might be very real.

Just as they finished reading, a racket outside made their hair stand on end. "Curse?!" they said, looking at one another in fright. Then they realized someone could be there to steal the diamonds.

Chapter 10

Miranda sat at one of the outside tables and scanned over the dinner menu. This was her last night in Galveston; tomorrow afternoon, she would be on a plane headed home. She was already making plans for her next cruise, hopefully with a companion. Her thoughts then wandered off to Sheriff Hill and his welcoming smile greeting her when she got home.

A commotion at the restaurant entrance to her left startled her from her daydream. Her table was in a row of outside tables beside the building. She turned as the tables between her and the door were shoved into hers by a man. Sunlight reflected on what she thought was a Glock .45 in his hand.

One waiter grabbed the assailant, wrapping him in a bear hug from behind, while the other tried to get the gun away from him.

She managed to get up and away from her table before it was shoved against the building, trapping her in-between. To Miranda's amazement, someone the size of a football player ran from around the group towards her. He tackled her, and they fell to the ground along with her table. Her purse and water glass were tossed into the air and came crashing down, spilling their contents on the ground almost out into the road. Her phone bounced and landed in a puddle of water.

During all the commotion, the football player who tackled her pushed himself up and grabbed the crystal bracelet from the contents on the ground. The bracelet attached to her keys fell just out of reach. When he got up, he stumbled over her, picked up the keys, and ran off.

The waiters finally wrestled the armed guy to the ground. When they got the gun from him, someone helped Miranda up. She brushed the debris from her skirt and elbows. When she gathered her purse and items, she discovered her keys missing and her phone's screen broken.

They heard sirens in the distance, indicating the police were on the way. The subdued man twisted and struggled against his captors, getting loose and escaping just before the police arrived.

"What was that all about? Why was that guy going into the restaurant with a gun?" Miranda said to no one in particular.

"Ma'am, are you all right?" a man in the group asked her.

"Yes, yes. I'm fine, thank you. But I'm afraid my phone didn't make it out so well," she said, putting everything back in her purse. She took a quick glance to be sure she still had a billfold but couldn't find her keys. Then she realized her lucky charm was missing.

When the police officer finally finished taking her information, she called her uncle to have her house keys and church keys remade.

"I will be back tomorrow around four from the airport, so I'll meet you at the diner. I had my car keys on a different key chain so, thankfully, only my house and church keys were stolen," she said. "That was really strange, Unk. There was an altercation at the front of the restaurant, and at the same time someone stole my lucky charms." *How odd that the pirates didn't snatch my bling, but they were snatched at this restaurant. Interesting.*

Chapter 11

During her dinner, which the restaurant owner bought for her and the other guests, her thoughts bothered her. Not to mention, the angels were still trying to get her attention.

She glanced around the restaurant, noticing a magazine rack; the top magazine's pages mysteriously fluttered in the breeze. She got up and walked over to check it out. The top magazine was a weekly news brief titled "The Sign Of The Times." The cover had a picture of a mule on it with the title "To Mule Or Not To Mule." She stared at the article, then realized she might know what was going on.

She went to her table and looked at her purse. What would someone want with her lucky crystals? She wondered again, why they weren't taken during the pirate attack on the ship and why they were taken now. It must have had to do with where she was.

She remembered after the incident with the pirates, she had put the bracelets in her small travel bag. But, when she packed to disembark the ship, she had pulled the two out of her suitcase and put them back in her purse and key ring.

Then a thought hit her. *The two charm bracelets that were stolen are the two that were in my suitcase when the pirates came aboard. So the two bracelets that are in my small bag right now are the ones that were left in my room.* "The ones the thieves passed up before," she said.

So now all she had to do was see if her hunch was right. After dinner, she went back to her hotel, pulled the other two lucky charms from her small travel bag, and looked at them very closely. "What's so special about you guys?" she said.

Miranda got up early the next morning and went to the nearest jeweler. According to the jeweler, her bracelet wasn't crystal, "but the best diamonds this ol' jewelry dealer has ever seen!" He even asked if she would sell them.

She went back to her hotel room and made a couple of calls, then gathered her luggage for her ride to the airport. The hotel bellhop called to let her know her taxi arrived, and she quickly came down, meeting him at the canopy. As soon as she got in the back seat, she knew she'd made a mistake. A passenger in the cab had a gun pointed right at her.

"Be quiet, lady, and don't make any stupid moves," the gunman said. After a brief ride through town, they put a blindfold on her, then came to a stop. From the smells and nearby screeching of seagulls, Miranda guessed they were by the shipyard.

They led her in and forced her to sit in a hard, straight-backed chair. Her captors removed the blindfold; an elderly man sat before her. "Ma'am, let me introduce myself. I'm Mr. Master. And I brought you here because we have a problem." Pointing at himself then back at her, he said, "You and me. You have something I want, and I have something you want."

"Sir, I don't have a clue what you're talking about," she said.

"I have two young men who unfortunately tried to keep half of the loot, and I want what they gave you for safe keeping. In return, I will give the two kids to you."

"What? I don't know what you're talking about. No one has given me anything," she said.

The old man nodded to a goon behind her, and she heard him walk away. After a few minutes, the goon shuffled two young men and an old man in front of her. They were gagged, and the boys were wild-eyed.

"I've never seen these people before, sir," she said.

"Lady, look, I know you have the rest of the diamonds. I don't have time for all this mess. And I don't want to kill anyone today, so come off it, and tell me where the diamonds are!" he screamed.

Chapter 12

"The diamonds are cursed, lady, and if you don't give them up, you and your descendants will be cursed forever!" the old man hollered at her.

"Mister, like I said already, I don't have the foggiest idea of what you're talking about. I just got off a cruise, and I'm headed home. I've never seen these kids and this man before in my life! I promise!" Miranda pleaded.

She looked at the boys, who appeared to be in good health. She looked around the huge warehouse and tried to make sense of her surroundings. It looked and smelled like they were at a shipyard, but she wasn't sure.

Just then Joe from the Cozumel store came in, and she recognized him instantly. He walked up to the man and pleaded, "Mr. Master, I tried to get the diamonds to you. I planted them on her, but she must have realized the gems were real somehow and switched them. The diamonds we stole yesterday were fakes, just crystals," Joe said. "And the kids kept the other half."

Mr. Master rose from his stool and walked over to Miranda, getting in her face. "Lady, I'm going to ask you one more time. If you don't start talking, someone's gonna die right here and now."

"I-I'm not sure. The only jewelry I own are the crystal bracelets that I always keep with me—f-for good luck, ya know? And just yesterday, I was at a restaurant and someone tackled me down and stole them," Miranda said, blinking her eyes excessively.

A loud crash came from outside, and the old man stopped and looked in that direction. "Sylvester, go see what that is," he ordered and waved his gun towards the door.

Sylvester walked over to one of the big, dingy windows and tried to see outside while one of the other goons pushed the boys down to sit on the ground beside Miranda. "Sit down," he said. "Don't move. I wants to keep all of yous together within easy reach."

Suddenly, the door next to the big garage door opened, and two men in black stormed in. The first man fired a gun towards the ceiling.

"Put your hands in the air! Everyone! You're under arrest!" a third officer ordered, stepping in from a door on the other side of the warehouse. Bits of the roof rained down on them.

Miranda put her head down and hoped nothing was going to fall on her. More men in black stormed in through windows, surrounding Mr. Master and taking his weapon. Sylvester and the two other goons were rounded up and brought together in the center of the room.

"This is all we found, Detective," one man said as he shoved two goons closer to Mr. Master. Two more were brought in from the other side of the building.

"Finally, we've put a stop to you, Master." The detective glared. "Thank you, miss, for your information and cooperation. We couldn't have done it without your help," the detective said while keeping his eyes on the old man.

He walked over to Joe and said, "Joe, I can't believe you're caught up in all of this. But, if you hadn't have stolen the other half of the diamonds from Ben's place and tried to mule them into the country to rescue the kids, none of this would have taken place. We might not have found anyone alive."

The boys were helped up and untied. They looked at each other with puzzled looks and shrugged. "What happened?" they asked in unison.

"I just knew we were dead meat," Ben said.

The detective who untied Miranda said, "By the help and grace of God, we finally got the Master Dealer. For whatever reason, he's stolen every Mayan artifact from Cozumel to Belize and back. And these diamonds were the last of the great artifacts."

He walked over to Master and spoke to the boys while staring intently at him. "You two boys are very lucky. He's left several dead in his wake over the years. You two stumbled upon the mother lode. The diamonds you discovered have been hunted for hundreds of years, and by much smarter hunters."

Smiling, he walked around Master. "They are supposedly cursed. We heard on the streets that they'd been found by two kids who didn't have a clue as to what they'd found. So, this made you two an easy target. Miss Miranda here figured out the mule trick and told us of the pirate attack on her cruise ship. From there, we were able to piece together the story. We just weren't expecting to actually catch the famous Mad Master Antique Dealer himself."

The End

Connect with Elizabeth A. Rochel at the following links:

www.EARtheWriter.wordpress.com

WattPad: https://www.wattpad.com/user/Elizabetharocjel

Cover by Author.

Di Shona McKenzie's Guide to Bumping off Your Boss

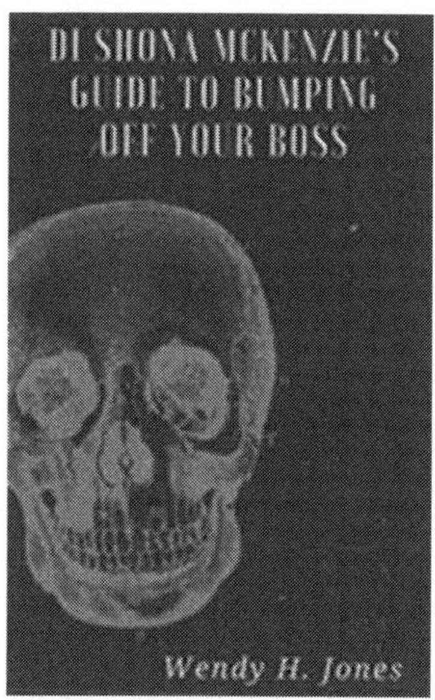

Wendy H. Jones

Award-winning author Wendy H. Jones lives in Scotland, and her police procedural series featuring Detective Inspector Shona McKenzie is set in the beautiful city of Dundee, Scotland. After a life in the armed forces and in academia, Wendy returned to Dundee to follow a lifelong dream to write.

Killer's Countdown was her first book and the first in the DI Shona McKenzie Mysteries. *The Dagger's Curse* is the first book in The Fergus and Flora Mysteries for Young Adults. This book is currently shortlisted for the *Woman Alive Magazine* Readers' Choice Award Book of the Year 2017. She is currently working on a new series called The Cass Claymore Mysteries. Cass Claymore is a red-headed, motorbike riding, ex-ballerina who inherits a detective agency. This will fit into the category of humorous crime. A highly successful marketer, she shares her methods in the book, *Power Packed Book Marketing: Sell More Books.*

My name is Shona McKenzie, and I am a Detective Inspector in Dundee, Scotland. I'm famous for investigating weird and wonderful murders, the likes of which the world has never seen. Dundee, the murder capital of Scotland, seems to have had more than its fair share of murders since I arrived. This leads to my nicknames of The Grim Reaper or Attila the Hun. Somewhat unfair I feel, as I am not responsible for the demise of any of the victims. Neither am I responsible for the grisly way in which they shuffle off this mortal coil. This does not stop people speculating. I head up a team of Dundee's finest boys and girls in blue. Or in civvies as we in CID do not wear uniform.

The worst offender is my boss: Thomas to his friends and Sir to me. I don't seem to say much more than 'Sir' to him. It's the only word I manage to insert into any conversation. These consist of him bollocking me—loudly and often. There's not a lot a mere Inspector can say to a Chief Inspector to calm him down. He informed me that sorry just doesn't cut it anymore. This leaves me to occupy my inner thoughts with ways in which I can get rid of the old goat. These are lurid, lucid and legal. If you use the term legal in its loosest sense that is. I, of course, choose to despite my career in law enforcement, as my American cousins would say.

Many people requested that I share my methods, and I did so in my first book, *DI Shona McKenzie's Guide to Killing Your Boss*. Before I sent it into the stratosphere I had it checked by a lawyer. No, I wasn't inciting anyone to kill. Yes, it was a bit of fun and definitely fine to publish. Same rules apply here, guys and gals: No copying what I am doing for real. That would earn you twenty-five to life at Her Majesty's pleasure. Also, arresting you is far too much like hard work. I've enough on my plate already.

"Stop wittering," I hear you cry. "On with the guide and less of the chat."

You raise a fair point so, without further ado, here is my "Guide to Bumping off the Boss."

Guns

This can be a tricky one for me, as Scottish Police are not armed. However, at the conclusion of a case, my little team of expert shots are given guns. Usually pistols but we have been known to carry rifles. The important point in this method is 'expert shots.' None of us are actually experts with a gun. We just pretend to be. Apart from

Jason 'Soldier Boy' Roberts of course, who was in the Territorial Army. That's a whole different story, and one I won't bore you with here. Given that when it comes to guns we are a bunch of bumbling incompetents, I fantasise about a misplaced shot, which dispatches the Chief in a manner that involves lots of blood. Sorry to the squeamish amongst you, but it has to be said. This is a particularly good one as it can be put down to an accident. Yes, it involves a huge investigation, but in the end, a new Chief Inspector would take up residence in the station.

There are a couple of Russian thugs rattling around in Dundee, and they seriously get up my bonnie Grecian nose. I have often fantasised about killing them off, but in this instance, they might come in useful. I am convinced, although I've never been able to prove it, they have hit men for hire. Just in case, I'm putting aside cash in a special savings account—in the Cayman Isles. It always pays to be prepared. The added bonus in this little scenario is that I will be able to lock the thugs up for millennia and rocket them straight out of my orbit. A winner on all fronts if I'm honest.

Water

I appreciate that water and murder aren't often seen in the same sentence. However, if you have ever been to Scotland, you will realise there is rather a lot of it. From bonnie wee burns (streams) to huge rivers such as The Forth, The Clyde and of course, Dundee's offering, the River Tay. We also have an inordinate amount of lochs. To those of you not in the know, a loch is a lake. There are 31,460 of them at last count. In order to keep all these waterways topped up and looking at their finest, God saw fit to give us rain—a lot of rain. In fact, Scottish vernacular contains 50 words for rain. Anyone resident in, or visiting, the country soon comes to realise that trickling brooks can become raging torrents at the first sign of a cloudburst.

I am sure we are not alone in this, and unless you live in the Sahara Desert you will get your fair share of torrential rain. This provides the ideal opportunity to bump off the boss. In whatever line you work, a swollen river must present itself somewhere nearby. A quick 'accidental' bump and in goes the boss. Now you see him, or her, floating down the river. Or rather rushing down the river, out of sight and out of mind. In my case, my wanderings are local before I trip over a waterway. I have a burn at the bottom of my garden that turns into a fully fledged, raging torrent at the merest hint of rain. I only have to invite him round for dinner, and he's a goner. The drawback with this one is that it's pretty obvious I might be considered instrumental in his demise. So maybe not the Fithie Burn then. Shame.

Lochs feature heavily in many of my investigations. They are always a good way to dispose of a body. Why be imaginative when there's a perfectly decent, if somewhat boring, solution right in front of your nose. Lochs usually mean boat trips. The following equation comes into play:

Water + Boat + Boss ÷ Quick Push = Successful Resolution To The Boss Problem

This equation works particularly well if the variable of atrocious weather is added in. Then the boat will be tossing around on the waves, so spectacular opportunity for an accident. However, make sure you are not prone to seasickness before carrying out this particular method. Vomiting tends to leave a lot of DNA around the place.

Another variation involves a boat and a strong tide. This works better for disposing of a body rather than bumping him or her off to start with. Pop the corpse in a boat and give it a quick shove, and it might be in America before the body is discovered. If you're in England that is. Doing the same in Scotland would net you Ireland or one of the Scandinavian countries. The net result is still the same. The boss is off your hands and in a country far, far away.

This next one could cause maximum chaos. Stuff him down a *cundie*. My sergeant, Peter Johnston, tells me this is Dundonian for drain. No, I don't know why either. Probably comes from the French word conduit. Anyway back to killing the boss. Shove him down the drain, and the flood waters will drown him. You've probably guessed the downside of this. Yes, you are likely to flood the city, but you need to be ready for a little collateral damage when considering these things.

Rain and mudslides go well together. Again this one might be a trifle difficult to pull off depending on the terrain around you. However, with a little thought and imagination, you might just be able to pull it off.

Snow

If you think there are a lot of words for rain in Scotland, try the ones for snow. Go on, have a guess? Nope, nowhere near. There are 421, no less. I kid you not. That's more than the Inuits. We do weather in rather a grand way in Scotland. Snow provides endless fun when it comes to bumping off the boss. However, I appreciate that this will not be a method that will suit everyone. Too cold for a start, and you're scuppered if you live in a country where it does not snow. For those to whom it does apply, here are my tips.

This one involves bumping him off in the first instance and then placing his very dead body inside a snowman. Preferably in an out of the way spot, ensuring he won't be found until spring. Do this early enough and it gives you several glorious, peaceful months until the investigation starts. Bliss.

Dump his body in a snow grave. Again it will not be found until spring with the same result as the previous method. This one is for those who are not keen on building snowmen and think it is too much effort. Graves are much easier to dig and shovel snow back on top. Don't say I don't think of you.

Smack him in the head with a snow shovel then say he slipped and hit his head on a rock. What do you mean there is a flaw in this plan? Oh, all right. I'll give the point to you. There would be blood on the shovel. This one might need a little thinking through. However, I can't feed you everything. If you do a little work yourself, the revenge will be sweeter.

Along with snow often comes ice. Couple this with the water in the previous section and the boss could disappear under the ice forever. A hole in the ice and shove him through, and he's gone until the ice melts. If you're in Alaska, this one is particularly suitable.

If snow is hard to come by where you live then sand would make a superb substitute. If you haven't got snow or sand then, quite frankly, you're not trying hard enough. Get a grip and think of something in its place. Either that or stick with the boss you've got and carry on grumbling.

Countryside

Of course, countryside is a method of murder. It is in Scotland anyway. Use a little imagination, and you'll find it's a method in your country as well. Unless you live somewhere so densely populated that countryside isn't a word in the dictionary, there is always somewhere remote to go. Even Hong Kong and Singapore have remote areas. Anyway, I digress.

Many of the bodies I deal with in the course of my work are

discovered in the remotest places possible. Even I wonder why anyone goes there and how he or she gets there. A team building exercise in a desolate location and you and the boss can find yourselves alone. I fantasise about this one a lot, and it's not in any sexual way. The ways in which I could kill him are many and varied. They usually involve rocks, caves and mysterious strangers. How about bumping him on the head, dragging him into a cave and blocking up the entrance? Or chuck him into a crevasse and throw the rocks on top. Another variation is to shove him into a deep crevasse and run crying for help. Or forget the cry for help and look as puzzled and concerned as the others when the boss doesn't reappear.

Cliffs are numerous in Scotland, so a quick 'stumble' and the boss is over and, like the MacDonalds, gone forever. This is one of the easiest methods of bumping off the boss and the least likely to be seen as suspicious.

Building Sites

Building sites often feature in my books. These provide rich pickings in the body disposal stakes. Take the boss along to look at a body, shove him in the foundations and pour cement over the top of him. Oops-a-daisy, the boss disappears in a rather satisfying way. He would also come in useful to reinforce the hole. If he causes any subsidence, hopefully I will be long gone before they investigate.

Building sites also contain about a gazillion items of industrial machinery. Said machinery allows for a veritable plethora of accidents to happen. Especially when the boss has long forgotten how to look after himself at a crime scene. Let me ask you, when was your boss last on site? I thought so. He just sits at his desk. I arrest my case, M'lud.

Should you know how to tie a noose you could always hang him at the building site. A bit tricky this one as you would need him or her to comply. Not many people, even ones as thick as Thomas, are going to voluntarily place their head in a noose. On second thoughts, not the best idea I've had.

Ring the Changes

One of my cases involved a deadly game of human jigsaw. Body parts were turning up all over Scotland. Take the boss to a remote shed or bothy and kill them any old way you want. I'll leave this one up to you. Then using whatever implement is at hand, chop up the body. This one requires a great deal of strength and also involves a lot of blood. If you live near a zoo, you could lob the body parts into the various enclosures and let the animals polish them off. What a great way to get rid of the evidence. Inspired, if I say so myself.

In Dundee, crossbows are a popular weapon for causing death and destruction. No, I'm not kidding. I told you my cases involved the weird and wonderful. Take him out with a well-aimed crossbow bolt, and you've bumped the boss and pointed the finger at the criminal fraternity. Genius.

Castles

Castles are the most marvellous places to kill someone. They are usually built on a rock, ruined, or full of weaponry. In fact, positively stuffed full of ideas to bump off the boss. With this, my imagination runs wild. A stuffed animal head would fall off the wall and land on his head, and he's gone. In place of a stuffed animal could be a sword through the heart or a lump of masonry smacking him on the head. Chucking him off the battlements would give a sense of historic realism, which would be satisfying. I can't think of a country without a castle or palace that could be pressed into service.

So there we have it, my friends: A positive smorgasbord of ideas for you to choose from. Please enjoy these and mix and match them to suit your own ends. Think up your own, which is endlessly satisfying. The important thing here is to remember that these are fantasies. Not one person, including dear Thomas, was hurt in the making of this book. Don't go killing off the boss, or anyone else, in real life. That is seen as not playing nicely, and I will come knocking at your door. I will have a gun and some highly polished handcuffs in my hands. I've heard prison is a tough place to live your life.

The End

Learn more about Wendy Jones at the following links:

Website: http://www.wendyhjones.com

Amazon Author Page: http://author.to/WendyHJones

Facebook: https://facebook.com/wendyhjonesauthor/

Twitter: http://www.twitter.com/wendyhjones

Pinterest: https://www.pintrest.co.uk/wopnes64

https://www.instagram.com/wendyhjones/

Books available from bookshops both nationally and internationally.

Cover by Author.

Afterword

Please tell all your friends about the One Million Project and our aims for charity, both in raising money and highlighting worthy causes. Sharing, tweeting, face-booking, blogging and recommending the collection will help us achieve our goal of raising £1,000,000 for cancer research, and combatting homelessness.

If you liked the stories in this book, please check out some of the writers other work and drop by the OMP website to comment and chat.

http://www.theonemillionproject.com/

Twitter - @JayGreenfield

Books available on Amazon in the series

Thank you for reading the OMP Thriller Anthology. If you enjoyed it, please go to the Amazon page and leave a review. As you can see, we have two other books in the series for your consideration available on Amazon.